Archer of the Heathland

Book Three

Vengeance

J.W. Elliot

Bent Bow
Publishing, LLC

Bent Bow Publishing
P.O. Box 1426
Middleboro, MA 02346

ISBN-13: 9781723786556

Cover Design by Brandi Doane McCann

If you enjoy this book, please consider leaving an honest review on Amazon and sharing on your social media sites.

Please sign up for my newsletter where you can get a free short story and more free content at: **www.jwelliot.com**

TO MY CHILDREN

Book Three

Vengeance

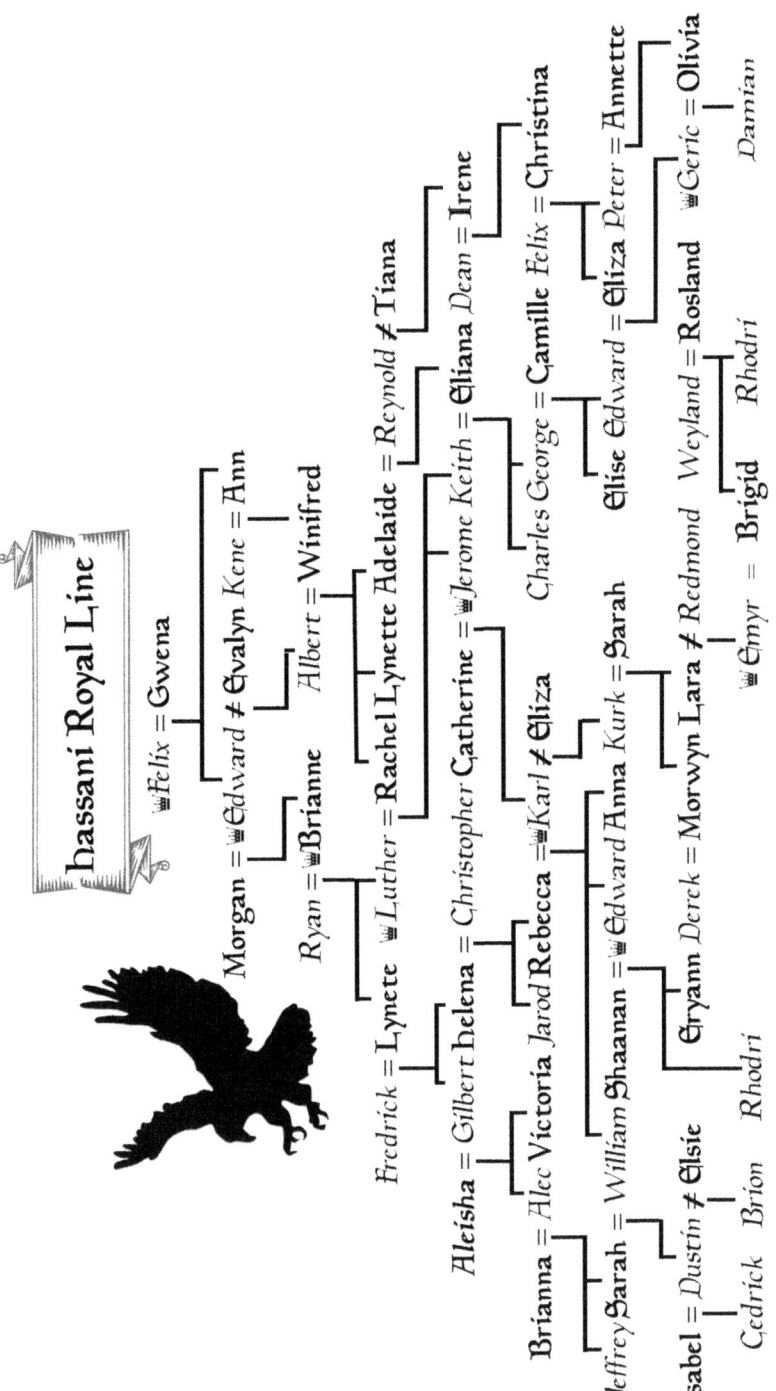

Chassani Royal Line

♔Felix = Gwena

Morgan = ♔Edward ≠ Evalyn Kene = Ann

Ryan = ♔Brianne   Albert = Winifred

Fredrick = Lynette   ♔Luther = Rachel Lynette Adelaide = Reynold ≠ Tiana

Aleisha = Gilbert helena = Christopher Catherine ≠ Jerome Keith = Eliana Dean = Irene

Brianna = Alec Victoria Jarod Rebecca = ♔Karl ≠ Eliza   Charles George = Camille Felix = Christina

Jeffrey Sarah = William Shaanan = ♔Edward Anna Kurk = Sarah   Elise Edward = Eliza Peter = Annette

Isabel = Dustin ≠ Elsie   Eryann Derek = Morwyn Lara ≠ Redmond Weyland = Rosland ♔Ceric = Olivia

Cedrick Brion Rhodri   ♔Emyr = Brigid   Rhodri   Damian

MAP OF
FREI-OCK ISLES

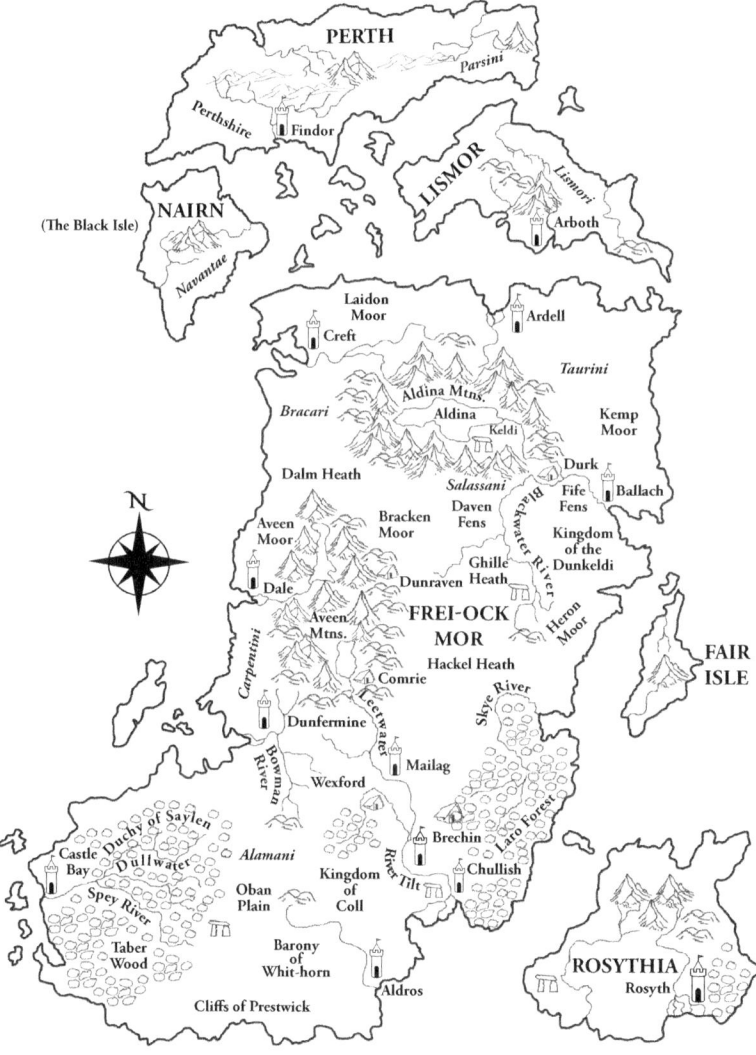

Chapter 1
The Bloody Brook

The brook ran red. York bent to collect a few more stones for his sling, but now his gaze focused on the red, swirling water. He glanced up at the stone walls of the little, round keep that peered out over the vale from the summit of the rocky hill. Purple and pink heather stood out in bunches amid the short, green grass of the heathland. The brook curled around the base of the hill and slipped into a stand of aspens, whose leaves quivered in the cool, morning breeze.

The guard on the walls stood erect, facing the snowcapped peaks of the Aveen Mountains to the east. A thin line of gray smoke had attracted the guard's attention. But the brook ran with blood. Surely, this was more important than a little smoke. York rose and strode up the creek, wondering what might have caused the water to turn red. His Carpentini boots pressed deep into the mud. The morning's mist had moistened the earth and dusted the leaves of the mahogany and bayberry with little teardrops. The heather glistened in the slanting light.

York passed under the stand of aspen. The lingering mist clung to his black hair. His linen trousers and shirt soon sagged about his lithe frame, heavy with moisture. The air tasted sweet and clean. York stepped through a land that had long been widowed of its inhabitants, as the ruined buildings and stone walls bore silent witness. The rotted beams of houses and barns stabbed out of sunken holes in the ground like bones reaching from the grave for the life that had betrayed them. York had come with his mother and sister to breathe vitality back into these mountain valleys, to seek a new homeland where his suffering people could find the strength to survive.

A wail floated to him on the morning mist. York stopped beside a crumbling stone wall and scanned the aspen grove, listening. The wail came again, ghostly and mournful as it pierced the haze. It had a strange, unearthly quality and was filled with pain and terror. York's heart beat faster, and he almost fled back to the keep. But maybe it was one of his own people. They might need his help.

York quickened his pace until he came to the great boulder that sprawled across the narrow valley. The brook spilled over one side of the boulder in a glittering waterfall. Something bobbed at the crest in a gentle, rhythmic cadence, like the slow, regular breath of life. The water that splashed over the mossy surface came with bold, red streaks. York scrambled up the boulder beside the little waterfall until he stood peering out over the pond where he and his baby sister had fished for brook trout the day before.

Horror gripped York's stomach. A dam of linen-clothed bodies clogged the channel as if they had been pushed up by the beavers in an attempt to stop the running water. Men, women, and children, all silent and staring in death, bobbed in the current, bumping against one another. Their blood spread like a stain to color the water as it spilled over the boulder.

The wail rose up again behind him. York tore his gaze from the gruesome scene in search of the pitiful creature that made that awful, haunting noise. A dark head shifted among the bushes where a little boy no more than three years old curled up in a tiny ball of ragged clothing. The boy had a ghastly wound on the side of his head that still dribbled blood.

Terror clutched at York's throat. Whoever had done this couldn't be far away. He scrambled along the top of the boulder and ducked into the underbrush to where the boy lay.

"Hush," York said as he reached out to touch the child. He needed to silence him. The boy jumped and cried out. York clamped a hand over his mouth and looked around.

"Hush," he said again. "I won't hurt you." He spoke in the Carpentini dialect because the boy wore the linen clothes and whip-stitched boots peculiar to the Carpentini.

The boy stared at him with big, brown eyes. York lifted the boy into his arms, when something splashed behind him. He pulled the child close and spun. A man with a dark streak of dried blood on his face stood with one foot on a log and the other in the water. He wore a long, green tunic with loose sleeves favored by the Bracari. His black hair that had been cropped short in front was matted with globs of mud. The Bracari had frozen in place to stare at York as if he expected York to miss him if he didn't move. York glanced at the bodies. This man had been injured in the fight. Where were the rest of the Bracari? York looked around as the hollow fear filled his chest. He was alone in the wood with an injured child and a Bracari who would not want to be discovered.

York hugged the boy close to his chest, slid down the boulder into the aspen grove, and sprinted for the keep. He had to warn the rest of the Carpentini that the Bracari had found them again—before it was too late. The boy whimpered as York's feet pounded the earth. Branches lashed York's face. He ducked and wove. A splash and heavy crashing sounded behind him. A rock flew past his head and slammed into a tree. He ducked, clutching the boy close to his chest. He broke from the cover of the aspens onto the dirt trail that skirted the stream. The top of the keep peaked over the valley, but no one was looking his way. The keep disappeared from view as York cut through the undergrowth, broke from the trees, and scrambled up the hill. The walls of keep now loomed in front of him.

"Bracari!" he cried out. But the word was lost as he gasped for air. "Bracari," he tried again.

A horseman appeared in front of him and then another. But they weren't Carpentini or Bracari. The bigger one held a huge longbow with an arrow on the string. The other was smaller, maybe as old as York, only fifteen or sixteen. He carried a short recurve bow and had long, blonde hair that he pulled back. York shied away from them. They blocked his approach to the keep—the only safe place he had. York leapt over a low, stone wall.

"Stop," someone shouted. But the accent was not Carpentini. York chanced a glance back to see the man with the longbow rein his horse around toward the trees. He dropped the reins and drew the bow. The Bracari dove back into the cover of aspens.

"I said stop!" the man commanded again.

York slipped on the damp grass and fell to his knees. A stone slapped the earth beside his hand. York struggled to his feet and scrambled up the hill, clutching the boy with one arm and tearing at the moist earth with the other as he strained to claw his way up the slope to the keep. His lungs burned. His arms ached from carrying the child. His legs had become so heavy. Shouts now came from the keep above him. But they would be too late. York would never make it with two horsemen and a Bracari on his tail.

Hooves beat the earth, and York tensed in preparation for the pain of the arrow. The string slapped. He cringed and stumbled, but the pain never came. York righted himself and craned his neck around. The Bracari that had been chasing him fell on his face on the green hillside with an arrow quivering in his leg. York blinked in confusion. The large horseman leapt from his saddle, jammed a knee into the Bracari's back, grabbed his hair, and yanked his head back. He pressed a blade to his throat.

"When I say stop, I mean it," he growled.

His accent was strange. York paused, then stopped. His chest heaved, and his legs trembled as the shorter rider rode up to him and slipped from the saddle. It was a woman—a beautiful woman—not too many years older than himself.

The concern on her face confused him.

"Are you hurt?" she said. Her accent was strange, too. He shied away, trying to shield the boy as she reached for him.

She paused and cocked her head. "May I?"

York pressed the boy close to his chest, uncertain. Who were these strangers? Why would they shoot the Bracari?

"I'm not going to hurt him," she said. "But he needs care."

York hesitated, glanced at the still-bleeding wound on the boy's head, and handed the child to the woman. She pulled the child close and whispered in his ear. She caressed his cheek and kissed his brow.

Then she knelt, swung her water skin to her front, yanked the plug with her teeth, and poured water into the boy's mouth. The boy sputtered and then began to drink.

"Are they all right?" the man called.

York glanced over to see the Bracari tied up like a pig for roasting. He bent over with his hands on his knees and tried to catch his breath, trying to understand what had happened. Sweat dripped on the grass to join the glittering drops of the morning rain. He was alive, and that was something.

Vengeance

The jangle of weapons brought York's head up. Two dozen men rushed down from the keep and formed a semi-circle around them. Reed stood at their head. He was a big man with a fiery beard and a temper to match. York had never seen the man who could stand up to Reed. Reed waved, and half a dozen men raced down the hill into the woods. They would be searching for more Bracari.

"Lay down your weapons," Reed ordered.

The young woman ignored him. She poured water over the gash on the child's head and cooed to him.

The man with the longbow raised his hands. "We're not Bracari," he said. "I'm Brion of Wexford. I'm not your enemy."

"Enemies are all we seem to have these days," Reed said. "I want to see that bow on the ground."

For a moment, York thought Brion might refuse. But he sighed and laid the bow on the ground. The Bracari squirmed, and Brion set his boot on his back and pressed down. York saw the smile twitch on Reed's lips.

"I've never heard of Wexford," Reed said.

Brion shrugged. "It's not much to talk about. More a collection of shacks, really. Most people in Wexford don't even know where they are."

Reed didn't seem amused with the answer. He waited, fingering the edge of the long knife he held in his hands.

"It's in Coll," Brion said, "on the edge of the Oban Plain."

"An Alamani this far north?" Reed said. "Either you're crazy or you have a death wish."

"Neither. I'm looking for someone."

"And your new king sent you?"

Brion shook his head. "King Emyr knows that I am here, but he didn't send me. I came on my own."

Reed scowled as a murmur swept through the men. They shuffled their feet, and a few advanced toward Brion.

"Didn't he live with the Salassani?" someone said.

York had heard of this King Emyr. He had been raised a Salassani and had led a coup to seize the crown of Coll. Rumor said he was planning an invasion of the heathland.

Reed pursed his lips. "Spy? Scout?"

Brion smiled and shook his head. "I told you. It's a personal matter." The Bracari captive wiggled again, and Brion shoved him back to the ground.

"Look," the young woman said as she stood. "This child needs care. I want hot water and clean bandages, now."

Reed studied her for the first time, then glanced back to Brion with raised eyebrows.

"My wife, Finola," Brion said.

"You brought a woman into a land spilling over with blood?" Reed scowled. "You don't look like a fool, but—"

"She's not that easy to leave behind," Brion interrupted.

"I'm going to the keep," Finola said and strode off up the hill with the child in her arms.

"Hold!" Reed bellowed, and York thought he might attack the woman. But Reed seemed more confused than anything.

Finola paused and glanced back at him with a defiant smirk that dared him to challenge her. York looked at Brion, who was smiling.

Reed sheathed his knife and waved toward the Bracari. "Bring him," he said and stalked up the hill past Finola without looking at her. Two men grabbed the Bracari and dragged him toward the keep. The rest of the men followed, leaving York and Brion alone.

Brion pursed his lips at York and cocked his head to one side. "Do you think that means I can pick up my bow now?"

York smiled despite himself. "Probably," he said.

Brion snatched the bow from the grass, gathered the reins of the two horses, and led them towards the keep. York noted that the horse Brion rode was a black mare with a silver-speckled rump and Finola's was a buckskin. They were beautiful horses, and York secretly longed for one of his own. They had lost their only horse months ago to the Bracari.

"Is he always that friendly?" Brion asked in a conversational tone.

"No," York said. "He's usually a lot meaner."

Chapter 2
The Keep

Gwyneth haunted the shadows of the doorway as the men dragged the Bracari inside the walls that surrounded the keep. She had seen York's desperate flight and the rescue by the two strangers, and she wanted a closer look. None of the Carpentini men spared Gwyneth a glance, which was fine with her. When people ignored her, it meant they weren't going to spit insults at her or hurl stones at her head. Gwyneth waited for the beautiful young woman with the blonde hair who still carried the child in her arms. She couldn't be more than nineteen or twenty—three or four years older than Gwyneth—and she was dressed like a man. She wore a loose tunic with a leather belt tied around her waist and trousers that she tucked into the high, brown leather boots. A quiver full of arrows was strapped to her back, and a long knife dangled from her belt. Gwyneth caught the bulge of another knife sticking out of the top of her boot.

The woman paused and nodded to Gwyneth, who glanced down at her own dirty blue dress covered with patches and grease stains and knew she looked like a beggar. Well, she was a beggar. She always had been. The handsome young man stopped behind the young woman to peer over her shoulder. He carried a longbow in his hands, which was something Gwyneth had never seen before. He was dressed like the young woman, and he had a strong, kind face— the type of face that made Gwyneth wary. The ones that looked nice were the most dangerous. They were the easiest to underestimate. They could get a woman to drop her defenses.

When the young man saw Gwyneth, he nodded and touched

his brow in the Carpentini fashion. Gwyneth frowned. No one had ever given her this most basic sign of respect in all her life, except for her long-dead uncle. Carpentini saluted one another as a form of greeting, but only when they wished to express respect or intimacy. Gwyneth narrowed her eyes.

"Hello," the young man said. "I'm Brion."

Gwyneth ducked through the doorway and scampered across the courtyard between the walls and the keep. She wouldn't let him deceive her that easily. She had seen enough of men to know they were all the same.

Cow and horse dung made the going treacherous in her bare feet. The day was beginning to warm, and the reek of man and beast was starting to become oppressive. So many people and their animals had to be packed inside the walls at night that there was hardly a place to lie down. No one wanted to be found outside the walls after sundown for fear of Bracari raids.

Gwyneth darted into the keep and slipped into the shadows away from the fire. She wanted to see what was happening—not be seen. The strangers entered the smoky shadows of the keep and waited. Reed, the big, red-headed leader of this little village, glared at them.

"I'll deal with you in a minute," Reed said to the strangers.

He turned to York. "What happened?"

York passed a hand over his head that caused his sweaty, short-cropped hair to stand up all over the place. Gwyneth thought he looked comical that way. But otherwise, she liked the look of him. He was small for his age and slender, but he had a strong jaw, and she had seen him work just as hard and long as any man. He also had eyes the color of a chestnut. If he hadn't been a boy and she hadn't been half-Bracari, they might have been friends.

"There was blood in the brook this morning," York said. "So I followed it to the little falls. They were all dead, clogging the stream." York gestured to the boy who clung to the young woman. "He was the only one alive."

"You should have called for help," someone said.

"And who would have heard me?" York demanded. He glared at them.

Reed chose to ignore the exchange. "And him?" He jabbed a

thumb at the Bracari who lay on his side watching with wide eyes. Blood soaked his pant leg to stain the wraps he had wound around his lower legs just above the short-topped boots the Bracari liked to wear. Gwyneth wondered if the man knew he was going to die. The Carpentini had long ago stopped showing mercy to Bracari captives because the Bracari had shown none to them.

"He chased us," York said. "He tried to kill us."

Reed nodded and gave York an annoyed look. "I gathered that," he said. "Did you recognize the folks in the stream? Were they any of ours?"

Gwyneth figured that Reed was thinking of the six families he had sent into the next valley to prepare some fields for planting. They were long overdue.

York frowned and glanced at his mother who sat hunched over against the wall watching him. Gwyneth didn't know her well, but she didn't like the way she glared at her son. Her expression was always accusing, as if she blamed him for something. York swallowed and looked away.

"I've seen one of the women before," he said. "She was at the first village, when—" he glanced at his mother again, "when the Bracari killed my father."

Reed twirled a finger through his beard as he studied York. Then he spun and kicked the Bracari's injured leg. The Bracari yelled and bent over his leg, grimacing in pain.

"Speak, swine," Reed said. "Where are the rest of your men?"

Brion studied the keep and the crowd of Carpentini that had gathered. The air smelled of wood smoke and sweat. He looked up at the scaffolding and bare beams where the upper floors should have been. The keep was still under reconstruction. These Carpentini hadn't been here long. Brion had seen the piles of newly cut stone and the heaps of sand and clay for mortar in the courtyard outside the keep. He had also seen the jagged, unfinished walls and scaffolding where men kept working despite the turmoil. They had selected a good place, and they were desperate to secure it before a new Bracari threat found them. But they were too late. The only reason a Bracari would have risked his life to chase and silence a mere boy was that he was trying to protect someone. There had to be more Bracari about.

Dozens of Carpentini had gathered in the keep. Their gaunt faces and bodies showed the strain of a people under assault. Far more women than men crowded inside. The children huddled close to their mothers' sides, casting furtive glances at the Bracari that Brion had shot. Brion found himself wondering if any of these Carpentini were related to him, if any of them could be his own mother.

Only a few months ago, he had discovered that his mother had been a Carpentini healer who had worked for the Duke of Saylen. And now he had ventured into the heathland again to look for her. He had been taken from her as a baby and given to Weyland and Rosland to raise. The Duke's legitimate son, Cedrick, had made it his business to find them all and kill them. He had succeeded in killing Weyland, Rosland, and the Duke. Now Brion hoped that his mother had escaped—that she was with the rest of the Carpentini hiding in the Aveen Mountains. The problem was that he had no idea what she looked like—only that her name was Elsie.

Finola had carried the child to the fire where she set about heating water without asking anyone's permission. Brion smiled. When it came to children, Finola didn't stand on ceremony. In her mind, the needs of children always superseded anyone else's. Finola wanted children more than anything. Brion's smile faded at the thought, and he turned his attention back to the gathering as a Carpentini scout rushed into the keep.

Reed whirled to face him.

"It's an army," the man blurted, "at least two hundred strong."

"Sound the alarm," Reed said. "Gather our people in."

Then he spun on Brion. "I'll be needing those weapons now," he said with a gesture of his hand. "Even your King Emyr wouldn't let armed strangers remain inside his keep when he was under attack."

Brion glanced at Finola. She had bandaged the child's wound and set him down on a pile of clothes beside the fire. She reached to pick up her bow and backed toward the door. Carpentini warriors drew their weapons, and those with bows pulled arrows from their quivers. This would not end well for any of them.

Brion raised his hands as the calls from the alarm horns echoed through the keep. "You can't defend this keep," he said. "Those Bracari will trap you inside and starve you out. How many months' supplies do you have stored?" He knew the answer by the nervous glances some of the men and women exchanged.

Reed laid his hand on his sword. "You can give up your weapons, or I can take them," he said.

"We'll take the third option," Brion said. "We'll leave the keep with our weapons and let you fight the Bracari alone, but I warn you that if you let them trap you inside an unfinished keep with no supplies, you won't survive."

Reed strode up to Brion and stood so close that Brion could smell the fish and onions Reed must have eaten for breakfast. Brion tensed, ready for action.

"What do you propose?" Reed growled.

"Delay them," Brion said. "Draw them onto ground you choose where their numbers will be a disadvantage."

"Such as?"

"About a mile from here there's a narrow canyon of tumbled stone. You can lure them in and trap them."

"I know the place," Reed said.

Reed glanced around at the crowd of men, women, and children. Brion felt nothing but pity for him—to have so many people depending on him to make the right decision—to protect them against such overwhelming odds.

Reed stepped back from Brion and turned to the scout. "How long do we have?"

"Maybe two hours before they arrive. They're moving slow, burning as they come."

Reed studied Brion. "Can I trust you, Brion of Wexford?" he asked.

Brion nodded. "The Carpentini have done a great service to friends of mine. I will fight with you."

Reed spun. "Alec, form a rearguard of no more than twenty men to harass and delay the Bracari. Karney, leave a token force in the keep. As our people come in, send the women and children ahead and organize the men. Then retreat to the canyon. Bring all the supplies and weapons you can carry."

Reed faced Brion again. "You and I will go to this canyon and organize the defenses."

"I want to fight," York said. Reed glanced at him, and Brion could see that Reed discounted the boy—even after he had bravely saved the child and given them warning of the Bracari presence. With so few men, Brion would have thought that Reed would accept any boy big enough to fight.

"You go with the women," Reed said. "There will be plenty of fighting for everyone soon enough."

York frowned, and Brion followed the direction of his gaze to where a woman crouched against the stones of the keep and glared at York.

"How old are you?" Brion asked.

"Sixteen," York said.

Brion considered him. He was small for his age, but he had courage. "You come with me," Brion said and nearly smiled as York's face lit up and he stood taller. Reed gave Brion an appraising glance and turned away.

"Move!" Reed bellowed. "Take only food and weapons."

Chapter 3
The Hounds of War

York struggled up the steep incline over the moss-covered boulders and into the stand of shaggy evergreens. Great clumps of pale green moss drooped from the branches. The air had that sharp taste of pine mixed with damp earth. Below in the narrow crevice, water rushed and gurgled as it cut its way relentlessly through the soft stone, slicing a deep but narrow gorge filled with twisted cutaways, jagged boulders, and the skeletons of fallen trees.

Reed's voice echoed over the rush of the water below as he barked orders to the women and children who struggled through the narrow opening. They worked their way over the jumble of stones and piles of debris that littered the floor of the crevice. York paused to catch his breath as he surveyed the scene that spread out around him. Men piled stones at the lip of the canyon, while others dragged logs and boulders to bar the entrance so that only one man could enter at a time. Brion had climbed the rock face ahead of York and was positioning archers and slingers. The Carpentini straggled in over the green slopes from all the tiny hamlets Reed had been trying to establish—a ragged, discouraged line of refugees without a home.

In the distance, the smoke curled up from the dozens of fires the Bracari had set as they burned their way through the newly constructed Carpentini homes. The thought of the Bracari brought a snarl to York's lips. He had not forgotten, nor would he ever forget, what they had done.

It had been a cool, spring day high up in the foothills of the Aveen Mountains when York's father, Lucain, had burst into their make-shift hut and rushed

13

to snatch his sword from the rafters.

"Run!" Lucain cried. "Take Bethann and run. Find your mother and get into the woods."

York glanced at his four-year-old sister, Bethann, who sat in the corner on a pile of blankets that she used for a bed. Her bright, blue eyes watched him.

Lucain was a big man and a great warrior. He had fought alongside the legendary warrior, Lotrel, and his son, Edrick, at the Battle of Bloody Creek that had saved the Carpentini from destruction fifteen years before. Lucain buckled the sword belt around his waist and scowled at York.

"I told you to run." He shoved York toward the back door. York staggered a few steps and stopped. He didn't want to run. He was big enough to fight. They had been running and hiding from the Bracari ever since he could remember.

Lucain drew the sword—the one that had been wielded by Lotrel and later by Edrick. Lucain had promised York that someday the sword would be his. To York, the sword had always been a symbol of the strength and determination of his people. He was proud of his father and determined to be just like him one day—strong, confident, a defender of his land and his people.

"I'm coming with you," York said. He pulled his sling from his pocket. It was nothing more than two leather chords attached to a leather pouch. But York was the best slinger in the village and regularly brought home meat for the stew pot. He could kill or injure a Bracari just as well as a man with a bow or a sword.

"Go now," his father ordered as he swept out the door.

York hesitated. If he were just a few years older and a little taller, his father wouldn't be treating him like a child. But he couldn't leave his mother and sister unprotected either.

Cries and screams shattered the quiet of the village. York grabbed up his little sister, kicked open the back door, and rushed into the cool light of early morning. The smell of cooking food and wood smoke filled the air like any other spring morning. But the sounds were different. The clash of swords, the shouts of men, and the cries of the wounded filled the village. How had the Bracari found them in this secluded mountain valley?

Bethann wiggled in his arms. "Momma?" she whimpered.

"Shh," York hushed her as he glanced around, trying to decide which way to go.

The makeshift village had been erected in a clearing deep in the pine forests that covered the slopes of the Aveen Mountains. Ever since the recent heath war that King Tristan had started with the Alamani the previous summer, the Bracari had been invading Carpentini lands claiming them as their own.

"York," his mother called.

York spun to see her rushing toward him—her hands were still wet from washing clothes and her sleeves still flecked with suds. Her black hair spilled from the hasty knot she had tied to get it out of her way while she worked. She yanked Bethann from York's arms and raced into the milling crowd seeking to escape into the shadow of the trees. York followed as she ducked into the underbrush.

"This way," York said. He led them to the pile of boulders where he had been practicing with his sling the day before. They clambered through a gap in the stones to a little overhang where they could hide.

"Wait here," he said.

"Save him," his mother whispered. York nodded and raced back toward the village. He couldn't abandon his father to fight alone, without his only son beside him.

As he ran, York slipped the loop from one end of the sling over his middle finger, pulled a stone from his pocket, settled it in the leather pouch, and pulled the other string through his fingers until he grasped the familiar knot. He ducked under a branch and slid to a stop on the edge of the clearing. A big Bracari warrior in a long, green tunic laughed as he chased after a Carpentini woman, who clutched her blue skirt high to free her legs for running.

York swung the sling once over his head and snapped it forward with all the strength he could muster as he let go of the loose end of the string. The sling cracked as the stone flew true to slam into the side of the Bracari's head. York gave a battle whoop as he watched the Bracari stumble and fall without a sound. He thought his father should have had more faith in him. He was small, but he was skilled enough to be a warrior. York grabbed another stone from his pouch and prepared to throw again when the snarl of an enraged dog reached his ears.

He spun as a great black beast leapt onto a shrieking child. The horror of the scene almost paralyzed him. But York snapped the sling again, feeling the reassuring weight of the stone in the sling as it spun over his head and flew toward the dog. The stone slapped into the dog's neck and knocked it off balance. The dog snarled and sank its jaws into the child's upraised arm. The child screamed. York swung again, this time taking the care to be sure of his aim.

The stone cracked against the dog's head. The dog released the child and staggered sideways. Then it turned, and York looked it right in the eyes. A low rumble escaped the dog's throat as its lips lifted in a snarl. The child tried to crawl away without using her injured arm.

York realized with a sudden sinking feeling that he was about to face the *rush of an enraged Bracari hound. The Bracari had been breeding these massive war dogs to hunt and kill Carpentini. The dog's hackles raised, and the muscles rippled beneath its black fur. It charged. York stood his ground as the beast bounded toward him.*

His mouth went dry, and he struggled to breathe. York snapped the sling. The stone struck the dog full in the forehead. The dog stumbled and plowed head-first onto the trampled earth. York shrieked in triumph and rushed the dog. He yanked his knife from its sheath, leapt onto the dog's back, and plunged the blade into the dog's heart. The dog's huge muscles rippled as he tried to throw York off. It jerked and struggled. But York clung to its back and drove the blade home again and again in desperate terror.

As the dog's death struggles slowed, York rolled from its back, sheathed his knife, and scrambled to the weeping child. He carried her into the trees and set her in a little hollow.

"It'll be all right," he said before he sprinted back into the village.

His father's hoarse cry roared over the tumult of battle, and York zig-zagged in between the huts until he found his father locked in combat with three Bracari warriors.

York prepared his sling, but he didn't dare throw. The men were weaving and dodging, exchanging blows and backing off in the weird choreography of battle. Two Bracari lay bleeding on the ground, and York felt a sudden pride in his father. He was a great man. A skilled warrior. No Bracari pig would ever defeat his father.

A Bracari swung a great sword in a powerful stroke for this father's head. His father flicked his sword to parry the blow, while he kicked a second Bracari in the groin. Then, the unthinkable happened. The famous sword his father wielded snapped at the hilt. The Bracari's sword drove through the broken sword and bit deep into his father's shoulder.

York screamed as the third Bracari drove a blade into his father's belly. The horror of it tore the tears from his eyes and gripped his stomach in an agonizing knot. York swung the sling. The stone glanced off the Bracari's shoulder. York loaded it again and swung. This one caught the Bracari in the face. The Bracari dropped his sword and clutched at his head. The other Bracari charged at York. York didn't have time to load another stone, but he couldn't leave.

He couldn't let his father die like that—alone and unaided. York dodged behind a hut, trying to slip a stone into his sling. A dog rushed past him, apparently intent on some other prey. The Bracari came around the hut, and York snapped the sling. The stone caught the Bracari in the chest. The Bracari roared

Vengeance

in pain, and York slipped away into the milling crowd of fleeing Carpentini. He circled back to find his father, but the village had been overrun. The Bracari warriors had formed a line and were capturing and butchering as they came. York could see his father's body lying in the dirt beyond the Bracari line, but he couldn't reach it.

York ground his teeth and screamed in frustration. He had no choice but to retreat into the woods. The tears blurred his vision and the sobs burned his chest. He had failed. His father was dead. If he had been a true warrior rather than a child playing with slings, maybe his father would still be alive.

The deep-throated bark of a hound rang over the hills as York watched the last of the men Reed had left at the castle break from the trees and sprint across the green, sloping hill toward the crevice. York scrambled up the final ten yards to the ridgeline to stand beside Brion. They were a good fifty feet above the opening to the crevice.

"Can you use that sling?" Brion asked.

York nodded.

"Good. I want you over there by the boulder where you will have a clear area to swing it." Brion laid a hand on York's shoulder. "I imagine you've already seen battle," he said.

York nodded again.

"Keep your wits about you, and don't forget to pay attention to what is going on around you. If they come up the hill, you don't want to be taken by surprise."

"I'll kill them," York said. He hadn't meant to sound like an immature teenager spoiling for a fight. He wanted to sound resolute and determined because he knew men judged him because of his size.

Brion appraised him and nodded. "They haven't left you much choice, have they?"

The bay of the hounds rang out again, and York scrambled to the area Brion had indicated. The Bracari burst from the tree line below and spread out over the open ground before the crevice. Their green tunics blended with the vibrant green of the heathland in spring, but the white leg wrappings they wound around their calves just above the short-topped boots seemed unnatural as they churned their way toward the crevice. They kept coming—at least two hundred of them.

The breath caught in York's throat. His pulse pounded at his temples. There were so many of them. The black shapes of the hounds bounded through the purple heather that dotted the green hillside. The sudden terror at the Bracari arrival gave way to a trembling anger. York hated them. He would kill as many of them as he could. But they were still too far away.

York was surprised to see Brion draw his bow to his ear, pause, and loose. The quiet thrum of the string sounded as the arrow leapt from the bow. York followed the arc of the white goose fletching as it lifted into the gray sky to plummet toward the on-rushing Bracari. One of the leaders stumbled and fell. York glanced back at Brion in shock. He had never seen a man who could make a shot like that. Brion drew and loosed two more times before the Bracari were within the range of the other archers. A shower of arrows fell among them as the last of the Carpentini slipped into the crevice. York placed a stone on his sling, whirled it once over his head and snapped it.

He lost sight of the stone as it sailed over the green land and so had no idea if it struck a Bracari. But he kept slinging, one stone after another. The flood of Bracari reached the crevice, and York realized how ingenious Brion had been in choosing it. The slope up to where the archers and slingers stood was steep and slippery. Any Bracari who tried to scale it were picked off by the archers or the men who tossed rocks down from above. Those that struggled to break through the barricade into the crevice faced the rocks from above and the arrows and swords from the men inside the barricade.

The crashing roar of battle surged about the stone outcrop and the crevice. Blood stained the rushing creek. The cries of the wounded and dying filled the air. A shout rose up from the Bracari as they tore at the barricade and part of it crumbled into the creek. The Carpentini fell back as the Bracari rushed in. York's sling and the bows of the archers from above were of no use. They couldn't shoot down into the crack.

Brion gestured for York to pick stones from the piles by the lip of the crevice, while he discarded his bow, drew his sword, and slid down the slope into the Bracari that were clambering over the barricade and into the gap. Some men followed him, but others rushed to the piles of stones and began dropping them to bounce and ricochet onto the heads of the Bracari. York joined them as the cries of the women and children echoed through the crevice.

Gwyneth crouched in the corner of the overhang, breathing in the damp air. Her shirt was wet and muddy, her bare feet scratched and bleeding. The sounds of the battle at the entrance rang off the dripping stone walls. Women and children clung to one another, whimpering in the shadows, knowing that none of them were safe. Gwyneth kept her gaze on Finola, the young warrior woman. She had her bow strung and paced the entrance to the overhang. She seemed so strong and confident.

The women had spent the last hour erecting a makeshift barricade out of fallen trees and boulders. But Gwyneth knew it would be no use. If the Bracari reached them, they would be enslaved or killed. Men were always men. She had learned this from her earliest experiences. Men had preyed upon her mother, despised her because she had failed to bare a male child. Gwyneth remembered it well. She had been only ten when her Uncle Edrick died. The vile men had started in on her mother at once.

"You won't get a better offer," the man had said. He was a tall, wiry man with short, dark hair and a wispy beard. Gwyneth tried to understand what he was talking about. She had seen the man around the village and had noticed that he had taken an interest in her mother, Aila. Most men either ignored her mother or seemed to think she was some dog they could order about.

Aila tried to twist her wrist from the man's grasp. She stared up at him with her one good eye. The patch she wore on the other had slipped aside, revealing the hole where the other eye should have been.

Gwyneth rushed past the pile of straw in the barn where the man had cornered Aila. "Let her go," Gwyneth yelled. She kicked at the man's shins. He backhanded her across the face, sending her sprawling onto the hard-packed earth. The reek of horses and manure filled her nostrils. She tasted blood.

"You're damaged goods," the man said. "No man will marry you. I offer you a home and food and clothing. I only ask a few favors in return."

"You're a brute and a villain," Aila said. "Let me go."

The man laughed. "You'll come around," he said. "You have no protector now that your dear brother has gone the same way as your useless father."

Aila spat in his face.

The man raised his fist and swung. The slap of flesh on flesh echoed in the barn. Gwyneth scrambled to her feet and rushed the man again as the harsh tears streamed down her face. She was only ten and small for her age, but she latched onto his leg and sank her teeth in as hard as she could bite. The rough linen fabric tasted of sweat and horse. She refused to gag in revulsion as she ground her teeth, desperate to save her mother.

The man bellowed, grabbed her by the hair, and yanked her off his leg. He flung her to the earth. "Bracari dog," he yelled. The wind flew from Gwyneth's lungs. The man kicked Aila one last time.

"Next time," he said, "you won't refuse."

Gwyneth watched him stride out of the barn as she gasped for breath. Why did everyone call her Bracari? She was half-Carpentini. Why didn't that matter? And why were men like this? Why did they only want to abuse and control women? Her uncle hadn't been that way. He had been gentle and kind. But Gwyneth had never met another man like him. And now that he had died in battle, they had no one to provide for them, no one to protect them.

Gwyneth crawled to Aila's side. Aila sobbed quietly into her hands. Gwyneth draped her thin arm over her mother's shoulder. Her mother jerked and glanced up. Tears spilled from her single bright green eye. She clutched at Gwyneth and pulled her close. "My baby," she sobbed. "My poor child."

A roar echoed down the crevice and children began crying. Gwyneth watched as Carpentini men fell back toward the deep overhang where the women and children crouched in terror. The Carpentini warriors stumbled over the rugged ground and slippery stones. Water splashed around their feet. There should have been more warriors. Why were there so few?

Finola stepped up to the barricade, nocked an arrow, drew, and released. A Bracari slumped over, clutching at an arrow in his chest. Finola drew and released again and again.

Several Bracari men clambered over the makeshift barricade as others pushed the Carpentini back. One of them grabbed up a little girl and held a knife under her chin. Gwyneth stared for a moment. These were the Bracari, the people she had been identified with all her life. She was hated because her father had been a Bracari. Now, here they were, killing and kidnapping. A strangled cry escaped Gwyneth's throat as she seized a rock from the floor and hurled it at the Bracari. It struck him in the back. Gwyneth grabbed up another stone and launched herself on the Bracari, beating him over the head in her desperate fury. He dropped the girl and stumbled backward, tripping over the wall of stones.

Finola drew her sword and leapt into the Bracari men who were attempting to snatch up the women and children. A cry of despair and rage rose up from the rest of the women who snatched up rocks or drew hidden knives. They rushed the Bracari warriors and swarmed over them in a hail of stones and slashing blades.

From where he stood on the lip of the crevice, York could see the battle raging below. Brion and two dozen other Carpentini struggled with the Bracari that still clustered around the mouth of the crevice. The tan-clad Carpentini mingled and struggled with the flood of green-clad Bracari, surging back and forth in a desperate fight. Reed stood with his legs planted astride the gurgling creek, swinging the great battle-axe for which he was famous. He reminded York of his father, and York wished he had big, burly arms so he could pick up a heavy axe and cut down the Bracari. Dogs growled and snarled as they dragged men down and clamped their jaws on their throats.

Bracari had penetrated all the way to the overhang, and the women had joined their men in the fighting. It was a desperate struggle, and York realized that they might lose—that Reed's entire village and all the Carpentini with him might be killed or captured. York dropped rock after rock onto the Bracari heads below, frantic to do something to stop the slaughter of his people. But he couldn't aim in the narrow gap. His stones deflected off the walls of the crevice and, more often than not, splashed into the creek.

The cries of the women and children filled his ears. His mother and Bethann were down there—the last of his family. He had to do something more to protect them. The horror of the scene choked him. York decided to scramble down the hill and join the men fighting at the entrance, when a growl sounded behind him. He spun to find a huge, black Bracari hound bounding up the hillside. He looked around and realized that all of the men who had been with him dropping stones on the Bracari had left the lip of the crevice and joined the battle below. He was alone. The hound cut off his escape.

Terror tightened York's throat. He had no time to use his sling.

In desperation, York grabbed a root that had crept over the edge of the crevice and swung himself over the side. The hound's jaws snapped at the hem of his tunic. York dangled over the chasm. His boots could find no purchase on the moss-covered stone. The hound snapped at him again, and York grabbed at another root and lurched downward. He glanced down at the struggling men and the rushing water. The hound snarled and pawed at the ledge, sending a shower of moist earth into York's face. Drool dripped from its jaws. York's hand slipped.

The root gave way, and he was crashing down into the chasm, clutching and clawing at anything that would break his fall. Stones tore loose, and he ripped off fists full of moss. He snatched at roots and bushes, slowing his fall to a jerking, lurching cascade of soil and rock.

York crashed onto the head of a Bracari and tumbled into the creek on top of him. York lay in the icy waters of the stream as they flowed over him for a moment before he realized that he was looking at the white leg wrapping of a Bracari standing over him. York jerked his head from the water as the Bracari raised a dripping sword for the killing stroke. York rolled free of the creek as the steel rang off the rock.

He struggled to get his knife free. The Bracari sprang after him, when a rock slammed into the side of the Bracari's head. He reeled. York freed his knife and slashed at the Bracari. He felt the knife bite into flesh and glance off bone. He scrambled away as the Bracari staggered backward, staring in horror at the gaping wound York had ripped across the man's chest. Men surged about York, jostling him in their desperate struggle.

The Bracari began retreating toward the entrance under the combined assault of the men and women, only to mill about near the entrance because there was no escape. Reed's battle cry rang out as he burst through the makeshift barricade, driving the last of the Bracari before him. The Bracari were trapped, and the Carpentini would show no more mercy than the Bracari had shown them.

Chapter 4
Vengeance

York trembled as he clutched Bethann to his chest. He stumbled over the heathland, trailing behind the rest of the injured and exhausted people as they filed back to the keep and the burned out homes they had been building. He was bruised and scraped from his terrifying plunge into the crevice. As they trudged along, they passed trampled fields and slaughtered sheep and cattle. Recently constructed buildings still smoldered.

The Carpentini had spent the night and the better part of the next day at the crevice as Reed sent parties out to see if it was safe to return to the keep. While they waited, they treated the injured, buried their own dead, and stripped the Bracari dead of all their clothes, weapons, and supplies. The silent, marching people reminded him of their flight from the last Bracari raid that had killed his father. It had been late winter then, and many had suffered from the cold.

York crouched over the tiny fire trying to coax it back to life as the chill wind blew through the makeshift lean-to he had erected against a boulder. His mother sat in the corner, her clothes torn, her face streaked with dirt and soot. Bethann, his little sister, chewed a root and stared hungrily at the skinned squirrel that York stretched out on the stone slab beside the few roots he had managed to pry from the frozen ground. They were all hungry.

It had been two days since the attack on their village and the stragglers were working their way through the pass to the other side of the Aveen Mountains in the hope of escaping the Bracari and their vicious dogs. York and what was left of his family had joined a band being led by a big, burly man with a red beard named Reed. He promised to rebuild a new village that would be safe from Bracari raids. York didn't believe him, but he understood why people grasped at the pitiful hope Reed offered them. The only other option was to lie down and die.

York had spent the last two days trying not to think of his father, but the image of him sprawled on the ground as his life's blood pooled underneath him would not leave York alone. He bent and blew into the fire as he added a few more sticks. The rich smell of burning heather filled the lean-to.

The air still possessed the bite of winter. Patches of snow clung to the shadows. York pulled the pot toward him and lifted his knife to cut the squirrel into pieces.

"Why didn't you save him?" his mother's accusation was soft as if she hadn't expected him to hear.

York turned from the fire in surprise. Had he heard her right? Bethann kept chewing on the root. The hilt of his father's sword lay beside his mother, as if she had just been holding it. Did she expect him to answer?

"I—"

"You were there," she said louder. "You are his son."

York stared in disbelief. She had hardly spoken a word since the battle. They had buried his father in a quick grave beside the others who had died and then had fled deeper into the Aveen Mountains.

What could he say? A knot tightened in his throat. He blinked at the sudden sting in his eyes. His own mother blamed him. How could he live with the shame and the guilt?

"If you had been a true warrior," she whispered, "he wouldn't have died."

York slumped against the cold stone of the boulder as the tears dripped into the pot. If even his mother condemned him, no one would ever let him forget that he had failed. He had let his father die.

Brion sat on a pile of stones just inside the entry of the keep. He rested his elbows on his knees. It had been a savage fight. The Carpentini had left no one alive. Every Bracari that had been trapped in the crevice had been slaughtered and their bodies stripped and burned in a huge bonfire that left a sickening haze over the valley. Brion had never seen anything like it. The horror of it still filled his chest with a peculiar dread. Something had changed in the heathland. The different tribes had long preyed upon each other for slaves and land and to win the right to wear the Salassani war paint. But they did not try to annihilate one another. Brion stood. He had come to find his mother and now discovered that he was caught in a vicious civil war. He needed to know what was happening.

The injured and dying lay scattered along the inner walls, too many to fit inside the keep itself. It was a pitiful sight. So many had been killed, so many maimed. Those men who were still fit continued to work on the walls while the women cooked over small fires and tended the wounded. The weapons and usable clothes taken from the Bracari dead lay stacked in a heap against the wall. Reed had allowed his people to claim whatever booty they could from the bodies.

The air had cooled as evening crept over the foothills of the Aveen Mountains. A breeze picked up the smoke from the fires and flung it about the enclosure, but it couldn't conceal the stench of human filth.

Finola busied herself tending to the injured—especially the children. Gwyneth followed her around like a shadow. She had picked up some Carpentini boots and a pair of Bracari trousers and a tunic from somewhere. She had also found a belt and a knife that she strapped around her slender waist. Brion smiled. The girl was trying to imitate Finola.

Brion found Reed in the keep with a group of men gathered around him. York sat by the fire cradling a girl in his arms. A woman worked over the fire beside him. Reed had ordered the most seriously injured to be brought into the keep. As putrid as the air outside had been, the keep was worse. Sick and dying people filled the enclosed space with a sickly, sweet odor.

Reed glanced up as Brion entered and gestured for him to join them.

Brion strode up to Reed. "Why are the Bracari attacking you?" Brion asked without any preamble.

Reed stared at him as if this were a stupid question.

"I mean, they weren't just raiding," Brion said. "They came to kill."

Reed scoffed. "While you Alamani have been celebrating your victory, Tristan has been seeking his revenge."

"Revenge? On you? For what?"

"Most Carpentini and Salassani refused to support him in the war. He says we betrayed him. He blames us for his defeat."

"That's ridiculous."

"To you maybe," Reed said.

"So, he convinced the Bracari to attack you?"

"He's done more than that," Reed said. "He's given them our land. Made us outlaws."

Brion stared. "He isn't the king of the Carpentini."

Reed gave Brion an ironic smile. "Maybe you should go tell him that."

Brion shook his head in confusion. "Can you please explain what is going on?"

Reed glanced at York and his mother as if they had something to do with it.

"The Bracari have long sought our lands," Reed began. "About two months ago, we captured a wounded Bracari that had raided our village. He had certain papers on him."

Reed glanced at York again.

York remembered the day they had learned what King Tristan had done to them.

He held his little sister close. The Bracari captive spit the blood from his mouth. It dribbled onto his green tunic. His hands were bound, and he was propped up against a pine tree. Reed stood over him with a club in his hands.

York recognized the prisoner as the man that ran his sword through his father's belly. He would never forget the broad scar on his cheek that made him look like he was permanently laughing. The man had been captured the previous evening by the scouts Reed had sent out to search for any more Bracari bands. If Reed hadn't been standing there with a club, York would have slipped his knife between the man's ribs. But he couldn't afford to be banished from the small community. He would never be able to keep his mother and sister alive on his own.

York leaned to whisper in his mother's ear. "He is the one that killed father."

His mother jerked her gaze from the Bracari to stare into York's face. She didn't have time to say anything before Reed started speaking.

"Why are the Bracari invading our land?" Reed demanded.

The Bracari sneered with his ruined mouth. "You have no land." He gestured to a leather satchel with a nod of his head. York picked it up and handed it to Reed, who flipped it open and drew out a bundle of papers.

"What do they say?" Reed asked as he shoved them toward the girl named

Vengeance

Gwyneth. She unfolded them with nimble fingers and began to read. York experienced a pang of jealously. How could this poor orphan girl know how to do something most Carpentini men didn't know how to do?

"I Tristan," Gwyneth began, "King of the Dunkeldi and Lord of the Heathlands, in consequence of the treasonous rebellion of the Carpentini and the Salassani clans, who not only refused to protect our lands from the invasion of the Alamani —"

"We bled as much as any of the tribes," someone shouted.

Reed waved him to silence and bade Gwyneth continue. She cleared her throat.

"—but in some cases conspired with them to overthrow our lands and to enslave our people, do hereby outlaw all clans of the Carpentini and the Salassani." Murmurs of disbelief rippled through the crowd, but Gwyneth continued reading. "They no longer enjoy the protection of my laws or of my arms. The names of their clans shall not be spoken. Their men shall be executed on sight, and their women and children sold into slavery—"

A general murmur of horror swept through the gathering. "By what right?" someone demanded. Reed shushed them and gestured for Gwyneth to continue reading. She licked her lips and glanced around at the crowd of angry onlookers. Her eyes were wide as she looked back to the page and continued reading.

"In recognition of faithful service in the late war, I hereby grant all Carpentini lands to the Bracari and all Salassani lands to the Taurini. Clan chieftains may seize these lands, and, after holding them for six months, the lands will transfer to that clan."

Pandemonium erupted. Someone kicked the Bracari, and he fell heavily on his side.

"Tristan isn't our king," someone shouted. "We have never accepted him as king. We are a free and independent people."

York's gaze focused on the face of the Bracari, who lay on his side with blood dribbling from his mouth. The Bracari was laughing at them.

Reed yanked the Bracari to a sitting position.

"Shut up," Reed bellowed over the tumult. "Explain this," he said to the Bracari.

The Bracari laughed again. The blood gurgled in his throat.

"Tristan couldn't seize your land if you were men enough to keep it," he said.

York jerked his knife from its sheath. He had heard enough. This man had killed his father, and now he mocked them. York stepped forward, but a blue-clad form streaked in front of him. Before he realized what was happening, York's mother stabbed a knife into the man's throat. Reed gave a shout and pulled her off, but it was too late. York's mother kicked and fought until Reed released her, and she stumbled to her knees.

Reed yanked the knife from the Bracari's throat and tossed it on the pine needles beside York's mother. York stared in shock for a moment before he slipped his knife back into its sheath and bent to help her to her feet. She grabbed his hand and squeezed it tight. Her lip lifted in a sneer.

"I had to do it because you couldn't," she said.

York's insides melted into a hot, painful glue that made it hard to breathe. He glanced around to see the entire crowd of silent, watching people. They all knew that he had not avenged his father. That he was no warrior.

"Well, this isn't what I expected," Brion said. He sat beside Finola under the little lean-to they had constructed down by the creek at the base of the hill. The keep was overflowing with refugees who kept pouring in. Word had gone out that Reed was gathering the Carpentini. Finola had also insisted on escaping the constant reek of the keep and the noise of the injured and dying. She had spent all day giving what help she could with Gwyneth in her shadow and the little boy Finola had named Iain clutching at her tunic.

The evening air was chill this far up in the foothills, and Brion's breath came in little white clouds. The air tasted sweet and fresh compared to the fetid stink of the keep. The gurgle of the creek softened the harsh crack of the hammers as Reed's men worked furiously to complete the walls.

"I've never seen savagery like that," Brion said. He still couldn't rid himself of the memory of the piles of mangled corpses and the stink of death. It was always the smell that clung to him. He would never get used to it.

"Even the women were so. . ." Brion fiddled with the handle of the knife in his belt as he struggled to find the words to describe what he had witnessed.

"Desperate?" Finola said. "Terrified? Full of vengeful hatred for men who had been killing their husbands, fathers, brothers, and children before carrying them off to rape them and sell them as slaves? I know exactly how they felt."

Vengeance

Finola gazed at Brion. She wasn't chiding him. She was just reminding him that she understood how deeply that hatred could push its roots into a woman's soul. Brion nodded. He understood all that, but what he had seen had been so vicious. Finola smiled at his silence.

"Seems like we've gotten ourselves in over our heads," she said. Iain, snuggled in Finola's lap, staring at Brion with wide, brown eyes. Brion had constructed a long fire before the lean-to with a firebreak to reflect the heat back into the shelter. He had also built a low-lying shelf for a bed, which he had covered with pine boughs and furs. They would be warm tonight despite the chill.

Iain clung to Finola with a desperation that made Brion pity him all the more. What must this child have seen? Finola smoothed his hair with a gentle hand.

"He's such a clever thing," she said.

Brion had seen Finola growing increasingly attached to the boy. He needed to do something about that.

"Finola," he began.

"Don't," Finola said without looking at him.

"You know he can't stay with us," Brion said. "These are his people."

Finola glared at him. "He has no one else," she said. "His entire family is dead."

"But we'll have to leave," Brion said. "I know how much you want a child—"

"Don't," Finola snapped. "Don't pity me."

Brion touched her leg. How could he explain to her that he didn't blame her or pity her? Ever since they had received word that Brigid was expecting her first child, Finola had grown increasingly frustrated and withdrawn. She seemed to see her lack of ability to conceive as a personal failing that she could not forgive. When Brion reminded her that her mother had only been able to bear one child, Finola had simply turned away.

"If I can't have my own," Finola said, "then I'm going to help the ones that I can."

Brion watched her, uncertain how to convince her that the child would be better off with his own people. He also hoped to dissuade her because he was desperate to find his mother, Elsie. All this unexpected turmoil and commotion was only going to make it more difficult. Brion pushed a log deeper into the fire.

"What do we do now?" he asked. "Do we stay here or move on?"

Finola shook her head. "If your mother came north, she must be around here somewhere. She could hardly go to the Bracari or the Aldina. I think she's hiding in the Aveens. With all the Bracari around, she'll have to come where the people are gathering sooner or later. We have a better chance of finding her here than wandering around the foothills."

"How will we recognize her?" Brion asked. "All I have is the ring and the old man's description of her as tall and slender with dark hair and dark eyes. That could describe most of the women here. She could be here now, and I wouldn't even know." Brion wore the ring on a chain around his neck.

"Didn't the Duke say you looked like her?" Finola said.

Brion grunted. "That's not much help."

"Maybe you should just ask Reed if he has heard of her?"

Brion scoffed. "Reed is only tolerating us because we helped them. When he finds out who we are, we aren't going to be safe."

Brion wanted to conceal his true identity as long as he could. In a twist of fate that still left him bewildered, he had become a duke when his father, the Duke of Saylen had legitimized him and given him his title. His younger sister, Brigid, was now the queen, and Emyr, the man who had led the raid that killed his adopted parents, sat on the throne. Brion had only visited his estate in the south once and left his friend, Owen, to administer it for him. Brion wanted to be free.

He was not cut out to be a noble, constantly pouring over ledgers and accounts and seeking favor at court. He wanted to roam the wild heathland he had come to love, and he wanted to find his mother. He had tracked her to the village in the southern Aveen Mountains only to be told by an old man that she had escaped Cedrick just before the war began and fled north. He had also stated that the Carpentini were gathering near Comrie, and so Brion and Finola had ridden north to find them.

Still, it would not be wise to let the Carpentini know that he was a duke. It might make him a target for anyone still upset by the last war or anyone who wanted to capture him and use him to influence Emyr.

"You think the Carpentini would sell us to the Bracari?" Finola asked.

"Why not?" Brion said. "We would be a valuable bargaining chip for Tristan."

Something rustled the leaves outside the lean-to beyond the fire. Brion squinted to try to peer past the blaze from the long fire, but the light of the dancing flames obscured everything in the growing darkness beyond. Brion slipped his knife from its sheath as Finola set Iain aside and picked up her bow.

Gwyneth stepped into the firelight. She still wore the long tunic and trousers she had been wearing earlier in the day. She had added a sword that dangled at her hip and a bow and a quiver of arrows.

Behind the dirt and grime on her face, she was a beautiful girl with long black hair and green eyes. It was an odd combination, but it was also striking. Brion glanced at Finola, who set her bow down and smiled at Gwyneth. Gwyneth glanced at Brion as if she didn't trust him and stepped into the lean-to to sit on the wooden bed frame next to Finola and as far away from Brion as she could get. Brion realized that Finola had planned this all along and shook his head in disbelief. He should have known.

"Hi," Brion said to Gwyneth.

Gwyneth scowled at him.

"They call you Gwyneth, don't they?" he asked.

She continued to glare at him with lips pinched tight. Brion shrugged helplessly to Finola.

"Yes," Finola said. "Her name is Gwyneth, and she's alone, too."

Brion grunted as he realized he would be sleeping on the ground tonight. Was Finola going to collect every orphan she found?

"Things are going to change around here," Finola said.

Brion glanced at the ground before the fire, trying to decide where he should make his new bed.

Finola laughed. "I'm not banishing you to the dirt," she said. "I'm talking about the way these Carpentini men treat their women."

"Should I be frightened?" Brion asked.

"No man is safe," Finola said with a wicked grin.

Brion tried to appear innocent as Reed glanced at Gwyneth who had just entered the keep the next morning with the sword on her hip and a bow in her hands. Reed scowled and gestured to Finola.

"What are you doing to my household?" he asked. He nodded to the men around him, and they dispersed. Some hurried out the door of the keep as though they had been sent on errands.

Finola gave him a pretty smile and batted her eyelids at him playfully. "I don't know what you mean," she said.

Brion pitied any man who tangled with Finola when she had set her mind to something. And he was anxious that she not upset the guarded acceptance they had achieved from Reed and his band.

Reed smirked at her. "I'm not blind," he said. "Gwyneth did not stay in the keep last night, and now she returns this morning armed for war?" He glanced at Gwyneth again. "Can you even shoot a bow?"

"I will be able to," she said, standing tall and defiant.

Finola gave him a satisfied expression. "It's time you trained your women to fight," she said.

Quiet settled over the occupants of the keep as the murmuring ceased and all eyes turned to Finola. Brion wondered how all these people could stay inside the keep with its horrible stink.

Finola kept talking. "The battle at the crevice proved that we can fight and that we will have to fight again before this is over." She scanned the men, daring them to contradict her. "If you want your women to survive and avoid slavery, you need to make sure they know how to defend themselves."

"I'm not sure I like that idea," someone called out.

Brion glanced around to see a woman punch a short, round man in the arm. He grinned.

"She's ornery enough without a knife," he said.

"We have a right to defend ourselves," a tall, thin woman with graying hair said. She had a bandage around her arm, proof that she had participated in the battle.

"But if you're all out fighting, who's going to care for the young'uns and cook the food?" It was a young man with long, black hair, and he appeared to be in earnest.

Vengeance

The tall woman smirked at him. "Wouldn't do you any harm to learn to cook," she said. A ripple of laughter followed her words. "Besides," she continued, "if it hadn't been for us, you would have lost at the crevice."

Several men exchanged glances. Her words were true enough, and everyone there knew it. Reed studied the woman. He clearly respected her opinion.

"Very well," Reed said. He turned to Finola. "I assume you're volunteering to train them?"

Finola grinned. "You have plenty of weapons now."

Reed nodded and faced the tall woman who stood with her hands on her hips. "Just make sure the men working on the keep are fed and that your training doesn't interrupt our preparations for next winter."

Then Reed motioned for Brion to approach. Brion stepped around a woman holding a child. "I'm trusting you and your wife," Reed said. "I don't need any more problems. If this training gets out of hand, I'm putting a stop to it."

"Fair enough," Brion said.

"And," Reed continued, "it might interest you to know that a large party of Salassani with their women and children will arrive here this afternoon. It appears they're searching for a Brion of Wexford."

"This can't be good," Brion said to Finola as they left the stifling air of the keep.

"You think the Salassani mean trouble?" Finola asked. Iain clung to her tunic as she carried him on her hip. Gwyneth trailed behind.

"They probably blame me for what Tristan is doing to them," Brion said.

"But how would they know you are here? We didn't tell anyone but Emyr and Owen that we were coming north."

Brion sighed as he gazed out over the mist-covered hills that rolled up to the snowcapped peaks of the Aveen Mountains. It was a beautiful land. His mother was out there somewhere, struggling to stay alive. With the Bracari roaming the area seeking to pick off unprotected Carpentini, she was in real danger, and he was helpless to do anything about it. Brion nodded toward the distant peaks.

"Do you ever get the feeling that some evil spirit is sitting up there on those mountains reporting to our worst enemies every move we make?"

Finola laughed. "Now you're getting paranoid again," she said.

"Yeah, well, I'm thinking maybe we should get out of here before the Salassani arrive."

Finola shook her head and grinned. "I have an army to train."

"You're enjoying this, aren't you?"

"We start with the Carpentini and then we move to the Alamani. Men everywhere are going to learn to respect women."

Brion held up his hands. "You and Gwyneth are going to start a civil war between men and women if you're not careful."

Finola wiggled her eyebrows at him. "Admit it," she said. "You still get nervous around dangerous women."

"I get nervous every time you have a big idea," Brion said.

"Because you know I'm always right."

"No," Brion said with exaggerated patience, "because I know it's usually going to make my life more difficult."

Finola nudged Brion and nodded to where York was climbing the hill towards them.

"I think," she said, "that you had better decide what you're going to do for that boy."

"What?"

"He needs you," Finola said. She gestured to Gwyneth to follow her, and she headed down the hill toward their lean-to. Gwyneth gave him a reproachful glance as she passed.

Brion scowled after them for a moment before striding to meet York.

"Morning," Brion said. "How are your mother and sister?"

York gave a noncommittal shrug. "Fine," he said.

"Your father?"

"My father was a great warrior."

Brion hadn't missed the way York spoke of his father as if he were gone. "It's your mother, isn't it?"

York snapped his head up to stare at Brion before he looked away. "She thinks it's my fault," he said.

Brion studied York. He was small for his age, but he had shown as much courage as any man who had fought at the crevice.

"Will you help me?" York said.

"If I can," Brion said.

"I need to be a warrior," York said.

"You've already been one."

York shook his head emphatically. "No. I mean, I need to be like you. I need to be able to use a sword and a bow."

"What do you mean, you 'need'?"

York gazed at the ground.

If he agreed to help this boy, he was committing to remain with the Carpentini and postpone his search for his mother. He was also agreeing to remain and face the Salassani. Brion glanced up at the Aveen peaks again.

"All right," Brion said. "But I want something in return."

York's eyes widened, and he began to fidget. "But I don't have anything."

"Do you know how to swim?" Brion asked.

York stared in surprise. He had apparently been expecting something different.

"Yes," he said.

"I'll teach you what I know if you'll teach me how to swim," Brion said.

A broad grin crept over York's face. "Agreed," he said.

Gwyneth joined the other fifty women gathered at the base of the hill below the keep who had come to be trained by the fiery young woman. A big Carpentini woman shouldered Gwyneth aside to get a better position. Gwyneth stepped back. She had always tried to be invisible. When people didn't notice her, she experienced less trouble. Still, things like this happened all the time. No one thought twice about insulting her. And no one would come to her defense. Gwyneth shifted so she could see around the woman as Finola raised her hand to quiet the crowd.

Finola had selected an open space between the creek and the trees where there was room to spread out. The women milled about whispering to each other as they waited for Finola to begin. They were dressed in the traditional blue dresses that the Carpentini women wore. Gwyneth moved to the front of the crowd of women. She held the sword she had picked up off the battlefield and the bow and quiver of arrows she had pulled from the pile of weapons Reed had deposited in the keep. Other women came with a variety of weapons they had also collected. Small groups of men loitered nearby, acting as if they were working. But Gwyneth knew better. They had come to gawk. Men were so predictable.

Finola stood in front of the women, slender and confident, but she had not brought her weapons. This confused Gwyneth. She had come to learn how to use the bow and the sword, how to wreak vengeance on any man that tried to abuse her the way they had abused her mother.

"Ladies," Finola began, "let's start by being honest with ourselves. In most cases, the men who are going to attack us will be better trained, more experienced, and stronger than we are."

The women exchanged glances. This wasn't what they had expected.

"It also takes years of training to become competent at the sword or the sling. We don't have years. We have weeks, maybe days."

"So, what's the point of this?" a short, round young woman called. "You just said we don't stand a chance."

A sad expression swept over Finola's face before she replied. This also confused Gwyneth, she had thought Finola was a hard woman, made of steel. That's what she liked about her. She couldn't understand why she would show this sign of weakness in front of the women—women that Gwyneth knew could be vindictive and unforgiving. They had never been able to forgive Gwyneth for being born half-Bracari.

Finola shook her head. "I'm sorry for what the Bracari have done to you," she said. "I'm sorry for what they have done to your children and your husbands. But let's face it. You have so few men left now. If you hope to survive, you'll have to learn to fight."

The woman who challenged Finola put her hands on her hips. "So let's get on with it," she said. "What's the point of standing here talking?"

"The point is," Finola shouted over the commotion that followed, "that all of you have seen combat. Most of you have already had to fight and kill to protect your children and your families."

Vengeance

"So?"

"So, the most important thing you bring to any fight is your determination to conquer. If you have already decided that you're no match for a man, then you have already lost."

The women shuffled their feet, but no one spoke.

"You have to decide that your life and your person, that the lives of your children and your menfolk are worth fighting for." Finola paused and considered for a moment. "Well," she said, "some men really aren't worth protecting, but most of them are. And all of them would be lost without us, but you have to decide that no Bracari pig is going to steal you away from your own people and live to brag about it."

The women chuckled. Someone shouted, "Here! Here!"

Finola surveyed them. "I've seen what you are capable of back there in the crevice. You know that you have a right to your own body, to decide who can touch it and who cannot." Finola glanced at Gwyneth as if she knew Gwyneth's history. Gwyneth's chest warmed with the hatred for the men who had tried to steal that right from her mother.

"I've also been told that Carpentini women of old used to be great warriors," Finola continued. "That they used to fight alongside their men. Is this true?"

The women nodded. Gwyneth had heard the tales of the women who rode into battle with their husbands. Her mother, Aila, had told her how her own grandmother had stood against Bracari warriors and won. Gwyneth had always wanted to be like her.

"Then let's reclaim that Carpentini tradition and train to be warriors," Finola said.

"Nice speech," said a scrawny woman with short-cropped hair who stood on the front line. "But you have only told us how weak we are compared to men."

"I told you to be honest about your abilities," Finola said. "To deceive yourself that you have more skill and strength than you have will only get you killed. Can anyone think of one of the greatest advantages you have in a fight against the Bracari?"

Gwyneth glanced around. The women looked at each other. Some shrugged. No one spoke.

"Remember that the Bracari think of you as the prize they get to take home," Finola said. "They aren't here to kill you. They're here to capture you."

"So?" the scrawny woman said.

"They aren't going to try to kill you outright, or even seriously injure you," Finola said. "Crippled slaves are no use to them."

"You mean we should take advantage of that and kill them first?" someone asked.

"Exactly. They might expect you to try to run, or to claw and bite. But they won't expect you to stand your ground and to fight to kill."

"But we don't know how to use a sword," someone said.

"That's why we're going to focus on two weapons that give us an advantage," Finola said. She pointed to a pile of wooden poles about six feet long that Gwyneth had helped her and Brion stack.

"The staff?" someone scoffed.

"The spear," Finola said. "But I don't want you killing each other while we learn to use them."

"What's the other weapon?" someone asked.

"The knife," Finola said. "We use the spear to kill them before they can get too close. If they get past it, we kill them with a knife."

"What about the bow and the sword?" Gwyneth blurted. She hadn't meant to say anything, and she realized that everyone was now looking at her. Gwyneth felt the embarrassed heat rising in her face, but she glared at Finola. She wanted to be a real warrior, not some child playing with sticks.

Finola studied her. "How many of you already know how to shoot a bow or use a sling?"

A scattering of hands crept up. Gwyneth didn't raise her hand. She had never had the chance to learn anything about real fighting.

"Good," Finola said. "We'll use you. For now, set your weapons aside and grab a staff."

The scrawny woman who had challenged Finola stood with her arms folded, while the other women collected a staff.

"Do you have something else to say?" Finola asked.

"We won't stand a chance without swords," the woman said.

"What's your name?" Finola asked.

"Meredith," the woman replied.

Finola picked up a shorter stick about the size of a sword and tossed it to Meredith. Then she picked up a staff.

"Okay, Meredith," she said. "You have a sword. Protect yourself."

Finola lunged, driving the staff at Meredith's stomach. Meredith stumbled backward, swatting clumsily at the staff with the stick. She managed to knock it aside, but before she could do anything else, Finola tapped her on the arm and then the leg with the staff before driving the tip into her stomach. Meredith collapsed to the ground.

"What's the matter with you?" Meredith panted.

Finola reached out to help Meredith to her feet. Meredith slapped her hand away.

"It's about reach," Finola said. "A spear or a staff gives you longer reach. A man with a sword can't touch you if he can't get past the tip of your spear."

Meredith lunged to her feet with the stick in her hand. She slashed it toward Finola who jumped back just in time to miss the stroke that would have slammed her upside the head. Finola brought the staff down with a crack on Meredith's wrists. Meredith cried out and dropped the stick.

Finola picked it up the stick and tossed it to another woman. "Come get me," she said.

The woman hesitated before charging at Finola only to be stopped by the tip of Finola's staff at her throat. "Keep coming," Finola said.

"This is pointless," Meredith said. "None of us knows how to use a sword."

Finola snatched the stick from the woman's hand and held it out to the crowd of men. They all looked sheepishly at each other. Gwyneth knew what they were thinking. None of them wanted to be shamed by a woman.

Finally, the young man who had spoken earlier in the keep stepped forward. He spread his hands. "This is just for demonstration purposes, right? I don't need any more bruises."

Finola tossed him the stick without comment.

The young man assumed a fighting stance and then dashed in. Finola blocked the stroke and slashed at his neck. The young man parried her stick and swung again. Finola reversed her staff and struck the young man's knee. He backed up and grinned at her. Then he rushed in. Finola retreated but always managed to keep the staff in the young man's way. After several more exchanges, he grabbed her staff in frustration, and Finola jammed the end of it into his chest. He cursed and tossed his stick on the ground.

Finola faced the ladies. "It's about reach, not strength," she panted. "Now pick up your staves."

Gwyneth picked up the staff and examined it with new respect. She had to start somewhere.

"Let's see you use that sling," Brion said to York. They had left the women practicing the staff and crossed the creek to the back of the hill to a large cutaway with a bare, earthen wall they could use as a backstop. The creek gurgled behind them, and the earthy smells of the exposed bank surrounded them.

"I already know how to use a sling," York said. This was a waste of time. He needed to become a warrior as fast as possible. He didn't have time to mess around with slings.

"So, show me," Brion said.

York suppressed the frustration that warmed his chest and placed a stone in his sling. After the battle at the crevice, he had spent several hours replenishing his bag of small, round stones. He had learned long ago that rounder and smoother stones flew straighter. But this isn't what he needed. York glanced at Brion, half-expecting to see that look of derision he so often received from other men. But Brion was watching him with interest.

"Try that large root, about halfway up," Brion said.

York took one step forward as he swept the sling in an arc around his head and snapped it forward. The stone tore a chunk of bark from the root and slammed into the earth, creating a cascade of loose soil.

Brion pursed his lips and nodded.

"Can you do that all the time?" he asked.

York nodded. "Almost."

"Again," Brion said.

York snapped the sling and tore another chunk of bark from the root.

"That's really impressive," Brion said. "I don't know anyone who can use a sling like that."

"But it's just a sling," York said. He didn't try to hide the scorn in his voice. The sling was the weapon of boys and men too weak to wield a sword or a bow.

Brion studied him. "Why do you say that?"

"No real warrior uses a sling." York had been ridiculed for years for being too small to use a man's bow. His father had taught him to shoot a bow, of course, but he hadn't been allowed to use it much because they only had the one bow. It had been broken in the raid that forced his family to retreat into the Aveen Mountains months ago.

"A warrior uses the weapon that suits his purpose," Brion said. "Let other people underestimate you, but don't ever undervalue yourself." Brion gestured to the sling. "With that kind of skill at hitting your target, you have nothing to be ashamed of."

That was easy for Brion to say. York had seen that his sling was no use against a man with a sword at close range. It didn't matter how good he was at the sling. He hadn't been able to save his father.

York glanced at the recurve bow Brion had brought with him. He wanted to get started on the real weapons. York had watched Brion dig through the pile of weapons at the keep, testing each bow until he had the one he wanted and then testing several quivers of arrows until he was satisfied.

"We'll get to that," Brion said, motioning to the bow and arrows. "I can't teach you anything about a sling. You're already better than I ever could be. But to be a warrior you have to know how to use a variety of weapons. You have to know how to track, hunt, hide, and move quietly. You've got to learn to think like your prey, and you have to be prepared to kill and to be killed."

York kicked a clump of grass. "I just want to be a warrior," he said. He didn't care about hunting, he was already good enough at that. He just needed to be able to fight like a man.

Brion frowned. "You seem to have a twisted idea about what a warrior is," he said. "What do you mean when you say 'warrior'?"

"A warrior destroys his enemies," York said. "He punishes those who insult his family."

Brion kept frowning. "You think being a warrior is about revenge?"

York nodded. This made perfect sense to him. What was the point of knowing how to kill people if you couldn't use it to maintain your family's honor and seek vengeance on those who hurt you?

Brion gazed off over the green hills toward the north. Then he bowed his head.

"Look," Brion said. "Vengeance is one of the things that drove me to become a warrior. Salassani killed my parents and kidnapped my sister. I thought killing as many Salassani as I could would make things right—that I would find some satisfaction in making them suffer the way I had suffered."

Brion shook his head sadly and looked back to York. "It didn't work," he said. "In the process, my friends Neahl, Lara, and Tyg were all killed. I'd like to see Tristan punished for his role in their deaths, but killing him won't make me or you happy. It won't take away all of your problems. It won't bring your father back."

York swallowed the sudden knot that rose in his throat. There was nothing in the world he wanted more than to have his father back—to feel his strength and courage. York looked everywhere but at Brion.

"Anyway," Brion said, "you have to channel this anger, or you'll make foolish mistakes that will eventually kill you. You can't fight based on emotion alone. You have to use your head. You have to be smarter, more devious, and more cunning than your enemies. If all you can do is wield a sword or shoot a bow, you'll eventually meet someone who is better than you, and you'll die. It's as simple as that."

York scowled. This isn't what he wanted to hear.

"So," Brion continued, "as I said, you need to develop every skill you can because you never know when you might need it."

"Okay," York said.

Brion smiled. "All right then. Your first and most important lesson is to never underestimate an opponent the way people keep underestimating you."

This surprised York. How had Brion known?

"I've seen how Reed pushes you aside," Brion said.

"They think I'm too small," York said.

"Learn to use that to your advantage." Brion grinned and laughed. "I knew a great, big, bear of a man who was whipped by a man about your size. I also knew a man who was an accomplished assassin who looked like a sot and could disappear into any crowd. Never let anyone tell you you can't."

York nodded.

"Try to hit me," Brion said. This gave York pause. He wasn't sure Brion meant it.

"Try," Brion said again.

York lunged, swinging wide. Brion blocked the strike and tripped York. York hit the ground hard, but he scrambled to his feet and put up his fists.

Brion nodded. "I like your spunk, but you underestimated me," he said. "And you announced your first move. You dropped your shoulder before you attacked, and you swung wide and slow. Anyone with a little training would have bested you."

York scowled. Brion had cheated. "But you knew I was going to swing," York said.

"Granted," Brion said. "But what I said is still true."

York kept scowling.

"What's the problem?" Brion asked.

"I don't see the point in this," York said. "No Bracari is going to try to punch me when he has a sword."

Brion picked up the recurve bow and spun on his heels. "If you already know everything about being a warrior, you don't need me," he said.

York watched Brion leap across the creek, expecting him to turn around and come back. This could only be a bluff. Brion wouldn't leave him. But Brion didn't turn back. York waited until he was a hundred paces away and ready to round the base of the hill before jogging after him.

"Wait!" York called.

Brion stopped.

"Please," York said.

Brion turned. "I've better things to do than to argue with a boy who thinks he already knows everything," he said.

York waited. He needed Brion. No one else was going to help him.

"You train my way or not at all," Brion said.

York nodded.

Brion came back and set the bow down. "Warriors don't always need or want to kill," he said as if nothing had happened to interrupt his teaching. "A battle with weapons can become a hand-to-hand fight in an instant. A warrior who has no skill without a weapon is no warrior at all."

York nodded again.

"So, let's begin," Brion said. He taught York how and where to strike, and how to read an opponent's intentions. Then he picked up the bow and taught York how to stand, how to hold it, how to draw it with his back muscles, how to look down the shaft without seeing it. But he wouldn't let York aim at anything.

York began to protest but stopped himself.

"Not yet," Brion said. "We don't have much time, and I'm not worried about you striking your target after what you did with that sling. I want your form to be perfect before you start worrying about hitting anything. A perfectly executed shot will almost always fly true."

Brion watched him shoot at the bare, earthen wall of the cut-away, offering him little corrections.

"Don't squeeze the bow like you're trying to strangle it," Brion said.

"But it wants to jump out of my hand when I shoot," York said.

"Relax your hand," Brion said. "If you put pressure on the bow with your thumb, your arrow will shoot to the left of your target."

York drew the bow until his shoulders burned and his fingers were raw.

"You're getting the hang of it," Brion said. "Now that we're good and hot, let's have a swimming lesson."

A slow smile spread across York's face. It was his turn to order Brion around.

Chapter 5
Old Enemies, New Friends

The crowd of Salassani straggled along the creek just as the sun began to slip behind the Aveen Mountains. Brion kept to the shadows of the trees and studied them as they passed. They looked much like the Carpentini—haggard, dispirited, on the run. Armed men on horseback flanked the ragged line. Travois tied to the backs of horses carried the sick, injured, and old. Children clung to their mothers' necks, casting frightened looks at the crowd of Carpentini who had gathered to watch them arrive. The women Finola had been training broke off to join the crowd of onlookers. Finola and Gwyneth made their way toward the trees where Brion and York watched.

The Salassani men tucked their trousers into the high-topped boots that went almost to the knee. They wore dun-colored tunics secured with wide leather belts. Some had donned black cloaks against the coming chill of evening. Many of the women also wore trousers like the men's, though their tunics were longer and their belts slender. They preferred brightly colored tunics of red and blue. Most of the men, women, and children had dark hair with the occasional sandy-brown or blonde head that indicated the descendant of an Alamani slave.

Brion's attention was drawn to two figures. The first was an old woman riding a tan colored pony. Even from the shadows, it was obvious she was weeping. But she smiled through her tears in a way that made Brion think she wasn't crying for sorrow.

The other was a tall, slender man who rode a black pony. His complexion was too dark to be a Salassani, and he carried a recurve bow that was quite different from the bows the Salassani carried. His bow had been lacquered with a black varnish that did not reflect any light. His cloak was mottled with a dark gray and black pattern. If a man wanted to move unseen at night or in shadow, this is how he would dress. Even though the man tried to appear disinterested in what was going on around him, Brion could see that he was alert and watching. Brion decided to keep an eye on him. This man was dangerous, and he was no Salassani.

Brion elbowed York, who was standing beside him with his hair still dripping water onto his tunic from their swimming lesson. He gestured to the tall warrior.

"What do make of him?" Brion whispered.

"He hunts at night," York said.

Brion glanced at York. "Why do you say that?"

"He's dressed for the dark. He's probably an assassin."

Brion considered the man again. York kept surprising him with his ability to see through things. Maybe Brion was underestimating the boy the same way everyone else did. If York was right, and the man was an assassin, he wasn't good at blending in the way Tyg had done. In fact, he stood out. He drew attention to himself.

Finola arrived and followed the direction of their gaze. She scowled. "I don't know if I like having my old masters this close," she said.

Brion was still concentrating on the man in the mottled cloak. "I like that cloak," Brion said.

Finola wiped at the sweat that still beaded on her brow. "We're watching a line of homeless refugees who enslaved your sister and your wife, and all you can think about is some guy's fancy cloak?"

"Well," Brion said. "I could use one like that."

Brion glanced at Gwyneth. She still carried the staff she had been using, and she had picked up a small mail shirt from somewhere. Like many of the women Finola was training, Gwyneth was picking up bits and pieces of armor and weapons from the dead. Her cheeks were flushed, and she had a fire in her gaze that made Brion study her more carefully. He wondered if Finola understood how much anger this girl had bottled up inside her.

Finola gave a sudden cry and sprinted from the cover of the trees. Brion tried to catch her, but she bounded beyond his grasp.

Vengeance

Salassani men whirled their horses and some drew their weapons as Finola vaulted the creek, scrambled up the hillside and embraced a young girl in the plain clothes of a slave. The line stalled for a moment and then continued as everyone realized that nothing threatened them.

Brion raced after Finola. He should have considered that Finola might recognize some of these Salassani. She had lived among them for four months. But he hadn't wanted to draw attention to themselves. He wanted to understand who was looking for him before he revealed himself.

The girl was speaking in rapid Salassani as Brion approached.

"They killed my master," she said, "and kidnapped Ithel's wife and her baby. I hid in the grass by the river until they were gone. My new master is good to me."

The girl glanced up at a young warrior who stood over them. Brion nodded a greeting to him, but Finola scowled at him. She stood to face him.

"If her master is dead, she should be free," she demanded.

Brion placed a restraining hand on her arm. The warrior glanced at the girl. "She is free," he said. "I just give her a place to sleep." He waved a dismissive hand at them and followed the line of Salassani.

"What does he mean, Clidna?" Finola asked.

Clidna grinned and gave Finola a wink. "I just call him master, because it makes him feel good," she said. "His wife is pregnant and I help her out."

"Brion," someone called.

Brion turned to find one of Reed's close associates jogging toward him.

"Reed wants you," he said.

Brion nodded and gestured to Finola and York. When they stepped up to him, he bent close to whisper to them.

"I want you two watching my back," he said. "York, keep that sling ready. Finola, your bow."

"What about me?" Gwyneth demanded. Brion glanced at her. She was so desperate to prove herself.

"You stay with Finola," he said. "Watch the crowd for anything suspicious. I don't know who is looking for me or what they want, but we can't take any chances."

They all nodded and followed Brion up to the keep where the Salassani grouped together and milled about as they rested, waiting to be told where they could make camp.

Brion found Reed conversing with a short, balding man who hefted a double-headed axe like Reed used. The old woman Brion had seen weeping stood behind the Salassani.

Reed motioned for Brion to approach. Finola, York, and Gwyneth fell back to examine the crowd.

Brion noted that the man in the mottled cloak still sat astride his horse a good forty paces away from Reed, but Brion felt his gaze as he approached the small crowd.

"This is Brion of Wexford," Reed said without any ceremony. The short, bald man studied Brion, then he gave a sharp command to a boy standing next to him. The boy raced off.

"Brion, this is Hugh," Reed continued. "He is the leader of this group. He says several more bands are moving south."

"The whole of the Salassani nation is moving south," Hugh said.

"We're coming home," the old woman muttered.

Brion and Reed glanced at one another.

"All this land from Ghille Heath to the Leetwater used to belong to my people," the woman said. "I played at this castle as a girl. It was called Dunraven Keep. It guarded the pass to Crystal Lake and then on to Dale."

Reed's eyes narrowed, and he scrutinized Hugh as if sizing him up. Reed clearly saw this Salassani interest in his keep as a threat.

"The Carpentini are here now," he said.

Hugh was already shaking his head. "We've no grievance against the Carpentini," he said. "We've all been driven from our homes and so should not quarrel over past wrongs we did not commit."

"We'll have to establish terms if you are to remain with us," Reed said.

Hugh nodded again. "How long we remain in this area depends on him." He pointed at Brion.

Brion glanced around to be certain that Hugh was talking about him.

"Um," Brion stalled. "I'm just a guest here myself."

The boy returned with a tall, dark-haired Salassani that Brion recognized. His hand dropped to the hilt of his sword. But the man smiled and extended a hand to Brion, who hesitated. This was the man who had attacked Brion the night when he, Redmond, and Neahl had been camped by an old, burned-out farmhouse. It had been Brion's first real battle. The first time Brion ever killed a man. Brion had dislocated this man's shoulder. Redmond had treated him, and they had left him to find his own way home alone.

"We've met," the man said. Brion shook the man's hand, ready for any treachery. But the man nodded to Hugh. "This is him."

Brion stepped back and gripped the handle of his sword, but Hugh made no move toward him. Instead, he laid his axe on the ground at Brion's feet and bowed low. Brion looked on in confusion.

"My Lord Duke," Hugh said.

Reed scowled. Brion glanced at him and rolled his eyes. He had avoided his lands in Taber Wood for this reason. He preferred to be anonymous. He had never wanted to be a duke in the first place and still thought of the nobility as parasites that lived off the labor of others. Brion had left Owen in charge of his lands because he couldn't face the people who lived and worked on those lands. Redmond had despised the nobility, and Brion had good reason to distrust them.

"What's this?" Reed said, raising his bushy eyebrows.

"You didn't know?" Hugh asked.

Reed frowned. "I think we should take this discussion inside." He glanced up at the man in the mottled cloak. "For now," he said, "you can tell your people that they can camp in the meadow at the bend over yonder." He pointed to the spur of the hill that forced the creek to swing wide around the knoll upon which the keep stood.

Then he spun on his heels and lumbered into the keep. Brion hesitated. He needed to know where these men stood. He had defeated one of them in battle and left him injured and alone on the heathland. If the man was seeking revenge, Brion needed to know before he was caught off guard inside the keep.

"I see you made it home alive," Brion said.

"My name's Daren," the man said. "I'm not here to get revenge."

Well, at least he goes straight to the point, Brion thought.

"Sorry about the shoulder," Brion said.

Daren waved his comment away. "It was a fair fight. We attacked you."

Brion wasn't so sure an ambush could be considered a fair fight, but he shrugged. "How did you know I was the Duke of Saylen?"

"Word travels fast in a defeated army," Daren said. "I heard the others call you Brion, and we knew that the new duke had rescued his sister from the Great Keldi."

Brion questioned the wisdom of traveling so far north into the heathland. He had never intended to do it. His only thought was to find his mother who was supposed to be in the southern Aveens. But when he found that she had fled north, he had followed.

"Well," Hugh said after he finished giving his orders, "shall we join Reed and see what he's got caught in that beard of his?"

Brion glanced at Finola who had her bow ready with an arrow on the string. She nodded that she would follow him. York slipped inside the keep ahead of Brion, and Gwyneth stood in the shadows of the portcullis with her staff in hand. Brion smiled to himself. He and Finola were acquiring a little army of their own.

Brion followed Hugh under the portcullis into the courtyard and on into the keep that still stank of human waste and wood smoke.

Hugh paused and surveyed the lines of the injured and dying. He frowned. "You've been attacked here, too," he mumbled.

"Two days ago," Brion said.

"All right," Reed said as he sat on a low wooden stool before the fire. "What's this about?"

Hugh glanced at Brion and Daren. "We have a proposition for King Emyr," Hugh said.

Reed smirked. "Of course you do."

"Emyr lived among the Salassani," Hugh continued. "He was one of us and was expected to become a headman of his village."

"So?" Reed questioned.

"So, he knows the Salassani ways. He might send us aid."

Reed glanced at Brion, who shrugged. Brion had no idea what Emyr might do.

"If the Duke of Saylen will go to him," Hugh continued, "and explain what Tristan has done to us, maybe he will send men or weapons and food, at least."

Brion groaned inwardly. He didn't have time to go to Chullish. He needed to find his mother before some Bracari captured her or killed her or she simply disappeared forever.

"Ask him to give us back our homeland," the old woman said.

Reed stood. "If you've come to lay claim to this land, you had best turn around now."

Hugh raised his hands in a gesture of surrender. "She's not talking about the land around Comrie Lake. We mean the southern Hackel Heath and the Skye River."

"We mean," Daren cut in, "to offer ourselves as a first line of defense against Dunkeldi raids into Coll. If King Emyr will allow us to occupy the old fortress and places of refuge, we'll agree to accept him as our king."

Brion stared at them, stunned. "You mean to abandon your lands in the Fife Fens and move permanently south? To become vassals of Coll?

"We have no other choice," Hugh said. "If King Emyr won't take us, we'll be destroyed."

"You realize that King Tristan will see this as treason," Brion said.

Hugh scoffed. "What do I care what Tristan thinks?"

"Brave words," someone said, "for a man who was driven from his home because of what Tristan thinks."

Brion found that the speaker was the man in the mottled cloak he had seen earlier. The man leaned carelessly against the stone doorway to the keep. His cowl was up so Brion couldn't see his face. His voice was deep, and he spoke with an accent Brion didn't recognize. Hugh wasn't surprised by the man's presence, but he didn't seem eager to contradict him. In fact, Hugh eyed him with uncertainty as if measuring his response.

"Who are you?" Brion demanded.

The stranger raised his hands in a dismissive gesture. "Just a friend."

"I want a name," Brion said.

"Arno," the man said.

"We have no choice," Hugh interrupted, apparently anxious for them to stay on topic. "Tristan has left us no choice."

Reed grabbed Brion's elbow and pulled him aside. "Why didn't you tell me you were the Duke of Saylen?"

"Would it have made any difference?"

Reed considered. "Not really."

"Then what's the problem?"

Reed grunted as Hugh stepped up to them.

"Will you go?" Hugh asked.

"No," Brion said. He would not abandon the search for his mother. Not after coming so far. Not without knowing that she was safe.

A murmur swept through the crowd.

Brion raised a hand to quiet them. "But I will write to Emyr if there is someone who will carry the message."

Daren stepped forward. "I'll go."

"You'll never get inside the walls of Chullish," the man in the mottled cloak said.

"I can get him in," Brion said.

"How?" Hugh asked.

"Don't worry," Brion said.

Hugh gestured to Daren. "You leave in an hour."

As Brion neared the door where Arno still leaned against the stone wall, Arno straightened and inclined his head. Brion stopped.

Arno lowered his hood. He had a narrow, angular face with a close-cut beard and black hair. Arno scrutinized Brion from head to foot. "So, you're the famous Brion of Wexford, the Duke of Saylen," he said.

"No one has ever accused me of being famous," Brion said. "I'm just an archer."

Arno had a casual way of standing that made him appear relaxed and unintimidating. Once again, Brion decided that this man was dangerous.

"Ah, but you are the man who plucked two women from the heart of the Great Keldi, bested a king renowned for his swordsmanship, defeated or evaded every Salassani war party sent against you, and then placed your brother-in-law on the throne of Coll."

"Stories are seldom what they seem," Brion said. He wasn't about to get into a discussion of his experiences in the heathland here. If Arno was fishing for information, he would be disappointed.

"Well at any rate," Arno said, "I look forward to seeing you in action." Arno smiled, spun on his heels, and strode through the door.

"You're sure you want to do this?" Brion asked as he approached Daren and Hugh, who waited for him beside a small, brown-speckled Salassani pony.

"I think he'll listen to us," Daren said.

Brion handed Daren the folded letter that he had sealed with the signet of the Duke of Saylen—a stag in a teardrop shield. The wax was still warm. "The letter explains what Tristan has done," Brion said. "I asked Emyr to consider your proposal and said I supported it."

"Thank you," Daren said. "I knew that night when you let me live that our paths would cross again."

"Don't thank me yet," Brion said. "You still have to survive to deliver your message, and the people here may not have time enough to wait for assistance."

"He won't abandon us," Daren said.

"Why are you so sure?"

"Because he's one of us," Daren said. "We know him." Daren glanced around. "People whispered before he left that he should be the king of the Salassani."

Brion scowled. "He wasn't even twenty," he said, "and he was an Alamani slave."

But Daren was shaking his head. "He was Mortegai's son, and Mortegai trained him to become the head of the Salassani."

"So, you think he'll be expecting you to come with an invitation to make him your king?"

"He will."

Brion shook his head in disbelief. "Good luck," he said. Emyr had never hinted at such a thing, but Brion had given up trying to predict the way the future would unravel itself. It never seemed to follow any of his plans anyway.

He handed Daren a small golden eagle. "You'll need this to get into Chullish. Demand to see the master of the guard. He'll recognize the symbol and take you to Emyr."

Daren leapt into his saddle. "Thank you," he said again. He touched his head in the Carpentini salute and galloped away.

Brion watched him disappear over the rise. Had he made the

right choice? Would Emyr send soldiers and so start another war?

"Well," Hugh said as Daren disappeared over the rise. "There goes our last hope."

Brion studied him. He might be right. And Brion's mother was still out there.

"Who is the man in the mottled cloak?" Brion asked.

Hugh passed a hand over his balding head. "No one to mess with," he said. "I think he has powerful friends."

"But who is he?" Brion insisted. "Why is he with the Salassani?"

"I don't know," Hugh said as he turned back toward the keep. "He joined us a couple of weeks ago." Hugh's eyes narrowed. "He knows more than he should."

York rose before the sun was up, strung the bow Brion had given him, and slipped the quiver over his head. Bethann was still sleeping, snuggled up against their mother's back. York paused to gaze at them in the pale light of the fire that still burned against the wall of the keep. Several people huddled around the flickering flames, trying to eke from it what little warmth they could.

His mother's face had lost the tight worry that made her appear so much older than she was. Her dark hair spilled over her neck. Bruises from the battle at the crevice blossomed purple and blue on her neck and cheek. Brown scabs had closed the scratches and cuts on her hands and arms. Seeing her like this, peaceful and unconcerned, York could almost believe that she still loved him. He bent to caress Bethann's cheek before striding to the still unfinished portion of the wall. He paused to nod to the men guarding the gap before he slipped out onto the dew-covered slope.

The air still held that early spring chill with the fresh scent of wet heather and moist earth. A few stars twinkled overhead as the gray of morning slipped into the eastern horizon. York stole into the shadows of the wall to circle around to the embankment where Brion had been teaching him how to shoot. He knew that Brion and Finola had set up a shelter at the base of the hill, and he wanted to avoid drawing their attention. He wanted to be alone. The Bracari had slaughtered the last few sheep they had left, and he was going to have to find some way to feed his mother and sister. Spring was not going to bring the respite Reed had promised—that much seemed obvious now.

"Boy."

York jumped and spun to face the voice. A shadow parted from the wall and advanced toward him. York stepped back as he drew an arrow from his quiver and placed it on the string. The figure chuckled.

"You have no need of a weapon, son," he said.

The man's accent was strange, but York knew he was the man Brion had pointed out who wore the mottled cloak.

"Who are you?" York demanded.

"A friend," the man replied. "You can call me Arno."

York glanced around, trying to decide if he should call for the guard and make a break for it.

"Relax," Arno said again. "I'm not going to harm you."

"Then what do you want?"

"I hear you're pretty good with a sling."

"So?" York didn't release the tension on the string of the bow. He was ready to shoot at the slightest provocation.

Arno extended his hand. "Stones are never perfect," he said. "And so, they never quite fly the same, do they?" When York didn't answer, Arno continued. "I can teach you to make lead shot that will fly true every time and penetrate as deeply as an arrow."

York glowered. He didn't want to admit that he was curious. He was careful about selecting the stones for his sling. Any irregularity in form could give the stone a wild, uncontrolled flight. But it took hours of persistent searching to find the right stones. What if he could simply make them himself? He hesitated. The man opened his hand to show York three pale, silver, conical balls with pointed ends.

"Give these a try," Arno said. "If you like them, I'll show you how to make more of your own."

York released the tension on the string and grabbed the lead shot. They were remarkably heavy for their size.

"You'll find me in the Salassani camp." Arno strode away.

York placed the shot in his pouch as Arno disappeared down the hill. He didn't trust the stranger, but maybe his fear of the Bracari was starting to make him paranoid. He slipped down the slope and circled around to the embankment. He would wait to see what the new shot did. For now, he had come to practice archery.

His shoulder muscles complained when he drew the string to his ear and his fingers ached. But he was careful to practice everything Brion had taught him the day before. He drew in his breath, relaxed, increased his back tension, and let the string slip from his fingers. The arrow leapt from the bow and disappeared into the shadows of the embankment. But York didn't care where it went. All he wanted was a perfectly executed shot, and he had done it.

The arrow slapped into the damp earth, and York drew another. He knew he would have to resharpen the broadheads, but it didn't matter. He was going to be a warrior before the next band of Bracari came.

York stiffened. He had heard something or rather felt it. He nocked another arrow and crouched. Maybe Arno had been waiting to catch him far from the keep where no one would hear his cries.

"You shoot me, and I'll slit your throat." The voice was quiet and feminine.

"Gwyneth?" York said. Gwyneth's slender figure materialized from the shadow of a boulder and splashed across the creek. She was carrying a bow of her own.

"What are you doing?" York demanded.

"Following you, obviously," Gwyneth said.

York turned back to the embankment. "Leave me alone," he said. He had known Gwyneth for almost a year. She was quiet and watchful, but she had a reputation among the Carpentini. She had a temper, and she was the half-breed that had caused the death of so many Carpentini warriors sixteen years before. People blamed her for the Carpentini weakness that had allowed the Bracari to push them out of their own lands.

"Show me everything Brion taught you yesterday," Gwyneth said.

York smirked at her. She had combed her hair and pulled it back like Finola did. And she had washed her face. York had always thought she was pretty, but she was even more beautiful without the ragged dress, tangled hair, and grimy face.

"I don't know anything," York said. "Go ask Finola. She's training the women."

Gwyneth stepped up to him, and it angered him that she was an inch taller than he was.

"Don't be such an idiot," she said. "Just show me what he taught you about the bow."

York let out a long dramatic sigh. Of all the girls in the Carpentini band, he liked Gwyneth the best. But she could be trouble. Only Reed would take her in after her mother died. No one wanted anything to do with the half-breed. York had never understood it since there were lots of people who had Bracari blood among the Carpentini. And what if Reed found out that York had seen Gwyneth in private and he didn't like it?

"Just leave me alone," York said.

"All right," Gwyneth said. "Then I'm going to tell Brion that you've been having secret meetings with that big man in the cloak."

York stared at her. Where had she been hiding? How come he hadn't seen her or heard her following him? Had Arno seen her?

"I wasn't having any secret meetings," York said.

"Sure," Gwyneth said.

"All right," York said. "But I wasn't having any secret meetings. The guy was just there."

"If you say so," Gwyneth said. "Now show me how to shoot this thing."

York taught her the steps Brion had given him, and they stood side by side, shooting arrow after arrow into the embankment as the gray light of morning brightened to full day. The Salassani encampment awoke as did the Carpentini in and around the keep, and people began moving about.

In the morning light, York noticed that Gwyneth wasn't bringing her bow to full draw. He stepped up to her and placed a hand on her arm. Gwyneth jerked and jumped sideways. She drew the bow and aimed at York, who stood there in dumb confusion until the wild look left Gwyneth's face and she let the bow down.

"Don't touch me," she said.

"What's your problem?" York demanded, the color rising in his face. "You could have shot me."

"I'll kill any man that touches me," Gwyneth said.

York smirked. "I'm not much of a man yet, in case you haven't noticed, and besides, you asked me to help you."

Gwyneth stared at him. "Just don't touch me," she said with a little less conviction.

"You're going to have a hard time training to be a warrior if no one can touch you," York said.

"Men are all alike," Gwyneth said.

"Like what?" York scoffed.

"Never mind," Gwyneth said. "What were you going to tell me?"

York scowled at Gwyneth. She was hard to understand. He couldn't even figure out why she had chosen him to teach her. As she had just demonstrated, she had a wild, unreasonable hatred of all men, except Reed.

"You have to draw all the way back to your ear and anchor your hand on your face," York said, "or your arrows won't fly the same."

Gwyneth nodded. "Okay. Thanks."

She drew and released while York watched.

"That looks right to me," York said. He picked up his bow.

"What did that man want anyway?" Gwyneth asked.

York fidgeted. She was just trying to detract his attention from her nearly shooting him. "He just gave me some better shot for my sling."

"That's not what I asked," Gwyneth said.

"What are you talking about?" York nocked an arrow and drew it to his ear.

"People always want something," Gwyneth said. "He's just acting like he wants to help you so he can make you think he can be trusted. Then he's going to ask you to do something for him."

York released the string and scoffed at Gwyneth. "You're paranoid," he said.

"No, I'm realistic," Gwyneth snapped. "Nobody ever gives you something for nothing—especially not a stranger. I should know."

Chapter 6
Victims and Rescuers

Brion bent to examine the muddy tracks. He had left his horse, Misty, with Finola and had taken York out on foot for the day to train him in tracking in the hills away from the distraction of all the people collecting at the keep. At least that's what he told himself. But it had been an excuse to continue his search for his mother. Finola refused to come, saying she needed to keep training the women. And Brion had left her there once he had extracted a solemn pledge from Reed that he would protect her.

"I hardly think she needs my protection," Reed had said. "I've seen her fight."

"You know what I mean," Brion said.

Reed nodded. "You've both earned that at least. No Carpentini under my command will harm her."

Reed's pledge gave Brion little comfort, but he trusted Finola, and he knew she was rapidly developing a rapport with the Carpentini women. More and more of them were gathering for her training.

But Brion had allowed himself to be distracted for too long. It had been more than a week since he found York racing toward the keep carrying Iain. He needed to search for his mother before things got completely out of hand.

When he asked Reed about her, Reed simply shook his head. "I know of no Elsie," he said. "But the Carpentini have been seeking refuge in the Aveens for months. She could be anywhere. Why do you want this woman anyway?"

Brion had held his tongue. If his mother was in hiding, it would do her no good for folks to whisper that the new Duke of Saylen was searching for her.

Brion gestured for York to join him beside the tracks. They entered the lower end of a gulch several miles south of Dunraven Keep and followed it. A recent rain left the ground moist on the narrow game trail that wiggled its way amid the fallen timber and the rocky outcrops. The trail had widened as the feet of at least a couple dozen people swung onto it from an adjoining gully. They had been traveling north.

This far up in the Aveens, the land was wetter and more densely forested in pines and oaks. Birds called to each other and hopped about from branch to branch. Squirrels chirped and flashed their silver tails. Rabbits and whitetail deer frequently disappeared into the trees and sometimes simply stopped to watch as Brion and York made their way under the canopy of pines. The occasional wolf trotted across an open space following the line of the trees. Pheasants and grouse burst from the underbrush in a flurry of wings. The land had been so long without human inhabitants that the animal populations had rebounded. It was a hunter's paradise.

Brion pointed to the tracks pressed deep in the mud. "See the whipped stitching?" Brion said. "Only the Carpentini do that to their boots."

"I know," York said. Brion gave him an annoyed glance. York was smart, but he hadn't yet learned to let people think they knew more than he did—especially when they were supposed to be teaching him something.

"They have women and children with them," Brion continued. "See how the smaller tracks tend to point forward, while the larger ones point more outward?"

York nodded.

"It isn't always so pronounced," Brion said. "But women almost always walk with their feet pointed more forward than men. Now look at their stride. How were these people moving?"

"They were running," York said.

"That's right. And what were they running from?"

"Bracari," York said. Brion nodded. York had certainly recognized the more square-toed shape of the Bracari boots pressed into the earth on top of the tracks of the fleeing Carpentini.

"How many?"

York studied the ground and shook his head. "I don't know, maybe ten or twelve."

"Sounds about right," Brion said. "And these tracks are fresh, not more than a couple of hours old. Look how the edges are sharp and there is no debris in the prints."

"They're in trouble," York said. "We should help them."

Brion nodded. "I was thinking the same thing. But we have a problem."

York glanced around as Brion leaned in close to whisper to him.

"Someone has been following us since we left the keep." Brion didn't tell York, but he was fairly certain it was the stranger in the mottled cloak. The stranger had taken an unexplained interest in Brion, and Brion suspected there was much more to him than met the eye.

Motioning for York to follow him, Brion continued past the trail they had just crossed as if he meant to avoid it. Once they had gone a good half a mile, Brion led York off the trail behind a fallen pine tree. Then he slipped off his pack and pulled out four thick pads of felt with straps sewn onto them. They strapped them to their feet and then covered them with a sack of thin felt that they tied around their ankles.

York grimaced as he stepped about in the funny footgear.

"An old friend once told me," Brion said, "that felt booties were the only way lumbering oafs like me could walk quietly." He smiled at the memory. Tyg had taught Finola to creep silently but somehow had never gotten around to showing Brion. "They also will leave very little sign to follow," Brion said as he shouldered his pack. "Now let's see who's following us so we can go after the Bracari."

Brion led York up the hillside under the canopy of shaggy pines. Their felt-covered boots made little sound on the blanket of pine needles and left no discernible impressions. If they avoided any patches of snow or muddy areas, their passing would go unnoticed and be virtually undetectable by anyone trying to track them.

Once on top of the ridge, Brion circled back to a huge boulder they had passed. He motioned for York to lie down, and they both crawled to the edge where they could peer down on the narrow trail they had been following. A few minutes of watching rewarded them with the sight of a short, round man dressed in Carpentini clothing bent low following their trail. This surprised Brion. This wasn't the man in the mottled cloak. Why would a Carpentini be following them?

Brion shifted until he could whisper in York's ear. "Who is he?" York shook his head.

Brion considered confronting the man, but his mind was still uneasy about the Carpentini heading north pursued by Bracari. For all he knew, his mother could be with them. This problem seemed more pressing than the curiosity of a single Carpentini. He could deal with him later. He nudged York, and they slithered back down the rock.

"Now let's find those Carpentini," he said. "Keep your sling ready. We may need to fight."

York nodded. Brion didn't relish the idea of taking York into combat. He considered sending York back to warn Reed that small bands of Bracari were still operating in the area, but he didn't dare send York alone with someone trailing them and Bracari hunters about. They might already be too late to help the Carpentini, who had probably come north to join Reed.

Brion set off parallel to the valley the Carpentini had entered. He left the felt over their boots because he needed to make good time while making as little noise as possible. The crest of the ridge was rocky and strewn with fallen pines. The valley below narrowed, and Brion became increasingly worried the Carpentini had chosen a path that would leave them trapped. The women and children would not be able to scale the moss-covered rocks. He became so intent on navigating the broken ground of the crest that he almost missed the quiet slap of a boot on the moist ground. Brion froze.

York stepped up to him and pointed. In the valley below, a good thirty paces away, a party of Bracari worked their way back down the valley. Their long green tunics stood out in the deep browns of the forest. Three Carpentini women stumbled along in their midst with their hands tied in front of them. One clutched a baby to her chest. Another was an older woman with graying hair. She was tall and walked with her head held high. Warm anger spread through Brion's chest. He would not sit idle while the Bracari enslaved these women. Ever since Finola and Brigid had been enslaved and he had gone deep into the Aldina Mountains to save them, he had no patience for the practice of slavery.

Brion glanced at York and drew his bow. He counted ten Bracari warriors. Brion aimed low to compensate for the elevation and loosed. The bow thrummed, quieted by the beaver fur silencers he had tied to the string. Before the first arrow struck, Brion had a second in the air. Two Bracari clutched at the arrows that ripped into their bodies. York's sling snapped, and something silver flashed as it flew through the trees. A crack echoed up the canyon as a Bracari dropped silently to the trail.

The remaining Bracari dove for cover as they searched for their assailants. A young warrior tried to drag the youngest female captive away, but Brion dropped him with an arrow through his back while York's sling snapped again and another Bracari fell.

The Bracari found them and arrows began arcing up the slope to skid and scrape over the boulders. Brion ducked as an arrow deflected off a branch and narrowly missed his head.

"Stay here," he whispered to York as he scampered up the ridge for a better position and shot two more Bracari. Then he worked his way silently down the slope in search of the last three. An arrow flew up at Brion, and he dropped behind a tree for cover as York gave a cry and slid down the slope as if he meant to engage the Bracari hand-to-hand. Brion cursed and leapt after him.

Gwyneth knelt beside Finola as she washed the old woman's forehead with a damp cloth. They had been working their way around the inside of the keep, offering what help they could to the injured and dying. They had found the old woman by the portcullis lying on a pile of old skins. Gwyneth knew this woman. She had come to her aid at the lowest point in Gwyneth's life. The memory was still so vivid that it jerked the tears to her eyes and wrung her insides. How she wished she could forget, but the images and feelings came in a rush.

Gwyneth cradled her mother's head in her lap as the burly man stocked away. The cold mud from the street soaked through her skirt. The pain in her ribs where the man had struck her as she tried to fight him off stabbed every time she took in a breath.

"Momma," she whispered. She brushed the hair from her mother's bruised and bloody cheek. A big gash had opened over the socket of her missing eye.

"Someone help me," Gwyneth bawled.

The crowd of people who had watched the man beat her mother unconscious stood silent. They hadn't raised a finger to intervene. But she needed their help now. She was barely fourteen, with no money and no home. They had lived by begging from village to village since her Uncle Edrick had died in battle four years before.

"Please," Gwyneth whispered.

"It's the Bracari child," someone said.

"She started the war that ruined us," someone else said.

Aila's one good eye opened. It was startlingly green against her pale skin. Aila swallowed and tried to move. But Gwyneth could see the odd angle of her leg and tried to hold her still.

"Shh," Gwyneth said.

Aila blinked slowly.

"She was always too proud for her own good," a woman said.

The hateful words had followed Gwyneth her entire life—at first, only in whispers for fear of her Uncle Edrick's wrath. But after he died and the Bracari had finally overrun their village so they had no home and no land to support themselves, the whispers became louder. People called her mother "the one-eyed whore" and her "the offspring of devils." Gwyneth had never understood their venom.

Aila had been sent to live with a Bracari leader in a desperate attempt to achieve peace. If she delivered a child, they would marry and the peace would hold. But when Gwyneth had been born, the chief refused to accept a female child, blinded Aila in one eye, and sent her back tied to a horse. He had followed with a Bracari army. The Carpentini only survived because her grandfather and her uncle had fought the Bracari off. But everyone said that battle had been the beginning of the end. They called it the War of the One-Eyed Woman or the Battle of Bloody Creek.

Gwyneth tried to keep in the sob. This wasn't the first time her mother had been assaulted. Every man they had ever met thought they could demand favors of her mother. When she refused, as she always did, they beat her. Some tried to rape her, but Gwyneth had always been able to cause enough trouble to stop them.

Now Aila lay in the muddy street, pale, haggard, and shattered.

"Gwyneth," Aila whispered. "Something is broken." She grimaced as she swallowed. "Inside."

Tears slipped from Gwyneth's eyes to drip onto her mother's cheek.

The crowd dispersed until only a bent old woman stood there staring at them. Gwyneth blinked up at her uncertainly as she shuffled over.

Vengeance

"Come with me," she said with a wave of her hand.

"She's hurt," Gwyneth said.

"You can't stay here," the woman said.

Gwyneth struggled to her knees and tried to lift her mother. Aila cried out and went limp. Gwyneth pulled Aila into her arms and lifted her. Her mother was surprisingly light. Gwyneth could feel her bones through her thin clothes, which confirmed her suspicions that her mother had been giving her most of the food.

The woman led her to a shack on the edge of the village and helped Gwyneth lay her mother on a wooden pallet. Aila groaned as they stripped off her clothes and began cleaning her wounds. Gwyneth gasped at her mother's wasted body, and the tears burned her eyes with the shame and the anger. Her mother looked half-starved. A great purple bruise had formed on her left side where three ribs bent inward. A little blood colored her lips.

"Momma," Gwyneth whispered.

Aila opened her eye and reached over to grab Gwyneth's wrist.

"You haven't been eating, have you?" Gwyneth said.

"My poor child," Aila said. "I'm so sorry I couldn't give you a better life."

"Why do they hate us?" Gwyneth asked.

"It's not your fault," Aila said. "That brute wanted to start a war, and he used us as an excuse."

The woman brought hot water and cleaned the blood and grime from Aila's emaciated body. She paused over the expanding bruise on Aila's broken ribs and gave Gwyneth a nervous glance. But Gwyneth wouldn't consider what that glance told her. She couldn't. She avoided looking at the crushed rib cage. It was so unnatural that it was offensive.

"You are the daughter and the granddaughter of clan chieftains," Aila said. "Don't ever let anyone tell you that you're worthless."

Gwyneth nodded but didn't know what to say.

"I want you to go to a man named Reed," Aila said. "He knew your grandfather and your uncle. He'll take you in."

Gwyneth squeezed her hand. "We'll go together."

Aila's head rolled back and forth. "Not this time," she said. A violent cough wracked her body, and a dark red blood clot slid down her neck. She lay gasping as Gwyneth struggled to understand what was happening. The old woman shuffled over, wiped the blood away and drew a blanket over Aila's body.

Aila swallowed and fixed her one good eye on Gwyneth's face. She reached a trembling hand up to touch her cheek.

"I have lived only for you, my child," she whispered. "You are my life, my whole world."

"Momma," Gwyneth mumbled past the clutching, choking fear.

The old woman laid a hand on Gwyneth's shoulder. Gwyneth knew she meant to reassure her, but a wild rage burst through her. She shoved the woman's hand away and lunged to her feet.

"No Momma," she cried. "You can't leave me."

A single tear trickled from Aila's eye.

"I'm so sorry," Aila said.

Gwyneth spun on the old woman. "Do something!" she demanded.

The old woman shook her head. "She's gone," she said.

Gwyneth jerked her gaze back to her mother's pale face. Her eye was still open, staring. Gwyneth collapsed to her knees and buried her head against her mother's neck.

Men, she thought. Men had done this to them. It was always the men. They started the wars. They forced women into servitude. They demanded everything of women and gave nothing back. And still, all those women had stood around and watched while the men had abused her mother. The bitterness burned in her chest. The Carpentini were all responsible. None of them had stepped in to help. Gwyneth entertained the fleeting thought that she should just run off into the heather and leave them all behind. But where would she go? How would she survive alone?

Finola rose, and Gwyneth swallowed the knot in her throat. Gwyneth reached over to pat the old woman's hand. "Thank you," she whispered.

The old woman closed her eyes and took in a deep breath.

Gwyneth stood to follow Finola, when a cry caught her attention. She strode through the gate to see one of the newly arrived Salassani boys taunting a girl. "Bracari," they screamed. Anger flared hot in her chest. She had been training for over a week now, and she wasn't going to sit by and watch while some boys abused a girl, not now that she could do something about it.

Terror surged into Brion's throat as York careened toward the valley floor. A shower of rocks and mud cascaded before him. York hit the muddy trail and rolled out of the way of the debris that followed him. He came up with moss and twigs dangling from his hair and mud streaking his clothes, but his sling was in his hand.

Brion scrambled over the last boulder and dropped into the valley to find the three remaining Bracari each holding a woman with a knife to her throat. The two Bracari that York had struck with his strange, silver stones lay motionless, but several of the ones Brion had shot still groaned or struggled to get to their feet.

"Let them go," Brion said.

"There's only two of them," one of the Bracari said. The others searched the ridgeline as if they weren't so certain.

The older woman watched Brion intently as if she recognized him. Brion noted that she held a rock in her hands. Somehow, during the confusion, she had picked up a weapon and the Bracari hadn't noticed. The woman with the baby was crying, while the other slumped against the Bracari holding her. Her blue dress was soaked with blood. Brion considered shooting the Bracari, but he couldn't get all three before they injured the women.

"Let us leave here," one of the Bracari said, "and we'll return to Bracari lands."

Brion scoffed. "Bracari word doesn't carry much weight at the moment."

He glanced at York. If he could hit one with his stones, while Brion shot the other, only one of the women would be injured. It was risky. If the women moved or the Bracari dodged aside, it could all go very wrong. The older woman with the stone gave a long, slow blink and wiggled the rock in her hands so that Brion could see that she meant to fight. The injured woman saw the gesture and jerked forward against the knife pressed to her throat.

The knife sliced into her neck as she crumpled forward. Brion's bow thrummed at the same time York's sling snapped. The two men holding the other women barely had time to react before arrow and stone dropped them in their tracks. The older woman gave a cry as the Bracari holding her loosed his grip. She launched herself on the last Bracari who was just rising from the fallen woman as if he were still trying to work out what had happened. He spun to face the charging woman, who brought her rock down at the same time that he drove his knife into her chest.

The rock crashed into his head, and he stumbled backward, leaving his knife protruding from her body. She stopped to stare down at it. Brion shot the Bracari and rushed to the side of the woman as she crumpled to the muddy trail.

"Hold on," Brion said. He had suppressed the little suspicion that this woman might be his mother. Now that hope burst to the forefront of his mind along with the desperate horror that he would have to watch his mother die. Brion jerked the knife free and held a hand to the pulsing blood that poured from the wound.

"What's your name?" he asked, terrified to hear the answer.

"The Duke," she said.

Brion's throat constricted. Had he found her only to have her die in his arms before he could even tell her who he was?

"Are you Elsie?" he asked.

She blinked. "I know the Duke."

"I'm Brion," he said. "The Duke's son."

She closed her eyes. "Elsie is my. . ." Her head rolled back and her body slumped against his arms. Her breathing grew more shallow as the life faded from her body.

"No," Brion whispered. The pain of failure stung his eyes and burned like fire in his chest. What were the odds of him stumbling upon his mother by pure accident? He struggled to think what to do, but that knife had penetrated the heart. He couldn't save her.

Brion lunged to his feet, stalked to one of the injured Bracari who had propped himself up against a fallen log, grabbed him by the shirt and shook him. The man cried out in pain as the arrow that had penetrated his side scraped against the log. His tunic was stained dark with blood.

"Where were you taking her?" Brion demanded. He couldn't help thinking that someone in Coll was carrying on Cedrick's attempts to destroy him and everything he loved.

"She's just a slave," the man gasped.

"Who sent you?" Brion asked with another violent shake.

"Please," the man said. "Just kill me."

Brion ignored him. "Where are the others?"

The man jerked his head back up the trail. "Up there."

"Are you scouts? Is there another army coming?"

"We're just looking for slaves," the man said. "I don't know about any army."

The quiet swish of a blade being drawn from a sheath sounded.

Vengeance

Brion jerked around to find York standing beside him with his knife drawn. He had approached Brion on the silent felt shoes.

Brion stood to face him. "What are you doing?"

"They killed my father," York said. His chest rose and fell. Tears stained his cheek.

Brion glanced at the Bracari who stared up at them with wide eyes. He was a dead man. It was only a matter of time. It might even be an act of mercy to let York kill him. *But where does it lead?* he thought. Redmond had once asked him that question after Neahl had cut the ears off the Salassani who had attacked them. But Brion understood York's anger—the deep, driving hunger for revenge. The woman who might have been his mother lay dead with the gore soaking her chest. He understood, but he couldn't give in.

"You're not fighting with your head," Brion said. The woman with the baby was whimpering behind York where she had collapsed to the ground to hug her frantic child. Brion stepped up to York and grabbed the hand that held the knife.

"If you start murdering helpless, unarmed men, you're just as much of a monster as they are."

York brushed the tears with the back of his hand. Brion glanced at the older woman again. She was no longer breathing. He swallowed the lump of despair that rose in his throat. He couldn't help her anymore. He couldn't be certain that she was his mother and he needed to be certain.

"Let's go see if we can help the others," he said. "Then we need to get word to Reed."

York nodded, and Brion released his hand.

"Just kill me," the Bracari said again.

Brion ignored him and strode to the woman with the child. He cut her bonds and helped her to her feet.

"Are you hurt?" he asked.

She shook her head. Brion pointed to the woman who had been stabbed in the heart. "Do you know her?"

"No. She came to lead us to safety."

"What was her name?"

The woman caressed her baby's cheeks. "We've been running north and hiding for months. She found us and said there was a leader deep in the Aveens who would help us."

"Reed?" Brion asked.

"I don't remember his name."

Brion shook his head in disgust and frustration. How many more bands of starving women and children struggled through the heathland grasping at any tiny thread of hope? And how could there be so many Bracari this far south and on this side of the Aveens?

Tristan had done more than simply outlaw the Carpentini and Salassani. He had organized armies and bands to scour the land for them. It was like a giant deer hunt with the Taurini in the north and east and the Bracari in the north and west squeezing the Carpentini and the Salassani into an ever-shrinking area where they could hem them in and destroy them.

"How many men were with you?" Brion asked.

"Not many. Six or seven."

Brion gave her a drink from his waterskin and a piece of jerked meat. Her baby wriggled, and she pulled it close while she chewed. Brion and York removed the felt covers from their shoes. Brion collected his spent arrows from the dead bodies. Only two Bracari were still alive. Brion considered tending them, but he knew their wounds were mortal, and he didn't want to waste time when he might save a few Carpentini. Brion watched as York stuffed the felt booties back into the pack.

"What were you thinking?" Brion asked. "You thought you would take them on all by yourself?"

York held up the felt. "I slipped," he said.

Brion stared. "You slipped?" Then he shook his head. "Try not to do that. It's not usually good for your health."

"Thanks for the advice," York said. "But if you're going to put slippery pads on my feet and make me run, you can't blame me."

"All right," Brion said. It wouldn't do any good to argue with him. "Let's go."

He stepped to the woman. "We have to move fast. I'll carry the baby for you."

The woman scowled at him and clutched the baby close.

"There's no one there," she whispered.

"Some of them might be alive," Brion said.

"They won't be," she said. "She pinched her lips tight and stared at the ground.

"I can't leave you here alone," Brion said. "You have to come with us."

She nodded and struggled to her feet.

"You run ahead," she said. "I'll follow."

Brion hesitated.

"I'll follow," she said again.

Brion gripped her arm and led her up the canyon a hundred paces away from the Bracari bodies. Those that were still alive wouldn't last long.

"Okay," Brion said. "But promise me you won't go back to the Bracari. They could still hurt you. You have to follow us."

She nodded. "You had better hurry."

Brion didn't like leaving her there. Something wasn't right about her, but if he had any hope of helping the others, he needed all the speed he could get. By his count, most, or all, of the Bracari that had entered the narrow canyon had been with the women. But if the Carpentini had been attacked, some of them might still be alive. And he was certain more women and children had been with them. What had become of them?

Nodding to York, Brion jogged up the narrow gully following the muddy trail that splashed its way through the little trickle of water that slipped amidst the boulders and pines. The gully narrowed to a crack, and Brion had to pull off his knapsack and quiver to squeeze through. When he emerged on the other side, an eerie silence greeted him. The birds had ceased their calling and no insects buzzed. The gully widened into a small amphitheater that smelled of human waste and death.

It was dark under the canopy of pines and many trees had fallen across the top of the gully about forty paces above forming a dark ceiling dripping with pine resin. Brion hurried on. He came around a large boulder that sat nearly in the middle of the amphitheater and skidded to a halt. The gully ended abruptly in a sheer stone wall with dark stains where the water seeped through to trickle to the spongy ground.

A single Carpentini man sat on a log with his back to Brion. All around him in little groups lay the bodies of women and children with the occasional man. But none of the men were Bracari.

Brion stared in confusion until York stopped beside him.

"What happened?" York whispered.

"I don't know," Brion said. He stepped up to the nearest group of two women, three children, and one man. They had all been sitting with their backs to a boulder. The women had been holding the children, and they had all had their throats cleanly cut. Brion tried to swallow but couldn't. The sickness choked him. He had never gotten used to the sight of dead women and children, and the smell of death could never be forgotten.

The man's arms and face were sprayed with blood and a knife still balanced on the palm of his hand. Brion glanced at the others who were slumped over in a similar pattern. Only five men, including the one still sitting hunched over on the log, lay in the hollow.

York sniffled behind him, and Brion turned to see York sweep his sleeve across his face, smearing the mud on his cheek.

Brion began checking all the victims only to find that none were alive. He finally approached the silent man sitting on the log.

"Hey," Brion said.

The man didn't stir.

"Hey," Brion said louder. "What happened here?"

The Carpentini raised his head slowly. His face was ashen white and streaked with tears.

"Kill me, please," he whispered.

Brion knelt beside him. "What happened?" he asked again.

"I…I couldn't do it," the man stammered. Then he clasped his head in his hands and wailed a long, slow cry of anguish that raised a knot in Brion's throat and jerked the tears to his eyes. Brion blinked rapidly.

"I killed them," the man said. "I slaughtered my own children, but I couldn't kill myself."

Chapter 7
The Fury of Desperation

Brion stared in mute horror before glancing around at the groups of bodies. They each had a man with them, save one. Two little girls huddled in the lap of a woman in a blue dress now stained dark with blood.

"You didn't," Brion whispered. It was too horrible to imagine. What desperate depravity could lead a man to murder his own family?

"We all agreed," the man moaned, "that we would rather die mercifully by the hands of our loved ones than be butchered or ravaged by the Bracari." He rocked back and forth. "They watched me," he cried again. "They watched me do it. Oh, my innocent children." The man tore at his hair. "Coward!" he shouted. "Coward! Kill me! Kill me!" Then he fell on his face to grovel in the mud and pine needles.

Brion passed a hand over his sweaty brow only to realize that his hand was trembling. York simply stood with his head bowed, but his shoulders shuddered. Brion wiped at his eyes.

The horror gripped his chest. He thought the battle at the crevice had been savage, but this . . . this was beyond savage. It was depraved. These people had been pushed beyond all reason, beyond all humanity.

A scrape sounded above, and Brion glanced up. A figure appeared on the lip of the gully. Brion whipped an arrow from his quiver and nocked it. A wooden ladder slipped over the edge until it came to rest on a wide ledge in the cliff. Brion now noted that makeshift stairs had been cut into the stone below the ledge. A slight figure in a brown cloak that could only be a woman or a child began to descend. Brion surveyed the lip of the gully, but no one else appeared. He gestured for York to check the entrance. York slipped away but returned after a few moments and shook his head.

The woman reached the ledge, scrambled down the stone steps, and moved among the bodies—bending low to check each one. Finding no one alive, she stepped to the man who now lay prostrate on the ground. She wrapped an arm around his shoulders and whispered to him. Slowly the man crawled to his knees and then back to his seat on the log. The woman gave a piercing whistle and two men descended the ladder. Brion backed up, still prepared to fight, but he was more curious now than concerned.

The two men came to her, helped the Carpentini to his feet and led him to the ladder. The woman faced Brion and raised a hand to lower the cowl. She had delicate features and black hair and didn't appear to be more than forty years old. She wore trousers and boots like the Salassani women did.

"And who are you?" she said. Her voice was quiet, but it had a note of command as if she were accustomed to being obeyed. Brion hesitated. This woman didn't wear the blue dress traditional to Carpentini women. But she spoke with a Carpentini accent.

"A friend of the Carpentini," Brion said.

The woman nodded. "As am I."

They watched each other. This woman had a short sword at her hip, but no other weapon that Brion could see.

"Where are you taking him?" Brion asked.

"Somewhere safe." She glanced around the bowl. "Where are the others?"

"Other what?"

"Survivors."

Brion glanced at York. He didn't know these people or what motivated them. But the woman they had rescued at the entrance to the gully had said they had traveled here for safety. Had they been searching for this woman and her band? Or someone else?

"You should take your people to join Reed," Brion blurted. "He's only a few miles from here."

A wry smile touched her lips. "Everyone in the heathland knows about Reed. How long do you think Tristan will leave him be?"

Brion considered. "You're stronger together," he said.

"Not if we're all dead together," she replied.

The woman gave a shrill whistle again and signaled for the men to search down the gully and then whirled to leave. The men raced off into the trees.

"Wait," Brion said. She turned back to him. "What's your name?" he asked.

She smiled again, but said nothing. She offered him the Carpentini salute and then climbed up the ladder.

Brion didn't wait for her to reach the top. He gestured to York and began scrambling back the way they had come, leaving the shadowed amphitheater with its reek of death behind them.

They squeezed through the crack and raced down the gully in search of the woman and the child they had left behind. Brion scanned the ground for the tracks the men he had seen racing in this direction. But there were none. They knew this area better than he did. What if they found the woman and child first?

Brion redoubled his speed as a new suspicion formed in his mind. The woman with the child had not followed them. She may have gone another way and become lost and was now alone and undefended. But Brion couldn't see how she could have made a mistake like that.

As they slipped and splashed around the last bend before the hollow where they had attacked the Bracari, Brion slid to a stop. The woman was sitting on a log, cradling her child as if nothing had happened. Her blue dress was stained with blood. The two Bracari that had been alive when Brion and York had left her had been stripped and mutilated. Their green tunics and brown trousers had been cut to ribbons. Their square-toed boots were tossed about amid a pile of their leg wrappings. Brion grimaced as he surveyed the scene. Chunks of flesh had been cut from them in the most brutal manner.

York stepped up to him. "Did she do that?" he asked.

Brion didn't answer. Not only had the woman murdered two injured men, she had taken the time to strip and disfigure them before sitting down to cuddle her child. Brion had never witnessed this kind of cold brutality. He approached the woman, but she didn't look at him. She was humming a quiet tune to her child. He touched her arm. She stopped humming and raised her head. Her gaze found his.

It was distant and childlike.

"Are you all right?" Brion asked.

The woman started humming again. Brion exchanged a confused look with York just as the sounds of the men hurrying along the ridgeline reach his ears. Four men, dressed like Carpentini in their long, tan-colored linen shirts and wide belts, paused on the crest before working their way down. Brion waited until they had descended. They took in the horrible scene of the mutilated men with hardly a glance. But one of the men rushed to the side of the gray-haired woman and knelt. He glanced up at the others and shook his head.

Their leader, a large powerful man with a balding head and a thin mustache, stepped up to Brion and touched his own head in the Carpentini salute. Brion returned it.

"Who is she?" Brion asked.

"It's not my place to say," the leader replied. He nodded to the woman and the child. "We'll take them."

"Who are you?" Brion asked.

"Just Carpentini trying to survive," he said.

"Who was that woman in the cloak?"

"It's not my place to say," he replied again. The other men bent to examine the two dead women.

Brion glanced at the body of the woman with the gray hair. She had known about Elsie. She had known the Duke of Saylen. Brion's hand lifted to touch the ring that hung on the chain around his neck. It was his mother's ring. The only physical connection he had to her.

"Is her name Elsie?" Brion blurted.

All four men stopped what they were doing to stare at Brion. Their leader studied him more carefully. "It is not my place to say," he said more slowly. But this time, warning sounded in his voice.

Brion wanted to reach out and throttle him. If she was his mother, he had a right to know. But this man was clearly not going to tell him.

"How many have you gathered?" Brion asked, thinking he might get some information out of them if he kept them talking.

The man ignored him, stepped to the woman with the child, and whispered in her ear. She nodded and stood.

"We thank you for what you tried to do," the leader said. "But don't follow us." He gestured to the men, who picked up the bodies of the two Carpentini women.

"You understand what Tristan is doing, don't you?" Brion demanded. The leader waited for Brion to continue. "He's trapping you in the Aveens so he can finish you all at once."

"Maybe," the leader said. He nodded to Brion and York and led the woman with the child up the rise to disappear into the trees. The men carrying the dead women followed more slowly.

"Are we going to follow them?" York asked.

Brion hesitated. He wanted to, but he couldn't. "No," he said. "We need to inform Reed."

After York checked on his mother and sister and given them the rabbits he had killed on the way home, he went in search of the man that had given him those amazing stones. They had flown straighter and with more force than any stone he had ever thrown.

The stranger raised his eyebrows in mock surprise as York stepped up to his tent.

"Well?" the man said.

"I want to learn how to make them," York said.

"I thought you might," the man said. He rubbed his chin. "I'll make you a trade."

York stepped back. Gwyneth had warned him that nobody ever gave something for nothing.

"I would like to get to know your friend Brion better," the man said. "You answer a few questions for me, and I'll show you how to make the lead balls."

York shook his head. He shouldn't have come. Gwyneth was right.

The man raised his hands. "I'm not his enemy," he said. "I want to help him."

York scowled. "How?" he said.

"Unfortunately, I'm not at liberty to say. You'll have to trust me."

York wanted those lead balls. He needed them. If the man meant no harm, then…

"What do you want to know?" York asked.

"I'm telling you," Brion said to Reed, "he's herding you all into the area around Comrie and then he's going to send an army. You have to make contact with the other groups. You have to organize a defense."

Reed worked his jaw and rubbed his beard. "I thought we were organizing a defense," he said. He gestured to Finola. "Isn't she organizing a defense?"

"You know what I mean," Brion said. "If a combined Bracari, Taurini, and Dunkeldi army finds you, you won't stand a chance."

Reed stood, grabbed Brion by the elbow and pulled him to a corner of the keep. "Listen," he said. "These people do not need you telling them that they don't stand a chance."

"You have to face the truth," Brion said.

"I have been staring the ugly truth in the face for years," Reed snarled. "You come in here and presume to tell us how to survive. Unless your precious king is going to send us aid, we are on our own. You understand?"

Brion bowed his head. Reed was right. By what right did he instruct Reed how to lead his people? Without knowing it, Brion had come to identify with the Carpentini. He was one of them, after all—at least on his mother's side.

"I'm only trying to help," Brion said.

Reed released his arm. "I'll send someone to find these people and ask them if they want to join us. My scouts tell me that more Salassani are coming south. Soon we will not be able to feed these people. The Bracari and Dunkeldi aren't my only problem, Brion."

"I'll go," Brion said.

"What?"

"I'll go find these people."

"Why?"

Brion hesitated. "Because I need to find someone."

Reed smiled. "You finally admit that you didn't just happen upon us?"

"I never said I did."

"All right," Reed said. "You go find Elsie. Bring her here if you can."

Brion scowled, but Reed just grinned and shouted some orders to his men.

"Wait," Brion said.

Reed turned back to him.

"Who did you have following us?" he asked.

Reed frowned. "I had no one follow you."

Brion glanced around the keep. "A Carpentini was trailing us."

"Who?" Reed asked.

"If I knew, I wouldn't have asked."

"Have you seen him here, with us?"

Brion shook his head. "York didn't know him either."

Reed rubbed his beard. "Why would someone want to follow you, Brion of Wexford? You said you were taking York out for some training."

"I was," Brion said. Brion knew he still had enemies among the various tribes. It had only been a few months since the second Heath War had ended, and Brion had killed many men in battle, and he still had a price on his head. It had not been safe to come this far north, but now that he had found news of his mother, he couldn't turn back. No matter what the danger.

"I have to go," Brion said. "She's up there. I know it." Brion poked the needle through the leather harness he was sewing and pulled the line through. The buckles jangled as he jerked it tight and began another stitch. York tossed a branch on the long, log fire before their lean-to. He placed a small cast iron pot on the fire and dumped a bag of metal shavings into it. Brion was curious to see what he was doing, so he watched as they talked.

Brion and York had spent the last hour explaining what they had seen in the amphitheater. Gwyneth sat to the side running a stone over her knife blade. The scrape of rock on metal rang out in the quiet of the evening amid the popping of the fire. The sweet scent of burning heather and aspen filled the air.

Finola bowed her head. "You don't even know where they are."

"I can find them." Brion jerked at another stitch and watched as York stirred the metal shavings in his pot with a metal spoon. Brion was sure he could find them. He had studied the lay of the land. He knew that amphitheater was near the base of the larger mountain. The Carpentini had been using it as a meeting place for refugees and using the ladder to foil any attempt by the Bracari to track them. Brion knew where to begin his search. They must have found some hideaway at the roots of the mountains. They thought they were secure, but Brion knew better.

Finola raised her head. "I can't come with you. Not now." She glanced at Gwyneth. "You should see them," she said. Brion saw the pride in her face. "They're getting good. Really good."

"Even some men have joined us," Gwyneth said.

"I think they might actually be able to do something," Finola said.

York glanced at Gwyneth. "I heard Gwyneth has been beating up every boy in the village," he said.

Gwyneth scowled, and Finola laughed.

"Only the ones that deserved it," Gwyneth snapped.

"It is rather liberating," Finola said, "to be able to punish men and boys when they need it."

"Don't get too zealous," Brion said. "We need to have some friends around here."

"Reed likes us," Gwyneth said. "He says the men have never behaved better."

Brion smiled. "I imagine so. What with all the women packing knifes and carrying spears around with them. It's bound to make any man nervous."

"Only the tyrants," Finola said.

"Back to my point," Brion said as he tugged another stitch taut. "I don't know how long I'll be gone. I don't want to leave you here alone."

"I'm not alone," Finola said. She patted Iain on the leg, where he lounged on the bed half asleep.

"Finola?"

"I'm doing something important here, Brion," she said. "I know you need to look for your mother. Go check this group out if you have to. In another couple of weeks, Emyr will send help."

"You think he will?" Brion said. He tied off the last stitch and cut the cord.

"He has to," Finola said. "Or the Carpentini and the Salassani are going to be pushed into Coll."

York placed a black iron plate on a stone. It had a hinge on one end and a clamp on the other.

"I heard talk that the Salassani aren't going to wait," Gwyneth said. "They say they need to get crops in the ground before it's too late."

"Probably," Brion said. But his attention was now riveted on York who had just drawn a pair of tongs from his bag and reached into the fire to grasp the little pot with the metal in it. York poured the liquid lead carefully into the holes in the iron plate.

"What are you doing?" Gwyneth said. She leaned closer for a better look.

"Making stones," York said.

Brion remembered the silver stones York had thrown at the Salassani in the gulch, but he was sure York hadn't had them before. If he had, he had been hiding them.

York knocked the latch loose with the tongs and flipped the plate open to reveal six perfectly formed, oblong, pointed spheres.

"Where did you learn to do that?" Brion asked.

York shrugged but didn't look at him. "A man taught me," he said. "They fly better than stones."

Brion noted the furtive glance York shot at Gwyneth and her knowing frown. Why did that glance leave Brion feeling anxious? Why would York be so cagey about where he had learned to make the strange leaden stones?

Gwyneth sheathed her knife and stretched.

Brion gestured to her knife. "Can I see it?' he asked.

Gwyneth handed it to him. Brion slid it into the sheath that was attached to the harness he had been sewing. He stood and gestured for Finola to help.

"A friend gave me one of these," Brion said. "It saved my life." He reached to slip it over Gwyneth's shoulder, but she flinched away.

Finola stepped in to grab it from him. "Let me," she said.

Brion handed it to her and waited while Finola strapped it on.

"You wear it underneath your clothes," he said, "so no one knows you have it."

Gwyneth reached back and drew the knife from where it sat at the nape of her neck. She grinned.

"I told you," Finola said to her. "He's not like most of the men you've known."

"What's that supposed to mean?" Brion asked.

"It's our secret," Finola said. She batted her eyelashes at him. "You know, girl things."

"Uh huh," Brion said.

Finola bent to whisper something to Gwyneth. Gwyneth shifted nervously. "Thank you," she said.

Brion nodded. "Just be sure not to use it on some unsuspecting kid. Save it for when you really need it."

Gwyneth nodded and cleared her throat. Tears glistened in her eyes.

Brion led York and three Carpentini Reed sent with him deep into the foothills of the Aveen Mountains south and west of Dunraven Keep. He ignored the trails and cut overland toward the amphitheater where he hoped to pick up some sign of the Carpentini who were hiding in the mountains. Once again, he had chosen to leave the horses behind because he believed that they would be scrambling through difficult, broken country where the horses would have to be left behind anyway. He hadn't missed the fact that the Carpentini they had encountered in the gully hadn't used horses—probably because horses couldn't go where they were going.

A gentle rain trickled from the skies, casting up the rich scent of damp earth and heather. Brion loved the smells of the heathland. It had been one of the things he had missed all while he and Finola had wintered at the cabin in Wexford. The heathland had burrowed into his bones. He felt more at home here than anywhere else.

Brion slipped a piece of wax from his pouch and passed it over his bowstring as he walked. He gestured for York to do the same to the short recurve bow he was carrying. The water wouldn't ruin his flaxen string, but it could waterlog it and slow the cast. He didn't dare unstring the bow to protect the string when he knew that Bracari might be lurking about.

He wrestled with the nervous excitement that kept rising in his chest. He might find his mother today or the next. The farther he strode into the thickening forests that coated the upper foothills, the more certain he became that she was there. He became so obsessed with the thought that he almost missed the subtle shift in the sounds of the forests, the almost imperceptible awareness that someone was watching them.

York followed in the rear as the small company slipped through the pines and beech trees and worked their way deeper into the canyons and gullies cut by the runoff from the mountains above. The streams they crossed were swollen and treacherous. The roots and stones of the forest floor had grown slick with rain. But they struggled on.

York had wanted to tell Brion about the stranger in the mottled cloak, but the man had insisted that it would be better if Brion didn't know just yet. The man promised to tell Brion when the time was right. York didn't understand the need for secrecy. He hadn't told the man anything he couldn't have learned by simply asking around. York's hand strayed to the heavy leather pouch at his hip. He now had two dozen cylindrical balls for his sling. And the man had promised him more metal when he returned. York adjusted the quiver across his back and made sure the leather flap still covered the fletchings, protecting them from the rain.

The short sword and scabbard that Reed had let him pick from those seized from the Bracari slapped against his thigh. He wasn't good with the sword yet, but he would be. Brion had started to teach him. York stood taller as he realized that he was finally becoming a man. He was armed like a warrior, and he would soon be able to make the men that had killed his father pay.

Brion stopped and held up his hand. They all crouched low or shifted to find some protection behind one of the huge pines that towered over them. York strained his ears to listen. The rain pattered on the canopy above and dripped through it in a steady mist that dampened every noise in the forest.

They had just entered a wide depression where a creek gurgled through the thick underbrush. A small break in the canopy let in a ray of gray light from the overcast sky. Nothing stirred. Not even the red squirrels that had been chattering just moments before.

Brion motioned for them to spread out. He glanced back at York and gestured for him to get back up the slope and into the pines. York hesitated and then obeyed. Brion would have a good reason, and he knew he should trust him.

York scrambled up the side of the depression over the slippery bed of wet pine needles and oak leaves. He had reached the top when the shouting began. He spun around in time to see Brion release an arrow before crumpling to the ground. A red stain had blossomed on the side of his head. Brion lay still, too still. The sickening ache York had experienced when his father died filled his chest. Not Brion! Not again.

The three Carpentini were flinging arrows at a group of Bracari that had rushed into the depression. Two of the Carpentini fell with arrows protruding from their bodies, and the third was clubbed over the head before York could get an arrow on the string. He loosed, and the arrow slammed into a Bracari chest. York fumbled with the second arrow as several Bracari turned toward him. The sound of crashing to his right brought his head around. Panic gripped his chest. He was alone, and they were closing in. He would be surrounded.

York dropped the bow, slipped his sling onto his finger and jerked open his pouch. He placed the lead ball in the leather cup and snapped the sling at the nearest Bracari. The silver ball whistled before it slammed into the Bracari's head. York ducked an arrow that skipped off a branch and sprinted into the deeper shadows of the forest. Someone yelled. A scream of pain and the clash of steel rang through the woods. York didn't have time to figure out who the Bracari were fighting, but the ones that were pursuing him wheeled about and left him. York raced on. He tried to forget the way Brion had fallen like a rag doll. He tried to forget the horrible tightness in his chest. Instead, he focused on the thought that he had to warn Reed. He had to get help. He had to tell Finola that Brion was dead. Bitter tears slipped down his cheeks as he sprinted through the undergrowth. Branches snatched at his clothes. Roots and rocks tripped his feet. But he stumbled on, pushing through the burning in his lungs, the ache in his legs, and the despair in his heart.

Chapter 8
The Pursuit

What do you mean Brion's dead?" Finola snapped. Her gaze passed over York's torn clothing that dripped with rain. She had been working with some women inside the keep in hand-to-hand fighting. Gwyneth came to stand beside her, panting and sweating. Her smile faded as she heard Finola's last words. Reed stood behind Finola, peering over her head, his brow wrinkled in a frown.

"The Bracari," York said, still trying to catch his breath. His legs trembled from the exertion of racing back through the forests and over the heathland, sure that the Bracari were pursuing him. "They ambushed us. I didn't see how many. Our men are all dead." The bitterness in his throat choked him. Brion had been the best warrior York had ever seen, and he had fallen with a single blow to the head. It was impossible to believe, but he had seen it with his own eyes. "I think they were waiting for us. They knew we were coming."

"What are you saying?" Reed asked.

York stood straighter. "We weren't even on a trail. The only way they could have been there was if they knew we were going that way."

Finola sheathed her knife and began collecting her things. Gwyneth watched her for a moment before joining her.

"What are you doing?" Reed asked.

"Going after Brion," she said.

"You just heard York say he was dead," Reed said.

Finola straightened and fixed Reed with a smoldering gaze as tears slipped down her cheek. "I would know if he were dead," she said. "Don't try to stop me."

Reed raised his hands over his head in a gesture of exaggerated disbelief. "You're just going to get yourself killed or captured," he said.

Finola ignored him and finished gathering the gear she had brought with her to the keep. York tried to understand why Finola didn't believe him. Then York noticed Arno, the man who wore the mottled cloak, standing in the shadows. The suspicion blossomed in his mind. Arno had known Brion was going to find the other Carpentini, and he had kept asking York about Brion. A sick feeling burst into York's gut. Had Arno betrayed York's trust? York glanced at Gwyneth. She had warned him, and now he had allowed himself to be manipulated into betraying Brion. York's hand strayed to his sling. Should he kill Arno here and now?

Finola picked up Iain and strode over to where Clidna stood with the other women. "Take care of him," she said. "I'll be back in a few days." Then she spun to Reed. "What are you going to do about this?"

Reed shook his head. "I can't afford to waste any more men," he said. "If the Bracari are preparing an attack, I'll need every man I have."

Arno stepped forward. The mottled cloak made him seem like a wraith in the shadows. "I'll go," he volunteered.

York glanced at Finola, afraid she might let Arno join them. She appraised Arno and then shook her head. "Not with me you won't."

Arno raised his hands in a gesture of surrender. "Only trying to help," he said.

Finola gestured to Gwyneth. "She'll need a horse."

"Use one of your pack horses," Reed said with some annoyance. "There are a few spare saddles in the stable." Then he appraised her. "You really are going after him, then?"

Finola didn't even bother answering him. She swung her cloak over her shoulders, fixed the clasp, slipped on her quiver, and strode from the keep. York glanced at Reed, who shook his head. York followed Gwyneth and Finola out.

In twenty minutes, the three of them were galloping over the heathland beneath the leaden sky. The rain had stopped falling, but the ground was muddy. York rode Brion's black mare, Misty, as he led Finola and Gwyneth back toward the hollow where Brion's body lay. He didn't know what Finola expected to find, but he understood her well enough by now to know she would not turn aside until she had seen the corpse.

He wondered if his mother had loved his father with the same fiery passion that drove this young woman. Would she have braved the heathland alone to find York? Would she care if York never came back?

By the time they reached the hollow, the gray of day had faded to the shadows of evening. York pulled them to a halt, and they dismounted on the rise well back from the hollow. He signaled for them to be quiet as they crept through the sodden forest. But he needn't have bothered. Finola and Gwyneth were both more skilled at moving quietly than he was. He considered using the felt shoes, but he was too anxious to take the time to put them on. He reached the crest. His bow still lay where he had dropped it. He slipped to his belly and peered through the snowberry bushes into the hollow. What he found sent his mind reeling in confusion. Brion wasn't there. No one was.

Gwyneth glanced at York. Was he lost? There was no one down there. The creek gurgled quietly, but nothing else stirred. The smell of damp earth and rotting wood contrasted with the sharp scent of the pines.

Finola stood. She had an arrow on the string of her bow and Gwyneth followed her example. Gwyneth had become accustomed to the weight of the mail shirt and the short sword at her hip. The bow now felt natural in her hands. But she had little experience in tracking, so she determined to follow Finola's lead. Finola stepped over a log and began to work her way quietly down the slope.

"Wait," York said in a harsh whisper.

Finola paused.

York rose and bent close to the ground as he worked his way down the slope in front of her in a wide zigzag pattern. Gwyneth understood that York was looking for sign, so she waited with Finola. She kept her gaze moving over the brush on the other side of the hollow. Unless York was lost, something wasn't right.

York reached the bottom, circled around, and then gestured for them to come down.

"Here," he whispered. He pointed to a spot where a boot had ground the pine needles into the mud. Then he picked up a stone about the size of a child's fist and turned it over to reveal the dark stain of blood with a few bits of hair stuck to it.

"That looks like Brion's hair," Finola said.

York nodded.

"Then where is he?"

York shrugged. "The others are gone, too," he said. "There were three Carpentini with us when the Bracari attacked. I know Brion hit one Bracari, and I shot another one. There should be at least six bodies down here."

Gwyneth glanced around again. "Then they have to be here somewhere," she said. She stepped to the creek, trying to see through the undergrowth to the other bank. Something odd waved up and down in the current in a deep pool that swirled under the rotted end of a huge pine tree. She bent closer and saw that it was a human hand.

"Here," she called, forgetting that they were supposed to be quiet. The sudden terror that she had found Brion's body jerked the word from her throat.

York splashed through the creek and pushed the brambles aside to find a dead Bracari with one of Brion's arrows in his throat. But it wasn't just one Bracari. Half a dozen at least had been piled up behind the large rotten pine log as if someone had made a hasty attempt to conceal them. One of them had slipped down the hill into the stream. There were no Carpentini, only green-clad Bracari. For one moment, Gwyneth wondered if any of them were related to her.

"Someone else has been here," York said. He glanced back at Finola before pointing to a bootprint still visible in the muddy bank. "Carpentini," he said.

"Can you follow them?" Finola asked.

York shrugged. "Maybe," he said. "The rain will have washed away most of their tracks." He glanced up at the dark canopy overhead.

"Brion trained you," Finola said. "This time it matters."

York stared at her. He swallowed. "But we've only been out

tracking a couple of times."

Finola frowned. "Brion said you barely needed him you were so good. Well, now he needs you."

Gwyneth could see the turmoil in York's eyes. He was uncertain of himself. But she also saw that he no longer seemed like the boy who had cowered in the face of his mother's antagonism. The muscles in York's jaw flexed, and he splashed back across the creek. He fell to his hands and knees and began circling the hollow. Finola also dropped to the ground and moved in the opposite direction. Gwyneth watched them for a moment before she strode up the slope to retrieve the horses. When they found the trail, they would need to ride on, and she didn't know much about tracking.

Misty pulled loose of Gwyneth's grasp and walked over to nose around the ground where York had found the rock with the blood on it. She butted the rock with her muzzle and made a quiet purring sound. The sight brought tears to Gwyneth's eyes. Misty recognized Brion's scent.

Finola glanced up at Misty, but kept searching. She and York began moving in a wider circle. Gwyneth assumed that Brion had trained Finola, too, but Gwyneth had never seen anyone tracking. She wondered what they were looking for, and she determined to tell York or Finola that she wanted to learn.

York finally raised his head. "I think they went this way," he said. "They're heading deeper into the mountains."

Finola nodded her agreement and mounted her horse. "Lead the way."

Gwyneth admired Finola's quiet determination. She wondered if her grandmother had been like Finola. Gwyneth's mother, Aila, had told her many times how her grandmother had used a spear to kill two of the Bracari sent to kill them, thus giving them time to escape into the flume. A rush of anger swept through her at the thought. All of her suffering had come from those Bracari and what they had done to her mother. Gwyneth had always wanted to be like her grandmother—a warrior who could protect those she loved. Gwyneth mounted and followed York and Finola out of the hollow.

York didn't ride Misty. He led her by the reins as he bent low, working his way slowly into the darkening shadows. Misty bumped him with her nose and stomped her feet if he took too long reading the trail. The light was fading fast, and Gwyneth knew they would soon have to stop, or they would lose the trail in the darkness.

But York continued for some time, occasionally covering a dozen yards before pausing to pick his way an inch at a time. Misty kept nudging him with her nose as if she were encouraging him to continue. Eventually, York faced Finola. The shadows hid his expression.

"I can't," he said. "I can't see anymore."

Finola nodded and dismounted. "We wait until light, then," she said.

But Misty was not so easily stopped. She tried to continue until York tied her securely to a large aspen.

"She must miss her master," Gwyneth said.

Finola gazed at Misty for a moment and then strode up to her. She patted her muzzle and scratched her ears. "We'll find him," she whispered.

Gwyneth was too wet and cold to sleep. They hadn't built a fire for fear of attracting unwanted attention. Finola had been unusually quiet all day and had gone off to sit with her back to a big oak. She had pulled her cloak around her in a way that indicated she wanted to be alone. So Gwyneth slipped over to sit beside York, where he leaned against a tree running a file over his broadheads. She didn't usually seek out men—in fact, she never did. But of all the men and boys she knew, she liked York the best. He treated her like he treated everybody else, and he was fun to tease. He took himself too seriously and let other men get under his skin. York didn't even glance at her when she sat down.

"It wasn't your fault," she said.

York ignored her.

"None of it was your fault."

York scowled over at her. A mosquito buzzed between them, and he swatted at it. "You don't know anything," he said.

"I know you blame yourself for your father's death," she said. "And I know that you're trying to blame yourself for Brion's."

"Leave me alone," York said, turning his back on her.

"Now who's the unfriendly one?" Gwyneth said. Ever since his father's death, York had become as moody as a girl. Gwyneth understood why, but sometimes she just wanted to slap him.

York remained silent. The rhythmic swish of the file over the broadhead continued.

"I warned you not to trust that man in the cloak," she said.

York snapped his head up. His file paused in mid-stroke. Gwyneth smiled. York was so easy to figure out, and he kept thinking she was too stupid to see what was going on.

"What did he make you promise?" she asked.

A defiant glare swept across York's face before he bowed his head. "He just wanted to know what Brion was teaching me and how he joined Reed."

"He told you not to tell Brion, didn't he?"

York shrugged.

"He taught you how to make those weird metal stones, too, didn't he?"

York scowled at the broadhead as he pushed the file down the edge.

"You think he was the one that told the Bracari where you were going?"

York glanced at her and nodded.

"I don't think he did," Gwyneth said. She grinned at the surprised expression on York's face. "Honestly," she said as she pulled her knees up and hugged them close. "Finola's right. You men don't pay attention to anything."

"What are you talking about?" York set the file down and pulled another arrow from his quiver.

"Some Salassani warrior came in the day after the big group did," Gwyneth said. She had spent her life learning to read people, and she thought she had read Arno correctly. "When you and Brion went out yesterday, he disappeared all day. I didn't see him until the next morning when he was hanging back in the shadow of the keep, watching you all leave. But I saw the man in the cloak. He was hanging around Reed, asking questions. He didn't have time to go off and warn the Bracari."

York glanced around at the darkness as if he expected the Salassani to jump out at them. Then he slipped the arrow he had just taken out back into his quiver, picked up his bow, and stood.

"I'm going to look around," he said.

He was just trying to avoid the discussion, but there was no point in forcing it. "You make too much noise," Gwyneth said. "I'll do it."

York glared at her. Then he sat down, pulled two felt pads from his pack, tied them to his boots, and covered them with a felt bag which he tied at his ankles.

"What are you doing?" Gwyneth asked. "You look like some kind of jester."

York glowered at her. "They work," he said, before he set off into the darkness.

"Don't get lost," Gwyneth said. But she couldn't resist watching him pad around in those things, so she rose to follow him. Finola had been teaching her to creep silently through the woods, and she thought now might be a good time to practice. She was too cold and restless to sit around anyway. She placed her feet carefully, stepping on the front outside edge before slowly rolling it down to the heel. She could feel every stone or stick before she put her weight on it and so avoided making any sharp noises. The quiet sounds of the forest smothered the sounds she made as she crept behind York.

Gwyneth had followed him for a good hundred paces when he paused by a large oak tree. He glanced around and started fiddling with his trousers. It took Gwyneth a moment to realize what he was doing. She stood up.

"I really don't want to watch you pee on a tree," she whispered.

York jumped and spun. His pants were still down, though Gwyneth couldn't see anything in the shadows.

York cursed and spun back around, while Gwyneth shook with repressed laughter. York strode off again into the trees. He swung wide around the trail they had followed until he found a pile of boulders where they could hide. York acted like Gwyneth wasn't there as he settled down to wait. Boys and men were so desperate to be seen as manly and strong that they couldn't take a joke.

Gwyneth clambered up to sit beside him. "That was funny," Gwyneth teased. "Admit it."

"Not really," York said as he peered into the shadows.

Gwyneth clamped a hand over her mouth to keep from laughing out loud. York needed to learn not to take himself so seriously.

The moon had risen behind the clouds, casting a pale light about the woods. Gwyneth wasn't used to wandering the woods at night and began to question the wisdom of following York. After the merriment of the joke had worn off, the sounds of the forest began to excite her imagination. She should have remained behind with Finola and the horses. Creatures fluttered and chirped in the trees above them. An owl hooted and another answered. York listened as if he understood. Then a quiet thump sounded, followed by the clip of a hoof against stone.

York slipped an arrow from his quiver, and Gwyneth did the same. The dark shape of a man appeared, leading a horse as he studied the ground. York raised up on one knee, drew, and released. Gwyneth barely contained the gasp of disbelief. York had just shot a man without even knowing who he was.

The arrow bit into the man's shoulder. He grunted and spun around as he dropped the horse's reins and drew his sword. He was left-handed. Gwyneth scowled. It was the man she had seen watching Brion—the Salassani warrior.

York whipped another arrow from his quiver, drew, and released. The arrow slammed into the man's upper thigh. He stumbled sideways until he fell to his knees.

"What are you doing?" Gwyneth whispered to York. She couldn't believe he was attacking a perfect stranger. He ignored her.

"What do you want?" the man called. He laid his sword on the ground and clutched at the arrow in his leg.

"Why are you following us?" York demanded.

"I'm not following anyone."

York shot another arrow into the ground beside the man.

"One more lie, and I kill you," York called.

Gwyneth thought the man's hand slipped to his belt. He drew something out slowly.

"Reed sent me to find you," he said.

He jerked and threw something so fast Gwyneth could barely see the motion.

"York!" Gwyneth cried as she lunged on top of him, forcing him down.

An axe flew over their heads to crash against the stones with a shower of sparks.

"Get off," York grunted as he shrugged her aside. York raised himself to one knee and shot the man in the chest. The man dropped to his hands and knees with a gasp as the arrow passed through him to skip off a log and disappear into the shadows.

York leapt up and scrambled over the boulders until he stood over the man. He kicked him onto his back and stepped on his good arm.

"Why are you following us?" York demanded again. Gwyneth didn't miss the quaver in his voice.

"The ransom," the man said. "Brion of Wexford killed my brother."

The galloping of hooves rang through the night, and Finola swept into the space before the stones. She sprang from the saddle and stood staring down at the dying man. Then she spun on York. "What are you thinking?" she demanded.

"I was checking our back trail the way Brion taught me to," he said defensively.

"Who's he?" She gestured to the injured man.

York shrugged. "He wants the bounty on Brion's head."

Finola cursed under her breath and shook her head. "I told him we shouldn't come this far north," she said. "And you two. Don't ever sneak off again without telling me where you're going."

Gwyneth stared at the dying man, a little stung by Finola's scolding, and sickened by what York had done. The man couldn't be more than thirty or forty years old. If he had been seeking revenge for the death of his brother, he probably saw Brion as some senseless killer. She couldn't blame him for wanting to get revenge, not if he loved his brother the way Gwyneth had loved her mother. The man watched them without saying a word.

Finola knelt beside him. "Can you tell us where they've taken him?" she asked.

The man shook his head. "If I knew that, I would have his head already."

Finola flinched as if she were restraining herself. "How did you know he was here?"

The man sneered. "He always leaves a trail of blood wherever he goes."

Finola raised a hand as if to slap the man, but she closed her fist. "Tell us what you know," she snapped. "Who else is looking for him?"

"Why should I help you?" he said. "Your little man has already killed me." His gaze strayed to York, who scowled at his use of the word "little."

"We can make you more comfortable," Finola said.

"Leave me to die in peace," he said. He coughed and something gurgled in his throat.

Finola stood. She stared at the man for a long moment as if deciding what to do.

"Okay," she said. "As you wish." She gestured for York and Gwyneth to follow.

Gwyneth slipped the man's water bag from his saddle and placed it in his hand before she followed Finola and York back to where the other horses waited.

York stopped at the end of the wide canyon. Misty snorted and bobbed her head. She hadn't wanted to approach the boulders, and York had dismounted, tossed the reins to Finola, and advanced on foot. Misty's behavior continued to confuse him. She was never skittish like most horses. He had never seen a more sure-footed and intelligent beast. But ever since they had cleared the grove of aspens at the head of the valley, she had been fighting him—jerking at the reins and trying to turn around.

York stood beside the stream that gushed from beneath an immense pile of boulders.

He stared up at the rockslide that had spilled into the valley, blocking any easy exit. Behind the boulders, a steep, rocky slope lifted up into the gray sky. Deep green pines crowned the ridge. There was no way out.

"Are you sure they came this way?" Gwyneth asked.

York nodded, but he wasn't sure at all. He had lost the trail a few miles back and had been guessing what path they might have followed. It had stretched York's skill and imagination to the limit to follow the trail this far. They had already spent one night and an entire day in the Aveens. The sun was now slipping behind the mountains. The urgency to find Brion was picking at him. If Brion was still alive, as Finola thought, they needed to find him quickly. The longer it took, the worse his chances of staying alive. For all York knew, the Carpentini didn't know who Brion was and would mistake him for their enemy. They might have already killed him.

"We're exposed," Finola said. She shifted in the saddle and gazed up at the jagged slopes that were surrounded by a thick halo of pines.

York glanced around. She was right. They were standing at the base of the rockslide in a wide dish that had been stripped bare of trees. Thick patches of a shrub called mountain mahogany had claimed the floor of the valley. Farther back, the white trunks of mountain aspens stood stark against the fading light. Their leaves fluttered and rattled in the cool breeze that swept down from the ridge above, bringing with it the fresh scent of pine.

York strode back to Misty and swung up into her saddle. She bobbed her head, snorted, and spun away from the pile as if it scared her. He had to hold her back to keep her from galloping down the trail. York jerked at the reins impatiently. He couldn't understand where the Carpentini might have gone. He had missed something. Something important. Misty passed under the aspens and veered off the trail.

"Whoa," York said as he yanked hard on her reins. Misty shook her head and stomped her feet. "What's the matter with you?" York said.

"Having trouble?" Gwyneth said with a scornful laugh as she came up behind him.

"She's scared of something," York said.

"Not Misty," Finola said. She dismounted and placed her hand under Misty's jaw. She leaned in close to her. "Do you know where he is?" Misty nuzzled Finola's face. Finola glanced up at York. "Give her the rein," she said. "Let her go where she will."

York shrugged. "Okay." He dropped the reins.

Misty bobbed her head and pushed through the aspens. York bent low against her neck to avoid being dragged out of the saddle by a branch. Misty paused at the edge of the cliff face and then veered left toward the rockslide, plowing through the thick undergrowth.

"To think," Gwyneth said from behind him, "all this time I thought *you* were tracking the Carpentini when it was really Misty doing it."

York ignored her. But she was right. Misty had been following Brion's scent. York had heard of horses trained to do that, but he hadn't known any that could.

There was no trail along the cliff face, and Misty didn't care that York was clinging precariously to her back as she forced her way through the undergrowth. A branch grabbed York's tunic and plucked him clear of the saddle with a sudden jerk. He hadn't even had time to grab the saddle horn. York dangled awkwardly as the limb bent and bounced under his weight. Heat flushed his face as he tried to figure out how to retain his dignity in front of the women. He needn't have worried because Gwyneth wasn't about to let something like that go without comment. She had started being fresh with him ever since Brion and Finola had turned up.

Gwyneth laughed. "Look at the little pigeon in the tree."

"Get over here," York said to her. "Let me stand on your horse."

Gwyneth eyed him with a devilish expression. "I don't think I like the tone of your voice," she said.

York reached up to try to work his tunic free. His feet churned the air as he struggled.

"You really aren't going to say 'please'?" Gwyneth asked.

York gave up and gave Finola a beseeching look. She was smiling.

"I think I'd say please if I were you," she said.

"Please," he said in a flat tone.

"That's better," Gwyneth said. "A little humility is good for a young man to learn." She backed her horse under his feet and waited while he stood on the horse's rump and worked the tunic free of the branch. When he finished, he dropped a hand on her shoulder to steady himself, but Gwyneth jerked aside, sending him somersaulting off the horse's rump into the brush.

"What's the matter with you?" he demanded as he struggled to regain his feet.

Gwyneth glared at him. "I told you not to touch me," she said.

York threw up his hands and stomped off up the trail behind Misty—too angry to care if they followed or not.

Misty stopped beside the rockslide where huge limestone boulders barred the way. She bobbed her head again and laid her ears flat. She pawed at the jumble of rocks and dirt that skirted the slide. York just watched her. "You crazy horse," he said.

Finola came up and laid a hand on Misty's neck. "What is it, old girl?"

Misty bobbed her head and pawed at the rubble again. She bent low to sniff at a large slab of stone. Then she raised her hoof to step on it. A hollow thud sounded.

Everyone exchanged surprised glances. York bent to examine the stone, his frustration forgotten in his curiosity to discover what Misty had found. That's when he noticed the long, thin marks that suggested the stone had been slid into place. He grabbed the edge with both hands and leaned back.

"Jumping toadstools," he groaned. "That's heavy." He peered up at the women. "A bit of help—*please*," he said.

"Just when we think you're turning into a man," Gwyneth said, "you have to go and disappoint us. First, the tree and now this."

York smirked up at her. She wasn't finished taunting him. "Come on," he said.

Finola and Gwyneth joined him, and together they heaved the stone aside. A waft of cool air rushed out to greet them. It smelled of mold, soil, and wood smoke.

"Not again," Finola said, closing her eyes and taking in a deep breath.

York glanced at her.

"I do *not* like tunnels," Finola said.

York flopped onto his belly and poked his head into the cool darkness. To his surprise, he found a narrow tunnel that led under the rockslide. Rays of light slipped into the dark passage through the cracks in the pile of boulders above. He pulled his head out and scrambled to his feet.

"Well?" he said.

Finola clicked her tongue in apparent disgust. "They would have to use a stupid tunnel," she said.

"What's the matter with tunnels?" Gwyneth asked.

Finola scowled but didn't answer.

"We can't take the horses," York said.

"That's obvious," Gwyneth said, rolling her eyes.

"We'll hobble them in the aspens," Finola said. "And we'll need torches."

Vengeance

The valley came alive with the sounds of evening. Gwyneth rested with her back to an aspen as the warblers, robins, and nightingales broke out in song. Crickets and tree frogs joined the chorus, casting up a rhapsody of music that seemed to flow with the rhythms of the earth itself. The wind rattled the aspen leaves and the creek bubbled over stones. Gwyneth had never heard anything so beautiful. A lump rose in her throat. Her mother would have been thrilled with the quiet beauty of this valley.

The thought of her mother made her think of Finola. Only a few years separated Finola and Gwyneth, but Finola had become her mentor—the mother figure she so desperately needed. It had taken her a long time to realize what drew her to Finola. It was more than simply seeing her as the kind of strong woman she wanted to be. Finola had a way about her that drew children of all ages to her.

Gwyneth glanced around and realized Finola was no longer with them. York sat beside the fire brushing the last of the pine resin they had gathered on the torches. Gwyneth rose and stepped off into the trees. Once out of the circle of firelight, she found Finola's shadow down by the creek.

At first, she considered leaving Finola to herself, but Finola had said so little in the last two days. Gwyneth slipped through the underbrush to stand beside her. Finola jumped at the sound of her approach, and Gwyneth heard her sniffle.

"Are you all right?" Gwyneth asked.

"I'll be fine," Finola said. Her voice was thick.

"We'll find him," Gwyneth said. "The Carpentini wouldn't kill him."

"It's not that," Finola said. "I would know if he were dead. I would feel it."

"What do you mean?"

"The silence," Finola said. "I would feel the silence, the way I did when Tyg, Neahl, and Lara died."

Gwyneth had never been able to put her feelings into words, but that is exactly how she felt about her mother. A once vibrant and beautiful mind had been silenced, muted. The echoing stillness continued to haunt her. Where had her mother's beautiful voice gone?

Had it joined the music that filled the valley?

"That is the worst thing about death," Finola whispered. "I can hear and feel the silence."

"Yes," Gwyneth agreed.

"I don't know if I can tell him," Finola said.

Gwyneth realized she had not followed Finola's train of thought. "Tell who what?"

"Brion," Finola said. "I don't want to hurt him, but I've come to realize over the last two days, that if I don't tell him soon, I may never get the chance."

Gwyneth touched her arm. "We'll find him," she said again.

Finola wiped at her eyes. "My mother struggled to have children. I was her only one. And I bled once after a man called Ithel beat me," she said. "I haven't told Brion, but I don't think I can ever have a child now. I so wanted to give him a child, especially after all he has lost."

Gwyneth's stomach tightened as she remembered all the men who had abused her mother and that last horrible night when her mother had died with her ribs caved in.

"Why do all men hurt women?" Gwyneth asked.

Finola grabbed her arm and pulled her close. Tears glistened on Finola's cheek.

"Listen to me," Finola said. "You have to give up this hatred of men. Not all men are like Ithel or the men who attacked your mother. Brion is a good, honest man. He has never harmed a child or a woman. King Emyr is gentle and considerate. Neahl and Tyg were honorable men. They sacrificed their lives to save us." Finola choked on a sob. "Redmond loved Lara so much that he remained alone for years rather than betray her memory. When she died, he was broken."

"I—" Gwyneth began.

"No, listen," Finola cut her off. "Reed took you in even though all the women in the village complained. Has he ever beaten you?"

"No."

"York is full of anger and pain just like you, but has he ever tried to hurt you?"

"No."

"Ever been mean to you?"

"No."

"There will always be bad men, just like there are bad women," Finola continued. "You can fight them, but you can't control them. If you never give up this hatred, you'll probably die alone without the warmth of the love you so desperately want."

Gwyneth scowled as the shame and anger burned in her chest. By what right did Finola judge her?

"My own father blinded my mother and tried to kill us both," she snapped. "Men preyed on my mother until one beat her to death. My. Mother. Died. Alone." Gwyneth enunciated the last four words.

"No, she didn't," Finola replied. "*You* were with her. Who will be with you?"

Gwyneth stiffened as if Finola had slapped her. Tears spilled from Gwyneth's eyes. She spun to leave. But Finola grabbed her, yanked her around, and embraced her so tightly she couldn't breathe.

"Let it go," Finola whispered in her ear. "You deserve so much more than this pain."

Gwyneth resisted. She wanted to pull away and run screaming off into the trees. She wanted to lash out and hurt everyone and everything. The memory of Brion tucking Finola and Iain into their sleeping furs at night while he stretched himself on the cold, hard ground stirred in her mind. Finola's arms pressed against the knife sheath Brion had made for her even while he was so preoccupied with his own fears and sorrows. She recalled the touch of York's hand as he had tried to teach her how to shoot the bow.

Gwyneth's chest constricted with a sob, and she clung to Finola with a desperation she had not let herself feel in years.

"That's it," Finola whispered. "Let it go."

The torch sputtered and spit as the resin burned, casting up a cloud of black smoke into York's face as he peered into the tunnel. The tunnel was still empty, so he swung his legs around and dropped to the floor. Gwyneth handed down their gear and bows and the bundle of torches before she and Finola followed him.

Gwyneth wrinkled her nose. "That torch stinks," she said.

York shook his head. "Girls worry too much about how things smell," he said. He faced the dark tunnel.

"Boys don't worry enough," Gwyneth said.

York ignored her, which he was discovering was often the best thing to do, and stepped off into the darkness. The torch light flickered and wavered on the pale limestone. The tunnel was more of a passageway cleared around the great limestone boulders. It snaked its way deep into the rockslide, always tending to come back to the cliff face.

The uneven floor was littered with the refuse of human passing—bits of clothing and leather, pieces of wood, and even the occasional broken chunk of glass. Clearly, the passage had been used, and used heavily. York couldn't understand how the Carpentini hiding up here had managed to conceal the trail to the entrance. There had been no trace. Unless they used the felt booties Brion had given him, there was no way that many people could have left no sign of their passing.

A muffled yelp from Finola made him jerk around, terrified that they were being ambushed. But when the light of the torch flashed on her face, she was standing quietly with her hand on her throat and an expression of forced calm.

"What?" York asked.

Gwyneth shook with repressed laughter.

"What?" York asked again.

Finola brushed at a strand of hair that had fallen before her eyes. "Keep going," she said.

Gwyneth held up her fingers and wiggled them. "Think eight hairy legs," she said.

York chuckled and continued. How could Finola be afraid of spiders? Women didn't make any sense.

The air in the tunnel was fresh from the many gaps that opened above them. But it still contained the smell of wood smoke that grew stronger as they advanced.

York moved more slowly. He had no idea what to expect or how the Carpentini would respond to being followed. He thought he heard a faint sound in front of them and raised a hand to call a stop when Gwyneth's urgent whisper caused him to spin around.

"York," she said.

He found Gwyneth and Finola facing the way they had come with arrows nocked on the strings of their bows. Fortunately, their bows were the short Salassani recurve bows. A longbow, like Brion's, would have been no use in the confined space of the passage.

"Someone is following us," Gwyneth said.

Chapter 9
Failure and Friends

Brion opened his eyes to stare into the darkness. His head throbbed. His mouth felt woolen and dry. The sounds of human activity surrounded him. The smell of cooking food and human filth mingled with a moldy, earthy smell. The light of fires flickered off a damp ceiling of stone. Where was he? The memory of the last fight filtered into his mind in confused images and impressions. This wasn't the little clearing. Where was York? Where was Finola?

Someone touched his arm, and he turned his head to find a middle-aged woman with long brown hair and a kind face peering down at him. She held a finger to her lips to quiet him. Then she raised her head to watch something. The sound of human activity stilled until a hush filled the space, broken only by the popping of the fires and the sounds of nervous breathing.

Brion studied her. She looked familiar—something about the shape of her profile. He had seen it before. He wracked his brain, but he felt so sluggish.

"Who—" he began. But the woman clamped a hand over his mouth. She shook her head.

A commotion echoed in the cavern. Brion tried to sit up, but the woman held him down. She shook her head again. Someone shouted and a group of armed men carrying torches strode into the cavern herding three individuals.

"What are you thinking?" a female voice demanded.

"They're Carpentini," a man said.

"She's not," the woman said, stabbing a finger at Finola.

"He was with the other one," the man said again.

"I know that," the woman harrumphed. "How did you find us?" she demanded.

"A horse." It was York's voice.

Brion pushed the woman's restraining hand from his chest and sat up. His head throbbed at the sudden movement.

The woman he had seen in the amphitheater stood before the group of Carpentini men who surrounded Finola, Gwyneth, and York. The light of the torches shone on the woman's delicate features and black hair. Again, he noted that she wasn't more than forty years old. She still wore trousers and boots. She let out an exaggerated breath in disbelief at York's assertion that a horse had led them.

"It's true," Gwyneth said. "She's a better tracker than York is."

"Finola," Brion said. But his voice was scratchy and soft. He swallowed. "Finola," he said louder.

Finola's head jerked around. She rushed past the men who tried to restrain her and fell to her knees in front of Brion. She wrapped her arms around his neck and wept. He held her and stroked her hair.

"I'm all right," he said.

"I shouldn't have let you go alone," Finola mumbled.

"No, it's all right," Brion said. "Did York say a horse found me?"

Finola released her hold of him and brushed away her tears. She gave a short laugh. "Misty," she said. Her voice was still thick with emotion. "She followed your scent."

"Can she do that?" Brion asked.

"Apparently," Finola said.

By then, York and Gwyneth had come to stand beside him. The woman Brion had spoken to in the amphitheater and the large, balding man who had taken the woman with the child that Brion and York had rescued walked up to them.

"I told you, Taegan," the man said.

Taegan sighed. "Well, now that you've had your happy reunion," she said, "care to tell us who you are?"

"I was coming to find you," Brion said.

"Looks like we found you," Taegan said. "Now, who are you?"

"I'm Brion of Wexford," he said.

Taegan's eyes narrowed slightly, and she cast a glance at the older woman who had been kneeling beside Brion when he awoke. "And this is my wife, Finola, and our friends, York and Gwyneth," Brion continued. "They're Carpentini."

"I can see that," Taegan said, folding her arms. Her gaze lingered on Gwyneth, making Gwyneth shift her feet and glance around. She apparently noticed that Gwyneth wore a Bracari tunic and trousers. "What do you want with us?"

"What happened to the men that were with me?" Brion asked.

Taegan raised her eyebrows, apparently annoyed that he had refused to answer her question.

"Two were killed," she said. "The other was badly injured and is being tended to."

"And the man in the amphitheater?"

"He'll be fine. Now stop stalling and answer my question." Her brow furrowed, and she glared at him.

Brion hesitated but decided to throw caution to the wind. "One of the women I tried to rescue the other day said she knew a woman named Elsie. I'm looking for her."

Taegan stared at him stone-faced. "There is no Elsie here." The man beside her shifted his feet and averted his gaze.

"I've come a long way to find her," Brion said. "I mean her no harm."

"There is no Elsie here," Taegan repeated. "I'm sorry to disappoint you."

Brion understood that she was determined to steer him away from the subject, which only heightened his interest. But pressing the matter would do no good.

"Reed also sent me," he said.

"Yes?" Taegan said.

"He invites you to join him before the Bracari and Dunkeldi come. He's gathering an army."

"He's also attracting every Bracari pig this side of the Aveens," she said. "We were better off before he came poking around."

"You can't fight them alone," Brion said.

"We don't intend to fight them," she said.

Brion paused. What did they plan to do then? He glanced at Finola, who stood.

"You think you can hide?" Finola asked.

"We've done pretty well until now," Taegan said. "You three are the first to find us."

"It was the horse," Gwyneth said. York smirked at her.

"You said that," Taegan said. She scowled at them.

"You won't be able to hide forever," Brion said.

"I don't have to. Just long enough for Tristan to satisfy his thirst for blood."

Brion almost laughed. He shook his head and then blinked against the sudden dizziness. "I don't think you understand," he said. "Tristan means to kill you all."

Taegan stepped toward him. Her hand drifted to the knife at her belt.

"Listen, Brion of Wexford," she said. "Don't you dare come up here and instruct us when you can always scamper home to Coll when it gets too dangerous for you up here."

Brion struggled to his feet. A wave of dizziness made him stumble, but Finola caught him. He realized that the ring on the chain around his neck, his mother's ring, was dangling on his chest. He grabbed it and shoved it inside his tunic. The woman frowned. She had seen it.

"I'm half-Carpentini," he said.

"Congratulations," Taegan said before she spun on her heels. "We'll decide what to do with you tomorrow."

Brion awoke to the sound of a baby crying. Finola stirred where she lay curled up beside him with one arm draped over his chest as if she were afraid of losing him again. York and Gwyneth lay beside the tiny fire that had burned itself out. Harsh whispers carried to him in the quiet of the cavern.

"He's not our enemy," a man said. It sounded like the balding man from earlier that evening. "And after what he was carrying, maybe he can help us."

Taegan replied, "He's not who you think he is."

"How do you know?" the man demanded.

"It's just wishful thinking," Taegan said. "The Duke is dead, and so is his son."

"We should at least ask him."

Silence followed for a long while. When they spoke again, their voices were too low for Brion to make out what they were saying.

Brion stared into the darkness. They had lied to him about Elsie. Taegan, who seemed to be in charge, had recognized the name. She was about the right age to be his mother. She was beautiful and strong—just the kind of woman the Duke would have found attractive. That would explain her reticence to discuss Elsie. Brion wrestled with his suspicions until sleep overwhelmed him.

The pale light of morning filtered into the cavern through some opening in the ceiling Brion hadn't noticed the previous evening. People began to stir, and he sat up to survey the cavern. His head felt much better, but sitting up brought back a dull ache. Water stains darkened the walls of the cavern, which extended back into the mountain a good twenty paces.

Several gloomy passages led off each side of the cavern. Fifty or sixty people huddled around fire pits to fight off the damp chill. They were mostly women and children with few possessions and ragged clothes. They reminded Brion of the families he had found dead in the amphitheater. The sudden anger at what the Bracari and the Dunkeldi had done to these people drove Brion to his feet.

A stab of pain flashed in his head before it subsided to a throbbing ache. He picked his way amid the sleeping people until he stood at the entrance to the cave. The last time he had been in a cave like this he had found the old midwife dead after she had given him his mother's ring and told him about his father.

Brion had long wondered how the midwife had known who he was and why his father, the Duke of Saylen, had been so upset when she had been murdered. At first, he had assumed that the Duke had been afraid that his enemies had discovered his secrets. Now, Brion realized that his father had genuinely cared for the old woman. But how could he even have known her? None of this made any sense.

The mouth of the cavern opened into a large passageway that led off in both directions. A huge gap in the stones above let the light of day into the passage. The thin columns of smoke coming from various openings farther to his right indicated the presence of several more caves. Brion wondered how many people they had packed into these caverns.

He nodded to the guard and stepped off down the passage in search of a place to relieve himself. He passed several caves filled with people before he found a secluded alcove of rock that already smelled of urine. On his way back, he came up short and dodged out of the way as a Carpentini warrior rushed past him toward the caverns. He was followed by several men, one of whom appeared to be injured. Brion hurried to follow them. They disappeared into the cavern next to the one Brion had slept in. Brion lingered in the shadows of the opening, curious to hear what was happening.

They roused Taegan. A short exchange caused a commotion as she shouted orders. The balding man with the mustache dashed in and began to argue with her. Brion heard the words "Dunkeldi" and "army" but couldn't make out what they said. Men rushed in and out.

In the commotion, Taegan noticed Brion standing in the opening. Their gazes met, and Brion thought she might order him restrained or sent back to his cavern. But she paused. A strange expression passed over her face before she turned away. Brion didn't have time to consider what her expression might mean because Finola was barreling toward him through the crowd of warriors. He hurried to meet her.

"Don't do that again," she demanded.

Brion held up his hands to head her off. "Just taking care of necessities," he said.

"I thought they had taken you," she said.

Brion embraced her. "I'm glad you're here," he said. "We'll be all right."

Finola squeezed him and then pushed him away. "I have to tell you something," she said.

Brion waited in confusion as tears brimmed in Finola's eyes and her lips trembled.

"What is it?" Brion asked. He glanced over her shoulder to see if something had happened to Gwyneth or York. He grasped her hands. They were cool and calloused.

"I don't think—" she began. But she was interrupted by the arrival of the two Carpentini leaders.

"We need to talk," Taegan said.

Brion glanced at Finola, but she had turned away. He nodded and followed the woman back to where York was stirring a pot of soup over a small fire. They sat down and gestured for Brion and Finola to do the same. Taegan began without any preamble as Brion and Finola sat.

"They call me Taegan," she said. "This is Steffan." She pointed to the balding man who sat beside her. "We need to know who you are."

"I already told you," Brion said.

She gestured to his chest. "You have a ring that bears the coat of arms of the Duke of Saylen," she said. "I ask you again, who are you?"

Brion glanced at Finola. She shrugged. How had this woman recognized the Duke's coat of arms? Brion's suspicions returned in earnest. His chest warmed with the anticipation that perhaps she was prepared to admit that she was his mother.

"I'm Brion of Wexford," he said, "the son of the Duke of Saylen and a Carpentini woman named Elsie." He had tried to keep the anxious excitement out of his voice. He studied Taegan for any reaction. "I have inherited my father's title," he continued. "I am now the Duke of Saylen."

A commotion rippled through the people who had begun to gather. Someone gasped, but Brion couldn't see who it was. A rush of emotions swept across Taegan's face before she managed to control them. Steffan grinned.

"I knew it," Steffan said. "Will you help us?"

Brion kept his gaze fixed on Taegan, waiting for her to admit that she was his mother, hoping that he had finally found her. But her expression had turned cold. Brion couldn't help but glance at Finola as the realization of what had just happened overwhelmed him—his mother had rejected him.

Finola reached out to touch his leg. He hadn't told Finola his suspicions, but she knew him well enough to have guessed. A horrible emptiness swelled in his chest. He had come so far and risked so much to find her. He had just told her who he was, and all she could do was give him this stony-faced stare after her initial reaction had betrayed the truth. Brion almost stood and walked out of the cavern, but he forced himself to stay.

"The Dunkeldi are coming," Taegan said. "They will be at Reed's stronghold within two weeks."

York jumped up. "We have to warn them," he said.

Taegan gave York an impatient wave of her hand. "We will," she said. "Sit down."

Gwyneth grabbed York's tunic and pulled him down beside her.

Taegan focused on Brion without meeting his gaze. "The Duke," she paused, "your father, sent us aid before the war began—supplies and weapons."

"Why?" Brion demanded. His sense of rejection was turning to anger. "Why would he help you?"

"Because," Taegan began. Her gaze flicked to someone behind Brion. When he followed her gaze, all he found was a crowd of people.

Taegan pinched her lips tight for a moment. "I don't know," she said. "But will you honor your father's commitment?"

Brion scowled. She refused to admit who she was. She didn't care that her lost son had risked his life to find her. Maybe he had misjudged the type of person his mother was. Maybe she had only wanted the Duke's money and support. Maybe she had never cared about her child. That would explain why she had never searched for him, had never tried to make contact in all those years.

"There's nothing I can do," Brion said. He was ready to leave. He had been wasting his time and putting Finola in danger for no reason. It was time to get out of the heathland and return to Coll.

Taegan stared at him in open shock. Steffan stirred. "You can mediate with your King Emyr," he said. "You can ask him to give us sanctuary."

"I already sent him a message on behalf of the Salassani," Brion said. "If he accepts, I'm sure he won't mind a few more."

"But will you ask him?" Steffan persisted.

Brion nodded. "Now we need to leave to warn Reed," he said.

"There will be no need," Taegan said. "You will remain as our guests."

The way she said this made Brion study her more carefully. "That sounds like an order to be held as prisoners," Brion said.

"No," Taegan countered. "But these are dangerous times. We can't have people running loose all over the heathland who know how to find us."

Brion couldn't keep the sneer of annoyance from his face. "If you knew the Duke as well as you pretend," he said, "you would know that his son could never accept such an arrangement."

Taegan didn't smile. "I must insist," she said. "At least until we know what course your king will take."

"We may not know for weeks," Finola said.

Taegan shrugged.

"What about Reed?" York asked.

Brion knew that York was worried about his mother and sister.

"He'll be warned," Taegan said. "I've already sent runners."

"So, you expect us to just sit here and do nothing while our friends are in danger?" Brion asked.

Taegan nodded. "For now. Things may change more quickly than either of us would like." She rose. "Thank you for your assistance, Brion of Wexford," she said. "I am sorry we cannot help you in your quest."

Brion gazed up at her as the hurt and anger burned in his chest. When he said nothing, Taegan whirled and strode away. Steffan gave him an apologetic gesture and hurried after her.

Gwyneth dropped the shirt she had been mending and made sure her knife and sword were close by as Taegan approached from the mouth of the cave. Taegan was alone this time, but she bore a determined expression on her face. Gwyneth and the rest of them had passed the morning relating their separate adventures and caring for their gear. Brion always obsessed about his gear. He made them pull everything out and check it before repacking it.

Brion paused in straightening his arrows and watched Taegan as she came to stand beside Finola. Gwyneth hadn't understood why Brion seemed so upset by Taegan. She watched him now to see what his reaction might be. But Taegan barely glanced at him. She motioned to Finola.

"I need to talk to you," she said.

Finola glanced at Brion. He looked away.

When Finola stood, Gwyneth rose and followed them as they worked their way among the people milling about. Why would Taegan only want to speak to Finola? From the way Taegan had eyed Gwyneth's Bracari clothing, she obviously guessed that Gwyneth was part Bracari. Maybe she didn't trust her because of it. It wouldn't be the first time. But as Gwyneth made her way through the crowd of Carpentini, no one cast her sidelong glances or sneered at her. Up here with these Carpentini, she was just a girl. It was an odd feeling.

She tried to be inconspicuous, but she thought Finola noticed her. Taegan stopped Finola just outside the cave and pulled her into a cavity between two boulders. Gwyneth slipped up to the other side and pressed herself to the rock.

"Tell me the truth," Taegan demanded. "Is he really the Duke's son?"

"Why are you asking?" Finola said. Gwyneth could tell by the sound of Finola's voice that she was irritated.

"He doesn't look much like the Duke," Taegan said.

"That's not a reason," Finola said.

There was a pause. "I need to know," Taegan said.

"You didn't answer me," Finola said.

"I'm not free to say."

"Then neither am I."

Gwyneth flattened herself against the cold stone as Finola stepped out of the alcove. Taegan grabbed her arm.

"You don't understand." Taegan sounded desperate.

Finola yanked her arm free. "I understand that you've been lying to us."

"It's dangerous," Taegan said.

"Tell me about it," Finola said. "Like we haven't been racing from danger for over a year now."

Another long pause followed. "I'm sorry I've bothered you," Taegan said. She swept past Finola and strode off down the tunnel.

"Yes," Finola called after her.

Taegan paused and revolved slowly to gaze at Finola.

"He is the Duke's son."

Taegan didn't say anything. She just stared as if struggling with something. Then she wheeled about and stalked away.

"Are you his mother?" Finola called after her. "He has a right to know."

Taegan stopped again. She cast one hurried glance over her

shoulder before striding away.

Gwyneth remained motionless, stunned by what Finola had said and relieved the secret conversation hadn't been about her. They believed Taegan was Brion's mother? That explained everything.

Finola stared after Taegan before turning to find Gwyneth with her back plastered to the stone. She raised her eyebrows and made her way back to Brion. Gwyneth understood Brion's drive to find his mother. If she could have anything in the world, it would be just five more minutes with her mother's arms around her—to hear the sound of her voice—to smell the lavender scent that always seemed to follow her mother around.

York was just drifting off to sleep when the shadow of the boy loomed over him. York scrambled backward and drew his knife as he crouched, ready for the attack. But the boy just stood there. Brion sat up, and the boy gestured to him.

"Follow me," the boy whispered. His voice was so young he couldn't have been more than ten years old.

Brion shook Finola, and she roused Gwyneth. They had been trying to get a few hours of sleep before Brion planned to make a break for it. But now this boy had interrupted their rest.

"Where?" Brion asked.

York straightened, but he kept the knife ready.

"No time," the boy replied. "Come now."

Brion rose to follow, but the boy pointed to their gear. "Bring it," he said.

Now Brion bent to peer at him. "Why? Where are we going?"

"Out," he said.

Brion grunted and grabbed up his bow that the Carpentini had saved from the battlesite. He braced it, and York jumped to follow his example. In five minutes, they had all buckled on their swords, braced their bows, thrown on their cloaks, and shouldered their packs. Then they followed the boy as he picked his way among the sleeping groups of people that appeared as black shapes, bulging on the floor. It was dark in the cavern now. The fires had burned down to little piles of red and orange coals that flickered as they passed. A little girl complained when York trod on her foot. "Sorry," he whispered and kept moving toward the back of the cave. He wondered why no one tried to stop them.

The boy ducked into one of the side tunnels that York had noted before. The tunnel grew even darker without the benefit of the light from the coals. York collided with Gwyneth when they all came to an abrupt halt, and she shoved him away.

"Ouch," she whispered.

Someone drew the hood from a lantern. The sudden blaze of light blinded York. The woman who had been treating Brion's injuries earlier stood, squinting at them. Their shadows flickered off the damp stone walls of a tunnel wide enough for two of them to walk side by side. The woman checked to make sure they were all there. Then she laid a hand on Brion's arm.

"The Duke was a kind man," she said. "Taegan means well, but I think keeping you here is poor payment for what the Duke has done for us."

"You knew my father?" Brion asked.

She smiled a sweet, sad smile. "We were good friends, at one time," she said.

"Do you know Elsie, then?" Brion asked. His hand jerked out as if he meant to grab the woman, but he pulled back without touching her.

The woman shook her head. "Elsie didn't come with us. We lost her back at the village."

"You mean Taegan isn't really Elsie?" Brion asked.

"No."

"What do you mean you lost her?" Finola demanded.

"I mean," the woman said, "she knew that her presence was a danger to anyone who came near her, so she left."

The candlelight flickered off her face, and York thought he saw a deep sadness there. Her eyes glistened as if they had filled with tears. The look wasn't unusual among the Carpentini. Everyone had lost someone they loved to the Bracari.

"Where can I find her?" Brion asked.

The woman grabbed Brion's hand and held it. "You mustn't seek her," she said. "It's too dangerous for her and for you."

Brion lifted her hand and grasped it. "Why do you say that?"

"They killed our entire village." A sob escaped the woman's

throat. "They will stop at nothing."

"But Cedrick is dead," Brion said. "Emyr is king."

"They will never stop," the woman said. "The Duke had too many enemies."

"Please." Brion was begging. "Please, tell me where she is."

"I can't." The woman's voice broke. "I . . . I don't know. We lost her. She ran away." The woman passed a sleeve across her face. "We don't have much time," she said. "I've arranged to have the guards let you pass."

"You arranged?" Finola asked.

The woman's eyes twinkled. "I'm a healer. People owe me."

She wrapped an arm around the boy and squeezed him. "Jason will show you the way."

The boy began to lead them off, but Brion didn't follow. "What's your name?" he asked.

The woman paused. "Jenna," she said.

"Thank you," Finola said.

"You must hurry before they find you missing," Jenna said. She handed Jason the lamp, gave him a brief hug, and faced Brion. "May the souls of your fathers guide your feet," she said.

Brion hesitated, but Finola grabbed his arm and pulled him after the boy.

Water dripped from the ceiling that glistened in the flickering light of the lantern. Jason's bare feet slapped on the limestone floor. York struggled with confused emotions. Brion was so desperate to find his mother, while York only wanted to avoid his. Her hostile silence and occasional bitter comments made being with her simply unpleasant. It was worse because York knew that she was right. He had failed to save his father. He had failed to avenge him when he had the chance. If the chance came again, he would do it regardless of the consequences.

Jason led them on through the cold darkness as Finola clung close to Brion. York smiled again at the idea that the strong-willed young woman would be afraid of simple spiders when she would stand and fight a dozen Bracari warriors.

The passage narrowed and slanted upward until the pale light of the moon slipped through the cracks in the stone overhead. The air became fresh with the sweet taste of pine. Jason set the lantern down carefully to make sure it was out of the way and scrambled through a crack above them. His white face appeared a moment later, and he waved at them to follow. York slipped off his quiver and pack and clambered out through the crack.

The evening air was cool and crisp. Gwyneth handed up his gear to him and then her own. When he reached down to help her up, Gwyneth hesitated. She glanced at Finola and then stretched her hand up to his. Her hand was smooth and cool, and her grasp was strong. York hauled her up and helped her swing out onto the big boulder. Gwyneth's hand lingered in his for just a moment before he pulled away. He knew she didn't like to be touched, and he didn't want to get her angry. But Gwyneth gazed at him with a curious expression he didn't understand.

"Thanks," she said.

York nodded. He had never understood why Gwyneth was so defensive about being touched, but something had changed. He had noticed it coming on for a few days now, but he hadn't really thought of it until that moment. She had been unusually talkative and teasing lately and even sought him out when she avoided everyone else. It all started that early morning when she had followed him and demanded that he teach her how to shoot bows. Now York tried not to focus on the thrill the feel of her hand in his had given him. He tried not to notice how beautiful she seemed with the moonlight full on her face and her dark hair spilling before her eyes.

"Excuse me," Finola said. "If you two are finished, I would like to get out of this miserable tunnel."

York's face grew warm in embarrassment as he reached down to pull up their gear before lowering a hand to assist Finola. Brion followed, and they were soon standing next to the rockslide high above the grove of trees where they had left the horses.

The great, vaulted sky spread over them, a mass of stars twinkling in the inky blackness. The mountains rose up all around them, cutting through the stars as dark, hulking masses. It was a beautiful scene with only one problem.

"Um," York said, bending to peer over the side. "There's a cliff." A sheer rock wall cut the night to disappear into the shadows below. A wave of dizziness made York reel, and he stepped back.

"We noticed," Gwyneth said.

York scowled at her, but she was smiling. This new Gwyneth was a bit unnerving.

"This way," Jason said. "Step where I step."

"Why?" Finola asked. "There aren't any more tunnels, are there?"

"No," Jason said. "Just some pits with poisoned stakes." He said this like it was nothing unusual.

"You did say poisoned stakes, didn't you?" Gwyneth asked.

"Yes."

"That doesn't sound encouraging," Finola said.

"Poison?" Brion questioned.

"We have to protect our back door," Jason said.

"What kind of poison?" Brion asked.

Jason shrugged and stepped off over the broken terrain, picking his way carefully from stone to stone. Brion bent low until he stopped at a depression in the rocks and lifted a branch away. He sniffed the air. "Smells like rotting flesh," he said.

Jason stopped and looked back. "Yep," he said. "It's a special recipe Jenna makes."

"Are there traps like this down by the other entrance we came in?" York asked.

"Sure," Jason said and kept walking.

York exchanged a wide-eyed glance with Gwyneth as Brion straightened and followed. If they had stepped in one of those, they would be dead already.

"How did we avoid them?" York asked.

"You followed the trail we use along the cliff," Jason said.

Gwyneth gave a quiet laugh. "Misty was following Brion's scent," she said.

"Wait a minute," York said. "How do you know how we found the entrance?"

"We were watching you," Jason said. "No one comes into this valley without us knowing it."

"You mean all while we were wandering around collecting sap and birch bark for our torches, we could have dropped into one of your pits?" Gwyneth asked.

"Maybe," Jason said. "But they are all closer to the slide. There aren't any where you camped."

"That's comforting," Finola said.

Jason brought them to a crack in the rock that split the cliff face. A huge pine tree grew right up the inside of the crack. Its upper branches poked out well above the cliff top. The cliff was shorter here than at the head of the canyon, but it was still a good sixty feet. Jason slipped a coil of rope from out of a crevice, secured it to the trunk of the tree and tossed it down. It caught amid the branches.

"You have to shake it loose as you go down," Jason said. "When you reach the bottom branches, just shimmy down the rope."

"How far down is it?" Gwyneth asked as she peered over the lip of the cliff.

Jason shrugged. "I don't know. I'll pull the rope back up when you're down. Good luck."

He stepped back and waited expectantly. They looked at each other.

"After you," Brion said to York.

Chapter 10
A Carpentini King

The descent down the tree in the dark proved to be a frustrating and terrifying experience. The rough bark scraped York's hands. Pine sap stuck to everything, and the rope refused to be shaken loose from the branches. York almost plummeted to the ground as he struggled with it, but it eventually fell free. When he reached the bottom branch, York found that the rope was also too short.

York dangled with his hands on the end of the rope, swinging his feet in empty space before he gathered the courage to let go. He only fell about ten feet, but it was a jarring fall. When he tried to catch Gwyneth, her foot kicked him in the face, and she landed on his shoulders. He tried to protect her as she came down, but she just ended up on top of him.

"You know," Gwyneth said, "I think the ground would have been softer."

York crawled to his feet. He didn't bother trying to help Finola and Brion down after that.

"Well, that was fun," Brion said. "Where are the horses?"

York shrugged and pointed. "Over there, I think."

They set off, pushing their way through the undergrowth. The aspen trees stood out ghostly white in the darkness. They struggled for a good twenty minutes before Brion paused and whistled. A whinny answered and crashing sounded.

"There they are," Brion said. They angled off towards the sounds until they found Misty and the other horses clustered around the creek. The horses had broken loose from their hobbles, but the ropes had become entangled in the undergrowth. Misty's silver-speckled rump twitched as they approached her, and she shook her head. Finola's buckskin nibbled at Misty's ears, and Misty butted her with her head.

"That dumb horse won't leave Misty alone," Brion said.

"She's just teaching Misty some patience," Finola said.

Brion grunted in annoyance and bent to free the horses. As they tied on their gear, York realized that they had another problem. They only had three horses. He stood back awkwardly trying to decide what to do as Brion prepared to ride Misty.

Finola glanced at him and grinned. "You can ride with Gwyneth."

Brion looked around. "Oh yeah, sorry. I forgot that you had ridden Misty here."

York shrugged and looked at Gwyneth. She was scowling. She might have been willing to let him help her up through a crack and even to let him attempt to break her fall from the tree, but she didn't seem too excited about having to sit with him on a horse. He waited.

"You sit behind me," Gwyneth said.

"What?" York said. He wasn't going to let a girl control the horse.

"It's either that or you walk," Gwyneth said.

"Come on," York said.

Gwyneth spun and continued packing her saddlebags. She was as stubborn as a mule, and she would make him walk if he didn't agree to her terms.

"All right," York said.

He waited until Gwyneth swung up into the saddle. She pulled her foot from the stirrup so York could use it to hoist himself up to sit behind the saddle. He hesitated as he tried to figure out how to hang on without touching her. He had never put his arms around any girl except his sister, and he couldn't help but feel awkward with his body pressed against Gwyneth's. But he couldn't see anything to do but hang onto her. When he slipped his arms around her, she slapped his hands away.

"You hold onto the saddle," she snapped.

York looked to Finola and Brion for help. Brion smiled. Finola raised her eyebrow at Gwyneth, but Gwyneth looked away. So, he grabbed the back of the saddle as best he could. It didn't take long before the jostling of the horse trotting down the trail nearly bounced him off its rump. They angled downhill, and he struggled to avoid pressing against Gwyneth too hard while still staying mounted. He squeezed his legs tight and clung to the saddle, but it was no use. He slid to one side so that he was staring down at the dark, stony trail. The horse stumbled, and his grip slipped loose. He tumbled to the ground. Gwyneth glanced over her shoulder at him.

"Oh, all right," she said. "We're going to be picking you up every half mile if you don't hang on."

York climbed back up and slipped his arms around Gwyneth's middle. Her waist was slender and her stomach tight. Gwyneth shivered, and York felt his face burning. But he hung on as they trotted into the night.

Brion sat on Misty's back overlooking the valley around Dunraven Keep. It had filled with Salassani. The smoke from their evening fires lingered on the still air like a rain cloud.

"The keep isn't big enough for all those people," Brion said.

"It's gonna have to be," Finola said.

Their flight through the night had been exhausting, but uneventful. If any Carpentini from Taegan's band had pursued them, they hadn't tried hard to catch them.

Brion kicked Misty into a walk. He was ready for a hot meal and a long night's rest. His head still ached from the blow he had received, and he didn't feel like his old self yet. Still, he had to find Reed first. He needed to know what preparations Reed was making.

"I'll walk," York said, and he jumped from the horse's back. Gwyneth grinned down at him.

Brion shook his head. "There's no shame in relying on a woman," he said.

York adjusted his quiver and slipped the bow over his head so he could carry it in his hands. "I'd rather walk," he said.

Brion smiled, but he understood. York had been struggling to feel like a man and to convince others that he was worthy of being called one. To be seen riding into camp behind a girl who had been an outcast in their society would do little to help him.

Heads turned to watch them as they filed through the crowds that now encircled the keep. There were so many woman and children and so few men. This was becoming the pattern no matter where Brion went among the Carpentini and Salassani. It seemed as though Tristan had been trying to weaken them so much that they would not be able to resist when he finally decided to come out against them in full force. Brion feared that he might succeed.

Reed was standing by the entrance of the keep waiting for them as they made their way up the hill.

He was smiling. "Glad to see you're back from the dead," Reed said.

Brion dismounted. "I'm glad to be back. Did Taegan's messenger find you?"

"Is that what they call her?" Reed said. "Her messenger wouldn't say."

"They're secretive," Brion said. He reached to help Finola down from the saddle. Gwyneth dismounted beside her.

"Well," Reed said, "while you all have been sightseeing, we've been busy."

Brion glanced up at the walls of the keep. They were finally finished. "You plan to meet Tristan here then?"

Reed nodded.

"Any word from Daren?"

Reed shook his head. Brion knew that Daren couldn't have reached Emyr yet. It was a long way to Chullish and a lot could happen to a lone man in the heathland. He surveyed the valley, now filled with tents. They could sure use Emyr's help now.

"How many men is Tristan bringing?" he asked.

"He has nearly 4,000 Dunkeldi and a few Taurini and Bracari," Reed said.

Brion faced Reed. He tried not to show the concern he felt. "You're outnumbered," he said.

"We've always been outnumbered," Reed said.

"How many men do you have?" Finola asked.

Reed glanced at her. "With the Salassani, I figure I can field a little over 2,000 men."

"Two to one," Brion mumbled.

"What about the women and children?" Finola asked. "There

are too many to fit inside the keep."

Reed nodded and then he smiled. "Your little band of warriors has grown," he said. "You'll see tomorrow." Before Finola could question him further, Reed looked approvingly at Gwyneth. "You look more like your mother every day," he said. "She was a strong woman, and Edrick was a fine man. I wish he were here."

A look of surprise passed over Gwyneth's face, and she blinked rapidly. Reed didn't seem to notice. He was gazing out over the valley. "We've lost so many," he said. Brion had never seen Reed so thoughtful. Maybe the knowledge that the Carpentini were about to be destroyed once and for all had finally hit him.

Then Reed gestured to York who stood beside Gwyneth with his bow held loosely in his hands. "Your father would be proud of you," he said. "You may not be as large as he was, but you have his courage."

Before York could reply, Reed took a deep breath and clapped his hands. "Anyway, York looks like he's asleep on his feet. I heard you were coming and had someone prepare a hot meal for you. I know you don't like the keep much, so it's waiting for you down at your lean-to."

They turned to leave.

"Better be up at dawn, Finola," he said. "Your army awaits." He laughed as if this had been a funny joke and then disappeared back into the keep.

"He's in a strangely pleasant mood," Finola said as they led their horses down the hill.

Brion passed a hand over his aching forehead. "I'll grant him any mood he likes for a hot meal and a night's sleep."

The fire was burning as they approached the lean-to. A woman rose from before the fire holding a large spoon in her hands. York stopped just outside the ring of firelight. Brion glanced at him and then at the woman. It was York's mother. She still wore her faded and torn blue dress, and she looked even more disheveled than the last time Brion had seen her. Her gaze settled on York. She nodded, set the spoon back in the steaming pot, and walked into the shadows of the trees without saying a word.

Vengeance

Gwyneth stared in disbelief at the crowd of women that had gathered at the foot of the hill. An odd mixture of Carpentini women in blue dresses and Salassani women in trousers and blue or red tunics had gathered. Some were already practicing the knife and staff routines Finola had taught them. Others were shooting at bales of grass with bows. Still others were grappling. There must have been four or five hundred women down there, and the sun had barely risen.

Finola stood beside Gwyneth, apparently as surprised as she was. Meredith, the scrawny woman that had challenged Finola that first day, stepped up to them. She touched her brow to Finola in the Carpentini gesture of respect. Finola returned it.

"I kept them going while you were away," Meredith said.

A slow smile spread over Finola's face. "You did more than that," Finola said.

Meredith beamed. "Well, once the Salassani saw what we were doing, they asked to join." She shrugged. "I didn't think you'd mind."

Finola shook her head. "Of course not," she said. "Tell me what you've done. How have you organized them?"

She strode toward the women while Meredith explained how she had followed Finola's practice of rotating them between different skills. "I didn't really have anything new to teach them," she said. "But you can see we're better than we were when you left."

"Excellent," Finola said. She faced Meredith. "Will you be my second in command?" she asked.

Meredith chuckled. "I kind of already am," she said.

Finola clasped her hand. "We can do this," Finola said. "We can make these women a force to be reckoned with."

Gwyneth spent the morning rotating through the skill sets, glad to be back in training. It felt good to draw the bowstring to her cheek and watch the arrow zip through the air to bury itself in the bale of grass.

She had just finished a sparring match with a Salassani girl about her age and was refreshing herself at the creek when someone stepped up behind her. She spun, grabbing up the staff as she did. A tall, well-muscled Salassani boy stood smiling down at her.

"You're a bit jumpy," he said.

Gwyneth straightened. She was acutely aware that her sweaty

125

hair clung to her neck and that she smelled of sweat and dirt.

"I've been watching you," the boy said. "You're the best one out there."

"What do you want?" Gwyneth said. She bent and swung her quiver back over her head.

The boy shrugged. "Just being friendly," he said.

"Well, don't," Gwyneth said. She tried to step around him when he laid a hand on her arm. It was warm and rough with callouses. Gwyneth reacted on instinct. She twisted her arm free and swung the staff in an overhead arc that smacked the boy upside the head. He staggered backward with a cry of surprise. Gwyneth kicked his feet out from underneath him and pressed the end of the staff to his throat. He stared up at her with wide eyes.

"Don't. Touch. Me." Gwyneth said this slowly so that he was sure to understand. "Never touch me again."

She spun and stalked away. It was one thing to have York touch her, but no other man ever would. She remembered the closeness of York's body and the feeling of his muscular arms around her with a little thrill. York might be small in stature, but he was strong and brave. He was becoming a real warrior. And York never presumed to take liberties with her. He was awkward and grumpy sometimes, but he respected her, treated her like an equal.

The afternoon practice was interrupted by a long line of Salassani filing out of the valley. Gwyneth stood beside Finola, panting as they paused in their knife practice.

"Where are they going?" Gwyneth asked.

Meredith spoke from behind them. "They say they can't wait for King Emyr any longer. They need to get crops in the ground, so they're heading south."

"What if he doesn't want them?" Gwyneth asked.

"That's not my problem," Meredith said. "Reed wasn't happy, though. He's losing several hundred warriors."

"Just jump," York said. Brion poised on the edge of the huge boulder overlooking the pond where they had come for another swimming lesson. "Don't be afraid of the water."

From the boulder, York gazed out over the broad meadow and the rising hills beyond that swept up to the Aveen Mountains. They had left the ladies to their practice, while Brion and York had resumed their training in tracking, hand-to-hand fighting, and shooting the bow from horseback.

They had been at it all day while the sun burned down, hot and bright. After the last bout of fighting that had left York lying face-down in the dirt, he had suggested they go swimming to cool off. But he was interested in more than just cooling off. It was his chance to get even.

Brion smirked. "The water doesn't scare me. Drowning does."

"You already know how to swim, more or less," York said. "Now you have to overcome your fear." This was fun to say because Brion had just said the same thing to him when he told him to let go of the reins and trust the horse.

Brion glared at him. "You're using my own words against me."

York grinned. "No, just pushing you beyond your comfort zone because I see a lot of potential in you."

"Stop it," Brion said. Then he peeked over the edge. "How deep is it?"

"It doesn't matter once you're in over your head," York said. "Just jump in and swim to the other side. You can stand up there."

Brion leaned forward to peer down at the icy blue waters. "It looks cold," he said.

"Yep," York said, "that's usually the idea after a hot day in the sun." Then he gave Brion a violent shove to help him over the edge.

Brion let out a shout of surprise as he plummeted toward the water, his arms and legs churning. He landed on his belly with a loud splash and a geyser of water. York winced. That belly flop had to hurt. Brion came up splashing. He floundered, and it looked as if he had forgotten everything York had tried to teach him. For one wild moment, York thought Brion was in real trouble. He stripped off his tunic and prepared to dive in to save him, but Brion lay on his belly and stroked toward the opposite shore. York experienced the warmth of pride rise in his chest as Brion leveled off. Brion still swam like a fish with no fins, but York had taught Brion something.

When Brion reached the other side, he was spitting mad. He

lunged to his feet, spraying water all over the bank. His chest and belly were bright red.

"York!" he bellowed. He shook the water from his eyes and glared up at York who had remained safely out of range on top of the rock.

York raised his hands in surrender. "I told you not to be scared," he called down to him.

Brion paused and started to chuckle. "You're crazy," he said. Then he threw back his head and laughed. "You're as bad as Neahl. That's exactly what he would have done."

York stripped off his trousers, acutely aware of his skinny legs compared to Brion's, but he dove into the pond anyway. The cold water felt so good after the hard practice under the blazing sun. They swam around and jumped off the rock, seeing who could get the best splash for a while until an uproar from the direction of Dunraven Keep sent them scrambling for their clothes and to their horses.

Brion leaned low over Misty's neck, urging her on. That kind of commotion could only mean one thing—an attack. Maybe another band of Bracari had found them or Tristan and his army had not been two weeks away as they were told. It was not good either way, and, to make it worse, he had left Finola at the keep.

As they drew nearer, the sounds became louder and more confusing. They didn't sound like fighting. No swords crashed. No one screamed in terror and agony. Brion caught a glimpse of the tumult around the keep for just an instant as he crested the last knoll and plunged into a grove of aspens that covered the hillside. When he pounded out of the trees into the wide area below the keep where the Salassani had made camp, he pulled Misty to a halt. York reined in beside him.

"What's going on?" York asked, apparently as confused as Brion.

Salassani and Carpentini were swarming the hillside, cheering and calling. Someone was blowing a horn in long, deep-throated calls that echoed over the hills. A host of men on horseback with bows, lances, helmets, and swords was spreading out over the green in front of the keep. A line of wagons trundled in over the hills.

Above it all snapped the white standard with the diving eagle, its wings outspread and its talons reaching for its prey.

"Emyr," Brion whispered in disbelief. He looked at York. "It's Emyr."

How could it be Emyr? There was no way Daren could have reached Chullish and returned already. Brion kicked Misty into a gallop again and swept toward the milling crowd. Brion and York had to dismount once they reached the base of the hill because of the press of people, so Brion and York tied their horses near the lean-to and pushed into the throng. People he didn't even know hugged him and patted him on the back. "It's the king," they said. "The king has come."

Brion and York finally broke into an area around the entrance to the keep where soldiers in bright mail kept the crowd back. One of them stepped in front of Brion and York as they tried to hurry past and laid a restraining hand on Brion's shoulder.

"Stop," he said. His voice had a strong southern accent. Brion spoke to him in Alamani.

"I'm Brion of Wexford," he said.

The soldier gave him a stony stare. "You still can't go up to the keep," he said.

Brion sighed. "I'm the Duke of Saylen."

The soldier scowled in confusion. His gaze passed over Brion as if Brion's trail-worn attire and wet hair didn't make him look much like a duke.

"I'm the king's brother-in-law," Brion said.

The soldier still looked dubious. "Wait here, please," he said.

Brion considered ignoring the soldier and plowing ahead. He was anxious to see Emyr, but he understood why the soldier was being cautious. He didn't have to wait long. In a few moments, Emyr was striding toward him with a broad grin on his face. Gwyneth and Finola, with Iain perched on her hip, trailed behind Emyr.

Emyr wore a mail shirt like the rest of the soldiers, but otherwise, he was his usual self. His sandy-brown hair blew in the breeze that swept down from the Aveens as he strode with his usual fluid confidence. He reminded Brion so much of Redmond.

Brion ran to meet him. They embraced.

"I was starting to think you and Finola had gotten lost in the heathland," Emyr said.

"How is Brigid?" Brion asked.

Emyr grinned. "As redheaded as ever."

"And the baby?"

"Oh, that," Emyr teased. "She said I couldn't tell you."

Finola grunted. "Out with it," she said, "or we'll make you eat Brion's cooking."

Emyr raised his hands in mock surrender. "I yield," he said. "It's a boy. He's a redhead with a powerful set of lungs."

"It?" Finola said with a little smirk. "He does have a name, doesn't he?"

Emyr grinned. "Edward Kurk Hassani."

"That's a big name for a baby," Brion said.

"Well," Emyr said. "Brigid wanted to name him Kurk Redmond Weyland Brion Neahl Tyg Hassani, but I couldn't let her."

Gwyneth and York stood back, wide-eyed and confused at the playful, familiar way Finola and Brion bantered with the king.

Brion glanced at them. "Relax," he said. "He wasn't always a king." He gestured to them. "This is Gwyneth and York, two of the toughest Carpentini I know."

Emyr extended a hand toward them. They both hesitated until Finola nudged them. They shook hands.

Gwyneth reddened, and York kept his eyes on the ground.

Emyr clicked his tongue. "This won't due," he said. "If we're going to be friends, you'll need to remember that I'm just a man and that Finola could probably lick me."

Finola grinned and slapped him on the arm. "Don't forget it," she said.

Emyr laughed at the looks of astonishment that Gwyneth and York shared and grabbed Brion's arm to pull him toward the keep. "Come on," he said. "Reed says you've been causing problems."

York stared at all the important men and women seated in a wide semi-circle in the great hall of the keep. Unlike the Carpentini, the Salassani were accustomed to having their women attend councils since they were the ones who selected their male leaders.

The clusters of injured and terrified women and children that had first sought refuge in the keep had been transferred to the campsite and the buildings that were springing up in the valley below the keep. The keep had been cleaned and no longer smelled so much of human filth. Reed had ordered a new stone floor that was only barely started. A fire blazed in the hearth and a rug had been laid on the dirt floor. A huge map of Frei-Ock Isle spread out on the rug. York hovered at Brion's elbow, not wanting to miss a single word and still astonished that Reed had even allowed him to be present. Finola had given Iain to Gwyneth to tend while she engaged in the discussion. Gwyneth scowled at York, and he shrugged. It's not like it was his fault.

"Tristan has failed to keep the conditions of the peace," Emyr said. "He has sent Dunkeldi warriors into Laro Forest to drive our people out. What he has done to you is not only brutal and unjust, but he has pushed you against the borders of Coll, hoping that I will attack you and so give him an excuse to restart his war."

Heads were nodding, and the faces of the Carpentini and Salassani were grave.

"There can be no peace," Emyr said, "so long as Tristan and his family retain the Dunkeldi throne."

A few people murmured.

"What are you proposing?" Reed asked.

"I warned him," Emyr said, "that I would personally pursue him into the halls of his own palace until the line of the Dunkeldi kings was broken." Emyr paused and surveyed the gathering. "He has refused the peace I offered, and so this can only end in blood. He has left me no choice."

"You plan to kill the king?" someone asked. "And replace him with what?"

Emyr gazed at the man. "I have already granted the Salassani the lands their forefathers once held on the southern Hackel Heath and the edges of the Laro Forest on the condition that they accept me as their liege lord."

One old, wrinkled Salassani woman started crying. "Bless you," she mumbled. "Bless you." The rest nodded in agreement.

"After we have driven the Bracari and the Taurini back to their own lands," Emyr continued, "I will do the same for the Carpentini. The lands you have lost to the Alamani in the south and to the

Bracari in the north will be returned to you. You will be allowed to rebuild your towns and villages as my vassals."

One of the Carpentini leaders who had recently joined Reed spoke up. "How do we know that we are not trading one tyrant for another?"

The Alamani leaders murmured, but Emyr silenced them with a raised hand.

"It's a fair question," he said, "especially given the way you have been treated by a man whom you never accepted as your king."

"Why will you be any better?" the man demanded.

Emyr considered. "I can't promise you there will never be any misunderstandings or mistakes. But I can promise to listen to your concerns and to make every effort to attend to them and honor my word." He gave the man a moment to consider. "In truth," he continued, "you have little choice. If you do not join us, Tristan will see your women and children enslaved, your men killed, and your lands delivered into the hands of the Bracari. He is coming, even now, with an army to destroy you. In return for your allegiance, I offer you protection and peace. You will retain the right to name your own leaders, according to your traditions."

"Fairly spoken," one Carpentini said.

"I will not yield my freedom to any king," another said.

"The Salassani accept your offer most gratefully," one of the Salassani women said. "Tristan and his family have only ever been tyrants."

An argument erupted among the Carpentini and the Salassani until Reed rose to his feet and his great voice boomed over the crowed. "Silence!" he shouted. When the argument quieted, he spoke again. "The Carpentini cannot survive without the aid and the protection of some friend," he said. "Already, the Duke of Saylen has risked his life to render us assistance when the Bracari were poised to destroy us."

Reed strode to stand in front of Emyr. He drew his sword, knelt, and offered it, hilt first, to Emyr. "Never have the Carpentini recognized a king," he said. "But I offer you my sword and my life as my liege lord. I swear to serve you faithfully so long as breath remains in my body and strength in my limbs."

A hush fell over the gathering as if they were all holding their breath. York stared at Reed, shocked and confused that he would do such a thing. The Carpentini tradition forbade any act of fealty to a king. Reed was such a powerful man that York couldn't believe he would even consider becoming subordinate to any man. He wondered if his father would have done it.

Emyr rose and grasped Reed's sword. "I accept your sword and your service," he said, "and I name you Earl of Dunraven and Master of Dunraven Keep. I will reward fealty with protection, disloyalty with justice. You and I are now bound by the solemn bonds of brotherhood with the task of bringing peace and prosperity back to these lands and to your people."

York stood stunned. The sound of the fire popping in the hearth roared into the ensuing quiet. No one seemed to know what to do. Reed arose and embraced Emyr.

"Finally, a king worth following," Reed said. Then he faced the other Carpentini leaders. No one moved until the old Salassani woman rose to her feet and then fell to her knees. As one, the gathering knelt. Even Brion and Finola knelt before Emyr. York fell to his knees, struggling to understand the constriction in his chest and the burning in his eyes. For the first time since he was an innocent child, he discovered a glimmer of hope that the Carpentini might survive, that he would have his revenge at last, that he might be allowed to become a real man like his father.

"Well," Finola said to Emyr as they sat around the long fire before Brion's lean-to, "you seem to enjoy dramatic entrances." Gwyneth sat cross-legged before the fire, heating and straightening her arrows the way Finola had taught her. She had watched the day's events with considerable confusion. That the Carpentini would unite under an Alamani king was simply impossible, and yet it had happened—at least with the ones that had gathered at Reed's keep. She still found it surprising that the Alamani weren't much different from the Carpentini. Somehow, she had never quite thought of Brion and Finola as Alamani.

None of the Alamani looked askance at her, like the Carpentini did. In fact, they were interested in her because she was with Finola and Brion. She was experiencing again, like she had in the caves, what it must be like for other people who weren't Bracari half-breeds—polluted and despised. To be normal. To be just a part of the crowd. Gwyneth had never seen so many people in one place and so many fine clothes and regal horses. She glanced at Emyr to see how he would respond to Finola's teasing.

The firelight flickered in Emyr's dark eyes as he smiled. "Kings have to put on a show," he said, "or nobody would follow them. But I meant every word I said."

Emyr had sent his guards out of earshot so he could have what he called a "normal" conversation with his friends. York had gone off to check on his mother and baby sister.

"You think you can do it?" Brion asked. He sheathed the sword he had been oiling.

Emyr stopped smiling. "We have to do it," he said, "or Tristan and his fool of a son will leave us all so weakened that the Hallstat will invade and sweep over the island like they've wanted to do for years."

"Even with the Salassani and Carpentini," Brion said, "you can't field more than five thousand men."

Emyr permitted another smile to touch his lips. "This isn't my only army," he said.

"What?"

"Hayden is leading an army through Laro that is almost eight thousand strong."

"Hayden?" Brion said. "You let *him* lead an army?"

Finola had told Gwyneth how much Brion and Hayden hated each other, even though they had fought on the same side in the last coup.

"I know you don't like him," Emyr said, "but he has proven true to his word."

Brion didn't look convinced.

Emyr leaned forward, his eyes wide and face tight with excitement. "This is our chance," he said. "We're never going to get a better one. It's our chance to bring peace to the island, united under a single king."

"I never thought I would hear you say that," Finola said.

"You don't understand," Emyr said.

"Uh huh," Finola grunted.

"No, listen," Emyr said. "If Tristan had kept the peace, I would have left him alone. But I can't sit back while he slaughters the people who raised me and destabilizes the entire island. I don't care who the king is. But I want to see an end to the killing and the suffering. It has gone on far too long." He waited for Finola to respond. She didn't. "You have seen what he has done to the children," Emyr said. "To the women."

Finola pulled Iain close. "I'm not defending Tristan," she said. "I just never thought you would be so ambitious that you would try to seize control of the entire island. That's what Damian wanted to do."

"But this is our chance to have *real* peace," Emyr said. "Peace without fear. The kind of peace that lasts."

"Anyway," Brion interrupted. "What are your plans? Ten or twelve thousand aren't nearly enough to conquer the Dunkeldi, the Bracari, and the Taurini."

"I don't intend to conquer them," Emyr said. "Only the Dunkeldi."

"Why?" Brion persisted.

Emyr pursed his lips and shook his head. "I would rather discuss the details in a more secure setting," he said. "Even the trees up here can grow ears."

Brion scowled and fidgeted with his sword as if he were displeased.

"So, tell me about your hunt for your mother," Emyr said. "What have you discovered?"

Gwyneth quit listening. She slipped her arrows into her quiver and arranged her sleeping furs. Iain was already asleep with his head in Finola's lap. She was stroking his hair. Gwyneth lay down and pulled the furs over her. The men's voices became a low background noise to the commotion of her thoughts. She wanted to cling to the anger and hatred that had kept her alive all these years. But she had to admit that she felt a closeness to Brion and York and even, in a small way, to Emyr, which caused her to question all of her assumptions about men and women. And tomorrow they were going to war.

Chapter 11
The Coming of the Storm

What do you mean we have to stay behind?" Gwyneth stood with her feet wide apart and her hands planted on her hips. She had just finished packing all her gear. Brion had come back from his early morning meeting with the king, and all he had to say was that Finola and Gwyneth couldn't ride with the army. The women had been training for this very thing. They had a right to prove what they could do.

Brion looked pleadingly at Finola, but she wasn't going to give him much help. She just watched as Iain played in the dirt.

"What have we been training for for weeks?" Gwyneth demanded.

"It's an army," Brion said. "They can't take women and children along."

"What about him?" Gwyneth gestured to York who was cinching a saddlebag closed. If York was going, she was going. It wasn't fair. Women always got left behind. For once in her life, she wanted to join the men. She wanted to be free to make her own choices—to prove that she was no Bracari brat.

Brion looked at the ground and shifted his feet. "I'm going to ask York to stay behind, as well."

"What?" York jerked in surprise. "No." York had also just packed his gear while they waited for Brion. He even wore his quiver and had his bow strung.

"Please," Brion said. "I need you to stay to protect Finola, Iain, and Gwyneth." Before York could protest further, Brion rushed ahead. "I know you're more skilled than half the men we're taking.

This isn't about you. I just can't leave them behind again without knowing someone I trust is here to look after them, in case anything happens."

York shook his head.

"Please," Brion said.

York looked mutinous for a moment, and Gwyneth thought maybe the two of them could convince Brion they had to go. Besides, she didn't need protecting. Then York glanced at Gwyneth and Finola, and his resolve melted away. Gwyneth could see it by the way he held his shoulders. York was always so transparent. But this time, it made her angry. She had been counting on him. He was just like all the rest of the men. They were never there when you needed them.

"Traitor," she snapped, and she spun on her heels and stomped away.

Brion watched Gwyneth go and shrugged helplessly to Finola. York looked as though Brion had just slapped him across the face. How could Brion get them all to understand? This wasn't some foray into the foothills. It was a real army, like nothing Brion had ever seen before. He had always fought on his own or with small groups. He couldn't risk taking them with an army that might get routed on the field. He had to know they were somewhere far away from the battle when it took place.

Finola seized his arm and pulled him away from York. She stopped by a big beech tree. Robins fluttered around in the branches above them. "I told you she wouldn't like it," Finola said.

"I don't have any choice," Brion said. He tried to think how he might reason with Finola, but, instead of arguing, she said, "I know."

Brion stared at her. Had he just misunderstood something?

"Now listen to me," she continued. "There's something I need to tell you."

Brion remembered how agitated Finola had been up at the caves. He had tried to get her to talk about what was bothering her, but they hadn't had more than a moment or two alone in days. Finola stared over his shoulder as if she were afraid to meet his gaze. Then she looked at the ground. She kicked at a bunch of heather. Purple flower petals fell in a shower.

"I . . ." she began. But she stopped and swallowed. She glanced at him again and tears brimmed in her eyes. Brion lifted her hand. He was bewildered. Was it Iain or Gwyneth? Had someone said something to her?

"Once," she tried again, "when Ithel beat me. . ."

Brion clenched his jaw but kept his silence. Ithel had gotten what he deserved when Finola and Brigid had killed him after he tried to recapture Finola. But the way he had treated Finola while she was his slave still made Brion angry every time he thought of it.

Finola blinked rapidly, trying to keep her emotions in check. "I bled a lot," she said. "You know how much my mother struggled to have children. I think Ithel might have made it worse by damaging something inside of me. I think that's why I can't conceive."

Brion's anger melted away. He enfolded Finola in his arms and held her tight. A sob escaped her throat. Of all the things Finola had wanted in her life, it was to have children of her own. She had wanted this since she was a child herself. Brion remembered how much she had loved the village children in Wexford, and how she had played house as a little girl. When she had played, she always had a toy baby wrapped in some cloth that she carried around. Now she was admitting to him that she could never have children.

"It's okay," Brion whispered.

"You need an heir," Finola sobbed into his shoulder, "now that you're a duke."

"I don't care about being a duke," Brion said. "You're all I care about. Besides, there are plenty of children now who will need a home."

"It isn't the same," Finola said. "I wanted to give you a child after everything you've lost."

Brion squeezed her as a rush of emotion swept over him. Beneath her strong exterior, Finola had been hiding this anguish. Sometimes he took her for granted. He failed to realize how deeply she felt things. He had wanted a son, but did it have to be his own? Rosland had taken him in and loved him like her own. He had never noticed the absence of his real mother. The more he searched for his real mother, the more he appreciated all that Rosland had sacrificed for him.

Brion stroked Finola's hair. "It doesn't matter to me," he said. "I was raised by people who weren't my parents, and I was happy and loved. That's all that matters."

Finola drew in a shaky breath and pulled away from Brion. Her eyes were red and puffy. She wiped at the tears that dripped from her chin.

"I'm sorry," she said. "I've been dreading telling you."

"It really doesn't matter," Brion said. "So long as I have you."

Finola squeezed his hand. "Be careful," she said. "I want you to come back to me. I don't like being left behind, but I know I would only get in the way. Besides, I can't leave my ladies or Gwyneth, Iain, and Clidna. They need me."

"I know," Brion said. "Emyr will keep me out of trouble."

Finola smiled. "No, he won't. He's worse than you are."

She hugged Brion and squeezed him tight. "I love you," she said. "Make sure you come back to me this time. I don't want to have to come looking for you again. I don't think I could bear it."

"I will," Brion said. And he hoped he could keep that promise. "While I'm away," he said, "you might ask around and see if any of these women know an Elsie." He had come into the heathland to find his mother, and now he was being swept up in events that forced him to abandon his search. He didn't try to hide his frustration.

Finola laid a cool hand on his cheek. "Sometimes, you're still that little boy looking for acceptance," she said. "We'll find her."

Brion nodded. That's what he hoped and feared. Maybe they had already found her, and she had rejected him. He still hadn't forgotten how Taegan had reacted to the name Elsie. Jenna had tried to convince him that his mother had run off and that no one knew where she was, but he didn't believe her. Taegan knew something, and she was hiding it.

York stood on the walls of Dunraven Keep, peering through the battlements as the army filed away over the green foothills. The supply wagons trundled along behind them, flanked by their guards. The morning chill still hung in the air. The great blue vault of sky swung overhead, making York feel small and insignificant as he contemplated his situation. He had been left behind—again. Overlooked. Unwanted. Reed had left 500 men to guard the keep and to protect the several thousand women and children that clustered into and around it. York was apparently man enough to guard a bunch of kids playing in the grass but not to ride out to meet the Dunkeldi. He ground his teeth against the bitterness of it all and shifted his attention to the crowd of Salassani and Carpentini kids out on the green hill playing the leather ball game common to all the peoples of the heathland. He pondered on how strange it was.

For the first time in anyone's memory, the Carpentini and Salassani were living side by side and united against a common enemy. More surprisingly, they had also sworn allegiance to an Alamani king. York still hadn't overcome the shock of it. His father had told him that Edrick, Gwyneth's uncle, had tried to unite the Carpentini in a common stand against the Bracari and had failed. It seemed so senseless that they would only set aside their old quarrels and ancient traditions against kingship when they stared the reality of their own extinction in the face. York wondered what might have happened had Edrick succeeded. Would the Carpentini stay this course and remain loyal to a king if they had only accepted him out of necessity?

York glanced down at the men in the courtyard preparing cauldrons of fat to be melted down into oil, barrels of sand, and piles of stones. They were preparing for a siege that York no longer believed would come. With Tristan leading his army southeast to Dunraven Keep, all the Taurini and Bracari haunting the heathland would gather around him. Emyr would meet them in battle far from Dunraven Keep, and York was being left behind.

The breeze caught up the smoke of the morning cooking fires from the camp and the sounds of practice fighting. York walked around the battlements until he could observe Finola's army. She had collected around 700 women who now spread out over the green, wielding spears and knives. Some had bows and slings, and a few even had swords. Here was another oddity that York had never believed he would see—women preparing for battle. The old stories told of Carpentini women joining their men in war, but that hadn't happened in so long that only the vague rumors persisted.

York had overheard Reed telling Finola that the only reason he felt secure in leaving the keep with so few men to guard it was because of Finola's army. York turned away in bitterness and strode back to where he could see the last of the wagons disappear over the rise heading northeast.

Finola didn't need his protection. The war had moved away from Dunraven Keep and, with it, his chances of avenging his father. His mother would never let him forget that he had remained behind again. But Brion had begged him to stay. York had already betrayed Brion's trust once. He wouldn't do it again. York whirled away from the battlements to descend the stone steps when a movement caught his eye.

Down in the little hollow, barely visible from where he stood, Arno rode his horse into the trees. His mottled cloak made it difficult to make him out against the ragged backdrop of the aspen grove, but it was him. Suspicion blossomed in York's mind. Despite what Gwyneth said, York was convinced that Arno had been the one that had betrayed Brion to the Bracari. And Arno hadn't been around the keep after they came back from the caves. Now here he was sneaking away after the army.

York spun and leapt down the stone steps two at a time. Brion had almost been killed because York had allowed himself to be tricked by Arno. Now was his chance to make it right. He retrieved the horse Reed had given him, hurried to the lean-to, grabbed up his saddlebags, an extra quiver of arrows, and a bag of lead stones and tied them to the saddle. He mounted and jerked in surprise to find his mother standing there watching him. She had cleaned her clothes and washed her face and hair, which she hadn't done in many weeks. Bethann held her hand, gazing up at him with her big, dark eyes. They both stared at him as if they expected him to say something.

"I'll be back," he said.

"Avenge him," his mother said.

York scowled. What did she think he had been training to do all these weeks? It was like she had lost her mind, and it had become stuck on that one thought. She didn't even care what happened to York. How could he explain to her that he wasn't going off to avenge his father? He was going to protect Brion. Or was he? York decided not to bother with an explanation. He nodded and reined his horse around.

In ten minutes, he was ducking into the trees where he had last seen Arno. The aspens closed around him. The air hung moist and heavy under the canopy of rattling leaves. It smelled of earth and decay. York leaned low over his horse's neck, searching for some sign of Arno's passing. A few minutes of searching revealed a broken spider's web that had been pulled off in the direction Arno had been heading. Brion had explained to York that spiders spun their webs in the late evening. A freshly broken web indicated that someone had passed since then. Then York saw a clump of moss ripped off of a root and the recently disturbed leaf scatter. Now that he had found it, the trail was clear.

But York knew better than to underestimate Arno. He looked like a man who was accustomed to danger and conflict. York walked his horse slowly, keeping his eye on the lay of the land for those spots where a man might circle around to check his back trail. York swung wide to avoid those places before coming back to the trail again. He wasn't going to make mistakes this time.

Arno didn't follow the army as York had originally thought. Once he was under the cover of the trees, he angled west toward the Aveen Mountains, not northeast towards the Dunkeldi army. This confused York. Why would Arno be going the opposite direction the army had taken? But he didn't let his guard down. When Arno's trail cleared the tree line and led up and over a green hill, York paused to study the horizon before moving on. He never let himself be silhouetted on a ridge for more than an instant.

After a few hours of moving steadily west, Arno veered north into a narrow valley filled with aspen, beech, and pine to follow a little creek. The canopy opened up above the creek, allowing more light to filter to the forest floor. It was a beautiful, peaceful place, and York had to resist the urge to slip from the saddle and rest beside the gurgling stream.

The sun was dipped low in the pale blue, cloudless sky when York noticed the uneasy feeling. Brion had warned him to pay attention to those feelings. York pulled his horse to a stop behind a huge beech tree and waited—listening, searching for anything that might explain why he felt uncomfortable. But there didn't seem to be anything wrong. York slipped from the saddle and tied on the felt shoes and the felt booties before he bent low to skulk through the trees.

He would be less visible on foot and make less noise with the felt overshoes. The trail of disturbed leaves and bent bushes with the occasional horse track in the soft earth of an anthill led him on. York noticed that the horseshoe that made the print had a bent nail that stuck out to one side. It was a bad shoeing job, and Arno was lucky the horse hadn't gone lame. York had only gone a good sixty paces before he heard a horse whinny. Another replied. York froze, holding his breath, desperately afraid that his horse might answer. But it didn't.

York crept forward, placing his feet the way Gwyneth had shown him. He glided like a shadow through the forest, following the twisting stream until he spied a bright little glade with a huge boulder off to one side. Two horses stood nosing each other.

Beside them, two men conversed in tones so low that York couldn't hear. York slipped off his quiver, placed two arrows in his bow hand and crawled on his belly to the edge of the glade. Arno handed the man a piece of paper. York studied the stranger.

He looked familiar. He wore Dunkeldi clothes with a white tunic, a wide belt from which a sword dangled, tight trousers, and short boots. He had a fine horse. York worked around until he could see his face. It was the Carpentini man that he and Brion had seen following them days ago back up by the amphitheater where they had found the group of dead Carpentini.

York scowled. Why was he now dressed like a Dunkeldi? What could this mean? York crept closer until he lay behind a rock, straining to hear what they said.

"...trap," the Carpentini said. "He's leading them into a trap."

Arno nodded and mounted his horse. He tossed the man a small bag that made the clinking sound of coins. He said something York couldn't hear and then kicked his horse northeast again back under the canopy of mixed aspen and beech trees. York considered shooting an arrow in Arno's back before he could do any more mischief but decided against it. He didn't have time to get involved in a fight. If Brion and Emyr were being led into a trap, York needed to find a way to warn them.

York lay on his belly, breathing in the smell of cool earth and decaying leaves. What was he going to do? He could continue following Arno. He could wait and follow this Carpentini traitor. He could just go back and do what Brion asked him to do. Or he could catch up with the army and warn Brion and Emyr that they were marching into a trap.

Brion was relying on him to stay with the women, but if Brion had known about the trap, he would expect York to ride ahead and warn them. Wouldn't he? The Carpentini mounted and kicked his horse to the east. York retrieved his quiver and his horse. He mounted, and sat in indecision. He couldn't afford to make the wrong choice. Not now.

Finola and Gwyneth might come looking for him, but they would ask his mother if she knew where he was before they did anything rash. And if York went back to tell Finola that Brion was heading straight into a trap, Finola would insist on going after him, and Brion wouldn't want that.

This decided it for York. He would go after Brion himself. He didn't have any other good choice. He waited until the Carpentini and Arno would be out of earshot before he kicked his horse into a gallop. He had traveled an entire day in the opposite direction of the army. That meant he had at least two days to make up if he hoped to catch them.

Brion crouched in the grove of aspen and pine that clung to the shallow hollow just north of the bend in the river. It had been five days since he had left Finola behind at Dunraven Keep. He shifted under the unfamiliar weight of the mail shirt and the iron helmet that Emyr had carried north for him. The helmet obstructed his view and chafed the back of his neck. Brion had already received two serious head injuries, and, even though he hated the confinement of the helmet, he knew better than to take it off.

Nearly a thousand archers on foot spread out on either side of him, two ranks deep. The heathland was dryer up here on the northern edge of the Ghille Heath, and trees were scarce and much smaller than they were near the Aveens. This narrow grove clustered along a creek that fed the shallow river for a good mile. The advance columns of the armies had already clashed, and Emyr had sent out skirmishers to draw Tristan into his position.

On this bank of the river, Emyr had placed the main force in a long line, five ranks deep, between the grove of trees and a large rock outcrop on the right flank of the army. Most of his 2,500-strong Alamani army had dismounted to fight on foot with long lances. They wore mail shirts over padded leather jackets. The Alamani formed the first three ranks with their long spears and shields. Behind them, Emyr had placed two ranks of longbowmen. On either flank, he had his cavalry. He had hidden another thousand horsemen, mostly Carpentini and Salassani, behind the rocky crag.

Few of the Carpentini and Salassani wore mail shirts or iron helmets. Armor was expensive and difficult to maintain in the desperate conditions to which they had been reduced. Still they wore padded leather jerkins and leather helmets, because only a fool would go into a battle like this unprotected.

Brion marveled at Emyr's creativity. The woods and the crag forced Tristan to approach through a narrow shoot after they had to cross the marshy ground around the river. The army was arranged in a U-shape that could clamp shut as soon as the prey had entered. By hiding the archers in the trees and the Salassani and Carpentini behind the crag, Emyr gave the impression he was facing Tristan with a much smaller force. Brion waited as the skirmishers splashed across the little river, riding hard.

A band of horsemen crested the hill behind them, but they reined to a stop when they saw Emyr's army arrayed between the woods and the crag with the banners of Coll snapping in the late morning breeze. The Dunkeldi horsemen wheeled about and disappeared over the rise. Brion took a deep breath and tried to steady his nerves.

He had never engaged in a battle of this magnitude. He had never been trained for it. He didn't know what to expect, except that the outcome of no battle was ever predetermined. His mind drifted to Finola, and he was glad he hadn't brought her here, that she was safe at Dunraven Keep. A rider broke from where Emyr watched the proceedings on the top of the crag. He raced down the hill, around behind the lines, and disappeared into the woods. In a few minutes, the sounds of pounding horse hooves reached him, and the rider pulled up in front of Brion. He jumped from the saddle.

"The king commands you to hold your men until he gives the signal," he panted. "No one is to shoot until the Dunkeldi are committed to the battle."

Brion nodded. "Tell the king we're ready and waiting."

The rider remounted and raced back to the crag. Brion knew that the real danger of their position was that Tristan might refuse to give battle on the ground they had chosen. He could choose to circle around the crag or the wood and force Emyr's army to turn. With a river to their back, they would be vulnerable.

Brion was relying on the scouts he had sent out to cover their flank to warn him if any part of Tristan's army broke away from the main group. He glanced up to see the crows circling overhead. They, at least, were anxious for the battle to begin.

The Dunkeldi army appeared on the ridgeline and spread out on the opposite hill. They swarmed like a horde of ants spreading over the earth. Brion watched in amazement as the lines of footmen and horsemen poured over the hill to fill the valley on the other side of the creek. The reports had been wrong. Far more than 5,000 Dunkeldi, Bracari, and Taurini poured over the hill. There had to be seven or eight thousand at least. Murmurs erupted up and down the line of archers. Everyone could see that they were outnumbered.

Brion hissed some orders to the messenger standing next to him to check with the scouts to see if Tristan had sent any men around to flank them. The man sped away, and Brion stared at the flow of Dunkeldi soldiers dressed in brightly-colored tunics and shining mail with proud standards snapping over their heads. It was an awe-inspiring sight, and it made him sick. What were they thinking? Emyr should have brought his larger force to face Tristan. If anything went wrong, this battle could become a rout.

The army split in two, and a group of riders pushed through to the edge of the river and paused. Tristan's standard waved over them along with a black flag of parley. The banner of the Dunkeldi kings had a round tower with a crown perched on top. Tristan was easy to spot in his gold-trimmed helmet and gold-trimmed mail. Brion glanced up at the crag where Emyr's standard still fluttered. But no one moved. The entire Alamani, Carpentini, and Salassani line remained silent, as Emyr had ordered.

When it became apparent that no one would come to speak with him, Tristan cried out in a loud voice that echoed over the field.

"Deliver to me the impostor king of Coll and his upstart duke," he said, "and I will return the Salassani and Carpentini lands." A hush settled over the field broken only by the shuffle of feet and the creak of leather. No one responded. "I will also allow the Salassani and the Carpentini to reoccupy the lands they have lost to Coll." A flock of crows circled overhead and few ragged caws echoed in the tense silence that reigned over Emyr's army. "Would you fight against your own people in favor of the butchers from Coll?" Tristan yelled. "Is it not better to live free than to fight and die for this Alamani dog who hopes to enslave you?"

Brion glanced at the men from Coll and the Salassani and Carpentini archers mixed among them. Their faces were grim, but they all understood who the real aggressor was. They had also learned that Tristan's word could not be relied upon. The Bracari and Taurini weren't going to return lands if they didn't have to.

Quiet filled the valley, broken only by the whisper of the breeze in the aspens, the calls of the crows, and the blowing of the horses. The silent menace of Emyr's army seemed to pulsate in the air. The usual insults and jeers were not forthcoming—only the deadly hush of men who knew they must conquer or die.

"So be it," Tristan bellowed. "Your destruction is on your own heads now." He wheeled his horse, and his guard followed him back to his waiting army. A long blast of a horn echoed over the hills, sending a shiver up Brion's spine. Tristan's army gave a shout that sounded like the roar of some enraged beast and charged down the hill towards the river. Thousands of horsemen with long lances and glinting mail splashed into the marshy areas around the river. Their horses slowed as they forced their way through the mud and into the stream. They churned the soft ground into a quagmire that slowed the ranks of horsemen and foot soldiers behind them.

They were in range of the longbows, but Emyr waited. Brion's archers began to shift. A few pulled arrows from the ground where they had stuck them and placed them on their strings.

"Wait," Brion warned and raised a staying hand.

The horsemen plunged across the river, struggled through the muddy ground on the opposite bank, and then hit the dryer earth of the valley floor. Their speed increased and the thunder of their hooves shook the earth. Behind them, the foot soldiers splashed into the creek. Soon the entire army was forcing its way between the wood and the crag. The main body of horsemen had penetrated to within a hundred paces of the main line. Most of them were now in front of Brion's archers.

Two long blasts from a horn rang over the rising tumult. Brion nocked an arrow, pulled the string to his ear and loosed. Thousands of arrows filled the air like a flock of angry sparrows. One cloud came from the main line between the trees and the crag, and the other bit into the left flank of the army.

Horses stumbled and fell, tripping the horses behind them. Another shower of arrows arced into the air. Men and horses screamed in pain and terror. The entire Dunkeldi advance stalled amid a jumble of writhing men and horses. The riders in the rear smashed their way through and came on, now less than fifty paces from the line. A hail of arrows cut into them and then another before the horsemen crashed into the line.

The line wavered. Horses lunged and bit and screamed as they were impaled on the lances of the first two lines. The archers behind the spearmen poured a steady rain of arrows into the Dunkeldi. The mass of foot soldiers finally reached the lines and a melee ensued. The line heaved back and forth. The horrible clamor of battle filled the air. Brion and his archers continued to shoot into the flanks of the Dunkeldi throng.

A mass of Dunkeldi archers gathered on the far side of the stream and loosed arrows in a high arc into the ranks of Emyr's army. Some of the arrows fell among the Dunkeldi, but the archers didn't seem to care. Another group of men on foot splashed across the creek and advanced on Brion's archers in the wood.

Brion saw Emyr's banner flutter overhead as he led his cavalry in a charge at the center of the Dunkeldi line. The Carpentini and Salassani horsemen Emyr had hidden behind the crag swung out and slammed into the mass of archers by the river, and then Brion couldn't pay attention to anything but the screaming Dunkeldi that rushed his line.

"Swords," Brion called, and then he was among the Dunkeldi. The chaos of battle raged all around. Men fell screaming, blood gushing from horrible wounds. The stench of severed bowels mingled with the reek of blood. Brion's sword flashed. He lost track of time as the Dunkeldi came on and on. The ground grew slippery, and the forest rang with the clash of steel and the cries of the injured. His line broke, and the Dunkeldi rushed past him, sweeping his men before them. Brion shouted at them until he became hoarse as he fell back before the onslaught. The left flank was lost. The Dunkeldi had driven a wedge in his line and were pushing them back.

A boy, who couldn't be older than fourteen, rushed at Brion with wild terror in his eyes. The boy already had a wound on his head that dribbled blood down his face. Brion deflected the boy's sword into the ground, stomped on it, snapping the blade, and drove his knee into the boy's stomach. The boy buckled over with a groan.

"Stay down," Brion yelled in his ear before spinning to meet the next Dunkeldi.

The melee swirled around him. He lost track of his men but kept fighting, parrying and slashing, slicing and stabbing. In the chaos of battle, the occasional blade penetrated his defenses and slid across the mail shirt. A sword clanged against his helmet, and he whirled to face a new attacker as a wave of nausea swept over him. He still hadn't recovered from the blow to the head he had received a few weeks before. A painful headache throbbed behind his eyes.

Another sword slid across his mail shirt, and Brion realized that he was alone. A group of Dunkeldi men on foot closed in. They kept a wary distance from the point of his sword, but if they rushed him all at once, he was finished. The armor wouldn't save him.

A horse loomed over him, scattering his attackers. Brion spun to face the new threat when Reed's great voice boomed above the fray.

"For your families!" Reed cried. "For the ones you have lost to the tyrant!"

Reed's mounted Carpentini and Salassani warriors slammed into the Dunkeldi flank and cut through them. The Dunkeldi advance slowed, then halted and fell back. Brion's archers swarmed back out of the woods, retrieved their bows, and began picking off the Dunkeldi as they struggled against the Carpentini and Salassani horsemen. A new cry rose up over the melee. "Coll!" they shouted. "King Emyr!"

Brion paused to catch his breath and to wipe the bloody sweat from his eyes and the slippery blood from his hands. He gazed out over the struggling mass of men and horses, trying to understand how the battle fared. Emyr's banner had advanced to the middle of the field where Tristan's standard flapped overhead, but Emyr appeared to be surrounded. The Alamani line of lancers and archers advanced, struggling to reach their king.

Emyr's army pushed the Dunkeldi back against the creek, where Carpentini and Salassani warriors on foot and on horseback rushed back and forth, slaughtering any who came within reach. Reed leapt from his horse's back, jerked the double-headed axe from his belt, and waded into the mass of Dunkeldi warriors. The Dunkeldi line began to collapse and fold inward. Emyr's army pressed them against the crag and the river, encircling them on three sides.

A lone horse broke from the melee, dragging his rider with him, its tail trailing out behind it. Unhorsed men scrambled to escape the flailing hooves of their dying animals and staggered into the open, where Brion's archers mowed them down. Brion wiped his hands clean, found his bow, which had miraculously remained undamaged, and searched for a vantage from which he could stick an arrow in Tristan or his son. He understood that this war would continue so long as those two survived.

Tristan sat his tall horse with the gold-trimmed helmet glinting in the light. Brion grabbed a passing horse and leapt into the saddle. He galloped to the top of rise that gave him a better view of the battle. He found Emyr locked in combat with Tristan's guards as he tried to force his way to the king. Tristan was a big man, and he was no coward, but it appeared to Brion that he waited for something, that he held back rather than engaging. Something wasn't right. Brion craned his head around. His archers along the wood line had recovered, the Alamani still advanced. The Salassani and Carpentini were bottling the rest of the Dunkeldi up in the narrow valley. It appeared as if the battle would be won.

A horn sounded, and the front ranks of the Dunkeldi army disengaged and rushed backward as if in defeat. The Alamani paused in confusion at the sudden reversal. Then the ball of fire appeared in the sky. Brion watched in horror as the fireball arced overhead with a dull roar. Heads turned up. A cry rose from the Alamani as the fireball smashed into them, spraying burning liquid over everyone within fifty feet. It bowled a large gap in the Alamani line. The Alamani broke and fled from the inferno. Another fireball soared over the hill.

Brion spun to find Reed gaping in horror at the terrible scene. Their gazes met, and Brion kicked his horse toward the river. Reed grabbed a horse and galloped after him, calling the Carpentini and Salassani horsemen to follow him. That machine, or whatever it was, had to be destroyed. A line of Dunkeldi tried to oppose them, but Brion and Reed plowed through them. They splashed and slipped through the muddy river and pounded up the hillside. Brion's horse outdistanced Reed's and the others' as they galloped up the hill. Brion crested the hill just as another fireball launched from a huge trebuchet on wheels.

It roared overhead, leaving a black trail of smoke behind it. Brion reined his horse to a halt to survey the situation before rushing headlong down the hill. Two dozen oxen were staked nearby, and a guard of fifty or sixty men protected the machine. The bodies of several dozen Salassani and Carpentini lay around. They must have seen the danger and tried to stop it.

Brion aimed at the man winding the windlass to bring the great arm back down for another shot and loosed. His arrow dove over the heads of the guards and struck the man in the side. He toppled sideways, but another man leapt to the windlass. Brion shot him, as well. Then a guard with a shield jumped in front of the next man, and Brion shifted his aim to the guards. By then, Reed and the several dozen Carpentini and Salassani galloped over the hill. They didn't pause. They were outnumbered by the guards, but they rode on, heedless of their own lives.

Reed crashed through the first line of guards, bellowing like a bull. Brion shot three more before they were too mixed up with the surging mass of Carpentini and Salassani for him to risk a shot. He dropped his bow in the heather and kicked his horse down the hill. Reed had reached the trebuchet and catapulted from the saddle. He drew back his big axe and chopped at the timbers and the ropes that bound them together. Huge chucks of wood flew up into the air with each bite of the axe. Ropes snapped and frayed. The trebuchet groaned. The battle surged around him. Once the guards understood what Reed was doing, they rushed to stop him. He spun to face them, but there were too many. Reed wouldn't last.

Brion urged his horse on. He cut and slashed his way through the surging throng of screaming men and kicking horses before he swept into the men that had gathered around Reed. He rushed them from the side, and three were down before they knew what hit them.

A Dunkeldi drove a blade into the neck of Brion's horse, and the horse reared and flailed about. Brion slipped free of the saddle and tried to roll clear. A horse hoof caught him in the back and sent him careening headlong into the trebuchet. He lay stunned for a moment before he shook himself and climbed to his feet, fighting the pain in his ribs and a raging headache.

The men working the trebuchet struggled to prepare it to launch again. Reed battled with ten men with his back against the trebuchet. Only the reach of his double-headed axe saved him. Brion pulled his knife from his sheath, and, with it in his left hand and his sword in his right, he rushed at the men. Several Carpentini joined him, and, in a few moments, the Dunkeldi guards had scattered.

"Do it," Brion said, and Reed whirled back to the trebuchet and swung the axe in a terrific blow that caused the trebuchet to shiver.

Brion protected Reed's back while he worked. The guards charged again. But their numbers were much smaller now. The Carpentini and Salassani swept them from the field, and, yet, the men working the trebuchet continued to crank the windlass. Someone crawled up onto the trebuchet to attach the cables to the unlit fireball that rested in a steel net. Brion jumped to stop him, but the man lit the fireball with a burning brand, and it blazed. Brion stumbled back from the heat, and the man at the windlass yanked a lever.

The timbers of the trebuchet groaned. The machine lurched as the weight fell, and then the whole machine exploded in a burst of wooden splinters. Brion ducked as a splinter stabbed into his arm and another bounced off his helmet. The fireball ignited the ropes and timbers. The flames licked their way up and over the pile of ruined wood. Those Dunkeldi who had survived broke and scampered into the hills. Brion fell to a knee, panting and blinking at the bloody sweat in his eyes. Reed lay sprawled on the ground. A gash on his head dribbled blood, and his padded leather jerkin looked like a porcupine with all the slivers of wood protruding from it. Brion jerked the splinter from his arm and scrambled to Reed's side.

"Reed," he called. Reed didn't respond. Brion grabbed his shoulder and shook him in desperation. They couldn't lose Reed, not now. Reed's eyes popped open, and he grabbed for his axe. Brion pushed him back down, but Reed shoved him aside and crawled to his feet. He plucked the splinters from his chest and stomach. None of them appeared to have penetrated too deeply because of the padded leather jacket. Reed brushed at the blood slipping down his face to collect in his beard, grinned at Brion, and rushed back into the battle. Brion shook his head in disbelief. The big, red-headed Carpentini was crazy.

In a few moments, any Dunkeldi left at the trebuchet were dead, and Brion, Reed, and the surviving Carpentini and Salassani scrambled back over the hill to see what had become of the army. Their horses had either been injured or had fled the fire at the trebuchet. The sight that met his eyes caught the breath in Brion's throat. Emyr's standard was nowhere to be seen. The Alamani had been pushed back. The ground where the three fireballs had landed still blazed with a black smoke that filled the air with a horrible stench. Bodies lay everywhere. Some writhed in agony. Others crawled to escape the battle, while some lay perfectly still where they had fallen.

"Where's the king?" Reed demanded. No one answered.

Then Brion realized that the Dunkeldi were trying to disengage. The main body fought their way toward the narrow strip of land in front of the crag. Tristan, in his golden helm, led their flight.

"He's escaping," Brion said. He threw off the annoying helmet and searched the hillside for his bow. It lay in the mud, wet but undamaged. The arrows in his quiver had all broken in his fall from the horse, so he retrieved a spent arrow from the hillside, nocked it, aimed, and loosed. The arrow whipped from the bow and fishtailed wildly through the air. It was too weak for his bow, and it flew too far to the right, landing amid the men surrounding Tristan.

Brion cursed and searched for another. This one splintered as he released the string, sending a few bits of wood into Brion's bow hand. Brion dropped the bow with another curse. It was useless, without a proper arrow, he couldn't make the shot; but Reed didn't wait for him to find one.

Reed roared and raced down the hill with the rest of the Carpentini and Salassani behind him. Brion plucked the splinters from his hand, grateful for the thick, leather shooting glove he always wore and rushed after Reed. He barely felt the pain from his injuries, but his head ached and he felt lightheaded. His legs seemed heavy, and his lungs burned as he raced toward the Dunkeldi army. The unaccustomed weight of the mail and his head injury began to tell.

When they reached the remaining Dunkeldi, the battle was short and fierce. A few remained behind as a rearguard while the rest fled. Reed searched for a horse to pursue Tristan, but Brion had to know where Emyr had gone.

He grabbed an Alamani spearman who had fallen to his knees in exhaustion. "Where is the king?" he demanded.

The man shook his head.

"Where is he?"

"I saw him fall," the man said.

Chapter 12
Enemy in the Dark

York gazed at the great cloud of black smoke that boiled over the horizon with a sick feeling in his gut. He had ridden as fast as he could, without killing his horse, for four days. It was now the fifth day since Brion and the army had left the keep. He had tried to save time by racing cross country only to discover he had misjudged the route the army would take. This land was new to him, and he had managed to get himself lost until he stumbled on their trail—not that he would ever admit this to Brion. He had found them at last, but he was probably too late.

His eyes burned and his head ached from lack of sleep, but it had all been for nothing. Emyr and Brion must have already stumbled into the trap Tristan had set for them. York struggled with the despair as he urged his horse on over the rolling hills. He had to let the horse walk, despite his desperate urgency to find Brion. If he killed or maimed the horse, he would have to go on foot.

The heathland this far east had fewer trees and smaller heather. Despite the spring rains, the ground was dry. Water collected in the little hollows and dribbled through shallow creeks that tended east. The size and scale of it oppressed him. He felt like an insect crawling along the back of a tremendous beast that didn't know, or care, that he was there.

A few more hours passed, and he began to encounter the refuse of battle. Injured or riderless horses straggled about the landscape. Some had ghastly wounds. Others limped. Here and there, a body lay amidst the heather, crumpled in death. Some were Dunkeldi. Others were Alamani, Carpentini, or Salassani. A few Bracari in their green tunics and Taurini with their long, black hair also littered the earth.

The reek of the rolling black cloud filled the air. Bits of ash floated leisurely to the ground in a silent rain of despair. A peculiar quiet hovered over the heathland as if it knew that some terrible drama had just been enacted upon its surface. A black stain still smoldered where a fire had burned through the wood and out onto the heathland beyond.

York swung his bow over his shoulder and nocked an arrow as his horse's hooves crunched over the scorched earth. He had no idea what he would find, but he had to look. Still, it wouldn't do to be foolish. He nudged his horse toward the stand of aspens and pines that crowded near the base of a huge crag where the silhouettes of a few men stood out stark against the pale blue sky. York couldn't tell who they were, so he ducked under the trees to get out of view and let his horse pick its own way. He kept all of his senses alert for danger.

Slowly the sounds filtered to him through the wood. The occasional clang of metal, the neighing of horses, and the cries of injured men. A sick knot developed in his stomach as the charred bodies of burned men littered the woods. Some still smoked with that horrible stench of charred flesh. What had Tristan done? These men were mostly Alamani, judging by the remnants of their clothes.

Something rattled close by, and York reined his horse to a stop. The woods had closed in around him. A little creek gurgled its way through the ruined forest. York placed his fingers on the string of his bow and felt the reassuring presence of the nock between his fingers.

A splash sounded. York swung his leg over the saddle horn and slipped to the ground. He crouched. Something moved. York drew the bow and aimed at the sound when his eyes focused on the form of a crouching boy huddled against the charred trunk of a fallen tree. He let the bow down and stepped toward him. The boy's leg stretched out awkwardly to one side, and a dark stain covered one side of his face.

"Who are you?" York said. He glanced around to see if anyone else lurked in the woods.

"Please," the boy said. "I want to go home." He spoke Salassani with an accent that York hadn't heard before.

"You're Dunkeldi?" York asked.

The boy nodded. York experience the sudden rush of anger and the desire to let his arrow fly. Here was a Dunkeldi swine who had come to kill Carpentini. He raised the bow and then let it fall again. He was just a boy, not much younger than York.

"How old are you?" York demanded.

"Fourteen," the boy mumbled.

"What happened here?"

"King Tristan made us fight, and then he rained fire from the sky."

York glanced up instinctively before he realized he was being silly. Fire didn't rain from the sky, and, if it had, the tops of the trees would also be burned.

The boy saw his confused expression. "Trebuchet," he said.

York nodded. That would make sense. The Dunkeldi king had dragged a trebuchet all the way down here hoping to use it against Dunraven Keep, but King Emyr and Brion had foiled his plans.

"Sit still while I tend your wounds," York said.

The boy hesitated. "I just want to go home."

"I know," York said. "I won't hurt you."

The boy adjusted his injured leg with a grimace and nodded. York retrieved his kit from his saddlebag, dressed the long deep cut on the boy's scalp, and extracted the broken arrow shaft that had penetrated his upper thigh. Fortunately, the arrow wound hadn't been deep. While the boy ate and drank, York cut him a walking stick.

"How did you escape the battle?" York asked.

The boy swallowed. "A big man broke my sword and told me to stay down. So I crawled into the trees." He shrugged. "A stray arrow caught me."

"Well," York said, "you're lucky. Did you see who won the battle?"

The boy shook his head. "They've all gone quiet now."

A bitter terror gripped York's stomach. "I've got to go," he said. He had to find Brion.

The boy watched him with wide eyes.

"Look," York said. "You can stay by the stream until dark and then you can make your way back toward Dunkeldi. You're sure to find other Dunkeldi skulking about." He hated leaving the boy alone, but he had no choice.

The boy nodded. York left him with his spare waterskin and some food before he rode away toward the battlefield with the growing certainty that he had been too late—that Brion, Reed and King Emyr might already be dead.

He hadn't gone far when the sounds of raised voices reached him. York slowed. He dismounted and crouched low in the brush before skulking toward the voices. He paused by a large aspen that had somehow escaped the fire and leaned against the smooth, white bark. On the edge of the trees, a band of men had gathered to argue in animated voices.

"The king is dead, I tell you," someone shouted. "We should all go home while we still can."

The bottom seemed to fall out of York's stomach. King Emyr dead? Then everything they had tried to do was ruined. The Dunkeldi had won. The Carpentini and Salassani were doomed. York almost turned around and hurried back to Dunraven Keep so he could lead his family, Gwyneth, and Finola to safety before Tristan reached them, but the men kept speaking.

"Then where is his body?" another protested. They spoke in the common tongue used by the Alamani. Everyone in the heathland could use it, but most preferred the older Salassani language. Still, the common tongue always sounded strange to York's ears.

"I don't know," the first man said. "Maybe Tristan carried it away as a trophy."

"Where is his guard?" another demanded. "Their bodies aren't on the field either."

Desperate hope blossomed once again in York's chest. Maybe he was still alive, still fighting.

"I say we go home," the first man said. "This war is over, and, if we don't go now, none of us will survive to escape this barren heathland."

"We're not such cowards," someone else said.

"Coward?" the first man said. The quiet swish of a blade being drawn from a sheath sounded, followed by several more. The band of men split into two groups each facing the other with weapons in their hands. York didn't want to get caught in some dispute. If

Emyr had been killed or was missing, as these men believed, then it was even more important that York find Brion. York rose from his hiding place to back away when a familiar voice bellowed over the arguing men.

"Hold!"

The sound of that voice sent a wild thrill of joy surging through York.

"Reed," he called out, but Reed didn't hear him. Reed's head had been bandaged, and he had what looked like bits of wood sticking out of his padded leather jerkin. His beard had been singed, and he was covered in mud and gore.

"What is this?" Reed demanded. "We don't have time to fight among ourselves. Find your horses and prepare to ride. The Dunkel-di are in retreat, if we let them reach Ballach, it will go worse for us."

"The king is dead," said the first man York had heard speak.

"Maybe," Reed said. "But unless you want me to see that you are punished for desertion, you will do as you're told."

York could see through the trees that the man refused to give ground.

"Just because the king has elevated you doesn't mean that you can command any Alamani," the man said.

York advanced through the trees until he had a clear view of the speaker. He was a tall, thin man with a mail shirt. His head and arm had been bandaged. But he stood with his sword raised, pointing it at Reed.

Reed appraised him. His lip lifted in a snarl. York knew from long experience that it was never a good idea to challenge Reed's authority.

"You would betray your king?" Reed spat in the dust. "I expected more backbone from the Alamani." Reed sneered. "You will prepare to ride."

Reed reined his horse around to ride away. The man raised his sword and rushed at Reed, but York's arrow caught him in the throat before he had taken three steps. He staggered and fell with a horrible gurgling noise to writhe in the heather. Reed wheeled about as everyone's gaze found York standing beside a white aspen tree.

A smile played on Reed's lips, and he shook his head before he kicked his mount over to peer down at York.

"Nice shot," he said. "But what the blazes are you doing here?"

"Arno," York said. "I followed Arno and heard him say that you were being led into a trap. I came to warn you."

Reed appraised him. "Where's your horse?"

York gestured back into the trees.

"Go get it," Reed said before he faced the men who stood staring at the twitching body of the dying man.

"Any more complaints?" Reed asked. The crowd of men exchanged wary glances.

"Good," Reed said. "We ride in twenty minutes. Find what's left of your companies and meet me below the crag."

York hurried to his horse and led it from the trees. Reed waited for him to mount and then rode beside him as they walked toward the crag.

"What happened?" York asked.

Reed glanced at him before looking ahead. "We lost over a third of our force with at least that many injured, but we held the field."

"Where are the King and Brion?"

Reed glanced at him again. "I don't know where King Emyr is, but Brion has gone after the main body of the army that broke away. He thinks they'll circle around and try to trap us when Tristan decides to stand and fight again."

"It was a trap, wasn't it?" York said as he gazed over the smoking battlefield. Bodies of men and horses lay everywhere. Arrows protruded from the ground at weird angles. The crows and buzzards had already started picking at the dead. Groups of men searched among the bodies, occasionally pulling one free and carrying him off the field, but others raised their blades for the killing stroke on some Dunkeldi, Taurini, or Bracari warrior. York had seen plenty of bloodshed in his young life—but never anything like this.

"I wouldn't call this a trap," Reed said. "What else did Arno say?"

"I don't know," York said. "I couldn't hear. I thought he was sneaking after the army, so I followed him. He met that Carpentini that followed us, only now he was dressed like a Dunkeldi. Arno paid him, and the man said Tristan was leading you into a trap."

"He said those words?"

"Well, not exactly," York corrected. "He said, 'he's leading them into a trap.' Those were his exact words."

Reed glanced at York and pressed his lips tight. His brow furrowed. "And you thought he meant that Tristan was leading us into a trap?"

"Didn't he?" York began to doubt his own reasoning. It had seemed so obvious just moments before.

"Reed," someone called.

Reed looked over his shoulder at a young Carpentini that had recently joined Reed's band. He had been the leader of a small, desperate group that reached them just after the Bracari raid.

"We have word of the king," he said. "Follow me."

Reed kicked his horse into a gallop as the man led the way. York followed. They stopped next to a man who wore the red eagle on his purple surcoat. He had been one of Emyr's guards. Reed dismounted and knelt beside the man, who had a terrible wound in his neck and his leg bent at an awkward angle.

"You have news of the king?" Reed asked.

The man nodded. But his eyelids dropped, and his head bobbed as he struggled to remain conscious.

"He was unhorsed," the man said, "but the guard recovered him from the battlefield."

"Was he injured?" Reed asked.

The man shook his head. "I don't know," he said. "But the guard pulled him back behind our line. That's the last I saw of him."

Reed patted his shoulder and stood to gaze out over the battlefield. "That fool has gone off after Tristan by himself," he said. "I'd bet Dunraven Keep on it." Then he glanced at York. "Best not tell the king I called him a fool," he said.

York smiled. "You probably shouldn't make a habit of doing that."

Reed sighed. "This 'king' business is gonna take a bit of getting used to."

"How many?" Reed asked one of the captains of Emyr's army. The man had to be in his mid-forties, and his face was covered in scars.

"Twelve hundred dead, about the same number injured," he

said. His voice was deep and gravelly.

"That's half our force," Reed said.

"Some of the injured can still fight."

"How many Dunkeldi?"

"We're still counting, but it looks like nearly four thousand dead."

York knew that the much higher number of Dunkeldi dead came from the Salassani and Carpentini practice of killing every injured man they found. Their hatred and thirst for revenge ran deep, much deeper than King Tristan probably knew. York studied the battlefield. Bodies of men and horses lay scattered about in twisted clusters where the fighting must have been the most ferocious. Ravens and vultures hopped about, squawking at each other as they competed for the most tender morsels. The stench of the carnage mingled with the smell of burnt grass and flesh to make the air nearly unbreathable.

"How many do you think went with the King?" Reed asked.

The man shrugged. "I would guess about six or seven hundred, but it's hard to say."

"We need to catch them," Reed said.

The man nodded.

"We ride then," Reed said.

York watched the men gather. There couldn't be more than a thousand in addition to all the men Brion and Emyr had taken with them, but it was all they had. Few appeared uninjured.

Reed turned to York. "You've got to find Brion," he said. "Tell him what you told me and tell him that Emyr has gone after Tristan with a small force. We need him and his men back here as soon as possible."

"Which way?" York asked.

Reed studied him. "I told you you had your father's courage," he said. "Few men would so willingly ride off into unknown territory with a hostile army on the loose." Then he pointed south past the crag. "You'll find the trail there. It should be easy enough to follow." He nodded to York and trotted toward the rise beyond the river. The line of weary men and horses followed.

Vengeance

The sun sank low over the Aveen Mountains by the time York caught up with Brion. The trail had straggled over the heathland tending southeast until it had abruptly veered north to follow a shallow creek up a rugged valley. The refuse of a fleeing army littered the trail—cast off horseshoes, bits of clothing, armor, and weapons. But it was the torn-up ground and the dead and dying men that punctuated the path like terrible monuments to the horror of war that most disturbed York. The majority of the corpses were Dunkeldi, but a few were Alamani. Some of the injured men called to him for water or begged him to kill them. But he had ridden on, stone-faced and churning inside. He wanted to stop and help them, but he couldn't. More lives depended on him finding Brion before it was too late.

The creek York followed made a wide bend against a rocky bluff before plunging into a cluster of junipers and slipping down a long, steep slope to crash into a clear pool. York paused at the crest. The sounds of battle rang amid the rocks. A red stain had spread in the pool where bodies clustered and bobbed in the current. York worked his way down until the bench opened a clearing in the pines and junipers. Below, where the water cascaded over the boulders, Brion and several hundred men had pinned a larger force up against the rocky bluff. There was no way out. The Dunkeldi were trapped and fighting for their lives.

York dismounted. At this range he wasn't sure of his aim with the bow, and he wanted to save his arrows for when he needed them. But he was so accustomed to the sling that it would be easy to cast his lead stones amid the mass of men bunched against the rock. He just needed an area clear of branches so he could swing the sling. He scrambled down to a wide slab that stood just above the creek, pulled the sling from his belt, nudged open the pouch of lead stones, and seated one in the pocket of his sling. The old confidence warmed him. This was a weapon he truly understood.

He picked out a man in the middle who wasn't wearing a helmet, whirled the sling once over his head, and snapped it at the struggling throng. The lead glinted in the waning light to disappear as it sped down the creek. York lost sight of it, but the man he had aimed at jerked and slumped to the ground. York gave a grunt of smug satisfaction and began systematically casting his stones. With each

163

slap of the string, a man either fell or cried out and searched for the source of his assailant. York had slung twenty stones before the men in the battle realized that something strange was happening. They cast their gaze around, searching for the source of the silent death.

Five more stones, and York saw Brion pause and search the ridge line. York waved at him, but it took Brion a moment to see him. When he did, he didn't smile. He scowled and returned to the battle with renewed energy.

After another twenty minutes, the Dunkeldi began to plead for mercy, and Brion called a halt to the slaughter. No more than a hundred Dunkeldi remained standing. The rest groveled in pain or lay in grotesque heaps amid the stones and roots of the trees. York climbed back up to his horse and led it down the slippery slope to the clearing below. Bodies littered the ground and floated in the pool, twisting in the current created by the crashing of the waterfall.

Brion rushed up to him and grabbed his arm. "What happened?" he said. "Where is Finola?" His eyes were wide and his nostrils flared. His face was splattered with blood.

York stared at him in confusion for a moment before he realized that Brion thought York had come to tell him that something had happened to Finola.

York shook his head. "They're fine," he said.

Brion stared at him. "Then why are you here?"

"Reed sent me," he said. "I came to warn you that Tristan is laying a trap for you. I heard it from a Carpentini."

"You left them?" Brion demanded.

"I had to," York said. "I had to warn you."

Brion passed his hands over his face, smearing the blood. "I asked you to stay back and protect them."

"From what?" York demanded. "I didn't see a single Bracari until I found the battlefield. They've all left."

"You don't know that," Brion said. He spun away from York to give some orders. The Dunkeldi were being disarmed and questioned about what they knew of Tristan's plans. York stood awkwardly, a little hurt and angry that Brion didn't recognize the sacrifice he had made to protect him. It hadn't been easy to ride alone over the heathland for four days and nights.

When Brion returned, he grabbed York's arm and dragged him

to his horse. "You have to go back," Brion said. "I need you there."

"You don't even want to hear what Reed sent me to tell you?" York said. The heat burned his face, and he scowled at Brion. How could Brion be so thick?

Brion let go of his arm. "All right," he said.

York had half a mind not to tell him anything, but he related what he had learned from Arno. Then he said, "And Emyr has gone after Tristan with only six or seven hundred men. Reed is riding after him. He wants you to bring your men and catch up with him as fast as you can."

"My men are exhausted," Brion said. He looked at them. "Gerold," he called. A short, stocky Alamani man who carried a longbow stepped over to them. "I've got to ride ahead," Brion said. "I need you to bring the men as fast as you can. Scatter the Dunkeldi horses and bring their weapons with you. Then ride as fast as you can to the river and follow it north. We should be able to meet Reed before he crosses."

Gerold nodded.

"Ride through the night if you have to," Brion said.

"Yes, Your Grace," Gerold said.

"Thanks, Gerold," Brion said, clapping him on the shoulder. "You're a good man."

Gerold glanced at him and smiled, apparently unused to having a nobleman thank him.

"Let's go," Brion said. He mounted Misty and trotted north. York followed. When they had cleared the little canyon and the stream slipped into the river, Brion stopped. "I'll go on alone from here," he said. "I need you to go back to the keep."

"Why?" York asked.

"Because," Brion said. "You've warned us that Tristan might be planning something, now you need to warn those left at the keep."

"What?" York couldn't understand.

Brion sighed, clearly trying to control his anger.

"You don't know that the trap wasn't being set for the people left behind at the keep," he said.

York paused. This hadn't even occurred to him. "But I want to fight," York said. "My mother . . ." He didn't finish the thought.

Brion simply stared at him. York bowed his head. Brion would think he was being a child, trying to please his mother.

"You've proven yourself many times over," Brion said. "If she can't accept that by now, she never will."

The words burned in York's ears. He had long thought it, but it was bitter to hear Brion say it out loud. It didn't matter what York did—it would never be enough. His mother would never forgive him. She would never let him lay his head in her lap while she stroked away the fear and the pain as she had done when he was small. She was pushing him away because she was ashamed of him. And since York couldn't bring his father back, nothing he did would ever make it right.

"She's sick," Brion said.

York nodded but refused to leave.

"Please," Brion said.

York reined his horse around without another word and headed up over the rise into the setting sun. He didn't look back. Weariness filled him to the core. He was physically exhausted, but the emotional weariness was worse. He was so tired of the disappointed glances and the occasional harsh criticisms. Everyone—even his own mother and now Brion—discounted him.

He paused at another little creek to fill his waterskin and to let his horse rest. He would steal an hour or two before pressing on into the night. For him, at least, the hurry was over. He was certain that the keep was safe, and, if he wasn't going to be allowed to join the army, then he might as well conserve his strength.

Dusk had fallen when York rose from his nap, stretched, and stepped to the creek for one last drink. As he bent to scoop the water into his mouth, he noticed the hoof print in the mud. He hadn't noticed it before, but it was only a few hours old, and several more led up the creek. York stood and surveyed the barren hills around him. He couldn't see much in the gathering darkness. It could just be a deserter or someone trying to find their way home from the battle. But then, why did the hairs raise up on the back of his neck? Why did he have the feeling that danger lurked about? He bent to study the tracks more carefully. What he saw sent his blood racing. The horseshoe that had made this print had a bent nail protruding to one side—exactly the same as Arno's horse.

York stood and peered down along the streambed. How could

Arno be here? He had ridden off to the west. York cursed himself for a fool. Arno had probably spied York from the cover of the trees and gone off to trick York into thinking he was going the other way, only to swing around and follow the army.

"Brion," York said. "Arno is going after Brion."

Gwyneth plunged into the chilly water for a much needed wash. She had crept away after dinner to a secluded pond well away from the keep. She needed some time alone—time to reflect and to settle her mind. Things had been moving so fast in the last few weeks that she was beginning to feel overwhelmed. She came up sputtering and shaking from the cold, but she grabbed up mud from the bottom of the pond and rubbed it all over her body. She scrubbed her hair for a long time because it was so dirty and tangled. Nothing compared to getting clean again, free from the weeks of dirt, sweat, and grime.

York had disappeared five days ago, and only after questioning his mother had they learned that he had gone after the army. Gwyneth had almost run off after him. How could he leave her here after all they had been through together? But she should have known. His mother constantly goaded him, and the men kept underestimating him because he was small. She wondered where he was now and if he had already been in a battle—if he was even still alive. She struggled to understand why she cared so much about a short, quiet, stubborn boy that most people ignored.

She had worked for years to keep from feeling anything for anyone because, when you did, you only got hurt. But now, she had come to know a sense of belonging, if only to Finola and Brion and the small group of misfits they had gathered around them. It was strange and comfortable all at once. It gave her a sense of purpose she hadn't felt in years. But it also frightened her. Was she just setting herself up for more pain? For more loss and loneliness? Would they all turn on her too, because she was a Bracari chieftain's unwanted offspring?

Something rustled in the bushes, and Gwyneth snapped her head up. She had just pulled on her clothes. She reached out and slipped her knife from its sheath and rose to stand in her bare feet in the tall grass. A crow cawed and wings fluttered as three crows burst from the undergrowth and flew to the other side of the pond.

What had disturbed them? Gwyneth stepped toward the tree, but she never got the chance to find out because Finola burst from the trees to her right.

"Come! Now!" she yelled.

Gwyneth stared at her, confused at how Finola had found her and then looked back to the spot where the crows had been disturbed.

"They're coming," Finola said.

The warning horn echoed over the hills.

"Come on," Finola said again.

Gwyneth scrambled into her boots and strapped on her sword. She grabbed up her bow and quiver, and rushed back to the keep. She and Finola joined the crowd of people gathering around the walls of the keep. Finola pushed through them and into the keep. Craig, the Carpentini leader Reed had left in charge, stood in conversation with one of the scouts and all the other Salassani and Carpentini leaders. Finola didn't ask permission to interrupt them.

"Well?" she said.

Craig gave her an annoyed glance. "Bracari are coming through the mountains. They were seen on the shores of Crystal Lake."

"How many?"

"We counted a thousand at least," the scout said.

"How long do we have before they get here?"

"Two, three days at the most," the scout answered.

"Unless we delay them at the pass," Craig said.

"What pass?" Finola asked.

"They're coming south, and they're in the central valley," Craig explained. "Unless they're going to swing farther south to the old Dale road, they will have to take the narrow pass one day north of here."

"What about Tristan's Dunkeldi army?" Gwyneth asked.

Craig shook his head. "We have no word of them."

"This could be a trap," Finola said. "Tristan may just be trying to lure us out of the keep."

"We thought of that," Craig said. "That's why we're only sending one hundred men to hold the pass. They might give us time to get word to Emyr and Reed."

"I'll go," Finola said.

"No, you won't," Craig replied. When Finola scowled at him, he continued. "I have strict orders from the king himself to keep you here." A smile played at the edge of Craig's mouth. "He even said I could tie you up if I had to."

"You don't want to try that," Finola said.

"Not really," Craig said. "But I need you here anyway. I want your ladies armed and prepared because we have another problem."

Finola glared at him, waiting for him to continue.

"This keep is too small to hold all of us," Craig said. He ran a hand over his head.

Gwyneth glanced around at the worried faces of the men and knew he was right. The keep was way too small. They wouldn't even fit, let alone have room enough to fight if they all crowded in.

"What are you saying?" Finola asked.

"I want you to take about half of the women and children to the crevice. If you follow it back about a quarter of a mile, it opens up into a series of grottoes. They're defensible."

"Alone?" Gwyneth said.

"I can spare one hundred men," Craig said. "The rest I need to defend the keep with the other half of the women and children."

"What about provisions and weapons?" Finola asked.

"I've already ordered the provisions to be packed and ready by tomorrow, but I suggest you start moving supplies and people by first light."

Finola nodded and spun to leave. Craig laid a hand on her arm to stop her.

"I'm counting on you," he said. "We'll do everything we can to keep the Bracari ignorant of your whereabouts, but if they find you, we won't be able to come to your aid."

"I understand," Finola said.

"And," Craig continued, "you already have the spirit of command, but remember that you are a duchess and these people have recently become vassals to your king. They *must* follow you. You have to maintain control, even when they're terrified."

"I understand," Finola said again.

Craig saluted her in the Carpentini way and then saluted Gwyneth. "May the gods of the Keldi guide your feet," he said.

Finola returned the salute and so did Gwyneth. It felt so strange to be respected by the people who had previously scorned her. She may be half-Bracari, but she was the niece and granddaughter of two great Carpentini chieftains. Now was her chance to prove it.

Brion had waited until York disappeared over the hill before riding north. Misty was tired, and he worried about the extra weight of his mail shirt and helmet. He had removed the uncomfortable helmet and tied it to the saddle long ago, but the mail shirt still sat heavy on his shoulders. He couldn't afford to run Misty, so he let her walk at her own pace. He needed haste, but it would do no good to kill his horse. He would ride late into the night to try to meet up with Reed before he reached the river. If Emyr was chasing Tristan back to Ballach, they had to cross at the great fork of the Blackwater River or just north of it. Brion had never been in this country, but he had memorized Neahl's map, and he had a good idea where he was.

As he rode, the sun continued to sink into the western sky, casting a soft orange glow over the heathland. At times like these, Brion remembered the strange enchantment he had felt for this land the first time he had seen it—wild, dangerous, and delicately beautiful all at the same time. He let his mind wander as Misty picked a game trail that followed the river and kept moving steadily north.

He couldn't shake the feeling that if Tristan had set a trap, they hadn't found it yet. The battle at the crag hadn't gone as Tristan had expected, but those men Brion had chased weren't just fleeing. He had become convinced of that when they had turned north. They were leading Brion away from the main army. If Emyr had taken another piece of bait, then the army was now split into three smaller units. They would be easy to isolate and wipe out.

Brion considered kicking Misty into a trot but decided against it. She had incredible stamina, as did most Salassani horses, but she also had her limits. He reached out and patted her neck when she bobbed her head and gave her quiet purring sound. Brion sat up straight, alert. Someone was out there. He faced forward but kept his eyes moving, trying to identify any sound or pattern that didn't belong. What had Misty heard or smelled?

A bowstring thrummed quietly. Brion flattened himself to

Misty's back and kicked her into a gallop. The zip of the arrow passed over his head to clatter amid the stones on the other side of the hill. Brion expected to feel the bite of the second arrow as they sped up the trail, but it never came. They rounded a bend in the river where the brush thinned, and Brion wheeled Misty across the river and up the hillside to circle back on whoever had attacked them. He leapt from Misty's back and pulled her down so that they lay side by side at the crest of the hill, waiting and watching.

Nothing stirred in the quiet evening except the night swallows and the mosquitoes that rose up in clouds from the creek. The sun continued to sink as Brion considered what had happened. The archer had shot at him from his right side. The only side from which Brion couldn't use his bow to return the shot. It had been an ambush, not some random Dunkeldi he had surprised on the trail.

Brion waited for almost an hour as the fiery glow faded from the western sky, but nothing stirred in the valley. Brion let Misty rise to her feet, mounted, and rode away from the river staying just below the ridgeline so he would never be silhouetted against the great ball of the moon that was already rising into the sky. There would be plenty of light for an assassin to see by.

Darkness settled, and the moon spread a pale light over the heathland. Rocks and boulders and even the heather cast long shadows. Brion dropped down into another valley, seeking the protection of the junipers that grew near a tiny stream. He had decided that he must have lost his pursuer, when Misty gave another purr of alarm. A bowstring thrummed to his right. Brion slipped from the saddle to cling to Misty's left side as he urged her into a gallop. The whine of the arrow sped over Misty's back. Brion dangled with one foot hooked on the saddle horn while the other leg clamped hard against Misty's belly. He clutched at her mane with both hands. It was all he could do to avoid being thrown to the ground.

When Misty had galloped a couple hundred yards. Brion dragged himself back up into the saddle and galloped up over the rise. Somehow, the assassin was riding around to get in front of him. He had figured out what Brion would do. So Brion dropped back down into the river valley where the light of the moon had not yet penetrated and pulled Misty to a stop in a small grove of junipers. He took off her saddle, turned it around, and replaced it backwards. Then he scooped mud from the river bank and wiped it over his face and hands. That way the assassin might not be able to tell that he was riding backwards. He climbed up and pulled his bow from his back and nocked an arrow. If the assassin attacked from the right side again, Brion would be ready for him.

Once again, he let Misty pick her way up the narrow game trail. Along the creek, the darkness deepened because the slanting moonlight had not infiltrated the thicket that hugged the creek. The small night owls began to call. Crickets chirped and clouds of mosquitoes swarmed him, seeking a meal. Brion found riding backwards awkward and uncomfortable. He often got clocked in the head by a low lying branch, but he kept his senses alert and his eyes searching, doing what he could to ignore the mosquitoes.

A good hour later, he experienced that uncomfortable sensation of being watched. Misty stepped around a boulder and splashed through a puddle when Brion saw the shadow not twenty paces away shift beneath an old gnarled juniper. Brion drew and released in one fluid movement. He had another arrow on the string before he heard the hollow thud of his arrow striking flesh and bone. He ducked as an arrow whizzed past his head.

Then he leapt from Misty's back and splashed across the stream and through the undergrowth. He had his sword in his hand as he exploded into the tiny clearing beneath the juniper. He stopped and stared in surprise.

Arno sat on the ground in his mottled cloak, smiling up at him. Brion's arrow protruded from Arno's shoulder, which meant, at that distance, that it had struck bone. Otherwise, the arrow would have passed through. This gave Brion pause. Even in the dark at this close range, Arno should have hit him if he was any kind of archer.

Brion leveled his sword at Arno's throat. "Give me one reason why I shouldn't kill you."

Arno smiled. "Would it matter if I said that you passed the test?"

Brion scowled. "Probably not," he said. "Who are you? Who sent you?"

"I told you I would be watching to see if you lived up to your reputation," Arno said. "I'm pleased to say you have surpassed it." Then he chuckled and winced. "You actually rode your horse backwards just so you could get a shot at me," he said. "I've never seen anyone do that before."

Brion shrugged, confused by Arno's manner. "It worked," he said.

"Yes, it did. Now would you mind giving me a bit of help in dressing my wound?"

"I might," Brion said, "or I might just kill you since you just tried to do the same to me."

Arno shook his head. "You're too valuable to kill. I shot to miss."

"Uh huh," Brion glared. "Flattery isn't going to save your life."

"I don't flatter," Arno said. "And I will tell you everything once you get your accursed arrow out of my shoulder."

"It's in the bone," Brion said. This much was obvious.

"I can feel that," Arno grunted. "I certainly hope you didn't ruin my bow arm."

"How do I know you're not just going to slip a knife between my ribs while I'm helping you?"

"Disarm me, then," Arno said. "I'm trying to be patient, but it rather hurts."

Brion smiled despite himself. An injury like that would more than hurt. He was surprised Arno wasn't groveling in the dirt. Brion sheathed his sword and bent to remove every blade he could find on Arno's body. He counted ten, and he was sure he had probably missed one or two. If Arno was anything like Tyg had been, he would have another knife somewhere. Brion whistled for Misty to join him, and she splashed across the river and came up to nibble at his ear.

Arno gave a short laugh that ended with him sucking in his breath. "You even saddled her backwards," he grunted.

"Made it easier to ride that way," Brion said.

The extraction took the better part of an hour since Brion couldn't push the arrow through. He widened the hole around the shaft with his knife, while Arno bit down on a piece of leather. Then Brion worked the shaft up and down and back and forth until the broadhead pulled free of the bone. It was a bloody affair, and, by the time he finished, much of the fight had gone out of Arno's posture and expression. He slumped against the juniper, breathing hard. Sweat dripped from his chin and plastered his dark hair to his head. Brion cleansed the wound and dusted it with the red powder

Redmond and Emyr used. Then he bandaged it as best he could, but he was not nearly as good a healer as Lara had been or as Emyr and Redmond were.

When he had finished, Brion sat back on his haunches. "So talk. I'm listening."

Chapter 13
Ambush

Gwyneth lounged by the lean-to, waiting for Finola to return from the council meeting. Gwyneth had tried to attend with her, but the men insisted that only the leaders could attend. Still feeling clean and refreshed from her bath, Gwyneth built up the fire, straightened her arrows, oiled her blades, and packed her bags. When she finished, she slipped off her mail shirt, and then lay back on the pine-bough bed lined with furs to wonder what tomorrow would bring. They were leaving the keep and going to hide in the crevice. She had never intended to return to the crevice after the last battle there. The horror of all the blood and the vicious killing of the surviving Bracari still haunted her.

She shifted to adjust the neck sheath that she always wore strapped to her back. It was the only gift she had ever received from a man. The hilt of the blade pushed uncomfortably against her spine, so she rolled to her side. This would be her last night at the lean-to and the keep—maybe forever. Tomorrow they would move to the chasm, and who knew if any of them would survive this war with the Bracari.

Gwyneth closed her eyes, enjoying the delicious warmth of the fire. It popped and crackled. The rich aroma of burning pine and aspen filled the lean-to. The furs were soft and warm. She pulled them over her and snuggled underneath them. She was drifting off to sleep when the furs were flung away, and someone grabbed her wrists while someone else seized a fistful of her hair and yanked her head back. A knife flashed, and cold steel pressed against her throat.

She froze, not daring to breathe, as the shadow looming over her came closer until the light from the fire illuminated his face. The handsome Salassani boy that had grabbed her a few days ago down by the creek stared down at her. She remembered the startled crows and realized that he must have been watching her at the pond. The sense of invasion filled her with anger and disgust. She jerked against the hands that restrained her arms.

"Let me go," she demanded.

The Salassani boy grinned. "We're all going to be dead in a few days," he said. "Don't you think we should have a little fun before we die?"

"I'll kill you," Gwyneth said.

"No you won't," he said. He withdrew the knife from her throat and sheathed it. Then he reached out to caress her cheek. She flinched at his touch and tried to pull away, but the hands held her.

"Hurry up," someone said behind her.

"Not this one," he said.

"I'll tell Craig," Gwyneth tried again.

The boy laughed. "Who will believe you?" he said. "From what I hear, everyone knows your mother was a loose woman and it's your fault the Bracari have been killing Carpentini."

Gwyneth jerked again.

The boy let his fingers slide down her neck. "You're the most beautiful girl in camp," he said. "It's a shame to let all that beauty go to waste." He gestured to his friends, and they dragged Gwyneth off the bed and onto the ground. The boy stood over her straddling her legs. He grinned.

Gwyneth struck out. She kicked him hard in the groin. He bent over with a cough, and she slammed her other foot into the side of his head. He sprawled into the fire with a cry of pain. Gwyneth swung her feet up and over her head rolling against the hands that held her wrists. She landed on a body and drove her knees down. The boy grunted. His hold on her hair released and one of her hands slipped free. She whipped the knife from her neck sheath and sliced it against the hand that held her other wrist. A boy screamed in pain and pulled away. The one underneath Gwyneth tried to grab her again, and she drove her blade into his belly, cutting a long gash.

By then, the handsome Salassani boy had pushed himself free of the fire. He came up with his knife in his hand. His tunic smoked and red coals still clung to the fabric.

"I'll kill you," he snarled and launched himself at Gwyneth. Gwyneth leapt off the writhing boy beneath her and rolled to the side. The Salassani boy spun to follow her, but she came up low under his guard and plunged her knife up under his ribs. She jerked it free as his blade cut a long, shallow gash on her arm. A fountain of blood pumped from the wound she had made in the boy's chest. Gwyneth lunged upward to rip her knife across his throat before jumping back as he staggered sideways and fell in a shower of blood.

Gwyneth stared in disbelief at what she had done as the boy twitched and gurgled. Her knees gave out, and she sank to the ground. A great sob escaped her throat, and she trembled uncontrollably. She raised her hands to stare at the dark blood that glistened in the light of the fire. Something crashed behind her, and she struggled to her feet to listen to the sounds of stumbling footsteps and then splashing. One of them had escaped.

The handsome Salassani boy quit moving. The other writhed and whimpered in agony. Gwyneth couldn't stay to listen as he died. She couldn't stand it. She staggered off into the trees until she came to a beech tree with big branches reaching out like arms to hold her. She slumped against the cool, smooth bark and wept.

Arno cradled his injured arm against his chest and gave Brion a wry smile. "First, let me tell you a few things you do not know," he said.

Brion nodded and folded his arms around his knees. "Make it quick," he said. "I'm in a hurry."

He had already lost a lot of time, but Arno intrigued him. He hadn't decided what to make of him. He had thought Arno was a trained warrior from the first time he had seen him riding towards the keep with the other Salassani, but he knew nothing else about him.

"You remember last summer when the Dunkeldi captured your sister and were carrying her to Dunfermine?"

Brion stiffened. How would Arno know about that? Most people knew the girls had been kidnapped and that Brion had gone into the heathland to save them, but very few knew about Brigid being carried toward Dunfermine.

Arno clearly enjoyed Brion's discomfort. "Didn't you wonder at the time why they would take her there?"

Brion didn't respond.

"She was a gift," Arno said. "Tristan was sending her as a gift to Cedrick, the Duke's son. Cedrick knew you would come for her no matter what the cost. He hoped to lure you to him. Then he planned to have his way with her, behead her, and send her head back to you and Neahl as a present."

Brion lunged to his feet and whipped his sword from its sheath. He leveled it at Arno's throat.

Arno eyed the blade. "I told you I knew things you didn't know," he said. "Cedrick was disappointed to lose his prize, but when you agreed to go with him into his father's camp, he was elated. He would be able to confirm his suspicions about his father's treachery and have you murdered at the same time." Arno pushed the sword away. "You don't need that," he said.

Brion kept it pointed at Arno's throat. Arno kept talking.

"After you kept him from raping that little girl, Cedrick was so enraged that he confronted his father and murdered him in his own tent, not an hour after you left."

"How do you know this?" Brion demanded. His hand gripped his sword, and he was tempted to run it home. He scowled at Arno. This man knew too much—more than he should.

"It's my job to know," Arno said. "You can sheath your sword. I already told you that you passed the test. I'm no threat to you." He gestured towards his injured arm and raised his eyebrows.

Brion didn't sheath his sword, but he did pull it away from Arno's throat. His mind raced. How could this stranger know about things that only a handful of people knew? How could he pretend to know what had happened in the Duke's camp at Dunfermine?

"I asked you a question," Brion said.

Arno raised his right hand. "I'm going to retrieve something from my pocket," he said. "Don't run me through."

He slipped his fingers into a little pocket stitched into his cloak and withdrew a piece of dark cloth. He held it up. Brion took it and adjusted it so the light of the moon that now stood overhead illuminated it. The cloth was dark, maybe red, and it had a black rook stitched into it. Brion flipped it over and then glanced at Arno.

"You don't recognize it?" Arno asked.

Brion shook his head.

Arno sighed. "When the Duke of Saylen himself isn't even impressed by our sign, it makes me wonder if we aren't too secretive."

"What are you talking about?"

"I belong to a special organization," he said. "We have made it our task to gather and sell information. You would be surprised what people are willing to pay." When Brion said nothing, Arno continued. "We have spies and assassins everywhere, in every land, in every capital, in every town and city. Little occurs in these islands or on the mainland that we do not know about."

Brion watched him, trying to decide if he could, or should, trust him.

"Unfortunately," Arno continued, "when you and Emyr led your little coup, you killed off most of our men in Chullish. We have a vacancy now, and I have been sent to offer it to you—if you proved that you were worthy."

"What?" Brion said.

Arno shifted and grimaced. "I'm offering you a place in our order," he said. "If you will keep us informed of the happenings at court, we will share what knowledge we have with you." Arno cocked his head sideways. "I think you'll find our knowledge quite useful."

"You expect me to spy on Emyr?" Brion couldn't believe what he was hearing.

"Not spy, exactly," Arno said. "That sounds so treasonous. Just pay attention to what is happening and let us know."

Brion shook his head. "I won't betray my friends."

"It isn't betrayal to share information in return for intelligence that could help your king save his throne."

Brion glared at Arno. "Now what are you going on about?"

"As a sign of good faith," Arno said. "I will share some of what I know with you, and you will see what our knowledge is worth."

Brion waited, trying to suppress his growing frustration.

"Emyr has enemies in Coll."

Brion grunted. "That's not news to anyone."

"They're organizing a coup," Arno said.

A hollow pit opened in Brion's chest. Brigid was down there all alone with her new baby. "When?" Brion almost shouted.

"Oh, they aren't ready yet. They're hoping he will get himself killed up here. In fact, they have been working with Tristan for just that purpose."

"Spit it out," Brion said.

"Well, I don't know what York told you about my little conversation he overheard, but Emyr is riding into an ambush at the fork in the river. Tristan is going to be waiting for him there. He has been trying to split your army to make it easier to defeat." Arno appraised Brion. "But I think you already figured that out." Brion nodded and Arno continued. "The conspirators also have a captain by the name of Ewan who is ready to betray Emyr if the opportunity presents itself. He is the one with the scarred face."

Brion knew the man.

"I imagine York didn't tell you about the Bracari army over a thousand strong marching on Dunraven Keep as we speak."

Brion stared. He didn't want to believe it. They had done everything wrong. Tristan and Emyr's enemies in Coll had been playing the tune all this time, and Brion and Emyr had been all too happy to dance. Now Brion understood why Emyr had refused to tell him anything about his plans. Emyr must have known that he had people working against him, and he was keeping his cards close. To speak it out loud would have meant potentially compromising everything he was trying to do.

"I will tell you one last thing," Arno said. "Your mother is alive, as I think you know, and she is hiding in the Aveens."

"Where?" Brion blurted before he thought better of it.

Arno shrugged. "That, I don't know."

Brion sheathed his sword and sat down. If this was true, he was a fool. If he had known any of this, he wouldn't have come north at all, and he certainly wouldn't have brought Finola with him. Now he had to choose between warning Emyr and saving Finola. At least he had sent York back, but York didn't know about the Bracari army. Would he even make it in time? What if he ran into the Bracari alone? Had Brion sent York to his death and left Finola and Gwyneth to die at the hands of the Bracari? It was too much to take in. He was days away from Dunraven Keep. He would never make it in time. What should he do?

"You see?" Arno said. "Knowledge is power. Knowledge is freedom. You join us, and we'll ensure you are the best informed, freest man in Coll."

Brion didn't care about that right now. Everyone he loved seemed to be in danger. At least Redmond was safe on the continent. Brion rubbed a hand over his head and let out a long sigh. He needed rest, at least for a few hours.

"I am no traitor," Brion said. "And I am no assassin. I doubt that I have anything to offer you."

"There is time to decide," Arno said. "You can finish this little war before you give me your answer."

Brion studied him while trying to keep his despair at bay. Which way should he go? He couldn't abandon Finola. He couldn't. But what if Emyr died in an ambush, and he could have prevented it?

"You won't mind of I tie you to the tree so you don't slit my throat while I sleep?" Brion asked.

Arno raised his good arm. "I've already told you that I'm here to recruit you—not to kill you."

"All the same," Brion said.

Arno grunted. "If you must."

Brion tried to hand him the cloth with the rook stitched into, but Arno shook his head.

"You keep it. You might need it sooner than you think."

Brion awoke as the blush of dawn spread over the heathland. Something had roused him. He lay still. Arno was still tied to the juniper where he had left him and apparently still asleep. Misty shuffled her feet. Brion rolled to peer through the heather. York was striding up the hill toward them with his bow in his hand. His horse grazed beside the creek.

Brion lunged to his feet. "Now what?" he demanded. He had expected York to be well on his way back to the keep.

York shrugged. "I came across Arno's tracks, and I thought he was hunting you." He glanced at Arno. "Looks like you got him first."

Brion sighed and shook his head. York was becoming too accomplished a tracker for his own good.

"Look," Brion said. "I appreciate your concern, and you are surpassing even my expectations of your skill at tracking, but you have to go back to the keep. You have to warn them."

York began to shake his head when Brion cut him off.

"There's a Bracari army heading there right now," Brion said. "Someone has to warn them."

Somehow, without realizing it, Brion had made his decision while he slept. As much as it tore at his insides to admit it, he couldn't let Emyr be killed. He had to choose the good of the kingdom and the lives of the thousands of people who would die if Emyr failed over his own interests. He had to trust Finola. He had to believe she would find a way to save herself.

"They'll be warned," Arno said.

Brion and York stared at him.

"I made sure their scouts would find the Bracari," he said. "They probably know already."

"Are you sure?" Brion demanded.

"Well, nothing's ever sure in war," Arno said. "But I'm reasonably confident that my plans worked. They usually do."

Brion smirked at the obvious arrogance. Perhaps a spy like Arno had to have that kind of arrogance to do what they did.

"Shall I kill him?" York asked.

Brion glanced at him. "Why?"

"He betrayed us to the Bracari when we were looking for your mother," York said.

But Arno was shaking his head before York finished speaking. "I keep telling you people that I am not your enemy," he said. "I haven't betrayed anyone to the Bracari. I'm working against Tristan. We've been paid handsomely to see that he falls."

York glanced at Brion for an explanation, but Brion didn't have one.

"Who paid you?" Brion asked.

Arno shook his head and pursed his lips. "Even if I knew, I couldn't tell you. Now, will you untie me? I'm a bit stiff."

Brion bent to untie him.

"Uh, I wouldn't do that," York said. "He's just going to cause more mischief."

Brion frowned at him. "I'm following my instincts," he said. Then he turned Arno. "Please, don't prove me wrong."

"I suggest you two get going," Arno said, "or you will miss Emyr and Reed."

Brion glanced at York. He wanted him to go back to do what he could to protect Finola and Gwyneth. But it would take him six days at least to reach them. If he was going to abandon them, he had to do something, anything he could.

"I'll go," Arno said.

"What?" Brion asked.

Arno gestured to his injured shoulder. "You've made sure I'm no use up here," he said. "I'll go back to Dunraven and do what I can to help."

Brion studied him. Did he trust him?

Arno smiled. "You can test *me* now, if you like."

The bodies of the two boys Gwyneth had killed lay on the green grass before the keep as the morning sun warmed the hillside and drove away the morning mist. Finola had insisted that they be carried before the leaders of the Carpentini and the Salassani. Gwyneth hung back behind Finola, trying not to draw attention to herself. She stared at the silent forms of the boys. Their faces were pasty and expressionless. Their eyes open. Dried gore soaked their clothes and colored their skin. Gwyneth fingered the shallow cut along her arm. Finola had treated it after she had found Gwyneth slumped against the tree.

Hundreds of people had gathered. Everyone had been preparing for Finola's group to leave for the crevice when Finola had appeared at the keep and demanded that all the leaders gather. It had taken them time to collect at the keep and none of them were happy about being summoned. Gwyneth hadn't wanted to come because she knew that no Carpentini was going to take her word for it—not the word of the half-breed. But Finola had insisted.

Another boy, much younger than the other two that had attacked Gwyneth, stood by some Salassani men cradling his bandaged hand against his chest. He pointed a finger at Gwyneth and sneered.

"She lured us into the trees and then attacked us," he said.

Gwyneth stepped toward him, but Finola restrained her. The hot anger and shame filled Gwyneth to bursting. Everyone's gaze shifted to Gwyneth. She wished she could just melt into the ground. She was surprised at the strange mixture of guilt, shame, and anger she felt. She hadn't done anything wrong. She had acted out of self-preservation, and yet, here she was cowering behind Finola, ashamed to look anyone in the eye.

"She's always attacking the boys," the boy continued. "She's a crazy half-breed."

"You lie," Finola said. "Every woman here knows what happened." She grabbed Gwyneth's arms and pulled up the sleeves to show the deep purple bruising on her wrists and the long cut on her arm.

"She was being held down by two boys, in the dark, alone," Finola said.

"Boys will be boys," a male voice called out.

"No," Finola snapped. "Boys and men will be vermin and tyrants if they're not constrained."

A muscular Salassani man stepped toward her, but stopped when a surge of men and women from all around the camp rushed forward to her defense. Gwyneth glanced around. Swords and knives were in their hands. The women lowered their lances to point at those on the other side.

"What are we fighting the Bracari for?" Meredith said. "If our own men can rape us and abuse us any time they like, we might as well join the Bracari and let them kill all the men. We get no better treatment from them."

A chorus of support rose up from the gathered women.

Craig raised his hands and stepped forward. "No man here is going to tolerate the rape of our women, are we men?" Not everyone looked convinced.

"She's a Bracari," someone shouted.

Gwyneth's cheeks burned with humiliation. How she hated being Bracari. Everything bad that ever happened to her had been caused by that one failing—the thing she could never change.

Craig faced them. "She is the granddaughter of the greatest chieftain the Carpentini have ever known," he said. "Her uncle and grandfather died to defend this people. You have shunned her and accused her for far too long. The blame for our defeat rests on our own shoulders. If we had stopped our squabbling earlier, we would still hold our lands." He revolved slowly to gaze at the crowd, daring anyone to contradict him. Gwyneth didn't know what to feel. No Carpentini had defended her in years.

"You see," Finola said. "This is why women need to be trained to fight." She gestured to all the armed women that surrounded her. "We are not your dogs, to be used and abused as you please. Every tyrant among you has cause to fear for his own life. Maybe now you will become the men you ought to be."

Craig nodded in agreement and faced the Salassani leaders. "He is one of yours," he said, pointing to the boy. "Do with him what you will, but if he comes near Gwyneth or any other Carpentini woman or girl again, I give them permission to kill him without question." The Salassani remained silent as the boy seemed to cower from Craig. "And if I hear of him or any other molesting our women or daughters, I will kill them myself."

Feet shuffled, but no one spoke.

"Now," Craig said. "We have a real enemy to prepare for."

The sun had already descended below the Aveens, before Brion and York neared the fork in the river. The shallow stream had deepened and widened. Willows and oaks clustered along its banks cut by the rocky outcrops of black stone. The water flowing over the stone appeared to be equally black, which was where its name the Blackwater River must have come from. They had followed the river north all day, moving as quickly as they could while sparing the horses. And they had avoided staying too close to the river. Now they lay on their bellies on a rise on the left bank, peering out to where another stream joined the Blackwater. It was a rugged landscape with piles of black boulders scattered amid low-lying shrubs, tangled junipers, and tiny heather bushes. A wide road crossed the Blackwater just north of the fork below a great black crag, but there was no one in sight.

"Where are they?" York whispered.

Brion shook his head. It was impossible to tell. They would have to cross the open country to examine the road. Brion tried to decide how he would set an ambush here if he were Tristan. It would be best to wait until the army was crossing the river and then attack them from both sides. Where could Tristan hide two armies in this open country?

"What was that?" York said. He pointed down by the river. A dark shape flitted in and out of the trees, heading south. Whoever they were, they appeared to be seeking concealment in the trees.

"It looks like something we should check out," Brion said.

They remounted and swung wide to enter the cover of the trees along the river so they couldn't be seen. Then they worked their way carefully from tree to tree. Brion signaled York to halt and dismount when they reached a place along the bank where the trees thinned and a rocky ridge came down almost to the water's edge. They led their horses up a narrow valley to hide them behind the ridge and crawled to a vantage point by a pile of black rock. The rock was rough, with sharp edges.

"What is this stuff?" York whispered after a sharp piece had cut his hand. Brion just shook his head and positioned himself so he could see both sides of the river. The fork was no more than two hundred paces before them. The black rock crag on the other side of the stream was crowned by a bunch of junipers. The Blackwater River snaked northward off to their right. If an ambush was being laid, the men would have to be concealed somewhere around here.

Brion waited, stifling the sense of urgency. He had to find Emyr before it was too late. The light was fading fast. He had expected to see an army or something, anything to indicate that Emyr had been here or that Tristan was lying in wait. Then he saw it.

What looked like a log had shifted and then a clump of grass. The man on horseback they had seen earlier appeared not thirty paces from where they crouched as he broke from the cover of the trees. The log shifted again. Brion watched in amazement as first one log and then two rose and rushed the man.

"What the…" York said.

A loop of rope appeared out of nowhere to sail through the air and encircle the man's arms. The line jerked tight, and the man was ripped from his saddle. The two descended upon him and silenced him before he could cry out.

Several more "logs," crowned with bunches of grass, rose and stalked over to where the first two logs stood beside the dead man.

"He suspects," someone said. "He's looking for us."

The voice had a Salassani lilt to it that was unmistakable.

Brion raised his hands over his head and stood. Two of the men disguised as logs raised bows to shoot, but Brion called out to them.

"I'm Brion of Wexford," he said. "I'm looking for Emyr."

One of the men threw back a hood to peer at Brion.

"It's him," he said, and he waved for Brion to come down.

Brion gestured to York, and together they clambered down the rocky slope.

The men threw back their grass-covered hoods. They were mostly Salassani with a few Carpentini. They all wore shaggy cloaks with bunches of grass, bark, and heather poking out all over. Brion had never seen anything like it.

"Where's the army?" the apparent leader asked.

"We left the main group to chase a few hundred that broke south to encircle us," Brion said. "I haven't seen Reed in a day and a half."

The leader glanced over Brion's shoulder up the river as if expecting to see the army filtering through the trees. "How many are with you?" he asked.

"I have about four hundred heading up the Blackwater now," Brion said. "They should be here by dawn at the latest."

"I hope that's soon enough," the leader said.

He glanced at York and then gestured to them. "Come on," he said. "You can't stand around looking like that. Call your horses."

Brion whistled and Misty and York's horse trotted out to them. The leader spun and led them into the trees.

"Where's Tristan?" Brion said. "I thought you were going after him."

The leader glanced at Brion as if he were deciding if he should trust him. "King Emyr rode on," he said.

"What?" Brion couldn't believe it. What was Emyr thinking? He was heading straight into the heart of the Dunkeldi lands with no way to reach Ballach without being seen. Even if he did, without an army he might as well slip a noose around his own neck and hand it to Tristan to pull.

"He left us here to ambush Tristan when he came," the leader said. "We had to ride hard to get ahead of him. We only got here a few hours ago."

"So Tristan isn't here. You weren't chasing him?"

"No."

"How many men did the king take with him?" Brion asked.

"Not quite two hundred."

Brion sighed. He should have insisted that Emyr tell him what he planned to do. Now he was blind to what was going on. Emyr was riding into the heart of Dunkeldi territory with less than two hundred men, and no one seemed to have any idea what he was up to. It sure looked like suicide.

"What's your plan?" Brion asked.

The leader signaled to one of the Salassani who guarded their supplies.

"I have four hundred men concealed along the river."

"Nice outfits, by the way," Brion said.

"They work," the leader said.

"Yeah, they do," Brion said, "I didn't see you until you moved."

"The Salassani know how to hide," the leader said with evident pride. "Anyway, we left one hundred men with the king's standard to act like they were pursuing Tristan, and we rode ahead to get in front of him. I'm hoping Reed isn't far behind."

"He left not long after the battle," York said.

"How many men did he have?" the leader asked.

"A little over a thousand, I think," York said.

"We've lost half our army," the leader said. "Tristan still has more than three thousand with him. Our scouts tell us that they should be here tonight. They'll probably camp on the northeast side of the crag so he can be concealed. He has reinforcements that should be here by tomorrow."

"Are you going to wait for Reed?"

The leader shook his head. "I have orders to attack tonight and to cause as much damage as I can."

"I have an idea," Brion said, "and it involves goose eggs."

The leader raised his eyebrows at him.

"It's a recipe one of my mentors taught me," Brion said. "It will burn like nothing else."

The leader looked interested. "Can you launch it from a bow?"

"That's the idea."

"I think I heard of this," the leader said. "Is it that fire you unleashed at the Great Keldi?"

Brion realized he shouldn't have been so nonchalant about it. These men probably had family or friends who were injured or died in that raid. It was so easy to forget that, for the Salassani, everything that had happened since the rescue at the Great Keldi had been nothing but a disaster.

"Sorry about that," Brion said.

The leader shook his head. "It is past. We're allies now."

"That's big of you to say," Brion said.

The leader smiled. "Emyr told me I had to be nice to you."

Brion nodded. He liked this Salassani who enjoyed a joke.

"I'll remember that," he said. Then he smiled at York. "Let's go egg hunting."

"Stay out of sight," the leader said. "Tristan has scouts about. While you're away, we'll get each of you one of our pretty cloaks."

York crouched in the darkness, draped in the heavy cloak the Salassani had made for him. The cloak smelled of earth and heather and dry grass. York had helped Brion gather a dozen goose eggs, poke holes in the shells and blow the yolks and whites out. Some had already had developing goslings in them since it was getting late in the season and they had to be tossed aside. Brion had heated a mixture of pine resin, quicklime, sulfur, charcoal, and something he had called saltpeter. The goo smelled awful, and York had plugged his nose as Brion made him hold the eggs while he poured it in. Then Brion pulled two copper cones from his bag and showed York how to pack the eggs in dry grass and birch bark soaked in pine resin. A flint and steel ignited the bark and the resin that now stuck to the egg. It was ingenious, but York couldn't figure out how they were supposed to shoot them from their bows.

"You just carry all this stuff around with you?" York asked.

Brion nodded. "Not always, but you never know when you might need it."

"And how do you shoot this from a bow?"

Brion pulled an arrow with no fletchings from his quiver. "I tie this to my string, put the cone on the end and when I shoot, the arrow stops and the cone keeps going."

"That actually works?"

"Yep. It's how we got the girls out of the camp at the Great Keldi."

Brion's men arrived a few hours after dark, and Brion led them across the small river and up the south slope of the rocky crag. They bedded down amid the juniper and birch trees to await Tristan's army. York dozed but couldn't rest. It seemed like a suicide mission to attack an army of three thousand with no more than four hundred men. But they were just supposed to hit and run. Still, things could go wrong so quickly. It was torture to just sit and wait, not knowing when Tristan's army would come and not knowing if he would survive when they did.

Not long after midnight, Tristan's army straggled across the river and made camp. They didn't even bother to set up tents. They simply picketed their horses in long lines and fell on the ground in groups. Only one tent went up in the center of the camp, and York watched its white fabric flapping in the breeze as the men worked to secure it to the ground. The moon was still full, and the valley below the crag flooded with bright moonlight. The army was settling in for the night when Tristan galloped in, riding toward his tent.

York watched in growing anger as Tristan dismounted his big horse and stepped into the tent. There was the man who had caused all of this suffering. There was the man responsible for his father's death. He couldn't just sit here while Tristan enjoyed a quiet night's rest. York checked that Brion was preoccupied with something else before he set down his bow and quiver of arrows and slipped down the hillside until he huddled in the shadow of a juniper just on the edge of the encampment. He hugged the cloak tight and waited until the sounds of a sleeping camp competed with the call of the crickets and the hooting of the owls.

He slipped off the cloak and stood. He gathered the cloak up into a wad and carried it with him, just in case he needed it. Then he strode right into the camp as if he belonged. The guards were too exhausted to notice him, and, within minutes, he found himself staring at Tristan's tent from behind a wagon. Guards stood all around it. Their armor glinted in the moonlight. There was no way to approach without being seen. That's when he stopped to realize what he was doing.

Vengeance

He had just walked into the center of the Dunkeldi camp without any plan how to get back out. Maybe he had never expected to get out. York ground his teeth. The time had come for this tyrant to be stopped for good.

He pulled the cloak back on and crouched under the wagon, peeking through the spokes of the wagon wheel, waiting for something to happen. York endured the long, uncomfortable wait crouched under the wagon in the grass that itched his skin where ever it touched. When the guards were distracted as they changed the watch, York crawled on his belly until he lay directly behind the king's tent. He lifted the edge and peeked in. It was dark, but a sleeping figure filled one side of the tent not five feet from where he lay. York raised the edge, rolled to his back and wiggled under. Sometimes it paid to be small.

He struggled to control his breathing and the nervous trembling in his hand. If he was caught in here, he was dead. They wouldn't ask questions, and they wouldn't care about his reasons.

Chapter 14
Unexpected Visitors

Ever so slowly, York crawled to his feet. He let his eyes adjust to the dark before he took one tentative step. His cloak jerked tight, and he experienced a moment of panic until he realized that he had stepped on the hem. He didn't dare breathe. He took one step and then two, doing everything Gwyneth and Brion had taught him about moving quietly. He wished now that he had thought to strap on the felt booties. The ground inside the tent had been covered in a rug, which helped. He stood over the shadow of a man who lay on his back with his eyes closed. His chest rose and fell. York bent. His heart pounded in his ears. His hand shook as he extended the knife.

He's a tyrant, York told himself. Tristan deserved to die. It was justice, and he might save thousands of lives by killing him here and now. Still, he hesitated. The man's eyes fluttered open.

"This is for my father," York snarled in a harsh whisper as he jerked is blade across the man's throat. One swift cut and York was racing for the back of the tent. The man came up gurgling as York slid under the edge of the tent, making more noise than he meant to in his haste. Someone thrashed about as the gurgling became louder.

"Guards!" someone called.

York raced to the wagon, slipped under it, and curled up beneath the cloak. Boots beat the earth. Shouts rang out.

"The prince," someone called. "Assassin!"

York realized his mistake. He pounded his fist against his forehead. *Stupid*, he thought. He should have known. The king hadn't been alone in the tent. But it was too late to do anything about it now.

The camp came alive as men kept calling to one another until the whole encampment seemed in commotion. York huddled under the wagon, trembling in terror. Even in the dark and confusion, there was no way he was going to escape the encampment.

"Fire," someone shouted and the cry rose up all around. York peeked out from under the cloak to see little balls of flame arcing through the sky. Several wagons were already in flames. The sounds of thundering hooves beat the earth. A flaming arrow pierced the tent, and the fabric caught fire. A huge man burst from the opening. He was still in his armor, and he had a bare sword in his hand. His face twisted in fury, making it all the more hideous in the flickering light of the flames.

A cry rose up from the side of the hill, and Tristan strode to his horse and vaulted into the saddle. He galloped toward the commotion. York slipped from under the wagon and darted in the same direction, hoping no one would suspect him. He circled wide to avoid the sounds of combat and was nearly to the cover of the trees when someone yelled at him.

"Hey, boy," the man said.

York sped as fast as he could.

"Hey!" the man called again.

York leapt into the trees and scrambled up the hill, fleeing the sounds of pursuit. He angled back toward the river until he found a good patch of thick brush. He jumped into the middle of it and yanked the cloak over his head. He waited, breathless and terrified. His pursuer thundered past him.

At that moment, another cry split the darkness. Emyr's men must have attacked from the other side of the camp. York listened to the sounds of the fighting until the horn sounded three sharp blasts. That was the signal to disengage. The sounds of fighting died down, and York rose from his hiding place. He retrieved his bow and quiver and joined the rush of men heading back down the river to conceal themselves in the woods.

Once York reached the river, he chanced a glance back. Great columns of flame leapt above the low-lying trees to cast a red-orange light dancing on the slope of the great crag.

What had he done? What would his mother say?

Gwyneth stirred with the first light. The pine branches she had cut to keep her body off the damp floor of the cavern poked into her back. She rolled free of the furs. Finola still snuggled with Iain on the other side of the little cave. They had spent the better part of the previous day hauling supplies and weapons. Wooden boxes and bags lay in disorganized piles. Gwyneth paused at the entrance to their little cave and stared out in awe into the diffuse light that filtered into the crevice.

A mist was lifting off the ground to rise up ghostly white. Little fingers of vapor curled around the tree roots that protruded from the crevice walls and slipped over the damp stones. Great clumps of moss hung from the boulders like the great shaggy beards of old men. And tiny, translucent moths hovered and fluttered amid the mist. When the light caught their wings, they looked like dancing teardrops.

The scene was so tranquil and so beautiful that it made Gwyneth's heart ache. She didn't know what it ached for, but to be privileged to see that much beauty felt like a priceless gift. She stood in silence just watching, enjoying the first real peace she had felt in her entire life. Then the guilt and shame overwhelmed her. She had killed two boys who had tried to rape her. Now, she felt dirty and tainted—unclean. She unconsciously wiped her hands on her trousers at the memory of the warm, sticky blood.

A messenger came splashing up the creek, and Gwyneth hurried to wake Finola. Iain refused to be wakened, and Finola wrapped him back in the furs before attending to the messenger.

"My lady," the messenger said. "The pass is blocked."

"Blocked?"

"Just as our men arrived," he said, "there was a great avalanche from both sides of the gorge. There's no way through."

"That seems like too much of a coincidence," Finola said. "They didn't see anyone else there?"

The messenger shrugged. "This means the Bracari will have to either go back and come around by way of Bracken Moor or go south to the Dale road. Either way, they can't get here for another three or four days at the earliest."

Vengeance

Finola nodded as Gwyneth suppressed a smile of relief.

"Craig asks you to continue with your fortifications at all possible speed."

"We will," Finola said. "Thank him for keeping us informed. I'll be down later today for another load of supplies."

The messenger bowed to her and saluted before hurrying back through the crevice.

"Are there Keldi gods or demons up there in that pass?" Finola asked Gwyneth.

Gwyneth shrugged. "I've never seen any of them," she said. "Until I do, I'm not going to worry about them."

Finola gave a short laugh. "That's probably wise," she said. "Well, how do you propose we keep the Bracari from coming down from above?" She gazed at the top of the crevice some fifty feet above them. "I was thinking of rock walls, but it seems like a bad idea to provide them with stones to drop on our heads."

"Pits," Gwyneth said. "To guard our back door." She was thinking about the way Taegan and her followers guarded the back entrance to their cave.

Finola elbowed her and winked. "I knew you had a soft spot for the cute little boy. What was his name?"

"Jason," Gwyneth said.

"Pits it is then," Finola said.

Worry gnawed at Brion as he sat wrapped in his camouflage cloak, peering out over the glistening waters of the Blackwater River. What if he had made the wrong decision? What if even now Finola was fighting for her life? He never should have brought her into the heathland again. He should have been more careful. And what of his mother? Arno had said she was hiding in the Aveens. What if the Bracari, or the men Jenna seemed to think were still looking for his mother, found her before he did? Now that the war had begun, Brion might never get another chance to find her. She might disappear forever. What if Emyr had underestimated Tristan and run right into his snares? So much was at stake, and it looked like Brion might lose everything.

The full light of morning rose over the heathland, casting a pale light over the still-smoking battlefield to their north. From the high ground where he sat with York and the Salassani leaders, they watched as Tristan's camp came back to life. They were prepared for him to send out patrols to locate their position, but they hoped to delay a confrontation until Reed arrived.

Brion glanced at York, who had remained silent since they returned from the raid. "Where did you go last night?" he whispered.

York didn't look up. He studied the toes of his boots that poked out from beneath his cloak.

"York?" Brion asked again.

"I killed him," York said.

Brion stared at him, trying to understand what he meant. They had all killed men last night. Then he understood. "The prince?"

York kept studying his boots.

"You thought he was Tristan?" Brion asked.

York raised his head. His gaze was steady. "I thought if I could kill Tristan, this war would end. He deserves to die."

Brion bobbed his head in agreement. "Probably. And if you had killed him, his son would have just kept fighting. I met him once."

"The prince?" York asked.

"Yep, and he was arrogant and murderous and intent on destroying Coll. He was one of those men who values no one's life but his own."

"Then it was good that I killed him?" York sounded like he needed Brion to give him permission to not feel guilty for murdering someone.

Brion pursed his lips. "I think Emyr would tell you that he had to die before peace would come to the heathland," he said. "But I have to tell you that I think you're either one of the bravest men I've ever known or you're completely insane."

York jerked his head up in surprise.

"You walked into an enemy camp and into the king's own tent to murder him in the middle of a desperate war without telling anyone what you were doing or having any idea how you might get out," Brion said. "That's either brave or crazy. And it's a little stupid."

York didn't smile like Brion thought he might.

"You would have done it too if he had killed your father," York said.

Brion opened his mouth to say that he wouldn't, but he closed it. He understood how York felt. He *had* felt it. He *still* felt it.

"Look," Brion said. "You can't keep doing things like that, or you're just going to get yourself killed."

York shrugged. "A man who can't avenge his own is no kind of man."

Brion nodded in understanding. Who was he to tell York he couldn't follow his conscience and avenge his father? Besides, Brion had felt exactly the same about Weyland and Rosland, his adoptive parents, and then about Neahl. He knew the hollow ache and bitter anger of having loved ones taken from you before their time.

"All right," Brion said. "But will you at least consult with me next time before you go off to do something crazy?"

Now York smiled. "Like running off into the mountains to look for my mother in the middle of a civil war?"

Brion shook his head and chuckled. "That's not fair," he said. "I didn't know there was gonna be a civil war going on."

York straightened and pointed down the Blackwater towards the ford. "What are they doing?"

Brion followed his gaze to see the Dunkeldi army marching off toward Ballach. Flankers spread out on either side, but they made no attempt to find those that had raided their camp in the night. They hadn't even collected all the horses that Brion's men had stampeded.

"Looks like a retreat," Brion said.

"But why? What about their ambush?"

Brion gave a short laugh. "I think you scared him," he said.

York gaped at him.

"I think Tristan understands that it is mere chance that he is alive this morning," Brion said.

"So he's just going to leave?"

"Maybe he knows about Emyr," Brion said. Then he looked at York. "You feel like a nice long ride?" he asked.

"You think Arno was wrong, don't you?" York said.

Brion nodded. "This wasn't much of an ambush. I think Tristan knows Emyr is up to something, and Emyr has left himself vulnerable."

"What about Dunraven?" York asked.

Brion frowned. "I have to trust Finola and Arno," he said. But that horrible, gnawing worry still clutched at his heart. If the Bracari had already attacked, there would be nothing he could do.

In another hour, Brion had divested himself of his heavy mail shirt and iron helmet. He had informed the Salassani leader that he intended to ride after Emyr, had captured six of the horses the Dunkeldi left behind, and set out with York over the heathland at a mile-eating canter. The horses would be able to keep that pace for a good while, and, when one tired, they could switch mounts. Everything now depended on speed.

The skies split open with a crack of thunder and a flash of light. Gwyneth scrambled off her bed to stand at the entrance to the cavern as the rain pounded the earth. It had been two days since they had come to stay at the crevice and seven since Brion and the army had left. The rhythmic hammering of the storm echoed in the crevice like the sound of a million drums. An oppressive darkness settled over the narrow canyon, illuminated only by the brilliant flashes of light.

"Let's go," Finola yelled over the noise as she pushed past her.

"What?" Gwyneth called.

"The supplies," Finola yelled over her shoulder. "We have to get the supplies up higher. This crevice is going to fill with water."

Finola called to anyone that could hear her. "Get the children to the higher caves," she said. "Then come back for the supplies."

Shadows scurried about in the darkness, lit now and then by a brilliant flash of blue-white light. The boom of the thunder shook the ground. Gwyneth followed Finola into the storm.

A flash of lighting revealed that the once-pleasant, little stream was now a rolling, bucking torrent that spit up spray as it crashed into the rocks and fallen logs. The supplies had been stacked at the base of the caves to be relocated the next day. They had already spent three days hauling them over from the keep and in fortifying the caves with walls of stone and logs.

People rushed past her, trying to keep their feet from slipping on the treacherously slick ground, carrying children and wooden boxes or bags of supplies. Gwyneth joined them. The rain beat so hard on her head that it hurt, and a wind ripped through the crevice, casting up a haunting moan that mingled with the hammering rain and the crashing thunder.

The work was only halfway finished when the dull roar penetrated the pounding wail of the storm. At first, Gwyneth thought she had only imagined it. But as she glanced over her shoulder, a flash of lightning that lingered and crackled as it spread its fingers across the sky revealed that the water was rapidly rising in the creek. Boxes lifted on the churning stream and floated away.

Gwyneth tried to scramble to safety over the slippery boulders, when someone screamed. The sound of it was barely audible in the tumult around them, but Gwyneth paused and gazed back up the creek. Another flash of lightning revealed a wall of water filled with debris racing toward them with an ever-increasing rumble of anger. In that instant of clear light, Gwyneth saw Clidna scrambling over a pile of rocks with a baby in her arms in a desperate attempt to escape the flood.

Gwyneth dropped her box and ran a few steps toward Clidna, but she slipped and fell hard. She slid a few feet over the moss-covered stones until her clutching fingers caught a root and jerked her to a stop.

"Clidna!" Finola cried. The agonizing despair in Finola's voice jerked the tears to Gwyneth's eyes before the growl of the flood drowned out the entire world. The gushing water snatched at Gwyneth's legs, and she scrambled and clawed her way up the impossibly slippery bank. The flood wanted her. It reached for her and clutched at her boots, trying to drag her down and swallow her alive. She held on with a desperation she hadn't felt since her mother died.

The next flash of lightning revealed that the place where Clidna had been standing was now a seething, churning rush of black water. Gwyneth buried her head in her outstretched arms and wept as the water licked at her boots.

Morning broke into the crevice with a pale gray light that revealed the scale of the destruction. The creek still churned its way through the chasm, skipping and spitting its way past new piles of debris. The stone and log barricades they had erected were gone. All around, the discouraged crowd huddled together, soaked to the skin and shivering.

Finola cradled Iain in her lap. She didn't speak, but her eyes were red and puffy. She had sent scouts out at the first hint of light to search for Clidna and the two dozen others that had been swept away in the flood. They had lost half of their supplies. If the Bracari came now, they could do little to oppose them.

Tristan, king of the Dunkeldi, swept through the gates and under the portcullis of his city of Ballach. His horse clattered over the cobblestone streets and up to the guardhouse. He had ridden hard for three days, leaving all but his close guard behind. His kingly clothes were travel-worn and battle-stained, but he didn't have time for the niceties of royal presentation. His army had been defeated by an inferior force, ambushed where no Alamani should have been, and his son murdered not ten feet away from him in his own tent. On his way east, he had received word that another Alamani army was even now marching on his city. His spy system had failed him. His intelligence had all been wrong, and someone was going to pay.

"Captain!" he bellowed.

When the guards recognized him, they scrambled to attention. Tristan sneered at them. These baser sorts were always the same. They shirked their duties whenever he wasn't around.

"Your majesty," the captain said. "We had no word."

"Clearly," Tristan said. "I want every soldier in the city prepared for a siege. Call up the militias immediately."

"My lord?"

"The Alamani are coming," Tristan said. "Now do it."

The man saluted and disappeared inside to scribble out the orders.

Tristan and his guard wove their way through the streets. The clip of their horses' hooves on the cobblestones rang off the buildings. Pedestrians struggled to get out of the way. Those that didn't were trodden down. Tristan had no time for nonsense. His throne was threatened. That upstart king who had been raised a peasant dared to invade the lands of the Dunkeldi.

"Open the gates," he bellowed as they neared the palace. Nothing happened until he pounded on the door.

"It's the king," someone shouted. The gates swung wide, and he galloped in. He leapt from the saddle, screaming orders to his steward, who rushed out to meet him in a flutter of robes.

"Prepare the royal carriage," Tristan said. "And supplies for at least two months. Send to have the treasury secured and prepared to be moved."

The horns sounded to signal the closing of the city gates. Tristan strode across the courtyard. He would hold the city to the last man, but he had to be sure that his line continued. If he had to ship his family to the mainland for safety, he would.

Someone shouted and pointed. Tristan gazed up at three flaming arrows that arced through the sky from within the city walls and toward the bay beyond. The clash of steel and the harsh cries of battle echoed from somewhere in the city. Tristan cursed. The traitors were already in his city.

"Where is the queen?" he demanded.

The steward bowed his head, unwilling to look at Tristan.

"In her chambers, I believe," he said.

"Do as I ordered," Tristan said and swept past him. How could he tell his wife that he had failed to protect their son—the heir to the throne? Still, it had to be done, and she and the children had to be spirited away before the siege began.

Tristan leapt up the stairs two at a time and rushed down the carpeted hallway. The guards at the queen's door saluted him, but he ignored them. He burst into the room and came to a stop. On a chair in his wife's antechamber, sat a trail-worn man with sandy-brown hair and a growth of fine stubble on his chin. He wore a simple mail shirt and watched Tristan with a steady gaze. Tristan stared, incredulous. It couldn't be.

Brion crouched on the banks of the Blackwater River, gazing over the water to the high walls of the city of Ballach. The smell of wet earth and fish filled his nostrils. The mosquitoes attacked with a fury that nearly drove him from the water's edge. Watch fires blazed on the ramparts, and the silhouettes of soldiers pacing the walls stood out against the graying sky of evening.

It had taken them three days of hard riding that had killed three of their horses. He had spared Misty as much as he could, but she was exhausted. They left her and the surviving horses to graze and rest along the bank.

The area around Ballach was thickly settled, and they had startled more than one farmer as they sped past his home. With so much movement coming to and from Ballach, the farmers and village people had simply ignored them unless Brion stopped to question them.

A steady line of country folk filed into the city because they had received word of Hayden's army. No one Brion asked could tell them about a Salassani party, and Brion was starting to wonder if they had miscalculated again. Maybe Emyr had gone to meet Hayden, and they had risked their lives for nothing. But Tristan was definitely there. A villager told Brion the king had entered the city not long before Brion had arrived. Apparently, Tristan had been riding hard and, by taking the road, had made better time than Brion and York.

A horn sounded clear and brassy on the still evening air, and the gates of the city began to close. A protest arose from the crowd still waiting to enter, but the gates snapped shut.

"Do you think Emyr is in there?" York asked.

Brion shook his head. "I don't know," he said. "Emyr had better be in there." If he had left Finola to fight on her own for no good reason, he would never be able to live with himself.

"You wouldn't happen to know how to get across the river and get into the city, would you?" York asked.

Brion scowled at him. "I might just toss you over the wall," he snapped.

York grinned. "You have no idea, do you?" he said. York tossed a stick in the river and swatted at the mosquitoes. "Looks like you're gonna have to swim." He said this like it would be a real treat to watch Brion swim the dark waters of the river. "It's only about a hundred paces across."

The river had widened considerably and flowed into a huge bay just visible beyond the city. This was the closest to the ocean Brion had ever been, and he had to suppress the desire to go down to see the bay. He had never been able to imagine what the ocean would look like. But now was not the time to satisfy his curiosity.

Several long wharves pushed out into the water with dozens of boats tied to them. A few boats still rowed about. The frogs had come out to fill the air with a deafening racket. One plopped into the water at his feet. Brion didn't know if he could swim that far. And even if they did, he had no idea how to get into the city.

"Let's try to find a boat," he said.

"Do you know how to row a boat?" York asked.

Brion regarded him. The one and only time he had been in a boat, Tyg had nearly drowned him.

"No," he admitted.

"Me neither," York said. He was clearly enjoying this. "We could just wait until daylight and try to sneak in with the crowd."

Brion considered. That way, he wouldn't have to risk swimming the river.

"You have to face your fear," York said.

Brion scowled at him. "I thought we already went through this."

"We did," York said. "But some people take longer to learn than others."

Brion smiled despite himself. "You're as annoying as Neahl used to be."

He gazed at the walls again, when three flaming arrows arced up and over the walls and out into the bay. Brion followed the arc of flame until they disappeared.

"What does that mean?" York asked.

"Listen," Brion said.

Cries and shouting rose up over the walls. Faint at first, but then they grew louder. The clash of steel rang over the water.

"He's insane," Brion said. "Emyr is completely insane. He's trying to carry out a coup in Tristan's capital city without his own army anywhere near the place. We have to find a way in."

York started stripping off his clothes.

Tristan waited, unsure what he should do as he stared at the man sitting in the chair in his wife's chambers. He didn't know where his wife and children were. If he attacked, they might be killed.

"It's over," the man said.

Tristan straightened. "Where is the queen?"

"She's safe."

Tristan stepped forward, and the man came to his feet.

"I want to see my wife and children," Tristan said.

"I can't allow that," the man said.

"What do you want?"

"Your surrender." The man gazed calmly at Tristan, as if the fact that he was sitting in the queen's chambers armed with a sword and a knife was a matter of little importance.

"Who are you?" Tristan demanded.

The man didn't move. His eyes narrowed. "You know who I am," he said, "and you know what has to happen now."

Tristan stepped back and drew his sword. "Guards!" he called. He was certain now. It was Emyr, the boy-king of the Alamani. The one who had helped the raiders escape after attacking the Great Keldi and trying to assassinate Tristan himself.

No one answered his call. Tristan turned to see the guards standing in the doorway with their own swords drawn.

"What is this?" he demanded.

"I warned you," Emyr said. "I warned you that I had lived under your rule and that I knew how to break it." He paused. "You have never learned to value human life or loyalty. Your rule is so weak that I had trouble finding anyone who *was* loyal to you."

"Get out," Tristan said. "You filthy upstart. You murdered my son."

Emyr showed no recognition. "I had nothing to do with your son's death, but you'll receive no sympathy from the thousands of mothers and wives who will be mourning the loss of their husbands and sons because you refused to accept an honorable peace when I offered it to you."

"You Alamani dog!" Tristan spat. "Don't speak to me of peace when the Alamani have been nibbling away at my kingdom for generations."

"What happened in the past," Emyr said, "neither you nor I can control. But your willful slaughter of the Salassani and the Carpentini and your butchery of the people of Laro Forest cannot go unanswered."

Tristan glanced at the guards.

"You would be unwise to resist," Emyr said. "Even now, I have three armies converging on Ballach. My fleet holds your harbor. I hold your palace."

Tristan spun and slashed at the guards. They fell back with cries of surprise, and he barreled past them. "Guards," he yelled as he ran.

They couldn't all betray him. He was their king.

"What are you doing?" Brion demanded as York stripped off his clothes.

"Unless you want to get everything wet," York said, "you're gonna have to strip."

Brion stared at him. "What about our clothes and weapons? You aren't seriously thinking of going in there with nothing but our skins?"

York laughed out loud, and Brion had to hush him.

"We tie our clothes and weapons in a bundle and carry them on our heads," York said. "That's how my family escaped the first Bracari raid that destroyed our village."

Brion wasn't convinced he could swim all that way with one arm, but what choice did he have? He couldn't leave his weapons behind, and he didn't have time to deal with a wet bow and bowstring. It was a good thing he had left his helmet and mail shirt behind. He couldn't swim the river with sixty pounds of armor on his head. Brion gathered his last quiver of arrows from Misty's saddle and stripped off his boots and clothes. He rolled the clothes around his sword and bow into a bundle, but he left the sheath knife strapped to the nape of his neck because one never knew. When he finished, he stood at the river bank up to his ankles in mud, feeling more vulnerable than he had ever felt in his life.

"You hold it on your head with one hand and swim with the other," York said.

"It's that easy?" Brion said.

"There's probably a current, but if you angle against it, you should be fine."

"Get on with it," Brion said.

York walked out into the river. His skin was so white that it almost glowed in the darkness. Brion often forgot how small York was. York slipped into the water and began to swim. Brion took a deep, steadying breath and followed. The cold nearly ripped the breath from his throat and his head almost submerged. He sputtered and splashed until he found the stroke, and he set out after York, who was a much stronger swimmer. Brion found himself carried downriver with the current and had to fight the panic that he would be swept out into the endless ocean. He kicked hard and tried to remember what York had taught him.

By the time he reached the shadows of the wharf and was able to get a hand on the ropes that trailed down in the river, he had swallowed a considerable quantity of water and was shivering with cold. He splashed and slipped his way free of the water and collapsed onto the grass. He hadn't kept his clothes dry, but at least his weapons weren't wet.

York strode up to him already fully clothed. "I was starting to wonder if you were going to make it," he said.

"Oh, shut up," Brion said.

From here, the clamor of battle from inside the city could be clearly heard. It sounded like a desperate fight. Brion glanced up at the walls. The fires still blazed, but he couldn't see any guards. He stood and slipped into his clothes and stomped into his boots. The clothes clung to his still-wet body, but he didn't have time to worry about it.

He strapped on his sword and slipped on his quiver before turning away from the gate to search for some way to scale the walls. He considered the refuse heap that protruded from beside one of the round bastions like a stinking cancer, but even if he could stomach the climb, he had no rope or hook to toss over the wall. He rounded the bastion and stopped. He pushed York back as York tried to step around him.

A group of men and some women stood at the foot of the walls. Someone was working their way down a rope that dangled from a window high above. A boat stood nearby, pulled up on the grass. Brion waited until the person was down and the others were pushing the boat out to the river. For a moment, he wondered if it was Tristan and his family trying to escape, but then he noticed that one of them wore a mottled cloak just like the one Arno wore.

Brion stepped out of the shadows. "Do you carry a rook?" he asked.

A woman covered a strangled cry, and the men jerked knives from their sheaths. But the man in the mottled cloak turned slowly to gaze at Brion. His hood concealed his face. Brion pulled the little piece of cloth from his pocket and held it out to the man.

Vengeance

"Mind if we use your rope?" Brion asked.

The man stepped up to Brion until the moonlight lit his face. He was young, not many years older than Brion, and he was smiling.

"Be my guest," he said. "But watch the trapdoor by the window. It isn't secure."

"Thanks," Brion said. He stuffed the cloth back in his pocket.

The man gave him a slight bow and returned to his group. Brion waited until they had pushed off and the current had carried them away before he stepped over to tug on the rope. It seemed secure.

"And you were worried we couldn't get in," he said to York.

York gazed up at the black window. "I went first last time," he said. "After you."

Brion grimaced and jumped up to pull himself up the rope. After the swim across the river, the climb was nearly more than Brion could handle. It never ceased to amaze him how tiring swimming was. He dragged himself over the sill of the window and searched the floor for the trapdoor the spy had warned him about before setting his feet on the boards. Once he found it and was sure he wouldn't plummet to his death, he clambered through and peered out the window as York began his ascent. Brion slipped to the door, opened it a crack, and peeked out. A set of wooden stairs led down over the top of structures built up against the walls. The fighting came from somewhere near the center of the city. A group of soldiers rushed past in the darkened streets below.

Three days after the storm, Jason, the boy that had helped them escape the caves, appeared on the lip of the crevice, gazing down on Finola's band of women. At first, Gwyneth didn't recognize him. He just stood there, motionless, as if he were waiting for an invitation to join them. When Gwyneth waved at him, he disappeared for a moment. Then he returned and tossed a rope over the edge. He slid down with practiced ease and ambled over to where Gwyneth and several ladies were piling the last of the logs and stones on one of the barricades they were erecting in the cavern.

"What are you doing here?" Gwyneth asked before he could even open his mouth.

Jason smiled at her. He had little dimples in his cheeks and dark hair with gray eyes. When he grew up, he was going to be a good-looking man.

"Taegan sent me," he said.

Gwyneth frowned. "How did you know we were here?" The thought that their whereabouts could be so easily discovered was not comforting. They had been expecting the Bracari to come any day now, and, if Jason could find them, no Bracari was going to have a hard time.

Jason shrugged. "The storm got you, too," he said as he cast his gaze over the piles of debris.

"Yeah," Gwyneth said. She had been trying not to think about it. They had found Clidna's body but not the baby she had been carrying. It was bad enough that the Bracari were trying so desperately to exterminate them. It didn't seem fair the land itself should attack them, too.

"Taegan says I have to talk to Brion or Finola," Jason said.

"Okay," Gwyneth said. "Come on."

They found Finola supervising the construction on the barricade at the mouth of the crevice. This one was massive with huge wooden beams and piles of stone. A pit with sharp stakes had been excavated in front of it, beside the creek, and carefully covered. Only a narrow pathway along the creek permitted access, up against the face of the rock. They had also been digging pits all along the top of the crevice, where the rock would let them, and filling them with sharpened stakes.

Finola gave Jason a surprised glance. "Didn't we leave you on top of a cliff?" she asked.

"Taegan let me come," he said.

Finola nodded. "She let you? You came alone?"

"Sure," Jason said.

"So is she coming, too?"

Jason shook his head. "No, just me."

"Okay," Finola said. "Why did she send you?"

"She says that the storm washed out the old Dale road, and the Bracari are having trouble."

"Which means?" Finola asked.

"It will take them longer to get here."

"How long?"

Jason shrugged. "With the rain and our traps, maybe a few more days."

"Traps?" Gwyneth asked.

"Taegan says we're going to make their lives miserable," Jason beamed. "Our warriors are ambushing them and setting traps for them."

"Okay," Finola said. "So we have a few more days to get ready. How many Bracari are there?"

"Our scouts counted fifteen hundred."

"That's more than Craig's scouts reported," Gwyneth said.

"Thanks," Finola said. "Are you going to stay with us?"

"No. I have to get back."

"By yourself?"

Jason scowled looked offended. "I go lots of places by myself," he said. He turned to head back up the chasm to his rope.

"Oh," he said and he spun around. "I almost forgot. Don't eat the meat."

Finola and Gwyneth exchanged glances.

"Our men will be bringing it," Jason said. "Just don't eat it, any of it. Don't even touch it." Then he jogged back up the crevice.

Chapter 15
The Storm

handful of guards spilled out of a nearby corridor in response to Tristan's calls.

"Yes, Sire?" one of them questioned.

"The palace is under assault!" Tristan yelled. "There are traitors behind me."

Some of the guards paused and looked back, but the rest fell in behind the king. Tristan sneered. That boy-king didn't hold his palace. The sounds of fighting erupted behind him, but he hurried on. A few more loyal soldiers and nobles joined him as he emerged in the courtyard just inside the gates, where his personal guards were looking on in confusion. The sounds of battle echoed through the palace and filtered in from the streets all around it.

"Traitors are in the palace," he said. "And they have kidnapped the queen."

"Uh, Your Majesty?"

One of his guards pointed, and Tristan spun to see Emyr emerge from under the far archway that led to the more private parts of the palace. Behind him filed several hundred men. Most of them were Dunkeldi, but a few Salassani and Carpentini were among them.

Tristan glanced at the handful of men that had joined him. With his guards, he didn't have more than a hundred. Then his closest advisor stepped out of the crowd surrounding Emyr.

"Lord Nelson?" Tristan said. "What are you doing?"

Lord Nelson was a tall, powerful man with a short-cropped beard. He wore his glittering mail and was prepared for battle.

"You have squandered Dunkeldi lives and treasure for far too long," Lord Nelson said.

"I trusted you," Tristan said. This betrayal was wholly unexpected. He had grown up with Nelson. They had played together as boys. He had honored him and raised him to the second highest position in the land.

Nelson laughed. "You never trusted anyone. Nor did you care who you hurt in your pursuit of pleasure and power. Do you want me to list the names of the girls you ruined or beat to death? Do you want me to list the men you have assassinated because they stood in your way? Do you want me to explain how your reckless attacks on Coll have led this kingdom to the brink of ruin and wasted the lives of our best warriors?"

"Shut up! Traitor!" Tristan yelled. He pointed at Nelson. "Seize them," he ordered.

Brion helped York scramble through the window, and they were soon hurrying down the stairs and into the dark streets heading toward the center of the city. The crowds of people rushing in their direction slowed their progress. The snatches of conversation he picked up as he ran confused him.

"The king has gone mad."

"Treason."

"The city has fallen."

"I saw them spirit away the queen."

Brion didn't know what to make of the panic, but as they progressed up the streets, he was reminded again why he didn't like cities. The crowds were suffocating. The stench of human waste and garbage filled every breath. The buildings blotted out the stars. Since most of the buildings looked the same, it was easy to get turned around and confused.

Ballach wasn't as large as Chullish, but it still took them a good twenty minutes to push their way through the desperate crowds and the piles of deserted carts and overturned barrels to reach the center of the commotion. Torches blazed in their brackets. Bodies littered the cobblestone streets in front of two square towers that guarded the gate to the palace. The gate had been flung open, and a few men milled about the entrance, apparently confused or uncertain what to do. The roof of one of the towers was in flames. The roar of it competed with the sounds of fighting, and its heat even reached the street where Brion and York stood.

Tristan's guard struggled with Emyr's men who fell back through the archway into the smaller courtyard beyond. The clamor of battle rang off the walls. Tristan watched as the battle surged back and forth before he spun to mount the stairs in the tower opposite the family quarters. He had to see that the treasury was still secure. Maybe he could bargain for the life of his queen and his children, or at least smuggle out enough money to raise another army. He would live to fight another day. He hadn't grown up in the rough and tumble of court politics without learning to respond flexibly to unexpected crises.

Three of his guards followed him as he raced down the hallway. Through the glass windows, he caught glimpses of the fighting that had spread out over the courtyard and burst into the rooms and buildings that surrounded it. Tristan had nearly reached the end of the long hallway when Emyr stepped out in front of him.

Emyr must be in there somewhere, Brion thought as he jogged up to the men who were loitering around the gate.

"What's happening?" he said.

The gate opened onto a wide, square courtyard lined by tall buildings all around. Great, decorative arches of black stone supported the buildings above. Opposite the gate, a narrow archway led into some other part of the palace. Bodies lay scattered in crumpled heaps, and the sounds of fighting still echoed from beyond the little gate. The upper windows of the buildings were covered in glass— something Brion had only seen in Chullish and Mailag. Clearly, this palace had not been attacked in so many years that no one had bothered to keep it defensible.

Either the men at the gate didn't notice in the darkness that Brion wasn't Dunkeldi or they didn't care.

"There's a coup," one of them said.

"I heard it was the Alamani king," another said.

"Where are they?" Brion asked.

The men shrugged. Apparently, they weren't too concerned about the coup. For them, it probably didn't matter too much who the king was, so long as they didn't get entangled in the bloodletting.

"Where are the king's chambers?" Brion asked.

One of them pointed to the buildings opposite them before another slapped his hand down.

The second one peered at Brion more closely. "Why do you want to know?" he asked.

"We're in the king's guard," Brion said.

The man's gaze ran over Brion's clothes. "Where are your colors?" he said.

"No time to put them on," Brion said.

York glanced at him and tried not to smile. Brion didn't tell them which king he had come to protect.

Tristan cursed.

"I told you that it's over," Emyr said.

"And yet you can see that it is not," Tristan said. "Now get out of my way or I'll run you through."

A smile played on Emyr's lips. "Before you die," Emyr said, "I want you to remember that Mortegai raised me and trained me. I claim your life in return for his."

Tristan had known Mortegai well. He had been agitating for Salassani independence and had been a thorn in Tristan's side ever since the last heath war when Mortegai had lost his son. Mortegai had needed to die.

Tristan rushed Emyr with a cry of rage, but the boy-king was swift and strong. In moments, Tristan realized that the boy was more than a match for him. "Guards," he yelled, and the three men with him rushed in. Emyr fell back as one of the guards slipped past his flurry of defense to wound him in the thigh. The blood darkened Emyr's trousers. Emyr didn't seem to notice. He swept in close and dispatched two of Tristan's guard before Tristan could stop him. Soon, only Tristan and one guard were left. Emyr occupied a narrow doorway that only allowed one of them to attack at a time. Then Tristan saw him.

A Dunkeldi warrior with a bloodied head skulked along the edge of the corridor. He had a sword in one hand and a knife in the other. Tristan renewed his attack to distract Emyr. The Dunkeldi raised his sword for the killing blow.

Brion sprinted across the courtyard and into the narrow stairwell. It wound around to the right and came out in a hallway paved with white stone. Oil lamps burned in sconces along the walls. Rich tapestries and fine furnishings demonstrated that Tristan didn't spare expenses on the outward display of his wealth and power.

York gawked. "People live in this?" he asked.

"Yeah," Brion said as he rushed down the hallway, checking the rooms on either side. Bodies lay in pools of blood, and men crouched against the walls, bent over their injuries. There had been fighting here, but Emyr was nowhere to be seen. Toward the end of the hallway, a door stood open, and a body lay across the threshold. Brion slid to a stop and stuck his head in.

The room was dark, but, as he scanned the room, his gaze was drawn through the window to the rooms on the other side of the courtyard. A series of windows blazed with light, and there in the middle was Emyr fighting for his life and apparently alone. Brion cursed. He couldn't reach him in time. He leapt through the doorway, grabbed up a chair, and threw it through the window. It burst in a shower of tinkling glass. A shadow appeared behind Emyr. A sword raised. Brion whipped an arrow from his quiver, drew, and loosed.

Glass shattered, and the injured man sneaking up on Emyr lurched sideways. Tristan jumped back. Glass shattered again, and his guard's cry of surprise was cut off by a strangled gurgling as an arrow appeared in his throat. Tristan glanced through the broken window to see a man and boy far across the courtyard. An arrow slammed into Tristan's side, driving through his mail shirt and padded gambeson. He staggered back but knew that it wasn't a killing stroke. His mail and padded shirt protected him. Something silver flashed. Glass tinkled. Pain slammed into his head, and he was falling—falling into darkness.

Brion stared as Tristan fell. Emyr turned toward Brion and York to gaze at them through the broken windows. A smile spread over Brion's face. He raised his bow in a salute to his king. York touched his forehead in the Carpentini sign of respect. Emyr raised his sword in return and then disappeared down the hallway.

Brion scowled at York. "You nearly took my head off with that stone," he said.

York grinned. "I knew you wouldn't be able to handle him without my help," he said.

Brion smirked at him. "Come on," he said. "Let's find Emyr before he gets into trouble again."

They found Emyr deep in conversation with a Dunkeldi noble. The man was tall and handsome. He wore bright mail that hung down to this knees and high leather boots. When Emyr saw them approaching, he waved them over.

"Thank you," Emyr said.

"You just ran off in the middle of the battle," Brion said. "We thought you had been killed."

Emyr ignored him. "This is Lord Nelson," Emyr said. "He will be acting as regent now that Tristan is dead."

Lord Nelson gave them a slight bow.

Brion returned it. Then he spoke to Emyr. "Can I talk to you alone?"

Emyr nodded, grabbed Brion's elbow and strode several paces away. York followed.

"You're crazy," Brion began without any prelude. "We've been chasing you halfway across the island, and you decide to take the king on all by yourself in his own palace?"

"Nice to see you, too," Emyr said. "But I was doing fine without you."

"Ha!" Brion laughed.

Emyr grinned at him. "Is he always like this now, York?"

York nodded. "You should see him when he's swimming."

Brion grimaced at York.

"Listen," Emyr said. "I'm sorry I didn't tell you what I was doing earlier, but I couldn't. It was too dangerous—and speed was of the essence."

"Yeah, I know," Brion said. "But, instead of riding off without a word to anyone, you could have least told us not to bother looking for you because you would be lounging in a palace while we were fighting for our lives."

"Well," Emyr said. "I'm not the only one with spies."

"Ewan is working for him," Brion said.

"I know," Emyr said.

"So how are you going to hold the city," Brion asked, "while you wait for Reed and Hayden to show up?"

Emyr gestured for Lord Nelson to rejoin them. "Lord Nelson has control of the city's guard," he said. "And my fleet is landing four thousand soldiers as we speak."

Brion gaped at him. "You must have emptied the whole of Coll to build this army. That makes more than fourteen thousand men," he said.

"Not quite," Emyr said. He smiled and winked at York. "While Brion has been honeymooning at Wexford and frolicking around the heathland, I've been building up my army because I knew Tristan wasn't finished."

"Right," Brion said with a smirk. "Now what?"

Emyr glanced at Lord Nelson. "We can handle it from here," he said to Brion. "I need you two to go back to Dunraven. Find Reed and take him and the army back with you."

Brion frowned. "You've heard about the Bracari, then?" he asked.

"Yes. And I'm afraid you might already be too late."

Brion nodded. "We'll leave now," he said.

Emyr grabbed Brion's arm and pulled him aside. "I'm sorry," he said. "I never should have taken you away from there."

"We didn't know," Brion said.

"I want you to know that I've named you and Brigid as regents for our child should I die," Emyr said.

This took Brion by surprise. "But the war is almost over," Brion said.

Emyr gave him a wry smile. "I have more enemies now than ever," he said. "And I can't leave here until the Taurini and Bracari are dealt with."

"Okay," Brion said.

"Now get going," Emyr said. "Take any horses you need from the royal stables. Tell Reed and the rest of the men with him that I order them to return to Dunraven to do what they can." He paused. "I just hope you're in time."

Brion hugged Emyr briefly, and he and York raced toward the city gates. It would take them at least seven days, probably more, to reach Dunraven Keep.

We can't go on like this, Gwyneth thought. She swallowed the bile that rose in her throat as she looked down with revulsion at the still-twitching form of the latest poison victim. Finola was already rationing the food, and people were scraping roots from the ground and picking every edible plant they could find.

A day after Jason's visit, the deer carcasses began to appear scattered throughout the valley. They had even been left on the green in front of the crevice. Despite Finola's orders not to eat it, the hungry people had collected some and now those who had eaten it were dying in droves. At least twenty people had died in the last two days.

The constant worry of the Bracari raid that never came, the pressing hunger, and living in the damp conditions of the crevice were wearing on everyone. Gwyneth worried that, if the Bracari didn't come soon, the people wouldn't be strong enough to fight— or worse, they would be fighting each other.

Gwyneth gazed out into the gathering darkness. The huge black stain on the hillside where Reed had burned the bodies of the Bracari after the first battle at the crevice marred the landscape. It had been twelve days since York and Brion had left them. She wondered how they had fared in the battle with the Dunkeldi king. Had York been in the fighting? It wouldn't matter if she couldn't survive this new Bracari attack.

She glanced at the dying young woman and turned away. She couldn't stand around watching them die any longer. If they couldn't eat the carcasses left near the crevice, then she would need to hunt for a deer that wasn't tainted with poison.

York learned how to sleep in the saddle. The exhaustion seeped so deeply into his bones, that it was easy so long as the horse didn't do anything unexpected. The heathland rolled under him without him even noticing. Mile after weary mile the horses alternated between walking, trotting, and cantering. Brion had found Reed and the army two days out from Ballach and had turned the entire column around. Reed and all the Carpentini, Salassani, and Alamani who had been in the first battle raced for Dunraven Keep. They seized every horse they could find and rode until it collapsed and then jumped onto another. Some men fell behind from exhaustion or lack of horses, but Brion, York, and Reed pushed on. Brion had left Misty behind after the second day rather than ride her to death.

"She'll find her way," Brion had said, but York had seen the look of concern in Brion's face. He loved that horse almost as much as he loved Finola.

Gwyneth knelt beside the little deer. It had bolted off into the trees after she had shot it, and it had taken her more than an hour to find it. It smelled of musk and blood. She suppressed the sense of pride that filled her chest as she looked at her kill. She would be able to feed many hungry mouths with this deer.

She had been delayed in setting out until late in the afternoon, but if she hurried, she could still return in time to provide a nice hot supper for all those hungry children. Gwyneth grunted as she hefted the deer over her shoulders and trudged back toward the chasm into the fading light. The sun's slanting rays sent long shadows stretching through the forest. A thin mist drifted in from the hills above. She broke from the trees and tried to pick up her pace as the shadows lengthened. The journey back was much farther than she had expected, and she knew that Finola would be wondering where she was.

A haunting noise rose up on the whisper of the breeze. Gwyneth stopped to listen. For a moment, it sounded like the low rumble of thunder. She glanced up at the cloudless sky. A few stars were beginning to appear. She faced the sound and realized it was a chorus of baying hounds. The sound rang over the hills.

Terror gripped at Gwyneth's throat, and she broke into a jog. The Bracari had finally come, and they had brought their war hounds with them. The weight of the deer slowed her progress, but she couldn't leave it behind. It meant too much to the hungry people in the crevice. They would need it now more than ever.

The warning horn from the keep echoed through the trees. They must have heard the baying of the hounds, as well. Gwyneth ran until her throat burned and her legs wanted to buckle. She slowed to a hurried walk, gasping for air as the baying grew louder. Almost everyone in the crevice had been out searching for food. They were scattered over the landscape. Would they make it back in time? The baying came from right behind her now, and Gwyneth realized she wouldn't make it—not if she kept trying to carry the deer, while still wearing her mail shirt. She dropped down into the last mist-filled hollow before the crevice and struggled over the jumble of stones and through the thick briars that tore at her skin.

Someone in the distance screamed before the sound was drowned in an eruption of barking and snarling. Gwyneth dropped the deer as the panic clutched at her heart. She pushed through the last of the undergrowth and sprinted into the fog that drifted over the green hill. The dark opening of the crevice stood two hundred paces away, like a yawning mouth. Something crashed into the trees behind her. Snarling sounded, and she could hear the bones of the deer snapping in the powerful jaws of the hounds. She chanced a glance back as two more hounds broke from the cover of the trees and rushed at her—dark wraiths in the rising mist.

Gwyneth ripped an arrow from her quiver and tried to nock it while she pelted through the moist haze. But she couldn't do it. The entrance was only a few more paces away when she spun, nocked the arrow, and loosed it into the lead hound. It yelped and careened off to the side, but the other came on. She struggled to get another arrow free of her quiver, when, as if by magic, an arrow appeared in the hound's chest. Its legs gave way, and it crashed to the earth, sliding right up to Gwyneth's feet. She stared at it.

"Get in here!" Finola shouted.

With one last glance at the twitching body of the dying hound, Gwyneth slipped around the pit and pushed through the gate. She glanced back to see groups of women and children rushing from all directions, pushing through the fog toward the chasm. Hounds bounded behind them. Their dark shapes disappeared into the mist only to reemerge and disappear again.

Some of the hounds stopped at the carcasses Jason's people had left and tore at the flesh, but others raced on. Gwyneth watched in horror as a mother struggling up the hill with a child fell under the weight of a hound. Her cry echoed over the hills.

Gwyneth whirled to stare at Finola and saw in her face the same horror that filled her own chest to bursting.

"We *have* to do something," Gwyneth said.

Finola nodded and called out to the women, "A dozen lancers and a dozen archers. Follow me."

Gwyneth followed Finola through the gate as the rest of the women rushed after her. They ran out about fifty paces from the gate to meet the terrified, fleeing women and children.

"Lancers, form a line," Finola ordered. "Protect the archers. Archers shoot them all."

For just a moment, Gwyneth thought she meant the people who were doomed to be killed by the dogs, but Finola was the first to shoot, and her arrow narrowly missed a young girl and buried itself in the side of a hound. The mist swirled, casting a ghostly, haunting aura around the chaos and terror that surged about them. Gwyneth aimed at a bounding shadow. She missed her first shot, but she made the second and third. People raced past them as arrows flew and dogs yelped in pain. Those hounds that had eaten the carcasses were stumbling about. Dogs surged around them, so many she couldn't keep track—all of them lean and hungry, looking as if the Bracari had starved them to make them more ferocious.

A hound snapped at the heels of an old woman and dragged her down. Her shrieks rent the air. The fog swirled in front of them, but Gwyneth shot at the shadow of the dog. It yelped and tore off into the mist. Then hounds were among them, bounding in and out of focus as the mist floated and swirled about them.

The lancers struggled to keep the hounds at bay as they retreated. Dozens of people collapsed under the snarling hounds without anyone being able to help them. Their cries filled the air along with the vicious snarling and barking. A hound leapt out of the fog and sprang onto a bowwoman with a snarl. Gwyneth spun and shot it in the back. Her arrow bit so deep that it punctured the bowwoman's hip. Blood seeped through her trousers. The bowwoman kicked the dog off and nodded her thanks to Gwyneth. She scrambled to her feet and limped back to join the rest of the women as they backed their way toward the entrance to the rock fissure.

The women guarded the gate as the stragglers who made it through the mob of hounds and the writhing vapor of cloud limped in. They waited. The cries and the screams of the dying filled the air. But there was nothing else they could do. A young girl staggered through the gate, weeping and holding one arm with a terrible gash. When no more figures waded through the fog, Finola ordered the women behind the barricade.

They closed the gate and barred it as dusk fell upon the horrible scene. Some of the hounds burst from the filmy haze to leap at the barricade, only to fall into the pit and be skewered on the sharpened stakes. Their whimpers of pain joined the terrible gut-wrenching noises of the dying out on the green field below the barricade that was now shrouded in concealing fog. Gwyneth sat on a boulder, dropped her head into her hands, and wept.

Cries of terror and shrieks of pain punctuated the long night as the hounds hunted down those who had tried to hide. Now and then, a hound would send up a long, deep-throated howl and others would take up the call. Some appeared to be haunting the crest of the keep as if they were searching for another way in. But the Bracari never came. They must have gone straight to the keep. Gwyneth drifted off to sleep near dawn, wondering how long the keep would hold.

All throughout the next day, the occasional sounds of battle would reach them, but mostly the keep was too far away for them to hear. Those with family in the keep begged Finola to send scouts to see what was happening, but she refused.

"With those hounds out there," she said, "and with the Bracari wandering the countryside, they would just be killed."

So they waited, hungry and exhausted, terrified of what the next hour might bring. Near dark, a man was seen just outside the tree line staring up at the crevice.

"They've found us," Gwyneth said.

The Bracari didn't come to the chasm that night. The next morning, a great booming echoed over the hills.

"What is that?" Gwyneth asked.

"A battering ram," one of the men said. "It won't be long now."

Finola ordered everyone to pull out the last of their food and prepare a hot meal at midday in preparation for the battle to come. At dusk, the figures began to appear, streaming from the forest in a long line. They came from the direction of the keep. At first, Gwyneth wondered why the Bracari would advance on them like that, until she recognized the women in the long, blue Carpentini skirts.

"It's our people," someone shouted. "They've escaped the keep."

"The keep has fallen," someone else said.

"Open the gates when they get here," Finola ordered. "We'll let in as many as we can."

They arrived in ones and twos and then in large groups. They crowded through the gate, and Finola sent them back up to the wide area farther in where there was more space. Gwyneth noticed that none of them brought much in the way of supplies. Soon, several hundred had crammed themselves through the gate. They kept coming long into the night. A few dozen battle-weary men made up the last of the stragglers, but Craig was not among them. By morning, the flood of refugees had ceased, and a deathly silence settled over the land around them.

Now they were alone. Brion, Emyr, and Reed had gone off with most of the warriors. The keep had fallen, and over four hundred men had fallen with it. It was only a matter of time now.

A trail of dead and lame horses straggled behind Brion and the scattered, disorganized column of riders. It was a grizzly testament to the desperation that drove them. Still, they covered in five days ground that should have taken them seven. On the sixth day, they encountered Carpentini refugees with the news that the keep was besieged. On the seventh day, the haggard survivors told tales of slaughter and butchery and of survivors fleeing to the crevice or being hunted and slain by the Bracari and their hounds. The keep had fallen and with it Brion's hopes that Finola was safe. Even if she was in the crevice, how long could they hold out with so few men and so many women and children? The agony of his choices drove like an arrow to his heart. Had he really sacrificed her to save Emyr and the kingdom? He should have gone back—at least he could have died fighting beside her.

The Bracari arrived on the open field before the crevice that afternoon sporting the heads of Carpentini and Salassani men on their spears as they gathered to taunt the survivors cowering in the crevice. They came dressed in their green tunics, surging from the trees along the bottom of the slope in an irresistible, green wave. Gwyneth struggled to swallow the knot of terror that choked her. How could the Carpentini survive? They were so weak, so few, and so unprepared. She and Finola had buckled their mail shirts about their waists, and Gwyneth had picked up some gauntlets. Other women wore the bits and pieces of armor they could find, but none of them were fully protected or even trained. Women outnumbered men by more than four to one. It was hopeless, but what choice did they have? There was nowhere left to run.

Finola arranged her archers so some could shoot over the barricade, while others were positioned along the crevice and the hollow to shoot any Bracari attempting to enter from the top. She had most of the men guarding the gate where the fighting would be the fiercest and where strength and experience would be needed. Lancers stood ready to thrust their spears through holes in the gate at any that approached too close, and slingers stood back from the barricade to take any that tried to clamber over the top. Barricades had been erected all along the crevice to provide places of retreat should the battle at the first barricade go ill.

The children were huddled in the deepest caves with a few women to watch over them. All the other women were armed—even those who hadn't participated in the training. Meredith commanded the women in the hollow. It was the best that could be done, and Gwyneth hoped it would be enough.

When their jeers and taunting received no reply, the Bracari dropped their trophies and made a few hesitant attempts at the gate.

Some climbed the hill and poked their heads over the rim only to receive an arrow in the face. They should have known they would be silhouetted against the sky.

Just before dusk, the Bracari made a concerted effort to overwhelm the gate. They roared as they rushed forward and threw themselves against it. The lancers thrust their spears through and the archers shot until they were exhausted and others climbed up to relieve them. The Bracari soon fell back, dragging their injured with them. Those that had died, lay in heaps before the gate. The stench of death lingered over the entrance as quiet settled over the chasm, broken only by the moaning and whimpers of the injured. Campfires sprang up across the field as the Bracari prepared for the night.

Finola set the watches, and they tried to get some rest. About midnight, a clamor rose up from the camp. Men shouted, swords clashed. "Poison," someone yelled. The cry rose up until the whole Bracari camp seemed to be awake. Torches flared and trailed off into the trees as if the Bracari were searching for someone.

"Do you think they found the poisoned meat?" Gwyneth asked Finola.

"If it took them this long to figure that out, then they're dumb as rocks," she said. "No, I think it was something else—poisoned arrows maybe."

Seventeen days after the army had gone north to fight Tristan, the morning dawned bright and clear. It would have been a cheerful morning if a Bracari army bent on murder hadn't camped on the pleasant green before the chasm. Gwyneth saw to her dismay that the Bracari had brought up their battering ram. A thousand of them spread out over the green hillside. Why did they even bother to attack? All they had to do was bottle them up in the narrow canyon and wait for them to starve.

"Target the men carrying the ram," Finola shouted as the Bracari advanced.

Finola's archers were so restricted by the narrow opening that they couldn't bring all of their archers to bear. The Bracari rushed over the narrow trail between the cliff wall and the pits where the carcasses of the hounds and men who had fallen in were beginning to stink. Some Bracari fell, but others replaced them. Bracari archers began picking off any archer that stuck their head above the barricade to shoot. Soon, it was too dangerous to shoot and only the lancers could resist the Bracari at the gate.

The Bracari struggled to bring the ram to bear, but it soon slammed into the gate. The entire barricade shuddered. It slammed again, and the gate cracked. The men rushed to shore it up, but the ram crashed again, and the gate burst open. The Bracari struggled to fight their way through. The men with swords battled, and the female lancers stood behind them, thrusting their spears through when they could. The entrance was so narrow that only one Bracari could try to force his way through at a time, but with the weight of the rest of them behind him, they couldn't be stopped.

Bracari appeared on the crest. Cries from above told Gwyneth that some had found the pits, but others still managed to avoid them and started raining stones and arrows down on the heads of the defenders.

The struggle for the barricade was desperate and terrible. Carpentini men spent their strength defending it until they were all cut down, and the Bracari pushed through. The female lancers and archers retreated to the next barricade. Bodies of men and women littered the crevice. The wails of the injured echoed off the walls. Children wailed and women screamed. Wounded women tried to drag themselves away from the fighting.

There was no hope now, and still Gwyneth struggled on. She spent all of her arrows defending the second barricade before she flung her bow aside and drew her sword. The creek ran with gore, and the stench of it soon overpowered the damp, moldy smell of the fissure.

They stalled the Bracari at the second barricade, but the stones from above and the Bracari archers now inside the crevice thinned their ranks so much that they were soon overwhelmed. A cry rose up from above, and Gwyneth thought it was a cry of victory. The Bracari disappeared from the crest for a moment and then ladders and ropes spilled over the sides. Horns sounded loud and shrill in the crevice.

Gwyneth's heart sank. It was over. Warriors clambered over the side and down into the hollow. They were lost. The pits hadn't worked. They hadn't even been able to hold for a single day. Gwyneth searched for Finola, preferring to die fighting by her side than anywhere else. When she rushed up to her, Finola blinked the tears from her eyes and placed a bloody hand on Gwyneth's shoulder. She took a deep breath.

"Let us die for the children," Finola said.

Gwyneth bit her lip and nodded. They faced the ladders, the ropes, and the men pouring in.

Chapter 16
Rage and Revelations

The smoke spilling into the clear blue sky over the green hillsides told York they were too late. It had been ten days since York had killed Tristan's son and seventeen since York had last seen Dunraven Keep. They had run as fast as they could, and they were still too late. His heart sank. His mother and sister had been there. Finola and Gwyneth had been there. Everyone he loved in the world, except for Brion, had been in that keep when he left. Brion urged his horse on, and York followed, fighting the desperate terror.

The keep came into view as they pounded around the last grove of trees. A knot clutched at York's throat. Bodies littered the hillside. Some dangled from the battlements. Crows and buzzards hopped about, feeding on the corpses. The gate lay in ruins and the portcullis was smashed. The rear gate had been torn off its hinges. The timber work in the newly-rebuilt keep still smoldered and burned. The rolling black cloud boiled into the air. A trail of bodies led towards the chasm where they had fought the first battle together against the Bracari.

A chorus of horns rang over the hills coming from the same direction. As the horn calls faded into the distant hills, the sound of harsh cries and clashing metal reached York's ears.

"They're still fighting at the crevice," Reed called. He kicked his horse into a gallop. The exhausted steed stumbled and almost fell. But he righted himself, and the two thousand men who had managed the mad dash across the heathland raced toward the crevice.

The carcasses of hounds lay everywhere, most of them ap-

227

peared uninjured. Here and there, the mangled bodies of women and children and the occasional man showed how the hounds of the Bracari had mauled their victims. Rage filled York's chest. He would avenge them all if it was the last thing he ever did.

The crash and clamor of the battle reached them as they rushed into the aspens and forced their way toward the caves—the clang of steel, the roar of men seeking courage, the snarl of the hounds. The screams of women and children sent York's blood racing. His exhaustion fell away.

"Bethann," he whispered. "Gwyneth."

"They're still fighting," Brion called. The desperate hope in his voice made York look at him. Brion's face was tight and his eyes were wide. He looked terrified. That thought nearly shook York's resolve. If Brion was that worried, then what hope could there be?

Brion and York broke from the trees to see the grassy slope littered with dead hounds and injured and dying men. The creek gurgled from the gate, carrying its bloodstained water. Brion and York didn't pause or give a battle cry. They simply raced into the battle as fast as their weary mounts would carry them.

The Bracari warriors milled about the barricade at the entrance while others swarmed on the crest. Bodies and timber filled the ditch before the barricade. The battle was fierce, but the image that arrested York's attention and haunted him was the sight of a dark-haired woman draped over the barricade in death. She still clutched a knife in her hand. For all he knew it was Gwyneth—but he didn't have time to reflect on it.

Brion and York slammed into the rear of the Bracari forces who were still trying to pass the wooden barricade. Others dismounted and scrambled up the hill to attack the Bracari at the crest.

A cry of surprise rose up from the Bracari who whirled to face the new threat. They soon realized they were outnumbered and backed up against the barricade. Though Brion's men were all exhausted, they threw themselves into the fray. Reed's roar rose above the tumult as he jumped from his horse, swinging the great battle-axe. Some Bracari tried to surrender, but they were cut down. Neither the Salassani nor the Carpentini were in the mood to show mercy to men who had shown none to them or their families.

York and Brion leapt from their mounts and waded into the

thick of the battle. Brion was incredibly swift with his sword, and they had soon splashed across the creek and pushed through the group at the gate. When they forced their way into the crevice, what they saw filled York with horror. Women and children lay sprawled in death. Hounds fed on their bodies. Their blood colored the waters of the creek. The stench of death poisoned the air, and the sounds of the dying rang in his ears.

With reckless fury, York rushed the Bracari who were now turning from a second barricade that had crumbled on one side to face the new onslaught. Brion was beside him, and, together, they hacked their way through the terrified Bracari. Bodies fell from above to crash into the creek and break upon the rocks. The Bracari scrambled back over the barricade and tried to find a defensible position. A few women who were backed up against a great boulder still struggled to fend off the Bracari attack.

York clawed his way to the top of the barricade and stood on the pile of logs and stones for a moment to survey the scene, searching for Gwyneth, his mother, or Bethann. Hundreds of Carpentini men and women held the hollow, and, in their midst, Taegan swung her sword. Clusters of women and children cowered behind them, packed into every nook or cave they could find to escape the fighting.

Then he saw them. Gwyneth and Finola perched on a large outcrop with a handful of women wielding lances as the Bracari tried to get at them. A sudden movement on a great boulder in the middle of the crevice drew his attention. A Bracari archer nocked an arrow. To York's horror, he realized the archer was looking at Gwyneth. York jerked his sling from his belt, struggling against the constriction in his chest and the panic that made his hands tremble.

He jammed a lead stone into the pouch and snapped the sling. The lead stone slammed into the Bracari's head. The archer released the string, and the arrow jumped through the air. Gwyneth looked up, and their gazes met just as the arrow buried itself into Gwyneth's leg. She let out a cry and stumbled backward off the boulder to disappear from York's sight.

York snapped the sling several more times until more of Brion's men arrived to rush over the wall, sweeping the Bracari before them. York splashed into the creek and bounded over the bodies. He rounded the stone where the archer had stood and slid to a stop. His mother was dragging Bethann's limp body up to a narrow ledge, out of the way of the fighting. Blood matted his mother's hair.

"No!" York screamed. His mother raised her gaze to his. She straightened, glanced at Bethann, drew a knife from her belt, and leapt off the rock into a bunch of Bracari who were struggling with the Carpentini from Taegan's band. She disappeared into the mob. York rushed to find her. Why would she do that? Why would she just throw her life away?

The horrible clamor of battle filled his ears so that he couldn't hear anything else. Tears stung his eyes and blurred his vision. He swung his sword in a desperate frenzy. He had to reach her. He had to save her before it was too late. The Bracari fell back, searching for some escape from the Carpentini that pressed them. York's mother lay on the stones at their feet. Her eyes were open, and she stared up at him. York cut his way to her and fell to his knees.

"Mother," he said.

She blinked and struggled to rise, but her arm looked broken, and she had a terrible wound in her neck that gushed blood. York tried to stop it. But she slapped at his hands with her good arm.

"Did you avenge him?" she whispered.

"Yes," York said.

A smile touched her lips. "Now you are his son," she said. She closed her eyes.

"No," York whispered. Something crashed into his shoulder and sent him sprawling amid the stones. He struggled to his feet and lunged into a group of Bracari as the tears spilled down his cheeks. The rage and despair blinded him to the danger of being so isolated. He just didn't care anymore. Three Bracari were down before they knew what was happening. Then he drove his sword into the last man and watched him slip to the ground to grovel in the bloody mud.

A Carpentini paused to look at him. The man touched his head in the Carpentini sign of respect before lunging into another group of Bracari. York recognized him as the man he and Brion had found in the amphitheater weeks ago. Apparently, the man had found his courage in killing Bracari. York scrambled up to the ledge where Bethann's body lay, her neck bending at an unnatural angle. Her eyes were closed. She looked peaceful, as if she were asleep. He touched her cheek with a bloodstained hand. Her flesh was already turning cold.

York let out a growl of pain and spun to search for Gwyneth. He couldn't lose them all. He couldn't.

The women at the cavern where Gwyneth and Finola had made their stand were fewer in number now, and Gwyneth had propped herself up against the wet stone wall as she did what she could to protect the women and children that cowered behind her.

York glanced at his mother. She no longer moved. He blinked at the tears that stung his eyes and jumped off the ledge to rush the Bracari that fought with Gwyneth.

He hacked at their backs until they spun to face him. When they did, the women jabbed their lances into them. The Bracari retreated, joining the rest as they scrambled over the bodies and stones, seeking a way out. Brion and the other Carpentini cut off their escape. Slowly, they were being forced into an ever-smaller area around the great boulder.

York clambered up to the outcrop, leaving a bloody stain on the stone from the many cuts and scrapes on his arms and legs. He reached Gwyneth and grabbed her arm to pull her away from the fighting. She shook her head.

"Come on," York shouted.

Tears streamed down Gwyneth's cheeks, and she pinched her lips tight. York tried to understand what she was trying to do until he realized that she intended to die. He shook his head—not after Bethann and his mother. He jerked on her arm again. "Come on," he yelled over the tumult of battle. Just then, several Bracari who had been pushed back by Brion's men stumbled past them. One of them glanced up and swung his sword at Gwyneth in a vicious strike that aimed to disembowel her from below. York flung himself in front of the blade.

The stroke slammed against his temple. A flash of pain lanced through his head, and he careened into the wall. He tried to blink against the dizziness and the nausea. The world collapsed into a dark tunnel. The last thing he saw was Gwyneth bending over him before everything descended into a swirling blackness. He felt the warm trickle of blood slide down his face, and he remembered no more.

Brion stood at the crest of the cavern gazing down upon the terrible scene. The heartrending sobs and moans of the injured and dying women and children reverberated around the hollow. The horrible, gut-wrenching reek of death overpowered every other smell. The horror of it still clutched at his chest. He had assumed he would get used to it, but he never did. Killing on the scale he had witnessed in the last couple of months left a strange, swooping, emptiness inside him—an emptiness bordering on despair. How could people be so vicious? What hatred could drive them to such depravity?

Carpentini and Salassani men picked their way through the piles of corpses, searching for survivors. When they found one, they lifted them and carried them to one of the larger caverns where Finola, Jenna, and any other woman who could still walk tended the hundreds of injured. Other men collected the dead and dumped them in the pits or dug new ones and covered them with dirt.

Brion glanced around at the pits on the ledge above the crevice. The bodies of the Bracari warriors and their dogs could still be seen through the thin layer of dirt. An awful stench rose into the air. Finola had been truly ingenious in the way she had organized the defense of the crevice. Brion stepped away from the trenches seeking air he could actually stand to breathe.

He didn't know what he had expected to find by climbing the hill and staring out over the country now ravaged by war and littered with the dead. The keep still smoked in the distance, and ravens and buzzards flocked to the field. Wolves lurked in the forest, coming out at night to feed on the corpses.

Why? Brion kept asking himself. Why would people allow themselves to become so driven by greed and hatred that they sought to destroy an entire people? Not a single Bracari who had entered the crevice left it alive, and those that escaped into the hills were being hunted by Taegan's warriors. More than fifteen hundred of them had died, and they had killed nearly two thousand men, women, and children, and left hundreds more crippled and dying. The Bracari had traveled several hundred miles from their homes to do this, and now their wives and children would be watching the horizon, waiting for them to return. Thousands of people all over the heathland were even now mourning the loss of loved ones.

The Carpentini and Salassani were broken, so diminished now that even if their lands were returned to them, it would take decades before they would ever be able to effectively occupy them. War was such a waste. Neahl and Redmond were right. Only the nobility benefited, and now Brion was one of them. He could use the war to expand his landholdings if he wanted. Emyr might even let him claim Comrie if he asked. But Brion wouldn't ask. He couldn't ask.

He gazed up at the Aveens and wondered if his mother had survived this war, and, if she had, how he would ever find her now. Brion pulled the little ring from inside his tunic and fingered it. He had found traces of his mother, but no trail he could follow—hints and whispers but no real information. Even now, she could be lying among the dead, and he would never know. Could he go back without knowing what had happened to her? Maybe he should. Jenna had said his mother had wanted to disappear, that she didn't want to be found.

Brion made his way down to the front of the crevice and found Finola sitting on a log with her head in her hands. She had several bandages on her arms and hands and one on her leg. A bruise was purpling on her cheek. Almost no one who had been in the crevice had gone uninjured. He sat beside her and wrapped an arm around her shoulders.

"I'm sorry," he said. "I never should have brought you here."

Finola raised her head to gaze at him. Her face was pale and haggard. She had large, dark circles around her eyes, which were rimmed with red. He could only imagine what she had gone through.

"If you hadn't," she said, "they would all be dead."

Brion considered and nodded. She was right. Her female warriors had held the Bracari long enough for help to arrive. If she hadn't been there to train them, they would all have been slaughtered.

Brion looked out over the disturbing scene before him.

"Why?" he asked.

"Why what?"

"Why would the Bracari pursue the Carpentini like they did? They already had their land. Why chase them into the Aveens?"

Finola surveyed him with a kind of pity. "Emyr would tell you that it is the way," she said.

Brion grimaced. "No it isn't. They've never done anything like this before."

"Maybe, but it *is* their way to hate each other. It's especially bad between the Carpentini and the Bracari. You've seen how they treat Gwyneth."

Brion nodded.

"We grew up thinking all the people of the heathland were savages, mere animals," Finola reminded him. "I remember being surprised when Brigid and I first arrived at Emyr's village that the Salassani actually lived in houses like ours."

Brion gave a short laugh. "Still," he said, "it isn't right. How can so much beauty be filled with such suffering and hatred, so much violence and horror?" He shook his head. "The heathland shouldn't be like this."

Finola glanced at him. "What? You want to tame it?"

"No," Brion said without looking at her. "I want to free it." Somehow, in the walk down from the crest of the crevice, he realized that what had been bothering him more than anything—that sense of being trapped, caged in, unable to pursue his own interests. That's why he had escaped into the heathland—to be free of the burden of being a duke, to experience the liberation of the open land that stood wide to embrace him, to be free of the guilt that he had failed so many people in his life, and now he had failed his own mother.

Finola reached over and squeezed his hand. They sat for a long while in companionable silence. She always seemed to know when words were of no use.

Brion sighed and stirred himself. "How are Gwyneth and York?"

"They'll survive," she said, "but York lost a large chunk of his scalp and a piece of his ear."

"That will make him a real hit with the ladies," Brion said.

Finola gave him a weary smile. "I think there's only one lady he wants to attract, though he doesn't know it yet."

Brion sat back and studied her. "Who?" he said.

Finola gazed at him and sniffed. "You know, sometimes you worry me. It's been happening right in front of your eyes for weeks, and you haven't noticed."

Vengeance

Brion tried to think if York had shown a preference for any young woman. York had been single-minded about learning to be a warrior.

"The tunnel?" Finola asked. "When York helped Gwyneth up, and then they rode together on the horse?"

"Nah," Brion said. As long as he had known them, they had either argued or ignored one another.

Finola grabbed his hand. "Come on," she said. She led him into the chasm. Brion wrinkled his nose against the smell. At least the bodies had been removed from this section so he only had to navigate the rocky trail. Pools of blood and bits of clothing and broken weapons bore grim testimony to the struggle that had so recently surged back and forth over this ground.

They found Gwyneth sitting with her bandaged leg outstretched. She was covered in grime and gore, but she had pulled her hair back and tried to wash her face. Next to her lay York. His head had been bandaged, but the stain of dried blood still colored his face and soaked his tunic. It had been a vicious wound. His eyes were closed, but he breathed slowly, rhythmically. Gwyneth glanced up at them. She, too, had been crying.

"How is he?" Brion asked.

Gwyneth shrugged. "He hasn't woke up yet."

Finola raised her eyebrows to Brion. Brion glanced between York and Gwyneth.

"No," he whispered. Then he considered the tender expression on Gwyneth's face, and he began to wonder.

Finola clicked her tongue at him and pulled him away. "Let's check on Meredith," she said. Brion glanced back and saw Gwyneth reach out to push a stray hair away from York's brow. How had he missed this?

Gwyneth watched Finola and Brion leave. She struggled with the horrible knot in her throat and the sorrow and fear that encircled her heart. York lay on his back with a bandage on his head and his clothes and face spattered in blood. Numerous cuts and bruises covered his arms and legs. He looked peaceful and pale like a sick child poised on the edge of death. Gwyneth struggled with the gnawing vulnerability. She hadn't felt this way since her mother died. The walls she had constructed to protect herself from pain had not worked. She had never let herself care about anyone after her mother had died. Caring meant you could be hurt. She had found comfort in her hatred of men and distrust of all Carpentini, which had given her life a strange kind of meaning. But when Brion and Finola had arrived at the keep, her walls had begun to fracture and crumble. Now they lay in ruins, and her heart ached for York and for Clidna and for all the women and children who had fallen. She didn't know what she would do if York died, too. Not since her Uncle Edrick had failed to return from battle had she felt so desperate for a man's companionship. She had thought she could live without a man, and yet, here she was waiting for York to wake up—waiting for proof that he would live.

Gwyneth touched a wet cloth to York's cheek to wipe away the blood. She let her thumb rest against his cheek and said the words she had never thought to say again. "I love you," she whispered.

Evening fell, and Reed returned with what supplies could be scavenged from the keep. He sent men out to hunt for food, since the Bracari had slaughtered most of their animals. Taegan's warriors returned with news that no more Bracari or their hounds could be found. Brion sat with York, while Finola made Gwyneth go lie down to get some rest. He pulled out his mother's ring and fiddled with it as his mind wandered over the events of the last few months.

Jenna came to check on York, and she sat on the other side of him. She wore the blue tunic and trousers that Taegan's women tended to wear. She had her hair pulled back in a thick braid. She was an attractive woman.

"He will wake," she said. "It'll just take time."

Brion nodded and sighed. "He's so young," he said. "But he's braver and more determined than most men I know."

Jenna's gaze strayed to the ring that hung from the chain around Brion's neck. "You still intend to find her?"

Brion nodded. "I have to know that she's safe."

Jenna reached out a trembling hand to touch the ring. Brion let her take it. Tears brimmed in her eyes.

"I'm sorry," she said.

Brion furrowed his brow in confusion.

"I'm sorry I lied to you," Jenna said again. Her voice broke, and she swallowed. "I am Elsie," she whispered. "I am your mother."

Brion's heart skipped a beat and then began to pound as if it wanted to break free of his ribs. He stared in disbelief. His mother? He leaned forward to get a better look at her, trying to see if there was any resemblance between her and himself. The Duke, his father, had said that he looked like her. Jenna dropped her hand to touch his. Her fingers were ice cold, and her hand trembled. A flutter rippled through Brion's stomach, and he struggled to think of something to say. He had spent all his energy in trying to find her. He had never considered what he might say to her.

"Is this true?" he stammered. For some reason he found speech very difficult.

She nodded, and her tears spilled from her chin to stain York's clothes. She sniffled and wiped at her eyes.

"I'm sorry," she said again.

Brion clasped her hands in his as he struggled to swallow past the tightness in his throat. His face burned, and he began to tremble all over. He was afraid to speak for fear it might come out as a croak.

"Why?" Brion asked. "Why did you abandon me? Why did you lie to me when you knew I had risked everything to find you?"

He had been laboring under the guilt of having left his mother undefended after failing to protect Weyland and Rosland, and now he learned that she had been lying to him just as much as the Duke had done. Parents weren't supposed to lie to their children.

A pained expression flashed across Elsie's face, and her lips trembled.

"I had no choice," she said. She squeezed his hand as if in desperation. "If I hadn't given you up, they would have killed you."

A sudden rush of heat swept through Brion, and he experienced the powerful urge to grab her and shake her. His whole life had been a lie, and it started when she had abandoned him. His breathing came faster as his pulse raced, and his hands began to sweat. Brion hadn't expected the hot, burning anger that filled him. She had lied even though she knew he had almost been killed trying to find her. He wanted to punish her. He wanted her to understand how much he had suffered.

"Can you forgive me?" Elsie said. She stared at him with a look of such longing and hope that Brion looked away.

Brion hesitated. He shifted in his seat and passed a hand over his brow. Could he forgive her? Could he forgive all of them—everyone who had lied to him by their silence as much as by their words?

"I just want to understand what happened," Brion said. But his voice was even with a hard edge to it.

A sob escaped Elsie's throat before she cut it off with a hand to her mouth. Brion experienced a little thrill and a moment of satisfaction at her pain before he realized what he was doing. By what right did he condemn her? He had no more idea of what she had suffered than she had of what he had experienced. Brion bowed his head. He swallowed the bitterness that rose in his throat.

"I'm sorry," he mumbled. "Please, tell me what happened."

Elsie glanced around to ensure they were alone. "Can I ask how you even knew I was alive?"

"Killian told me," Brion said. He had a clear memory of the old man lying broken and dying on the floor of Geric's dungeon.

Elsie smiled. "Oh, how is he?"

"Dead," Brion said.

Elsie's smile faded. "I'm sorry to hear it. I always liked Killian."

"He sacrificed his life so he could tell me about you."

Elsie swallowed and blinked rapidly. "So many people have suffered so much," she said.

Brion said nothing. He wanted to hear what she had to say.

Elsie clasped her hands in front of her. "My mother was a healer among the Carpentini," she began. "We were driven from our home by settlers from Dunfermine, and we left to wander in Coll, moving from place to place as she taught me her trade. We had been in Taber Wood for some time when soldiers came to take us to the Duke's palace. His wife was sickly and due to deliver his firstborn son. But the labor did not begin, and my mother was called away for another delivery. She left me to tend to the Duchess."

Elise shifted to a sitting position and straightened her blue tunic. "I spent a lot of time at his manor. The Duke and I fell in love," she continued, "and I soon learned that I was pregnant with his child. I was terrified and fled to my mother. I knew I could never marry a duke, and, if his wife found out, she could have me and my baby killed. We fled north to a village called Wexford where we hid in a cave until you were born. The Duke found us and begged us to come back to his manor, where he would protect us. But I refused."

She glanced at Brion as if she expected him to condemn her for refusing to stay with the Duke. When he didn't respond, she continued.

"He said he was involved in a coup, and if anyone discovered that he loved me and that we had had a child, they would kill us or capture us to use against him. I protested that I couldn't have you torn from me, but he begged me to at least let him conceal us. He hid us in two different places so that, if one was found, the other might live. He sent me to live among my people. My mother remained to watch over her grandchild."

Another shock swept through Brion. He stared in dumb amazement. "The old midwife was my grandmother?"

"Yes. She gave up her life of travel to be near you since I couldn't. She wrote and told me how you were growing, how you won the archery championship in your village. I was so proud of you."

"But why did Weyland and Rosland lie to me?" Brion asked.

"To protect us," she said. "You know what happened to my mother."

Brion nodded. He remembered it well. He, Brigid, and Finola had found her stabbed to death in her cave—the cave where he had been born.

"The Duke sent me a note," she said, "just before his son murdered him. He said he was proud of you and wished that you had been his heir. He told me my mother had been killed and that Cedrick would be coming for me. I fled the village, but Cedrick came anyway and butchered everyone. I was afraid if I let anyone know who I was, they might betray me. They might find you. I fled with my sister and everyone who would follow us as deep into the Aveen Mountains as we could."

"Sister?" Brion asked.

Elsie nodded. "Taegan is my younger sister, and you met my Aunt Shaunna."

"When?" Brion asked, but then he realized who she meant. "The gray-haired woman," he said. The one that tried to tell him about Elsie.

Elsie nodded. "She was my mother's sister. She took me in when I fled to the Carpentini."

"I tried to save her," Brion said. He wanted his mother to know he hadn't just let her aunt die.

"I know," she said, and she patted his leg.

Brion reached out and took her hand. The new revelations had been confusing, but now was his chance. A thrill of excitement swept through him. "Will you come with me?" he asked. "I'm the Duke now. You can come back to live with me. I'll take care of you."

A tear trickled down Elsie's cheek, but she shook her head. "My place is with my people," she said. "It took me a long time to realize that. I used to dream of going to you in Wexford. But it was too dangerous. And I couldn't go back to Taber Wood. It would be too painful."

The bottom fell out of Brion's stomach. The surge of disappointment brought a lump into his throat. She was rejecting him. She was forcing him to fail again. How could he protect her if she wouldn't stay with him? It didn't matter how hard he tried, he was always defeated in the end.

Brion blinked at the burning tears that welled up in his eyes. He wanted to order her to come back with him or maybe just beg her. He needed to make sure she was safe. He needed to be free of the guilt.

"But I can't leave you here alone," Brion stammered.

"I'm not alone," Elsie said. "I have my sister and my people. They need me. I'm good at being a healer. I enjoy my work."

"How will I know you're safe?"

Elsie squeezed his hand. "You have already helped make the heathland safe. I'm so proud of you." She paused. "You are a better man than your father was. He tried to do what he thought was right, but he used people. He used me, and he used you."

"And you loved him?" Brion asked.

Elsie nodded. "I still love him. I didn't always agree with him, but he was a good man forced into an impossible situation. He did the best he could."

Elsie leaned in and kissed Brion on the forehead. Her lips were soft and moist. "I love you, my son. That's why I gave you up—because I loved you too much to risk losing you forever."

Brion stared at her, struggling to understand how that logic could even make sense. He sat back feeling wrung out. He didn't have the energy to argue with her.

"Do you ever regret it?" he asked.

Elsie nodded. "Every day. I wish I could have done something else. I always worried that you would never be able to forgive me when you found out."

"But how do you live with it?" he mumbled.

Elsie scowled and looked as if he had slapped her. Brion rushed to explain.

"The guilt," he said. "How do you live with the guilt? Every night before I go to sleep, I see Weyland and Rosland lying beside each other in the grave I dug for them, and I know that I failed to protect them. I see Neahl bleeding to death and Redmond's despair at losing Lara. I failed them all."

Tears slipped down Elsie's cheeks. "I let go," she said. "I had to accept that I made the best choices I could under the worst possible circumstances, and I let go."

Brion bowed his head. Was it supposed to be that easy?

Elsie pulled the chain with the ring on it over Brion's head. She undid the clasp and slipped the ring from the chain. She lifted Brion's hand and slid the ring onto his little finger. Then she held his face between her hands.

"Stop wearing the past like a chain around your neck," she said. "There is so much in the world you can't control."

She leaned in and kissed him on the forehead again. "Be free, my son," she whispered.

York opened his eyes to stare into the shadows where the light from some flame flickered on the glistening drops of moisture that covered the stone walls. The murmur of disembodied voices floated to him. A moment of confusion resolved with sudden clarity into the last memory he had of the Bracari striking out to kill Gwyneth. York shoved himself to a sitting position and swayed with the sudden dizziness and nausea. He reached up to his head to feel the bandage. Dozens of other people lay in regular rows around him.

Women bent over some, while others sat up with their backs to the walls. But these weren't Bracari. They were Carpentini and Salassani. Jenna glanced at him, gestured for him to wait, and then turned to finish what she was doing. He tried to remember what had happened. The image of Bethann, prostrate at his mother's feet, and then of his mother, lying in a pool of blood, surged into his memory. The horror of it drove him to his feet. He staggered and careened into the wall. He had to find them. He had to find Gwyneth

Jenna jumped up and rushed to him. She grabbed a hold of him. "Not yet, Master York," she said.

"Gwyneth?" York stammered. "Please, where's Gwyneth?"

"She's gone," Jenna said.

The breath froze in York's throat. He leaned against the wall and slumped to the ground. Almost everyone he had loved was dead. Tears burned his eyes. Jenna knelt beside him, and he blinked at her through the blur of tears.

Jenna was smiling. "She's okay," Jenna said. "I sent her away to get some rest."

York stared. "She was here?"

"She hasn't left your side for two days. Brion just left."

"Finola?"

"She's fine, too."

York could breathe again. "The Bracari?" he asked.

Jenna frowned. "They're all dead. You arrived just in time."

"Where are my mother and my sister?"

Jenna shook her head. "I'm afraid they've already been buried with the rest."

York swallowed and struggled to keep the tears in. He couldn't blame them for not waiting to bury them, but he would have liked to have been able to say goodbye.

He would never be able to hold Bethann's soft hand in his or have her cuddle in his lap before the fire. His entire family was gone. Silenced. Vanished from the earth. All that was left were the memories, and, in recent weeks, the memories of his mother had not been pleasant. She had not been herself since his father had been murdered. But, at the end, she had accepted him.

At the end, she had approved of him. He had proven to everyone he deserved to be considered a man. Then why didn't it bring him the satisfaction and sense of belonging he had expected? Why did his heart still feel so empty?

Jenna lifted his hand. "I'm sorry. We've all lost loved ones."

York swallowed and nodded. At least Gwyneth was alive.

Jenna laid a hand on his shoulder. "She's quite the girl you've got," she said.

"I've got?" York blinked at her, trying to understand what she meant. Did she mean Gwyneth?

Later that day, Arno came riding in with the rest of Taegan's people. His arm was still in a sling. Jason rode behind him, holding onto Misty's reins. She pulled at the reins and jerked her head, nearly dragging Jason from his seat.

"Where have you been?" Brion asked Arno.

Jason dropped Misty's reins, and she trotted up to Brion and nuzzled his shoulder. Brion stroked her soft nose. "It's good to see you too, old girl," he said.

"We found her on her way here," Arno said. "Seems like she knew where to find you." Then he cocked his head sideways and raised an eyebrow. "You know, that horse has got problems."

Brion scowled at him. "Misty?" Worried that she had been injured, he looked her over, running his hands down her legs and across her belly.

"She wouldn't even let Jason ride her," Arno said. "She's as ornery as a mule."

Brion laughed and straightened. He patted Misty's muzzle again. "That's my girl," he said. Then he looked up at Arno. "You're avoiding my question. I thought you were coming to help them."

"I did," Arno said. "Who do you think told Taegan how to set off the avalanche, and who do you think convinced her to delay the Bracari army?"

Brion glanced up at Jason, who nodded his head as if to confirm Arno's assertions.

"I gave her a bit of help with the poisoned carcasses and poisoned arrows, too."

Brion pursed his lips. That wasn't the help he had expected, but, in the end, it had worked.

"Well, you didn't expect me to fight after what you did my shoulder, did you?" Arno said.

Brion shrugged. "I met one of your 'Brethren of the Rook,'" he said.

"Oh?"

"He was helping some people escape Ballach," Brion said. "I've been curious who they were."

Arno smiled knowingly but didn't say anything.

"I don't think Emyr is going to be happy," Brion said, "when he discovers your secret order kidnapped Tristan's family."

Arno considered. "Probably not, but bringing down Tristan didn't require killing his entire family. They might be useful later on."

"Emyr wasn't going to kill them," Brion said.

"No, but Lord Nelson was going to do it," Arno replied. "He's the one who paid us to kill them and dispose of them. We just decided to do it a little differently than he expected."

"Emyr knew?"

"He's no fool." Arno massaged his shoulder.

"You were wrong about the trap, too," Brion said.

"Nah," Arno said. "I was right. Emyr was just too smart for Tristan. That's all." Arno swung free of the saddle.

"You have an answer for everything," Brion said. "I just don't know if I can trust anything you say."

Arno didn't smile. "I have never lied to you," he said. "I may have withheld information, but that isn't the same as lying."

"Sure," Brion said. People lie by silence just as much as they do by words. "You told York to spy on me in return for the lead stones, didn't you?"

Arno shifted his eyes and shrugged. "Well, but that isn't lying. I paid him with knowledge and a new skill for a bit of information."

Brion nodded. "York was ready to kill you for it."

"I know," Arno said. "But he's a smart boy. In a few years, I might be recruiting him."

Arno gave Brion a questioning glance. "Do you have an answer for me?" he asked.

Brion glanced at his boots. "I won't betray Emyr," he said.

"I'm not asking you to," Arno said.

Brion studied him.

"Knowledge is power," Arno said. "Knowledge is freedom."

Brion didn't care about power, but he did care about freedom. Knowing what was going to happen before it did would give him the freedom to make his own choices—to act, rather than to wait around for other people to force him to respond. That's what he had been doing ever since the day he found Weyland and Rosland dead. He had never been in control.

"Okay," he said, "but I will only share information with you that does not endanger this kingdom or anyone I care about."

Arno grinned.

"However," Brion continued, "I will only do so if you give me any and all information that would protect my family, Emyr, and the kingdom of Coll."

"Done," Arno said. "Do you still have the cloth I gave you?"

"Yes."

"You'll need it again when you leave the island."

"I'm not leaving the island," Brion said.

Arno flashed his annoying smile. "Before I go, I'll teach you how to contact us."

"Where are you going?" Brion asked.

Arno surveyed him as if deciding what to say. "Nairn," he said.

"The Black Isle?" Brion asked. Redmond had told him that the people of the Black Isle were secretive and did not like outsiders. "Is that where you're from?"

Arno nodded. "When you've finished with this business, you should pay us a visit." His gaze strayed to where Finola sparred with Gwyneth and York. "You and Finola would be a real asset."

"Maybe," Brion said. He patted Misty again and led her away.

Gwyneth found York lounging on the crest of the hill above the crevice. He had been up and about for a few days, but she hadn't seen much of him since he had awakened. She couldn't still the little tremor of terror that rippled through her chest every time she thought of speaking to him about what had happened. He had sacrificed himself to save her, and she hadn't forgotten her whispered confession when she thought she might lose him. What if, somehow, he had heard her? What would he expect her to do? Even if he did accept her, would he be able to forget that she was half-Bracari—the same people who had killed his mother and sister? She almost left him to himself until she noticed that he was sitting with his arm draped over a huge Bracari hound.

"What are you thinking?" she demanded as she stomped up behind him.

York jumped and then relaxed when he saw her. The hound raised his head and examined her lazily for a moment before dropping it back down to rest on his paws.

"Jenna says I have to take it easy," he said.

"That's not what I'm talking about," Gwyneth said.

York gave her an annoying grin and patted the hound. "He's tame," he said. "I found him all chewed up in the woods. The other dogs must have gone after him."

Gwyneth drew her knife. She could never forget the sight of the hounds dragging down women and children. York jumped to his feet and stepped between the hound and Gwyneth.

"Calm down," he said.

"You can't tame a monster like that," Gwyneth snapped.

"Watch me," York said. "A good dog can be real useful."

"I'll kill it," Gwyneth said. She raised the knife and tried to step around York.

"Hang on," York said. His face flushed, and his brow wrinkled. "He's tame. He's not like the other dogs."

Gwyneth eyed him. She had half a mind to push past him and stab the dog, but the sight of York's ear with a piece missing and his bandaged head stopped her. York had risked his life to save her. She owed him. Gwyneth sighed. "If that thing growls at me just once," she said. "I'll stick a knife in it."

York smiled. The hound wagged its tail and padded around York to sniff at her. Gwyneth stiffened. The hound pushed his big, soft head under her hand and nuzzled her with his cold, wet nose, like he wanted her to pat him.

"See," York said. "He's just a dog. It was the Bracari who made them mean."

Gwyneth glanced at him when he said Bracari, but he didn't seem to associate her with them. She sighed, patted the dog, and sat down with her legs dangling over the edge of the crevice. York joined her, and the hound flopped down beside him.

Gwyneth glanced at York.

"Sorry about your head," she said.

York shrugged. "I'll just get a hat."

"You can grow your hair long," Gwyneth suggested. "Then you could hide it."

"I don't like my hair long," York said. "It tickles my ears."

Gwyneth laughed. "You're so pitiful."

Then she reached over to grasp his hand. It was warm and calloused. York stiffened as if unsure what she intended.

"Thanks," she said. She wanted to tell him that she had been prepared to die until her gaze had met his during the battle. All of a sudden, she had wanted to live. She had wanted to be able to hold his hand like this.

York's face reddened again, and he gave her an awkward smile.

"Sure," he said with a shrug. The way he said this made Gwyneth suspicious. He seemed to be hiding something. She had always been able to read him—but not now. Had he heard what she had whispered to him in her moment of terror and vulnerability? Should she tell him how she had felt seeing him lying at her feet with blood gushing from his scalp, how she had clutched desperately at the flap of skin the sword had sliced away? York watched her, waiting. Gwyneth withdrew her hand as the heat began to burn her face now, too. What was she thinking?

Chapter 17
Decision

igh summer arrived on the heathland with a flurry of lightning storms that traumatized the Carpentini and the Salassani who had experienced the flood in the crevice. Iain clung to Finola and whimpered every time the thunder rumbled through the sky. She shushed him and stroked his hair. So many children huddled together without parents. Reed and Taegan were working to find new families for them. Brion spent every available minute with his mother, knowing they would soon part and he might never see her again. She shared her knowledge of herb lore and healing with him, and he told her about his childhood and his adventures in the heathland.

The grass was turning brown. The heather and the green aspens, pines, and junipers provided the only bright color to the heathland. Reed's men were busy expanding and rebuilding the keep, while others tended the fields and constructed houses in the valley. A few stray Bracari had been found and dealt with before Reed could stop the Carpentini from killing them. Most of the Salassani had traveled south to join the others, though some who had lost all of their families remained with the Carpentini. Wagons with supplies arrived from Coll, along with news about Emyr's army in the north.

Emyr had used his army to drive the Taurini and Bracari back into their lands and to compel them to peace. One of the terms of the peace was that they free all slaves and either give them land, if they chose to remain, or allow them to return home. Consequently, Carpentini women and children trickled into Dunraven Keep in small groups to be reunited with their families or to learn that their families had been killed. Brion wondered when this horror would end for the Carpentini. Every day brought some new sorrow.

Gwyneth and York continued practicing with their weapons or followed Brion and Finola around. York had started wearing a felt hat to hide the bald spot above his left ear where the sword stroke had scalped him. The Bracari hound that he had saved never left his side.

Brion wasn't so sure it was a good idea to keep the dog—if for no other reason than the Carpentini who saw the animal were inclined either to run or to kill it. But York had his heart set on the creature, and Brion left him to it. The boy had lost too much already.

Late one evening, another group of Carpentini women and children arrived who had been enslaved. Finola strode out to meet them with Iain on her hip. Brion followed to see what he could do. They had barely approached the group when a woman let out a strangled cry and rushed at Finola. Finola spun away, and the woman fell to the earth. She crawled to her knees, weeping.

"Please," she said. "My baby, please let me hold him."

The woman was clearly Carpentini by her dress, and she appeared to be in earnest. Brion stared at Finola, uncertain how she might respond. Finola stepped back.

"Who are you?" she asked.

"Please," the woman said. Tears slipped from her eyes.

Iain reached out his chubby arms to the woman. "Momma," he said.

The woman sobbed. Finola scowled and glanced at Iain. Then she looked back to the woman. Brion could see the turmoil behind her eyes. She loved Iain. She had cared for him. She had planned to take him with them when she and Brion returned to Coll.

Finola glanced at Brion. A tear trickled down her cheek and her lips quivered. She handed Iain to the woman who clutched him to her chest with such passion that Brion felt a lump form in his throat. She must have been with the group that was coming to join Reed when the Bracari attacked.

Brion reached down and helped the woman to her feet.

"Thank you," she said. "Thank you for saving my baby. I thought he was dead. They killed everyone but the younger women. I thought he was dead."

Brion gripped her elbow and led her toward the keep where they could get food and water until a place could be found for them. Finola trailed along behind him with her head down. He reached out and took her hand. She stiffened and then let him take it. He squeezed it. Finola was a strong, passionate woman, but she was also kind and loving and desperately wanted to do the right thing. This had probably been the most difficult thing she had ever done. They walked in silence. There wasn't anything to say.

When they arrived at the keep, they found a messenger waiting for them. He bowed.

"My Lord. My Lady," he said. Brion frowned. He still didn't like being called a lord, but what could he do?

The messenger handed Brion a sealed note. It had the royal eagle stamped in red wax.

"King Emyr sends you his compliments and begs that you read this note at once."

Brion sighed at the formality, but he broke the seal and scanned the letter. Finola peered over his shoulder. It read:

> *Come to Ballach at once. Redmond is in trouble.*
> *I trust this job to no one else.*
> *E*

"No," Finola said. "He can't just order us around."

"Actually," Brion said, "he can."

Finola grunted in disgust. "I need a vacation from all these royal messes. Tell him to send one of his spies."

Brion pursed his lips. "I don't think he's inclined to accept that kind of answer."

"Oh? Then tell him to go jump in the moat," Finola said.

"I'll let you do that," Brion said. "What kind of trouble do you think Redmond could be in?"

"Who knows?" Finola said.

Brion turned to the messenger. "Can you wait a few moments?"

The messenger nodded.

Brion grabbed Finola's elbow and pulled her out of earshot.

"I'm sorry about Iain," he said. "I know that was hard for you."

Finola bowed her head. "He recognized her," she said. "I had no right to keep him from his mother." Brion pulled her into a hug and held her as the sobs wracked her body. He blinked at the sting in his own eyes. When Finola pushed away from him and wiped at her eyes, Brion pointed to where York and Gwyneth were shooting bows. They watched as York retrieved Gwyneth's arrows for her. When he gave them to her, the two of them started laughing at some private joke. Brion considered them. Maybe Finola had read them correctly. Maybe there was something there.

"Do you think they'll come with us?" he asked.

Finola gave him half a smile. "I think they'd follow us even if we tried to leave them."

"Should we sneak off tonight and see?" Brion asked.

Just then Gwyneth paused in her shooting and turned to stare at them with a scowl on her face as if she had heard every word.

Finola laughed. "It would be a waste of time."

ABOUT J.W. ELLIOT

J.W. Elliot is a professional historian, martial artist, canoer, bow builder, knife maker, woodturner, and rock climber. He has a Ph.D. in Latin American and World History. He has lived in Idaho, Oklahoma, Brazil, Arizona, Portugal, and Massachusetts. He writes non-fiction works of history about the Inquisition, Columbus, and pirates. J.W. Elliot loves to travel and challenge himself in the outdoors.

Connect with J.W. Elliot online at:
www.JWElliot.com/contact-us

Books by J.W. Elliot
Available on Amazon and Audible

Archer of the Heathland
Prequel: *Intrigue*
Book I: *Deliverance*
Book II: *Betrayal*
Book III: *Vengeance*
Book IV: *Chronicles*
Book V: *Windemere*
Book VI: *Renegade*
Book VII: *Rook*

Worlds of Light
Book I: *The Cleansing*
Book II: *The Rending*
Book III: *The Unmaking*

The Ark Project
Prequel: *The Harvest*
Book I: *The Clone Paradox*
Book II: *The Covenant Protocol*

Heirs of Anarwyn
Book I: *Torn*
Book II: *Undead*
Book III: *Shattered*
Book IV: *Feral*
Book V: *Dyad*

The Miserable Life of Bernie LeBaron
Somewhere in the Mist
Walls of Glass

If you have enjoyed this book, please consider leaving an honest review on Amazon and sharing on your social media sites.

Please sign up for my newsletter where you can get a free short story and more free content at: www.JWElliot.com

Thanks for your support!

J.W. Elliot

Writing Awards

Winner of the New England Book Festival for Science Fiction 2021 for *The Clone Paradox (The Ark Project,* Book I*).*

Award Winning Finalist in the Fiction: Young Adult category of the 2021 **Best Book Awards** sponsored by American Book Fest for *Archer of the Heathland: Windemere.*

Award-Winning Finalist in the Young Adult category of the 2021 **American Fiction Awards** for *Walls of Glass.*

Award-Winning Finalist in the Science Fiction: General category of the 2021 **American Fiction Awards** for *The Clone Paradox (The Ark Project,* Book 1).

Chet Kevitt Award for contributions to Weymouth history for the publication of *The World of Credit in Colonial Massachusetts: James Richards and his Daybook, 1692-1711.* Awarded by the Weymouth Historical Commission, 2018.

Writers of the Future Contest
Honorable Mention for *Recalibration,* 2018.
Honorable Mention for *Ebony and Ice,* 2019.

Printed in Great Britain
by Amazon

24703170R00148